Wake of the Sun

ISBN 978-0615961132

Cover Design and Artwork

Jon Campbell-Copp

Birch Island

First Edition

Printed in the United States of America and the United Kingdom

2014

For the lovely Sarah Jane.

Prologue

June 2012

Chainsaws coughed and screamed across the widening expanse. The men moved like soldiers clearing a battlefield of its dead. There were short bursts of silence as the trees fell, time acknowledging their final breaths. In several hours the forest was thinned to woody stubble.

Meredith witnessed the event from a small patio. The overlook would be a future viewing platform for the lightning fields. A few tables and chairs had been arranged on the newly placed concrete for expected visitors to the facility. Her tutor suggested that they retreat inside to escape the noise. The summer weather was bearable in the shade, but even from a distance the whine of the chainsaw teeth was hellish. Eight-year old Meredith asked that they remain there for her lesson.

After a session of multiplication and division, the tutor excused himself to go indoors. Meredith stood and walked to the edge of the patio. A black iron fence, thin and curling, enclosed the platform. She watched as the distant men slashed deftly at the wood, calmly slaying giant after giant.

Alika soon joined her at the fence and they went for a walk down along the edge of the shrinking forest. The men were on break. A haze of sawdust hung hauntingly in the daylight. Trunks, large and small, lay quiet. Stepping on twigs and mats of green leaves, they skirted the destruction and approached a large oak elevated slightly on a bank at the end of the field.

They sat at the base of the survivor, its large limbs chattering in the air. Around the trunk was tied a loose orange band; it was marked to fall as well. Clouds gently approached, members of the mourning party. A storm felt likely and the workers began to pack their gear. Alika observed the thoughtful face of his goddaughter.

Meredith touched at the design on her dress, its hem fallen about her as leaves against a tree. For the first time in months, she asked Alika if her parents were coming back. Alika reached out and rested a tender hand on her back. He still struggled to find the right words.

Thunder rumbled; the sound of someone breathing through a microphone. The rains came and they stood to go inside. Pools of water gathered in unusual places about the field. As they departed, Alika stopped and returned to the old tree. Its wrinkled skin was softer in the stormy air. In one swipe, he tore the tape from its waist.

March 15th, 2028
10,000 feet above Long Island, New York
11:50 a.m.

"Ma'am," said the flight attendant. "Ma'am."

Meredith woke in her seat aboard the descending airplane, a hand on her shoulder. She looked up at the middle-aged stewardess, the woman's make-up sanded down from a ten-hour shift over the Atlantic.

"We're landing in a few minutes," she said. "If you could just bring your seat all the way up for me—thanks."

Meredith obeyed, rubbing her eyes and pushing a lock of hair behind her ear. She stretched and glanced across the cabin. Drifting off had left her vulnerable.

The plane had slowed from its supersonic cruising speed and the woman beside her was looking out the window at the city skyline. The man across the aisle was signing the last of his customs forms as his son grudgingly put away a game tablet. Forward one row, a man removed his digital glasses and stowed them with a keyboard, while the couple ahead of her spoke suggestively in French. Other passengers were either returning from the lounges or gathering their things, eager to get off the plane. Meredith checked the Air Marshal at the back. Their eyes met and he returned to his magazine. She had spotted him in Paris.

The aircraft shuddered as it emerged through the last layer of clouds and approached the runway. The scurry of the city magnified steadily through its portholes. It had been sixteen years since Meredith had left America.

The landing gear extended and locked into place. The woman next to Meredith closed her eyes and began mumbling something of a prayer. Several rows ahead, a young child suddenly began to cry. The boy across the aisle snuck his tablet back into view. Air vents adjusted automatically at individual seats.

That same trepidation from the weeks before began ebbing back into her mind and stomach. Meredith assured herself that she would be detained, that the authorities, and one in particular, would seize her immediately. She doubted any drama—no guns, riot gear, or journalists—probably just a plain clothes FBI agent, an airport security member, or the Air Marshal sitting in Row K.

A twenty-something missing person, Meredith was not an obvious threat. To a select few, however, her mysterious return would be the most uncertain and troubling of dangers. By boarding this plane to New York, Meredith had been refocused in powerful eyes as a living liability to be eliminated by any means.

Chapter 1

March 15th, 2028
John F. Kennedy Airport, New York
12:15 p.m.

I imagine that the world used to sleep. Every evening, the sun going down, close her eyes in the comfort of the stars and sink into terrestrial slumber. It was possible then, of course, that was the way it was for millennia; when man was reverent to the sun, when the only human glow beneath the heavens that dared break the night was the light of fire.

Growing up on a busy avenue in the borough of Queens, night differed little from day. Only on the occasional urban-child rural excursion to places like Lake George or Gettysburg or Vermont, did I experience anything close to ancient dark. We'd camp out on summer nights in tents and there'd be a picture of us in the local newspaper. I'd try to stay up long enough to hear it—that stillness, the broad brushstrokes of nocturnal life, the sound of my own breath.

This fascination with the country and earth's native roots should have been a clear indication of what direction to point my life compass, but I stayed loyal to the city instead; first following my mother into psychology and then my father into the police force. And that's how I started—I examined the criminals, I discussed the atrocities, I testified in courts to the integrity of cranial constitutions—I dissected the accused, the confused, the undesirable. I was good at it too, numb to the horror, and I left my work at my desk. I got married in my mid-twenties, had a child, and then watched our family fall apart as my husband returned to the bed of his high-school sweetheart.

The divorce was how I ended up in D.C., working briefly for the State Department and then for the Federal Bureau of Investigation: Missing Persons Unit. I became *Agent Hanna Corsica* and joined the hunt for the lost. When we found them, I determined their distance from sanity. The FBI taught me to shoot a gun and deflect a knife, and in return I told them who was ready to return to society. Five years later, forty-seven cases have crossed my desk, from the mundane to the horrific, and all of them have been closed or transferred to another unit. My forty-eighth case arrived this morning just after Meredith Simon boarded a plane in Paris.

I was fifteen when Meredith disappeared. It was 2012 and only a few years before Hydrogen seriously entered the market. They said her father, Patrick Simon, was a murderer, a scientist gone off the edge. Evidence and sound reason showed that he'd arranged and committed heinous crimes, then violently sprung from hiding to abscond with his young daughter. The FBI led the resulting search, but the Simons were never found. I reviewed all the key details of the case on the journey up from Washington. My supervisor, Assistant Director Hugh Killian, says I'm on the lead for this one. Riding up separately, he called to tell me where to take Meredith after her plane lands at JFK—*Safehouse Five* in Brooklyn.

Two agents rode up with me from Washington and three others met us here at the terminal. It's not unusual for a large force to confront a single person, not in our line of work. We are standing near the gate and *PARIS (CDG)* is written in plain electronic type above the door where passengers have begun to emerge. A trans-Atlantic flight used to be a tiresome journey, but in just over two hours the supersonic trip is almost shorter than the drive out to Newark.

I look down at a security camera photo of Meredith, taken in Paris as she passed through customs. It's the first real picture of her in sixteen years, much better than our unflattering computer renderings and digital imagination. Her hair is shoulder length, wavy and brown. The curve of her eyes and nose are appealing, and I imagine her smile to be pleasant. She is slim, shapely, and the strength of her shoulders suggests dedication. Although the angle of the photo is limited, her posture is noticeably relaxed and does not suggest, to some surprise, that she is under duress.

I have stepped forward ahead of the other agents. If the situation appears hostile, then they will assist with force and hand-ties. If not, then Meredith is mine to guide away. Two Air Marshals on board the flight have been monitoring Meredith and one emerges now to signal that she is about to enter the terminal. I feel an unusual shiver of nerves. This is a high-profile case—the largest of my career—and I'm not sure why Killian has selected me to lead. I know little of Hydrogen or energy, and the closest I've come to the *environment* were those campsites in upstate New York.

As Meredith exits the door, her gait full of confidence, I straighten my face and take another step forward. She does not wait long to lock eyes, and once she has my estimations are confirmed—beauty, strength, health, happiness. I move forward again, but it's unnecessary, she is striking a direct path towards me. She has a handbag over her shoulder that swings lightly against her back. I half-expect her to hug me as one would a relative in the Arrivals Hall. I feel the agents rustle behind me, moving forward in support; rarely do people approach us with such confidence.

I stand my ground, chin raised. First impressions are crucial, vital in gaining trust and respect. When Meredith stops before me, her determined eyes even with mine, she is the first to speak.

"Hello, Hanna."

We don't use Hydrogen for everything, but a revolution is in motion. The coup began gradually, with little power plants springing up in rural areas across the US. Coal was the first to feel the heat as old power stations in states like California and Oregon gradually switched to Hydrogen. Federal legislation provided further momentum and Hydrogen stations now provide over 40% of US electricity, displacing aging coal and nuclear plants. There were features on TV that told how the technology worked, how the water molecule was split into Oxygen and Hydrogen using magnetism. To be honest, I never paid much attention. It was the same with coal plants and gasoline engines; I never knew how those worked either. We live our lives flipping switches, turning knobs, pushing buttons; it's a reflex.

Oil felt the next jolt as electric cars gained traction. Most energy companies adapted quickly, especially the larger ones with the capital to promptly enter a new market; ExxonMobil, Chevron, Shell, BP—these guys. The increase in Hydrogen power stations justified higher uses of electric power, and more importantly, the Hydrogen and electric vehicle lobbies joined forces at the Capitol. There's talk that Hydrogen-fueled cars will come next, but for the moment, electric cars seem to be doing just fine. I bought my first electric when I moved to D.C.—a 2023 Chevy Volt—I love it.

Fossil fuels have not entirely gone away. They still thrive in developing countries and within the burgeoning populations of China, India, and Indonesia—but Hydrogen is growing there too. It's the US and Europe, the descendants of the Seven Sisters, who have distanced themselves most from the black golds. There are more than a few people who say that the switch to Hydrogen resurrected the US economy. I don't doubt that they're right—the nation was in a rough way about the time Patrick Simon vanished with his daughter.

We go in a convoy of three vehicles; two agents, Meredith, and me in the middle car. I have not said much since our meeting in the terminal, but then again, protocol dictates waiting until you are in a controlled environment…or so I say to myself. In truth, Meredith has already taken the high ground. Having disappeared at the age of eight in 2012, she left before the spread of retinal scanners at airport security. The only tip to our foreign officers was that she used her real name and date of birth on a fake US passport. A quick examination of the facts might suggest delusion, but there was no *crazy* in those eyes when she addressed me by name.

The freeway into Brooklyn buzzes with common frenzy. Meredith looks out the window at her native land as I look back over her life on my tablet. I skim for details about her father, trawling through files and reports, hunting for ammunition, creating a backdrop. There is no shortage of intrigue in Patrick Simon's life—a script that has since been the focus of novels and movies alike. When we reach our destination, Safehouse Five, I will do the *interviewing*—a delicate term for interrogation. It is a skill I have been working hard to develop, one I feel that my son will come to resent. The key ingredient is material. You cannot read a person without context.

We hit heavy traffic on Atlantic Avenue and I recognize a particular clothing store. I grew up not far away, north a mile or so into Queens. My retired parents live in the same apartment, slowly improving its interior with the kids gone and their modest pensions arriving regularly. Meredith turns in her seat to look at me, as if sensing that my attention is no longer on her. I return to my tablet, skimming over an entry from an alleged journal of Patrick Simon. In his recordings, he repeatedly refers back to an event at *Pleasance Point*, calling it the epicenter of his career. Picking through the details of his youth, I see a pattern developing in his one-way carve through the dizzying world of energy. As with most passions, Patrick's fascination with energy began early on his life, sparked from little more than simple observation.

Chapter 2

May 1993
West Chester, Pennsylvania

Patrick was Prometheus in the school play. He was fourteen, and his was the generation rising with, not in, the shadow of technology. The drama teacher-director made this very clear in his pre-performance speech to the packed gymnasium.

"Bit of a windbag isn't he?" Mary whispered to George. She knew the premise of the play, while her husband did not. Their two younger daughters, Colleen and Kylie, 13 and 10, sat ambivalently beside them.

When Patrick had announced to the family that he had been given the lead part, George had not known what to say. He knew nothing of the theatre, and Patrick had never shown the slightest interest in acting. George was prepared to support his son, his first-born, and suppressed the traditional stereotypes about men of the stage. Nevertheless, leading up to Opening Night he chose to avoid the topic by insisting that the plot and all things Prometheus remain a surprise. Thirty minutes into the play, shortly after his son was chained to a rock, George was sound asleep. He woke to Mary's elbow, shamed, glimpsing the final torture of the well-meaning Titan.

Patrick had been handsome since birth, drawing first the coos of mothers and then the eyes of their daughters. He liked to swim, the individual nature of the sport fitting his ponderous identity. When comparing pictures, Patrick was a teenage version of his father, inheriting brawn, agility, and stubbornness. The placid kindness and appeal of his face, which shone through even as the eyes of Prometheus were gouged out by vultures on the stage, was courtesy of his mother.

"Can we go soon?" asked Colleen as the curtain was still falling. She was eager to get out of the humid gymnasium. Kylie, too, looked jittery.

Applause filled the room and parents rose to their feet as the young actors returned to the stage. George groggily stood and clapped. Mary was teary at his side as Patrick, unbound, came from the back of the stage for a solo bow. The clapping and whopping spiked, and a pride of girls sent a shrill up towards the stage. George nudged Mary. She slipped into his shoulder, wiping her eyes on his shirt.

They waited for him near the curtain, chatting with the other parents. George recognized a few of the faces from the rescue squad and police department. Other familiars had been in wrecks or happened by his office to spring their car from his towing yard. Kylie had found open space at the back of the gym, the gray folding-chairs receding towards the stage, and she chased paper airplanes made from abandoned programs. Colleen looked on, half-pretending that she did not know the little girl, aware that next year she would be a freshman.

Patrick emerged, ruddy and tired, his make-up scrubbed hastily away. George and Mary waited beyond the immediate crowd of parents and friends, allowing Patrick some final hand-pats and accolades before reaching their own open arms. Mary was first, rubbing at his unruly brown hair, followed by George who shook Patrick's hand before enveloping him in a hug.

"Great job Pat. You did great."

"Thanks Dad," Patrick said with a dry smile. "Hope you feel rested."

Caught out, George squeezed the boy into a more painful hug as a pair of girls walked by to wish Patrick good night.

Patrick looked after them and then back at his Dad.

"I suppose an hour on that rock might pay off," George whispered.

Patrick reddened as they began to walk for the exit.

"You want to ground our little air force, Mary, and I'll take Patrick," said George.

"That's fine. Should we stop at The Moo?" asked Mary in reference to the local ice cream parlor. "Patrick, you're the star?"

"Sounds good," replied Patrick.

"Then come young Prometheus," George played in a forced Greco tone. "Let us to iced cream go."

"Dad."

"Go to eat, that is."

The evening was starless and people filing from the gym sifted through the parking lot to their cars. Mary took the two girls in their white Ford Taurus, nicknamed *The Boat* for its hull-like hood and wide stern, while Patrick jumped up into the cab of George's tow truck, shutting the door on the yells, barks, and engines outside. He leaned against the hard back of the passenger seat, letting his eyes close in relief and accomplishment.

Patrick was no drama enthusiast. Indeed, this had been his first play. He had tried out on a whim because of a girl; Fiona Thompson, of whom he had been distantly fond since he could remember. It was a general rule that anyone who auditioned would receive a part and Patrick had sensibly expected a minor role. Getting the lead was a shock and a scare. A shock because of how close he got to be to Fiona—she was the make-up director—and a scare because he hadn't the slightest clue about acting. His mother had diligently run him through her own crash course on drama, sensing all the while that Patrick had ulterior motives for his sudden interest in the stage. Unfortunately, a week before opening night, Fiona got together with one of the vultures. Distraught, and much to the joy of the director, Patrick parlayed the tragic irony into his part.

Thunder rumbled as George climbed up into the truck. The older students hung by their cars eagerly awaiting the warm beer hidden in their trunks. It was Friday night and George felt guilty rushing Patrick away—surely ice cream with parents was not the only social reward available to the star of the show.

"Sure you're alright coming with us?" George asked, his eyes on the row of brake lights ahead.

"Yeah, I'm beat tired."

"Positive?"

"Yeah," Patrick confirmed.

"Still handle a little Moo?"

"Always."

"Good. Great job again tonight, I'm sorry I had to be old and fall asleep."

"Ah, I don't mind. It was good to have you there." Patrick paused. "Even if you were drooling."

"Ouch."

Patrick proceeded to recall a few of his mistakes that had gone unnoticed and George asked about scenes through which he had slept. By the time they reached the main road, father and son had fallen into silence.

The truck was getting old. George had owned it nearly thirteen years. His name was written plainly down the side along with his phone number and address. Nearly two decades previous, after his two tours in Vietnam, George had returned home visibly unscathed, the family house in Northern Philadelphia still peeling in all the same places, and taken a job with his Uncle Ernie's towing business. He met Mary shortly after at a garage sale and they married, choosing a poorly insulated apartment near the Eagles stadium as their first nest.

They moved out of the city because of Patrick. Mary had grown up in the countryside of Western Kentucky and believed in open spaces. Through his uncle, George arranged a loan to buy another man's business out in the suburbs of Philadelphia. Their current home had come with the tow yard, a modest two-story with three bedrooms and a back porch that leaked. It took George awhile to get used to the suburbs, especially the dark silences that abide beyond the flaxen glow and shadowing noises of the city. The town of West Chester was a far cry from Northern Philadelphia, but George liked it now and felt content to stay.

With a sudden whip of static, the truck's CB radio broke the silence of the cab. Patrick had been nodding off and jumped at the intrusion.

"George Simon, you there?" said a voice, distant and swept. It was not the usual West Chester police dispatcher.

"Who's asking?" George said warily, sensing a rouse. He knew most everyone who radioed him.

"This is Officer Trevor Cawley, Downingtown PD."

"Right, yeah." George knew right away that the call was serious. Downingtown was the next town over. "How can I help you, Officer?"

"That storm that just came through, not sure if it hit down there, well, it left us quite a mess," Cawley explained. "Our two guys, Rick and Paul, you might know 'em, they're going to be pulling all night at this rate. Trees down all over the place."

George knew where this was going. He looked at Patrick who gave him an understanding glance.

"What do you need?"

"Well, we just got an emergency call somewhat closer to West Chester, but still on our patch. Looks pretty bad. We were wondering if you could help us tow?" The officer then gave the location.

"How many vehicles?" Depending on their size, George could usually tow two cars at a time.

"Just one."

"Just one? Hold on a sec." He turned down the radio and looked at Patrick. "It's not far. I can drop you with Mom."

"It's fine."

"Your call."

"Can I come with you?"

"Um…sure. As long as you stay in the truck."

Patrick nodded consent.

"Okay," George replied, bringing the radio back up. "I'll be there in about fifteen minutes."

"Thanks, appreciate it. Crazy night over here. We'll have an officer there to meet you." Cawley gave the location again, said it was something to do with a lightning strike, and then cut off.

George reached back for the radio and punched in a few numbers. He had installed a radio in Mary's car and at home so they could talk when he was working.

In the summer of 1976, George had taken to searching for valuable second-hand books at garage sales throughout Philadelphia and then re-selling them to bookshops around the city. Although the hobby provided no substantial stream of income, George developed a knack for finding deals and it was a healthy diversion on Saturday mornings. Mary, meanwhile, was studying nursing at the Medical College of Pennsylvania, and spent her summers in the affluent neighborhood of Chestnut Hill with her Aunt and Uncle Bent. Humphrey Bent, Mary's uncle, also happened to spend his Saturdays scouring garage sales for vintage books. Some mornings Mary would go along with her uncle to half-assist, half-supervise—Uncle Bent was notorious throughout the second-hand scene for his questionable bargaining tactics and had even been banned from several flea markets.

During that summer of '76, Bent and George developed a cool rivalry over their mutual pursuit for discounted literature, taking turns at securing the best loot from the unsuspecting sellers. George had noticed Mary at a few of the sales, oblivious of her relation to Bent, and knew Mary only by her blue Chevy pick-up, long golden hair, captivating brown eyes, and delicate touch around antiques. Betwixt tables of lamp shades, photo albums and Frisbees, George eventually managed to speak with her. Soon they were taking coffee breaks at various stops throughout the city and having the occasional walk through Fairmount Park on a sunny day. It was not until George came to pick Mary up for their first official date that he learned her relation with his supposed nemesis. Uncle Bent nearly didn't let Mary out of the house; leaving George standing anxiously on the doorstep and struggling not to sweat through his navy blue shirt. One year to the day, they held a wedding for Mary and George at the very same home.

Mary's voice came buzzing through the speakers into the cab.

"Dang't George!" she yelled into the receiver. Despite being told otherwise, she still felt the need to speak extra loud when using the radio. "This thing freaks me out every time. What is it? We're almost there."

George explained.

"And you're fine with that?" Mary asked Patrick.

"Yeah, I'll probably just sleep anyway," Patrick answered, closing his eyes for effect.

"Well, the girls are expecting ice cream so I think we'll still go. Want me to pick up a pint for you two?"

"Moose tracks?" asked Patrick, opening one eye.

"Moose tracks for the hero," Mary blared into the speaker, jerking Patrick's other eye open. "See you boys at home."

The line crackled for a bit as she played with the knobs until the connection finally cut.

"You sure you're alright?" George asked, always hesitant about bringing family on a call. His work got ugly sometimes, even personal. The accident victims were not always anonymous faces in the paper.

"No prob. I'll hold down the fort," Patrick assured, shutting his eyes. "Or maybe just sleep in it."

They followed the local road down to a minor highway. Pleasance Point, their destination, was a well-known lookout, frequented by families during warm afternoons, but abandoned for lovers and couples in the evening. Or at least that was the way it used to be. George took the occasional break at a coffeehouse in town where he learned much of the community gossip, the majority of which he did not care to know. Word was that Pleasance Point had become an unofficial fighting ground of sorts. Kids, adults, men and women, could apparently go tussle there on select nights to make an extra buck. George came across a lot of these less rosy attributes of suburban Philadelphia on the job; chewed gum under pristine benches.

Pleasance Point was marked by an old wooden sign, erected in the Fifties for a young man's Eagle Scout project. The turning was just off the highway and led to a spiraling dirt road, worn flat over the decades. The road went around and around, circling the wooded hill, which emerged abruptly from the surrounding flat. Set apart from other land masses, the Point almost looked man-made.

Patrick slept against the window as they wound higher and higher. The shine of Philadelphia became steadily more striking as they neared the summit. While ascending the final incline, blue and red flashes of emergency vehicles came into view and George felt bark and chunks of wood beneath the tires. Patrick remained asleep.

The low beams on the truck illuminated a parked police cruiser. An officer was hunched over the passenger door, talking into a radio. He swiveled in the light, putting up his hands for George to stop. The officer set down the microphone and hustled to George's window. He was a short, middle-aged man that George had never met.

"Hey there pards'," said the officer He wore a police-issue poncho and spoke in a gravelly voice with eyes that hung like bare lamp bulbs. "You must be our tow man from over in Wes' Chester."

George immediately recognized the Kentuckian accent. Police could be deceiving: The mean ones looked kind and the cordial ones appeared sinister.

"Thanks for comin' up," the officer continued. "Ambulance is just loading up the boy now. Once they're on their way we'll have you in to grab the car. Didja' hear what happened?"

George shook his head.

The officer doffed his hat, running a hand down the bald spot where his hair had taken sides. Unknown to George, Patrick had woken up.

"So the boy here, I call him a boy but he's more like a young man, maybe in his twenties, he'sa up here with his lady enjoying the view and all that. You know, taking in the sights. Ya follow?" The officer gave a wink, his poncho rustling in the breeze.

George nodded patiently. "I follow."

"So this storm whips in and catches 'em by surprise. They were on the hood, by the way. And so the girl gets scared—least that'sa what she says—and goes back in the car. The boy, tough and all, stays out on the hood. Girl says he was shouting at the sky as the lightning and thunder get closer, probably puttin' on quite a show. You been up here before this?"

Though the place felt familiar, George shook his head—there were several years from his twenties for which he could not entirely account. He had inherited a taste for alcohol from his mother, a heritage he desperately wanted his children to disown.

"So there's a huge ol' oak tree that's been up here for years. Had carvings of everyone and their grandmother. Well, as the boy's dancing on the car, a bolt of lightnin' comes down and zonks that tree. Totally blows it to smithereens." The officer mimed the devastation. "Limbs and boughs thrown everywhere. Nuthin' left but a nine-foot trunk. That bark you was driving over was some of what's left. You'll see when you go up. I reckon a scientist or something would love to have a look."

The dense shrubbery behind the officer, affected by the flares of the cruiser, added an effective backdrop to his tale.

"So the boy and his gal were parked right up near this tree, and I dunno if it was the blast of the explosion, or if some of that 'lectricity got up into that car as well, but that boy got sent. I tell you, he was blown a good fifty yards into the brush. Girl said it all happened so fast. A flash, an explosion, but almost before the noise, her boy was getting cannoned away. Wild stuff, eh?"

"Is the boy alright?" Patrick asked from the passenger seat, his face flush with interest.

George flinched, forgetting that his son was in the truck.

"He's unconscious," the officer replied, un-phased by the teenager's presence. "But he'll live, paramedics say. Should be alright, least that's what they're telling the girl. Said she wouldn't stop screaming when they got here. Just hollering away. Luckily another couple came driving up shortly after the show. They drove down and called us."

"And the girl?" asked George.

"A few scrapes and cuts from one of the windows being blown out, but nothing that won't heal. She's gonna ride with him in the ambulance. Tell you what, she's mighty blessed a chunk of that tree didn't zip in and—"

An ambulance gave a *whop-whop* from out of sight. Without another word, the officer turned and started back up the road.

"You hear all that?" George asked Patrick, pulling to the shoulder.

"Yeah," said Patrick, watching the approaching rescue vehicle.

George studied his son. "Might be best if you don't mention it to your mother."

The ambulance passed in flashing silence, bobbling over the shredded wood, its occupants concealed.

The officer motioned for George to come along. Passing the cruiser, the Point came into view, as did the carnage of the strike. In contrast, the view of Philadelphia was spectacular.

The car was not charred or flaming as Patrick had expected. At first glance it looked fairly normal. George switched on the flood lights and the window damage became readily apparent. It was a red Chevy Cavalier that had seen better days, even before the recent shock.

The back of the car was closest to the tree, and glints of glass sparkled across the hood. Branches and sections of trunk were strewn about in a disorderly radius. It was as though someone had placed a bomb inside the tree.

"Those are some lucky kids," George said indirectly.

Patrick nodded, riveted by the scene.

George maneuvered about the wreckage until the truck faced opposite the Chevy.

"Stay in the car while I winch this up," George said as he hopped to the ground.

Patrick watched as his father began working out the chains. It was a rhythmic process, one that he liked to watch. Patrick cracked the window and felt the wind channeling in through the narrow slat. The siren of the ambulance reared from down on the highway.

Outside, George drew back at the wail, the wind whipping about him. This was his first lightning strike. Although common sense told him the car was safe, he remained cautious. Picking up a stick, he tossed it on the hood of the Cavalier. The wood bounced and thudded across the cold metal evoking neither snaps nor sparks.

George winched the car up onto its heels. Usually he would lift the vehicle onto the bed, but he was eager to chain tight and roll out. There was something about the location that made him uneasy. It was eerie, as if someone was watching from the bushes.

Everything secure, George hustled back to the cab.

"Ready to go Pat..."

The cab was empty.

George leapt from the truck. "Patrick!"

The wind had strengthened to a gale. Ominous clouds were regrouping. George looked frantically up the road, towards the bushes, and then back at the tree.

Silhouetted by Philadelphia, Patrick stood beyond the car, transfixed amidst the shattered frame of the great oak. There he ran his hand steadily along the shocked core of the tree, tracing the path of the strike and fatefully committing to memory the awesome power of a heaven-sent bolt.

Chapter 3

March 15th, 2028
Safehouse Five, New York City, New York
1:35 p.m.

Safehouse Five stands on a gravely avenue off Eastern Parkway in Brooklyn's Crown Heights. Four stories and worn, the tenement building appears to be just another brick of another New York City block. Litter lies in drifts against its sides and the front steps are stained and cratered. Trash cans are placed out front, the intercom system has names, and a mailman makes daily deliveries to a standard set of mailboxes. For fifty years, the building has been a regular member of the neighborhood. It's only on the inside, through the soundproof walls and past the holographic security measures, where the building is significantly different.

The structure was gutted when the FBI first purchased it under the alias of a ghost developer from Yonkers. In contrast to the usual hashed-up apartment plan, Safehouse Five was designed to be a single unit. The basement and first floor are buffer zones used primarily for storage and an impromptu recreation space for agents. A spiral staircase near the back leads up to the second floor, which consists of the main monitoring center, three small interview rooms, and a larger interview room where Meredith now sits. The third and fourth floors are split into mini-apartments, allotted for witnesses, detainees, or agents short of sleep.

Aside from the common entrance on the street, the building has another door at the back. This leads out to a two-vehicle covered carport and an alleyway. Most agents tend to enter through the front, always arriving in plain clothes, buzzing in, collecting mail, talking on cell phones, and altogether enhancing the façade. The back is reserved for visitors, who always come by car, shielded from sight by the plastic portico. Meredith is one such visitor, and it is FBI persons of interest like her that give Safehouse Five a purpose.

I watch her through the glass of the monitoring center as she goes through the final stages of identity confirmation. I'm debating my entrance. In all cases, I like to have an introduction which disarms the subject and allows me to more clearly assess their state of mind. With Meredith, I consider starting with some obscure facts about her father—lightning, alcohol, old friends—or perhaps something about Meredith herself—episodes from her childhood, her godfather, her mother. Then again, getting to the point may be more effective. I usually have more time to prepare for interviews, to create a backdrop and determine an opening gambit. The identity specialist wraps up his assessment with Meredith and I steady my file of papers.

Meredith checked one piece of luggage in Paris, a large padded suitcase. The item was removed as soon as the plane landed and brought here to Safehouse Five for inspection. I have yet to see the contents, but an agent on his break said there's about thirty years' worth of pre-digital paperwork. I don't envy that kind of analysis.

The door shuts behind the identity specialist, a lean black man with fashionable spectacles and strong cologne. He's from the New York office; everyone is local except me, Assistant Director Killian, and my two colleagues from D.C.—Agent Hanks and Agent Graham.

"That really is Meredith Simon," says the specialist.

Thanking him I push through the door into the interview room. When I am seated we make eye contact. Meredith smiles and the game begins.

How was your flight from Paris?

Shorter than expected.

Is that where you've been staying? You're quite tan for March.

It was on the way.

Have you been traveling long?

Not today.

Paris is a long way from Florida.

It is.

[Meredith studies me across the black Formica table. I move on.]

Ms. Simon, my name is Agent Corsica. I'm a member of the Federal Bureau of Investigation's Missing Persons unit. I'll be running you through a series of questions this afternoon, the answers to which are being recorded in the other room, and only there. Per federal guidelines, I'm required to tell you that these questions are optional. Should you prefer to abstain from answering, I can move on. This is not an interrogation; as far as I know, you have not committed a crime, nor should you feel any pressure to –

Thank you, but we can probably skip this part.

[I take the interruption well, half-expecting it.]

Are you in a rush, Ms. Simon?

Please, call me Meredith.

Okay, Meredith. What's the hurry?

That should become apparent soon.

I don't follow.

[Her speech is sure, feminine but not candied, and her accent has softened like one who has lived abroad. Killian has arrived in the monitoring center and his hoarse voice shudders through my earpiece: "Don't play dumb with her, Hanna, she's not our average kitten in from the rain." Although I don't appreciate the interruption, he's right.]

I presume that you're familiar with my story—my family's story?

I have a fair grasp of your background, yes.

Do you believe my father is a murderer?

[It is a question I have yet to ask myself.]

That's not my judgment to make.

Then what do you suppose?

Drawing on the conclusions of my colleagues, yes, I would suppose he is guilty of several crimes…one of which was abducting you.

[She accepts my answer with a nod.]

Is your father alive Meredith?

[Meredith says nothing. I study her clear eyes and squared posture. She has yet to show any symptom of concern or fear. What is it she wants? Clearly she has a prepared agenda for our meeting. She expected to be picked up at the airport, specifically by me, and then questioned.]

Why did you come back alone? Why now?

[I expect that Meredith wants to talk—she's come all this way—but only once she has established the importance of what she will share. Legitimacy must be earned and thus far she has made every effort to show composure and mastery. In most cases I am seeking the trust of the victim, but today the roles have switched. I do not know Meredith well enough to believe what she will tell me—but then again, I sense she is up for the challenge.]

Over fifteen years ago, at the age of eight, you mysteriously disappeared; allegedly abducted. A nationwide search was established, employing nearly every agency in the country. Your picture was regularly on the news, in the papers, placed on easels at prayer vigils. And in all this time, a decade and a half, nothing concrete was ever found to suggest where you'd gone. But today, out of thin air, you arrive on a transatlantic flight into JFK, grown up and traveling under your real name with a fake passport.

[Meredith watches me intently. Killian's voice returns in my ear. "Ease up, Hanna."]

Clearly you didn't come here on a whim. Very few 'Missing Persons' arrive after 16 years hauling a suitcase full of documents to greet their local FBI agent. If you're here because you want to come home and you want life to return to normal, then I can help. But if you're here to clear your father's name and liberate his reputation, then show me the evidence – because the evidence I have is less than flattering.

[Killian continues to breathe into the microphone and I recall from the briefing that the Simon case was his first with the Bureau.]

I'm not sure what you know about me, Meredith, or how you do, but I'm here to discuss your past and prepare for the future. And if that is so intimately tied to the events surrounding your father, then give me your side of the story – no one's ever heard it.

[Meredith smiles and leans back in her chair. I wait, unsure if I've just lost or gained credibility. After a brief silence, she starts talking about her parents. Killian sighs in relief. "Keep her going until we sort through her luggage—you would not believe what she packed." Meredith proceeds, speaking as if on the stand, charting the series of events, relationships, and experiences that would lead to her father's simple observation becoming a living idea.]

Chapter 4

November 2000
Boston, Massachusetts

Stroke. Stroke. Breath. Stroke. Stroke. Breath. Stroke…

Patrick Simon's hands made like blades through the water as he neared his final lap in the 800-meter medley. A familiar burn dug deeper into his lungs and he concentrated on the shape of the tiles at the bottom of the pool. His limbs felt drained of their muscle and yearned to be still. Ahead at the wall, a rectangular red board was lowered into the water to signal the last stretch.

Ducking beneath the surface, Patrick flipped, spun, and jettisoned off the wall. An onslaught of adrenaline flowed to dowse the flames in his chest. Pulsing and lunging, he breached the surface an impressive distance from take-off and continued his crawl, never looking to either side.

Halfway through the ultimate lap, he sprinted for the finish. It was no longer about the immediate pain, it was about completing the struggle. With five strides to go, he abandoned breathing and charged. The cheering and bursts of the crowd were swallowed in the beating water. It was just strokes now, a determined surge for the vertical stone.

Fully extended, Patrick's fingertips touched first. His body recoiled to narrowly avoid a full collision. The ceramic was like oxygen, and altogether his legs, arms, and back released their tension. Like a drifter come to shore, he clung to the wall gasping in short pants. Cheers and hoarse whoops rang out from The University of Pennsylvania section of the bleachers.

Patrick spit into the drain and raised himself from the water. He headed straight for the cool-down lanes, running a hand through dark brown hair and checking his time on the scoreboard.

On his way past, Patrick glanced at his coach, Jerry Cole. Coach Cole nodded to Patrick and turned back to the pool, holding back a grin. The closest competitor was a full lap behind.

The men's locker room rang and rank of the usual speech and scent; the same that makes it a playground for some and a dreaded part of team athletics for others. The Penn swim team had just beat Harvard for the third straight time, and this evening at the Crimson's home pool. The 400-meter relay squad was the most boisterous in victory, slapping and stinging bystanders with towels and profanities.

The hysterics subsided when Coach Cole entered. The Coach wore a tweed jacket over a black button-up shirt with the collar open. His nose was bent to one side from a fight during his youth in Scotland. He used his voice instead of a whistle during practice, roaring loud enough to make the divers flinch at the bottom of the pool. He was loved and hated, but always respected.

Joe Sharper, the team captain, clapped loudly to gain the room's attention. "Listen up!" Sharper barked, drawing a few scowls from his teammates.

The team huddled around a bench, Patrick amongst them. Towels hung haphazardly over shoulders and necks. Traces of chlorine, deodorant, and the scent of journeyed gym bags mixed in the air above them.

"A good swim ta'day gents," said Coach Cole, his hardy Scottish accent toned from two decades living stateside. "I know 'yer tired and will be wanting to get on to ta' buses alright, so I'll save my commen'tree for practice tomorrah'."

Eyes met in mutual disgust. Curses escaped under low breaths. Sunday practice after such a win seemed a bit steep, but it was common knowledge not to question Coach on his practice schedule. Nearly everyone held their tongue.

"Hey Coach," came the South Shore accent of Sam Nickels, vowels extended. He stood amongst a knot of juniors, a member of the 400-meter relay team who had been inciting chaos moments prior. He wore his athletics jacket over a pair of shorts. "You know, after such a victory, I think it would be appropriate if we had the day off."

The whole team turned to the Coach for his response. He did not take kindly to insubordination.

"I see," said Coach Cole. He leaned heavily on his right leg at all times and had a reputation of smiling when angry. "Is that your opinion?"

"Yes, Coach," replied Nickels brashly. "I'd say it was well earned."

"Aye," said the Coach, taking his gaze off Nickels and looking about the room at his team. For a moment, the team thought the bold negotiation was working, but no sooner had hope been permitted when the Coach began to smile. "It was a good swim, aye. But the pool is ours tomorrah'."

"Coach," Nickels began again to the surprise of the team. "I think we would all appreciate—"

"Silence!" burst Coach Cole, his voice chill enough to dry anyone fresh from the showers. "Nickels, get to the bus."

No one laughed. Patrick and the rest of the team looked over at Nickels as he solemnly bent to grab his bag.

"Leave that!" Coach Cole commanded. "The rest of you, clear up quick. Sharper, make sure everyone's 'oot. Simon, grab Nickels' kit. He can change on ta' bus."

Sharper and Patrick nodded.

Packing up took another half-hour. Patrick, the last to leave, pushed through the locker-room doors with a swim bag hitched over each shoulder. Singling out Patrick for such a menial task was Coach Cole's way of maintaining order. "Like the Lord Himself, I'm no respecter of persens'," Coach Cole would say, ignoring social protocol. "A God-fearing man is fearin' all 'ta time."

There were old black-and-white photographs on the wall near the exit. Patrick stopped to look at the antique Crimson faces. He always enjoyed swimming against Harvard. Not just for the revered name, but because of the pool, Blodgett Pool. It was not large nor new and renovated, or adorned with Ivy League frills. It was simply a pool, a place where you swam, and Patrick had become a great swimmer; dominant in his lane. A three-time, soon to be four, All-American, Patrick had not lost a race in two seasons. He had been named Pennsylvania Gatorade Athlete of the Year and missed the 2000 Sydney Olympic Team by one spot.

Yet for all these medals, Patrick could be disappointing to admirers. Unlike the fluid and graceful stride he used to decimate opponents, Patrick was less than exceptional on his feet. It was hard for his peers to describe. "Let's just say, things look bigger underwater," Patrick had overheard one girl say to another.

Since high school, this lingering expectation that Patrick would morph into some sort of deity, both wet and dry, had always built and then faded in the hearts of his fans, male and female. His features were subtly handsome. A strong chin held up a sloping nose, round brown eyes, a creaseless forehead, and a thick wave of dark hair. The longer someone looked at him, the more appealing he became. It was his hesitance in social situations that confounded, and his fascination of science was of little help.

Two buses waited for the swim team, their engines coughing into the face of a temperate November wind. They had parked across North Harvard Street amidst the avenues of the prestigious Harvard Business School. As Patrick left the building, just shy of 7:00 p.m., he felt taunted by the open space above the Charles River. It was a six-hour drive back to Philadelphia and his stomach braced itself against the unsettling ride ahead.

Of all the torturous duties that being a swimmer demanded, the long commutes rattled Patrick most. Several times, one to two hours into such a mammoth journey, he had sworn in a half-conscious, air-conditioned stupor that he was through with swimming. Yet his threats were baseless. He would never quit, nor would he lapse into indifference. For Patrick, there was more to swimming than a healthy dose of exercise, a satisfying extracurricular exertion, or credibility with peers. It was about his mother. She had loved watching him swim.

"Hey! Simon!"

Only a dozen paces from the exit, Patrick stopped and spun back towards the building. The sudden hail had come from behind him, somewhere in the darkness. Street lights and shadows made shapes along the natatorium and grounds.

A rustle perked Patrick's ears and Sam Nickels suddenly emerged from a set of small trees by the locker room exit.

"Come on!" Nickels motioned, looking around. His face was red and earnest. "Follow me!" Nickels then slipped back into the shrubbery.

Unsure if the chlorine had finally gone to his head, Patrick took up slowly after Nickels, obeying out of intrigue.

The sharp roar of an engine accelerating in first gear flared from the vicinity of the buses. Patrick whipped around, one of the bags flying free from his shoulder. Headlights traced the buildings of the Business School, their shadows swaying like boats in a steady breeze. Confusion gripped Patrick—his ride was leaving without him.

The buses reached the end of the Business School side road and began arching back towards the natatorium. Patrick realized that he could run to hail the bus or just stay rooted where he was; either way he would be illuminated by the headlights. The first bus began its turn. Patrick looked back to where Nickels had disappeared. He wondered how he could alert his teammate that they were about to be stranded.

At that same instant, the locker room door opened behind Patrick and out walked Joe Sharper. The team captain was dressed sharply, a little too sharp for the grungy bus ride home. Sharper paused when he saw the bag that had flung off Patrick's shoulder, the smug look on his face vanishing. He quickly tracked the bag to Patrick's curious frown and then onto the approaching bus. The headlights would be on them in seconds. Sharper's face tightened and he leapt forward, grabbing the bag and rushing at Patrick.

"Go, go, go!" Sharper yelled. Lights coated the side of the building.

Patrick, still failing to grasp what could possibly be going on, let himself be grabbed and thrown to the ground. A row of unsightly bushes cushioned their landing as Sharper dove and rolled past him.

The lights of the first bus passed over, then the second, and then it was dark. The sound of the engines faded slowly towards the highway.

Patrick laid on his back, not knowing what to feel—elation at not being on the bus, confusion at just being tackled into a row of bushes, or anger at just being tackled into a row of bushes. Patrick cocked his head towards Sharper who was getting to his feet and brushing at his pants.

"Simon," Sharper said tersely. "What the hell are you doing?"

Patrick felt like asking the same question of his captain.

"Simon, Sharper...you made it." The interruption was Chase Baker's, another Penn teammate who had now emerged accompanied by Nickels and two other swimmers. "Ready to go?"

The band of collegiates, six in total, was soon afoot and dashing towards Boston. Walking briskly with the pack, Patrick began to weld together the hot spurts of boasting from his teammate-conspirators. It seemed that their final destination was the city center where Baker's brother owned a night club. Along with Nickels and Baker were their close friends, Max Amado and Skip Turner, the final two members of the 400-meter relay team. The four junior-year swimmers had rarely strayed from one another since pre-season camp two years previous. Sharper and Patrick were the odd seniors of the group and Patrick assumed the captain was aboard only for his stripes. Except for Patrick, they were all twenty; Sharper, just one month shy of legal age.

The escape had been well planned. After the meet, Amado, Baker, and Turner had slipped out into the darkness to hide. Nickels then provoked Coach Cole, knowing the Coach would blow up and then send him to the bus. The buses were parked far enough away that it was effortless for Nickels to melt into the evening. In the interim, Sharper had arranged permission to return home with his parents, who had indeed been in attendance but not expecting to be collecting their son. Fulfilling his captain duties, Sharper issued the call to Coach in the front bus that everyone was aboard and then simply returned to the building where his parents were supposedly waiting for him. The plan had functioned flawlessly until Patrick, who usually lingered in the locker room, had frozen with confusion in plain view.

Not exactly the "clubbing" type, Patrick did like the idea of going to Boston. He was an academic at heart, a chemical engineering major usually consumed by thought or trial in a lab or library; places where he was comfortable. Besides hanging out with Alika and Ward, his two best friends at Penn, Patrick rarely strayed far beyond his routine of studying, swimming, and sleeping. His last girlfriend had been an awkward fling with an exchange student during sophomore year and his observance of the "dry-season" rule to not drink while the team was training—which was practically all year—made meeting new people increasingly difficult. Although affable, humorous, and engaging, it was a matter of priorities that stymied the social life of Patrick Simon.

Thc group shortly reached a more traveled road and Baker held up his hand. A street sign read *Western Avenue* and Patrick could feel that they had left the Harvard campus. They crossed the street amid the stutter of weekend traffic and gathered up around a lonely bus sign. A passing motorist would have described them as boys, not men, their wet hair frosted like grass in the yellow light of the street lamps.

Patrick stood off to the side while the four buddies kicked and shuffled around each other. Thanks to the balmy weather they wore short-sleeve collared shirts or button-up shirts with the cuffs rolled back to their elbows. Loafers snug under well-fitting jeans or dark khakis completed their nightlife look. Sharper kept aloof as well, occasionally checking his wallet, brushing at the two grass stains on his knees, and absently patting his hair. He had no desire to blend in with the junior band or partner with Patrick.

"Hey Patrick," Baker called through the din of traffic. "You don't mind paying the bus fare, do ya? It'll just be a few bucks—great investment too," Baker bargained. "But Pat, you gotta lose that tie."

Patrick considered the brown and white piece and then loosened it from off his neck. He always dressed up for meets.

The bus pulled up and the boys piled on. Patrick shelled out the $2.50 to pay his way, then followed Baker and the crew along the aisles of several buses, one of which took them the wrong direction and provoked some heavy cursing from Nickels. They grabbed dinner from a burrito cart near one of the bus stops, Amado spilling salsa all over his shirt as they entered the metro. By 10:30 p.m. they were walking past the Boston Commons along Boylston Street.

The Jade Club, owned by Baker's brother, had entered the Boston social scene by accident three years previous when several big names had dropped by the club on account of their drivers mistaking the Jade for another venue. Already sizzled with spirits, the celebs had remained at the Jade, and to the young owners' delight returned the following weekend with paparazzi in tow. Ever since, it had become a steady stop on the Boston nightlife circuit.

From the street, Baker led his guests out in front of the club. It was still early, but a line was already forming the sidewalk. Women of all ages were dressed in an array of revealing attire. Most stood talking, shifting, and anxiously scanning one another. Men smoked cigarettes, held their girls possessively around the waist, joked in groups, and generally tried to appear made, impressive, kings.

"Gents," Baker said with a showboat smile, his collar popped tight. "I think we better use a more suitable entrance."

Carrying on past the club, Baker continued to pomp the venue. Purple lights cast a sultry ambience upon the waiting crowd. A gold-rimmed balcony extended over the bouncers and valets that tended to the tide of arriving guests. A thin cursive sign to the left of the balcony read *The Jade Club.*

"They added that balcony this past summer," Baker commented. "And most of the bouncers are ex-NFL."

Amado and Turner were quiet and smiling. Nickels went back and forth playfully punching the pair in unusual glee. Sharper looked like he was about to pull a bank heist, his face stiff and guarded. Patrick brought up the rear thoughtfully observing their surroundings.

They finished off the block, passing two more bars, and then ducked down a side street. The alley was cobblestone and visibly old. Patrick imagined the work that had been expended in its original construction. It seemed a shame that such a deposit of effort was now merely an unused causeway.

Plodding round the buildings, the cobblestones ended abruptly in mottled pavement. Through a haze of milky floodlights, Patrick could make out the loading areas behind the bars and other stores. The back of the Jade Club looked weathered and pasty, a stark contrast to the side that entreated the public. A small sign was nailed to a post outside a loading dock with plastic doors. Block letters painted black by hand read *Jade.*

A man that looked part-bartender, part-troll was out having a smoke on the loading dock. Baker called up to him with his brothers' name.

"Whatchya' need wid' 'im?" the man asked Baker, looking into his crumpled pack for another cigarette.

"I'm his brother," Baker replied strongly, his lungs rich with pride.

"An' I'm his bahtendeh," the man spat back. "Go on and piss off."

The swimmers froze in surprise.

"No," Baker insisted. "He's expecting us. I really am his brother."

"Nevah heard of it," the bartender scoffed. "Go on and get out 'fore I call security to rough you." The bartender had given up looking for another smoke and flicked his spent butt into an old coffee can. He narrowed a hollow look at the boys and then turned inside through the plastic loading doors.

"Nice guy," Nickels said.

"Arrogant punk," Baker hissed in a low voice. "Thinkin' that he works here he can..." Baker trailed off into an imperceptible ramble of cursing.

A row of cars, trucks and SUV's were parked behind them on an old lawn that had become hard and gravely. Patrick looked the vehicles over, intrigued by their varying quality. A Beamer, an S-Class Mercedes, then a Toyota Corolla and a Ford Escort, the latter two rusting considerably.

The night grew quiet around the boys. Baker began to walk towards the door that the bartender had entered. No one else moved. The sobering reproof had shaken their spirits. Patrick was ambivalent, an observer only.

Baker reached the steps to the loading area. There was another door to his left that looked like it led into a kitchen where a faint light was on. Patrick imagined most of the Jade's business centered about the mug and glass rather than the knife and fork. Baker opened the kitchen door and quickly entered. Amado whispered something to Turner. Sharper fumbled with his belt. Patrick looked up into the sky. The city lights echoed an orange-gray glow that made the stars, and even the moon, imperceptible.

A slam came from the loading dock area and Baker suddenly emerged from the plastic doors. He was frenzied, off-balance, and spat curses back into the loading area.

Patrick could not see Baker's pursuer, but he could tell that Baker was intimidated. Indeed, Baker's face seized further as a large black man in a dark gray suit pushed after him through the hanging plastic flaps.

Baker hopped down from the dock and back onto the gravel. The man was a bear, bigger than Alika, and Patrick imagined the bouncer to be one of the acclaimed NFL alumni. Baker continued to back away, cradling his left arm slightly. The bouncer calmly walked towards the stairs that led down into the lot. Sharper and the rest began to retreat as well. Patrick remained still.

Baker had stopped about 20 feet from the base of the dock. "What are you gonna' do?" he spit, confidence failing. "I'm Seth Baker's brother!"

The bouncer walked past Patrick. His suit was pin-striped and his head perfectly bald. Patrick saw conviction in the bouncer's gunmetal eyes—this man was going to hurt Baker. Patrick shot a glance at the others. Their divine plan was unraveling; disappointment becoming fear as their leader cringed.

"Nickie!"

All heads switched in unison to the source of the voice. A man stood on the loading dock, his sharp dress in immaculate contrast to the building's drab exterior. Patrick recognized the matured face of Seth Baker. Seth had swum at Penn when Patrick was in grade school, and many of the school records that Patrick now held had previously belonged to Seth.

"Charles, it's okay. They're all right," Seth said calmly. The bouncer had stopped mere feet from his target. After a solid stare at the young Baker, Charles turned around and walked back towards the loading dock. Seth descended the stairs and gave Charles a pat on his way past. Patrick went unnoticed again.

"You can't do anything without raising hell, can you?" Seth said as he walked towards Baker, the younger brother's tongue held in the presence of his elder. Seth's face then slackened to just short of a grin and he pulled Baker into a mauling hug. "Glad to see you taking some initiative," Seth said in a fatherly tone. "Were you going to take on ol' Charles there? That would have been a sight."

Baker shrugged in humble silence.

"These you're guests for the evening?" Seth continued, taking in Patrick and the others. "Not a bad lot." There was a mark of confidence in the frame of Seth's speech and his demeanor suggested that he had appropriately adjusted to his own success. "Well come in out of the dark, got a big night ahead. Should get some liquor in you chaps. 'Specially you Nickie!"

They all laughed and moved forward for introductions.

Seth had been on the phone with a high-end agent when the boys arrived. Such calls were piped daily into his plush office on the Jade's top floor. Before seeing to more business, Seth set the boys up in an adjacent room. A round oak table topped with various bottles of liquor dominated the setting. Seth provided a collection of tumblers and shot glasses and invited the boys to tuck in.

From his spot at the table, Patrick could see through Seth's open office door. The room's design was simple and uncluttered with two low-slung black armchairs opposite a dark-stained wooden desk. A bookshelf held old and new volumes, several photo frames, and a few cultural souvenirs from time spent abroad. Seth sat behind the desk with his ear jammed into a phone, his feet occasionally propping themselves up on the desk.

Back at the oak table, the drinking game *Kings* was in full swing. Patrick had excused himself from the outset, choosing a can of Coke from the fridge instead. That he was observing the dry-season rule that the other boys should have been keeping enabled him to escape excessive ridicule. Patrick had drunk before, being startled by how promptly his body enjoyed and then craved the taste. As his father had warned, the damning habit was all too natural for a Simon.

With a substantial buzz achieved, Seth led his guests down into the club. The bodied scents of cologne, perfume and alcohol clouded about the boys as they melted into the swirling crowd. Lights flashed and faces lit to a steady beat. The anticipation of debauchery was palpable. Patrick trailed the group pensively.

The club had two main levels, a bar on each, and a VIP room with a drinks station of its own. The floors were sleek and black beneath the flood of mincing feet. The walls were a medley of white and dark-green tile, which whirled about in abstract patterns. They passed through the upper level, the lounge section of the club. Large cushioned booths and cocktail tables dotted the landing. Barmen dressed all in black dipped in and around the soft chairs to cater to the clientele. Steps led down on to the dance floor, which was surrounded by several more layers of light seating and high tables. The DJ was pocketed on a raised platform in the corner of the room. Head down, he bobbed loosely over his vinyl.

Seth continued down the steps and onto the floor, stopping intermittently to greet a strategic somebody. Their destination was the main level bar where Seth called one of the tenders and yelled something into his ear. The song changed and Seth swung back to the boys, telling them to get a good look at the bartender.

"This man is your gateway to all that lies beyond," Seth said loudly as the music rumbled about the room. "Order from him and there's no charge."

As Seth bid them a wild night, Patrick's teammates began busily placing orders with the bartender. They were not scheduled to leave until the following morning, the plan being to crash at Amado's Uncle's house and then commandeer the Nickels' old family mini-van for the return journey to Philadelphia. Beginning to wish that he had not dawdled in the locker room and missed the bus, Patrick maneuvered away from the bar, pressing awkwardly through couples and groups. A glowing sign for the bathrooms gleamed ahead and Patrick pushed towards it.

Women talked in groups, picked through purses, and casually waited in the long line extending from the Ladies room. Patrick edged past towards the Men's, which appeared to be less popular. Air fresheners and fans were hard at work in the hallway where the club's bump and beat was muffled.

As he came to the bathroom door, posted by a large triangle with a posh gentlemen, it opened towards him. To Patrick's surprise, a girl stood in the doorway. The combination of her gender and beauty made him freeze.

Roughly Patrick's age, the girl shouldered a purse. "What?" she shrugged, deflecting his gape. "It was empty."

Patrick wanted to say something, something witty. Her hair was long and brown, straightened and shiny. She wore a dark blue dress with a silver necklace.

She smiled at Patrick's silence and graciously stepped past him, her heels clapping on the tile, the scent of her perfume nicking Patrick as she walked back into the fray.

Patrick muttered something inaudible and pressed forward through the swinging door. The bathroom was empty. He stepped to a urinal and the image of the girl returned. The curve and sway of her face, the length of her neck, that pivot of her hips. The dress, and the way it brushed at her knees. She had been utterly stunning.

The porcelain sang and Patrick cursed himself. He was tragic with women.

Hadley Hannigan was frustrated. An wonderful evening that she had long anticipated was concluding in disgust.

Several weeks previous, she had been chosen to participate in a pilot column for The Boston Globe. The column was to feature aspiring journalists in Boston with local roots. As a graduate student in journalism, the opportunity was a heel-clicking break for Hadley. A man named Gary Coulier was the liaison between the journalists and the Globe. To kickoff the initiative, Coulier had invited all the selected journalists out for a meet-and-greet dinner at a restaurant near Quincy Market.

After the meal, which Hadley happily spent chatting with fellow writers, Coulier slyly pulled Hadley and several other more attractive female participants aside and invited them to come along later that evening to the Jade. Excited to go somewhere swank, and under the impression that all were invited, Hadley had arrived to find Coulier waiting with two other recruits. While the other girls heedlessly sank beneath their host's barrage of cocktails, Hadley gradually distanced herself and at last slipped away to the bathroom. Hadley realized there was nothing unusual about Coulier's advances, but she was bitter about the general decay of the evening—from an inspiring gathering of creativity to a carnal cacophony. She enjoyed the occasional taste of chaos and intrigue as much as the next girl, except preferably with the right company.

Reaching the restrooms, and not in the mood or state to wait, Hadley had entirely bypassed the Ladies and gone straight for the Gents, ignoring an over-powdered blondes' suggestions about how careless Hadley was with her virtue. She had used the facilities, finding them surprisingly clean, and encountered no one but the sober and surprised man on the threshold. He had been handsome and she had proudly left him in her trail as she marched to the coat room to get her things and leave.

Nearly there, she noticed Coulier seeking to interrupt her departure. Feigning that she had not seen him, Hadley dipped back into the club as if looking for something, weaving her way through the tables and chairs at the second level. Satisfied that she had eluded Coulier, Hadley nestled into an obscure booth at the rear of the club and waited. Dark bottles and empty glasses freckled the table, creating a still life in the vibrant movement of the club. A new song started and a group of girls about a nearby table squealed and oozed as one to the dance floor.

Casually observing the girls bump and grind, Hadley watched with further amusement as the same man from the bathroom awkwardly side-stepped through their group and made his way to a small curtain, above which hung a small sign that read *Smoker's Respite.* Hadley did not smoke, but she found herself intrigued by this character who looked even more miserable than her. Unsure if Coulier was still lurking, Hadley followed the same path through the curtain, entering onto a golden balcony where two dozen clubbers were milling around with drinks and tobacco.

The view looked onto the Commons and Hadley made a path through a pack of young professionals to an open spot by the railing. A slight breeze slipped up from the street and she folded her sleeveless arms. He was further down the railing, gazing out into the park as if thirsty for the outside world. Her thoughts danced creatively upon his brooding frame. He looked strong and athletic, and she wondered if his tousled brown hair was naturally untidy or if there was vanity in its preparation, if his clothes were unfitting to the venue because he had arrived unexpectedly or if he fancied himself a man of fashion. The profile of his face was soft and she imagined that his eyes were the same timber color as his hair. He reminded her of someone, someone with whom she was very close.

Patrick glanced down the railing entirely unprepared for the perfection that confronted him. Her hair was brown, shoulder-length, playful. Her eyes held their chocolate color even in the darkness of the night. Her features had a flawless flow; leading Patrick all about her face until gently returning him to her eyes. It was the girl from the bathroom, and she was walking towards him.

"Wingman?" she asked on approach, one hand on the railing.

"Wingman?" Patrick repeated, barely finding his voice.

"Not a wingman," she confirmed, smoothing her dress and then folding her arms, sizing him up like a tailor. "How about...your friend just made it big—maybe as a trader or a young exec—and he dragged you along tonight to prove how high he's risen?"

Patrick smiled. "Getting warmer."

"Am I?" Her voice was steady with a faint Boston polish. "Then one more guess." She locked eyes with his. "You got stood up. And in the process sank half your paycheck to get on the guest list. You figured you'd at least drown your sorrows, yet after that first drink the insatiable lust of those around you smothered even your deepest self-loathing." She paused to raise an eyebrow. "And so here I find you, standing alone on the balcony of one of the richest night clubs in the country, wishing you were somewhere else."

Patrick laughed. "I see you enjoy elaboration."

"Only on things I think I understand," Hadley replied.

Another couple shouldered past Patrick, nudging him closer to Hadley. "Meaning that you wish you were somewhere else too?"

"Correct," she said.

"Well, you were half-right at the end there," Patrick remarked after a brief silence, unsure if this meant she wanted to continue talking. He wanted to continue talking. "Although I didn't think I was being so obvious."

"Just a little."

"Did I meet you earlier?" Patrick asked, knowing the answer.

"I believe you did," she said, also appearing thoughtful. "Though we didn't really *meet* did we?"

"No, I guess not. But of all places to talk that was probably the quietest. Do you go there often?"

Hadley laughed, louder than Patrick expected, and she snorted slightly through her nose.

"I never caught your name," Patrick followed quickly, heartened by his rare word play.

"Hadley."

"I'm Patrick."

"Pleasure to meet you Patrick," she said, extending her hand.

"Likewise." Her hands were warm on his.

They both smiled and looked out on the pressing crowd below.

"So what do you do?" Patrick continued.

"I'm getting my MFA at Boston College," answered Hadley.

"Cool," said Patrick, unsure what MFA stood for. "Are you from Boston?"

"My accent doesn't give it away? Yeah, born and raised."

"Nice," said Patrick, suddenly forgetting everything he knew about Boston. "Do you want to stay and work here?"

"Probably. My family's all here and I love the city."

"Yeah, seems like a nice city." He gestured at the Commons, clutching for words. "Very green."

A group of girls skirted past, casting glances at the isolated pair. Patrick turned to ask another question, but Hadley was no longer leaning beside him. She was upright, brushing the back of her dress. Her face had straightened and Patrick assumed this was her exit. She had not asked anything about him, only guessed why he was moping about on the balcony—a question that did not really have an answer—and he imagined she was disappointed like the rest of them.

"Would you care to go for a walk?" she asked.

Patrick's face betrayed him.

"Good," said Hadley, already starting for the curtain. "I'll show you some 'green'."

She led the way back through the club towards the main door. Patrick followed, mesmerized, watching the way the hem of her dress flowed like a tide across the backs of legs. Glances naturally broke against her as she navigated the various islands of drink and gossip. The music continued to rage, but in her wake, Patrick felt a deep and unusual calm.

They strode into the Boston Commons around midnight. Hadley knew the grounds well and maneuvered them about the gazebos, large trees, and ponds. She had retrieved her coat from the check and Patrick had rolled down his sleeves against the new morning air.

It was Hadley's turn to ask questions; learning the events that had led Patrick to the Jade's golden balcony, laughing as he described being thrown to the ground by his team captain. She had noted his social hesitance back in the club and was still diagnosing it as he moved on to explain his engineering degree at Penn. It was not so much a stutter as a shyness, subtly avoiding eye contact and arranging his words like letters on a Scrabble board. Hadley knew other people that required a running start to enter a conversation, and she found with Patrick, as she had with others, that the awkwardness faded the longer he spoke.

"And do you intend to change the world?" she asked. He had just finished explaining a master's degree in renewable energy that he was thinking of pursuing the following year. It was their second lap around the park.

Patrick shrugged. "In the sense that everyone knows my name? No, probably not." They walked a few steps in silence, their elbows touching every so often. "But it would be nice, I suppose, if my work made some sort of impact."

"Come on," she said playfully. "You must think about it—conquering those evil, elusive oil tycoons, replacing the pollution of fossil fuels, being the Bill Gates of the energy world...something like that must have crossed your mind."

He played down a laugh. "In some form, yes, I've thought about it—the glory you describe—but it's never really distracted me much."

"So what motivates you then?"

Patrick cleared his throat slightly and absently raised his shoulders. It was a significantly deeper question. "I love solving problems," he said. "My friends say that's what 'makes me tick', and I assume they're right. Energy, too, it's been a mystery to me since I was a kid, and I can't seem to learn enough about it. I mean...there's so much to it and still so many questions about how to make it, how to store it, how to use it. It's not revolutionary—but I really think there's a better way we could be doing things. What exactly 'that way' is, I'm not sure, but it's the problem-solving mainly—something about finding a solution, and striking a path to get there, like a mountain climber scaling a peak, all of what's involved, that's what...I guess, fuels me."

Hadley waited a few seconds before speaking. "On a roll with the puns tonight, aren't we?"

He laughed and looked ahead. Another couple was walking up the path, arm in arm, and Patrick moved away from Hadley to let the other amblers pass between them. "So what brought you to the Jade?" he asked when they were side by side again.

"It's not as thrilling or mischievous a tale as yours," she began, "But not altogether uninteresting."

As Hadley recounted her evening up until their meeting at the restrooms, she regretted her flippant pun remark. She had known immediately that Patrick was opening up to her and likely in a way rarely displayed. There was honesty in his gestures and expressions, and everything he said to her felt real and free of deception. It stood in solid contrast to the marauding predators found in plenty at the club, the ones who crept up from behind or clumsily grabbed your hand. Patrick was also different than the men that Hadley had historically preferred. She was on a lawyers-kick of late and had just broken things off with a junior associate at a firm in Cambridge. He had treated her well, taken her to nice places, and was a decent lover, but something had been lacking—everything was too predictable.

They had circled the park again and Patrick checked his watch for the second time in as many minutes, acknowledging that he would have to meet his teammates soon. She sensed he was reluctant to leave, and she also felt resistance to parting. Since her account of Coulier, she had noticed with amusement how Patrick strained to keep his eyes above her neckline. He reminded Hadley so much of her Nicholas.

They entered a clearing by the frog pond where the city-glow sky nearly passed for moonlight. Barrels of clouds rolled slowly between the pair and the stars.

"A warm night for November," Hadley commented, wondering if he would try and kiss her, unsure whether she wanted him to.

"Beautiful," he echoed, looking up into the dark infinity above.

"PATRICK!" a voice maniacally yelled, breaking the charged calm. "Patrick! Is that you?"

They both turned to see the form of Joe Sharper stumbling through the park.

"Joe?" Patrick asked with some dread.

"Patrick!" the drunken captain confirmed. He stopped just short of a collision with Hadley. "Hello," he said, sloppily sizing her in all the usual places.

"Joe!" Patrick cut in, regaining Sharper's attention. Patrick looked apologetically at Hadley, whose face was a mix of amusement and concern. "What's going on?"

"Patrick, we couldn't find you," Sharper slurred. "And Skip and Sam, man, they got thrown out!" Sharper paused to burp, then resumed. "So we all left, and then we realized, 'Hey, we need

Patrick.' Well actually, it was more them that said that, because we need you Patrick…I need you."

"Thanks," said Patrick as Hadley suppressed a laugh.

"It's true man," Sharper continued, putting a sweaty arm around his teammate. "I mean...what would we do without you?" Sharper turned to Hadley. "Have you seen this guy in a swimsuit?" With surprising quickness, he lurched forward and threw his other arm around Hadley. "He looks alright."

"Hey," Patrick almost shouted, loosing himself and Hadley. "So where are you all going?"

"Back to Amado's, his uncle's or something," Sharper said, his voice wavering. "I'm really tired Patrick. Really tired."

"Can you tell me the address? I need to…" He looked at Hadley and she smiled. "I need to stay out a little longer."

"Address?"

"Yeah, to Amado's."

Sharper frowned. "I don't know." He was getting caught up on Hadley again.

"Can you find out? Being captain and all."

Beneath the glaze of alcohol, his formal title stirred a sense of responsibility in Sharper. He shot a look at Patrick. "Better believe it." Sharper then took off weaving down the path, yelling for Nickels and Amado.

"Sorry about that," Patrick said to Hadley.

"Not at all. Nice to meet a friend of yours," she grinned. "He has a certain charm. Found attractive, I'm sure, by other women."

A minute later, Sharper came rearing back with an address written erratically down his arm. After Hadley confirmed that she knew the street, Patrick excused Sharper. He gave them both a long wink and took off once more.

Patrick turned to Hadley. "Would you be able…?"

"To walk you home?" she guessed. "I'd love to."

Patrick woke to hot breath. He kept his eyes closed, opening them when he felt a tongue graze his cheek. The Labrador, black as a kettle, leaned in close to give Patrick a good sniff about the head.

"Bwah!" Patrick sputtered, wiping his face and sitting up. The dog took the hint and moved on with a wet huff.

The living room was lightly furnished with two couches, a coffee table, and a recliner. Faded magenta curtains hid the room from the morning light. The recliner was at full extension beneath the sleeping bodies of Amado and Turner; their noses inches apart. They had been fighting for the chair when Patrick arrived and appeared to have dueled to a draw. Sharper was passed out a few feet from Patrick on the floor. Baker and Nickels had swindled the two couches. The Labrador was honing in on Sharper now, his tongue probing about like a cane. Patrick checked his watch: it was 9:30 a.m.

Patrick lay back on his swim bag, which had debuted poorly as a pillow. A beautiful sensation stirred within him as he thought back on the night before. He had kissed her. *Hadley*—a name that meant little to him when he left Philadelphia the morning before. Now, all he could think about was the way he had brushed soft, silken hair out of her eyes so as to see her face more clearly when they kissed. Unsure if it was sensory, Patrick could still detect the playful tones of her perfume on his shirt, centered where she had pressed as they lingered on the steps of Amado's uncle's brownstone home.

It charmed Patrick to know that they had both been sober, that no artificial chemical had initiated their actions, and that the phone number in his pocket had been given with complete intent. He hoped that he could see her again. Chances were high, Patrick knew, that Hadley would be distantly cordial when he called, marking the evening down as a pleasant encounter and nothing more, but as much as he cautioned himself, he could not shake the hope that something amazing had occurred in his life and that the potential result would be worth a fight.

Sharper let out a disgusted yelp as the Lab smothered him with saliva. Baker had come alive as well and was sitting upright on the couch. He stood and yawned loudly at the ceiling, his hair askew in every direction

"Good morning Boston!" Baker cried with hangover bravado. Amado, Turner, and Nickels all jostled and stirred. Stumbling on a shoe, Baker pointed at Patrick. "Pat, you better drive."

Chapter 5

May 2001
Philadelphia, Pennsylvania

During his undergraduate years at the University of Pennsylvania, Patrick studied, swam, and had two best friends; Alika Tucker and Ward Prince.

Alika was Samoan, 6′6″, broad-chested, and wore glasses. He kept his tight curly hair short like a mat, played the drums in a band, and at 260 pounds was surprising agile on the volleyball court. He had first come to the United States as a foster child at the age of seven.

Alika also studied chemical engineering, although his first encounter with Patrick was outside the classroom. School had been in session for over a month and Alika had come to the swimming pool after playing pick-up basketball with a few guys from his freshman dormitory. Walking past the lanes where the swim team was practicing, two of Alika's friends got into a lighthearted shoving match. In the struggle, an elbow caught Alika in the face, knocking him off balance. He slipped on the tile, recovered, and then fell backwards into the pool—landing directly on top of Patrick. The aerial blow sent Patrick drifting unconscious to the bottom. Lifeguards blew whistles and coaches yelled, but Alika was already swimming down to collect the victim. Poolside, a lifeguard gave Patrick mouth-to-mouth and the wily Coach Cole brought him round with a mix of swear words and smelling salts. Revived, Patrick looked over at Alika, who was still in the water, clutching the side in angst. "Lane's all yours," he sputtered. They had been friends ever since.

Ward was a transfer student from Stanford who smoked when he played tennis, read the Wall Street Journal religiously, and had the looks of a daytime television star. He arrived at Penn in junior year, and despite his aura of finance and business, was also a chemical engineering major. Born and raised in the Bay Area, Ward hailed from a small affluent family with parents that liked to play. At boarding school, Ward had acquired a light drug habit, which persisted and developed until late in his sophomore year at Palo Alto when a Lab Assistant caught him sneaking an expensive scale from the equipment room. A search of his immediate belongings by two Stanford Public Safety officers recovered nearly a pound of marijuana. Despite family legacy, Ward was given the boot from Stanford. Chastened and humbled, he spent the ensuing months searching for a new academic home. He found acceptance on the opposite coast at Penn, subject to a pledge to undergo drug abuse counselling and keep clear of old habits.

Although buoyed by the miraculous transfer, most social groups had already formed and hardened by the time of Ward's arrival at Penn. His sandy brown hair and aristocratic snap allowed him some company, but no friends. Ward was enrolled in most of the same courses as Alika and Patrick, however they never formally met until an chance encounter between Ward and Patrick; again, at the swimming pool. Patrick had missed team practice that morning on account of illness and was fulfilling his training quota during the pool's evening open swim hours. Members of the public, faculty, and lay athletes occupied the various lanes displaying an array of swimming ability. Ward was among the patrons that evening and happened to be in a lane beside Patrick. Recognizing a fellow classmate, Ward called out to Patrick between laps, and ever the competitor, challenged the flu-inflicted Patrick to a 100-meter race. Accepting the invite, Patrick had decimated the able-bodied Ward, finishing so far ahead that he was sitting on the edge of the pool by the time Ward crumpled breathless against the wall.

"You swim well," Patrick had said as Ward pulled himself up out of the water.

"Not so bad yourself," Ward replied between gasps. "Ever think about trying out for the team?"

Patrick had smiled. "I did my freshman year."

"Tough luck," said Ward, shaking his head and wiping at the beads of water running out of his hair. "I'd say it's high time to try again."

They went on to chat by the poolside, touching on engineering classes, problem sets, irritable professors, and Ward's adjustment to Penn. As Ward went to leave and Patrick returned to the pool, Ward had glanced up at a distant wall covered with banners showing the championships won by the school and the various records held by students. Recognizing Patrick's name, Ward gave a short laugh as the semi-submerged form of Patrick pushed on through another lap. Together with Alika, the three would gradually become close friends, their companionship fulfilling for Ward a sense of reliability in which he found great comfort.

Throughout their fourth and final year at Penn, an establishment named The Kingdom was the trio's watering hole. Muddy, cold, and lost, Ward had found the place by accident on a damp December night after turning in at a splintering red door for directions. He had been leaving a Fraternity party at Delta Chi—of which he was not a member—where a gesture to a Brother's girlfriend had led to him getting tossed off the back porch into a puddle. Above the red door at which he entered was a painted white sign with dark blue lettering; *The Kingdom* it read, and in smaller letters, *Home to the Isles.*

He passed through another door, wooden and more worn, where the heat of a large paneled room brought feeling back to his face and the casual chatter of two dozen or so people was itself a welcome greeting. The smell of the bar was different than the ratty student dives and Ward figured it must be a private or locals-only venue. He moved towards the bartender, adrenaline still pulsing from the episode at Delta Chi.

Two hours later at last call, Ward was still perched by the bar. He had stayed the balance of the evening; making merry, drinking, telling stories, and finally hitching a ride home with an older gentleman who was also from the Bay Area.

Ward's first evening at The Kingdom had been a Saturday; by Wednesday of the following week, he had gushed about his night so incessantly that Alika and Patrick demanded a return trip, if only to pacify their friend. After a half-hour of retracing steps, The Kingdom was found. They arrived just past 10:00 p.m., entering into a lively atmosphere of clinking glass and hoarse laughter. Chelsea and Liverpool were playing on a large TV at one end of the room. At another, there were tables set out and customers, many of them families, finishing dinner.

"This is a pub," Alika stated, taking in the setting. "You found a British pub in Philadelphia."

"Amazing. Right?" Ward said, sallying up to the bar. The bartender, who Ward addressed as 'Phil,' amicably welcomed him back and two gentlemen down the way gave waves.

Ward ordered a round for Patrick and Alika and they settled into a booth at the fringe of the Premier League patrons.

"Not bad," Patrick said, sipping his half-pint. Following the events in Boston, Coach Cole had suspended Patrick and the others from competition until the spring. Given that he would not be competing for another two months, Patrick felt justified in bending the usual dry-season code. He nevertheless remained prudent with his intake, respecting past experience and a father's warning, drinking half-pints and nursing single bottles or cans for an entire evening. Patrick did miss the pool and the hunt for victory, but he was keeping in touch with Hadley, planning a visit to see her over the Christmas holidays, and he thought a brief suspension from competition to be worth the exhilaration he enjoyed from this new type of chase.

"Not bad at all," Alika echoed, looking about the room again. "Although we don't seem like their regular clientele."

The three continued to frequent The Kingdom, treating the mature setting as a symbol of their approaching life transitions. They learned that the bar was indeed a pub, an incredibly old one at that, and a well-kept secret of British football fans in Philadelphia. College kids would occasionally stray into The Kingdom, much as Ward had, and in a few words would be escorted right back out. There was no membership list, at least not a written one. Ward, having entered on a slow night with a pale complexion from the cold, had been unknowingly judged as 'all right.' The old man that had given him a lift home that evening was a regular named Ned, who had reportedly given his blessing for Ward and his pals to return.

In May, after graduation ceremonies were complete and the diplomas awarded, Ward, Patrick, and Alika rendezvoused at The Kingdom for a break from the bustle. The air inside the pub was as jovial as ever and Phil the bartender gave a salute when they entered. "Here's to the graduates!" he cried.

The pub rallied for a hail, extolling the next generation. The outcry earned the boys several rounds and it was a full hour later when the well-wishers left the three alone in their booth. Patrick and Ward shared a side while Alika stretched out on the other.

"Hard to believe it's over," said Patrick, wobbling his second pint on the table, the drink courtesy of a portly Penn alumni that would not be denied a congratulatory beverage. 'I went to Penn,' the man kept saying. 'Best institution in the world.'

"Four years down," Alika exhaled windily. "And now another two to go."

"Don't sound too excited," said Patrick. They had both been accepted for Master's courses at the Penn School of Engineering. Patrick had chosen to focus on methane recovery and fuel cells, while Alika would be pursuing research on drug delivery for medical applications. Both had earned generous grants and stipends to support them over the next two years.

"Well," Alika replied, leaning back into the booth. "When I hear Barton and Fulmer talk about their starting paychecks for next year, I can't help but wonder if I made the right decision."

"If it's money you're after, which I know is not the case, a graduate degree increases your yearly income down the road," said Patrick, taking a drink. "That's a statistic."

"If I survive the road," Alika replied. "And yes, it's not the money—it's freezing my Polynesian nay-nays off for another two winters on this campus."

"You did say that you don't feel ready to be out there building bridges and cleaning up rivers," recalled Patrick. "I believe your wording was: 'it wouldn't be ethical.'"

"In fairness, I was slightly drunk when I said that," started Alika. "But, sure, the last person I want cleaning my water is Barton or Fulmer. And even myself, I'm not sure I could trust."

"So do you think that the Fulmer's and Barton's of the world, be they in whatever profession, should stay in school longer?" asked Patrick.

"Not necessarily. I just don't think we graduate with the experience to start making decisions yet. Most of what we've done is theory, even the lab experiments." Alika paused. "Or maybe everyone's just winging it and are just as clueless as us."

"And experience?" continued Patrick. "Does this qualify you to be trusted? To perceive right from wrong?"

Alika frowned in thought. "It's not right or wrong, it's having the information to know what right is…so you avoid mistakes." He rolled an empty glass woefully on the table. "As in my last girlfriend."

Patrick nodded. "I don't think reason applies uniformly to relationships."

Alika smiled at Patrick across the table. "Too true."

Patrick returned to his question. "So do you think that right and wrong can be influenced by how much we know? As in someone's knowledge about pathogens, material structure, the moment of inertia."

"Not at all" said Alika, shaking his head, tiring of the conversation. "I'm saying that the more you know, the more informed you are, the more you can see the big picture, and therefore the better you can make a decision."

"Ah," said Patrick thoughtfully. "The *better* you can make a decision. Is this where your theory on non-profit energy comes in?"

Alika sat up and pointed at Patrick. "That's a good idea—an ethical idea."

"And it hasn't been done yet, because...?"

"Because the world ain't right," Alika concluded, taking another drink.

Ward had been quiet for the last few minutes, pensively studying the bar.

"What do you think?" Patrick said, nudging Ward. "You're going straight into work."

Ward had taken a job with a contracting company in San Francisco. It was an international firm that did work all over the Americas, particularly in Brazil. Ward had grown up with a Portuguese nanny, learning her language fluently during his childhood. Due to this skill and connections at the company, his application conveniently reached the top of the pile.

Ward did not respond. His gaze, unbeknownst to the booth, had narrowed on two individuals at the bar.

"I'll admit," Alika picked up, ignoring Ward's behavior. "For certain career paths, perhaps more education can be beneficial, but most vocations don't require much theory, and even in engineering, what good is a little more? Don't get me wrong, I'm excited about the research I'll do over the next two years, but that's hands-on work—that's experience."

"Which was born from theory."

"Yeah...but realistically, there is little I can readily do with the degree they handed me last week. It's all theory-based."

"Sure, but you have a foundation now. You can learn things faster, progress at a greater rate."

"I still say it depends on the subject. Besides," Alika said with another point of his finger. "Not everyone ticks by the same metronome as you."

Patrick shrugged and glanced back at Ward, then at the bar.

"Speaking of ticks," Patrick said. "Look who's at the bar," Alika made an unassuming glance. Ward had already been watching them.

Two of Patrick's former teammates from the swim team were trying in vain to get the bartender's attention.

"Chase Baker and Sam Nickels," Patrick confirmed with mild contempt.

"They got kicked off the team for that stunt in Boston, right?" asked Alika.

"No, just suspended for the fall season," said Patrick, absently beginning his third pint. Several full beers still sat on the table from their impromptu graduation party. "They ended up quitting anyway."

"That's right," recalled Alika, watching uneasily as Patrick took a larger than usual gulp. "But hey, if not for Boston, you'd have never met Hadley." Alika knew when Patrick was nearing his limit—the drooping eyelids, smiling with half a mouth, feeling the need to toast everyone—and for the past four years he had felt a responsibility to keep Patrick within his wits. It was a sensation common to those who grew close to Patrick; a soft pressing to act the mother.

Patrick raised his drink. "To silver linings."

"Weren't you going up to meet the parents soon?" asked Alika, reaching forward with a big hand and pulling Patrick's glass from his grasp. "Boston?"

"Yeah, Boston. I was supposed to go up last week." Patrick paused, accepting Alika's intervention without question. "I don't know..."

Alika waited for some elaboration, but nothing came. "Not feeling it anymore?" he offered. "It's been what, six months?"

"A little more."

Alika nodded candidly. "I like her, bro. She seems like a real chick."

"Thank you."

"So what's the problem?"

"The problem?"

"Yeah."

Patrick cleared his throat and leaned back in the booth. "Not to get all analytical but…we're different."

Alika gave a slight shrug. "Not necessarily a bad thing."

"Sure, but I sometimes wonder if, well, I might not be able to keep up."

"I see," Alika said sagely. He made eye contact with Patrick. "You mean like, physically?"

Patrick fired a kick beneath the table just missing Alika's shin and catching the edge of the bench. He was lining up for another strike when Ward suddenly grabbed his arm, whacking an empty glass across the table into Alika's lap.

"Jeez, Ward, watch what—"

"Those guys," Ward said tersely, marking Baker and Nickels. "Are they Delta Chi's?"

Patrick stopped to think as Alika thudded the glass back on the table. "I'm pretty sure," said Patrick. "Both of them. Why?"

Ward suddenly stood up and started towards the bar.

"Ward!" Alika yelled after him. "We got enough drinks…" Alika looked back at Patrick, and they both remembered at once—Delta Chi. They leaped from the booth.

Ward went for Baker first, whipping him around by the shirt collar. Although Patrick mildly enjoyed the look of surprise on Baker's face as Ward's fist hurtled towards his cheek, he was well aware that Ward was no match for Baker and Nickels. The pair had grown hefty away from the pool.

Baker reeled back from the first punch and Ward swung again with his left, landing a blow to the ribs. Baker doubled over. Nickels was off his stool before Ward could swing again, and in a mighty crash Nickels tackled Ward to the floor.

Nickels was up quick, sending shots to Ward's head and chest. Ward pulled his hands over his face to deflect the diving fists.

People yelled and Phil the bartender clumsily hopped the bar, sending pint glasses and bowls of peanuts crashing to the deck. The bartender grabbed Baker to pull him from the fracas, but Baker recoiled and caught Phil in the jaw, knocking him backwards over a table of bangers and mash.

Reaching the struggle, Patrick grabbed Nickels around the neck and yanked him off of Ward. In a scuffle of feet, they fell backwards toward the bar. Patrick hit first, smacking his head on a barstool. Nickels pulled free and wheeled around to where Patrick lay slumped against a stool.

Baker, meanwhile, dashed at Ward with fury in his eyes. Ward had recovered to a sitting position and braced for impact. Yells and curses made a fiery din about the impending collision. One stride short, Baker took a clothesline hook from Alika to the chest. He went to the floor, rolling and gasping for air. Alika took a step closer, daring him to stand. Baker took one look at the hulking Samoan and wisely doubled back onto his side.

Nickels was standing over Patrick by the bar. "Thought that was you," he scowled, setting himself to swing a kick into Patrick's dazed face. Instead a liquor bottle crashed down over Nickels' head, flooring him alongside his sputtering companion.

The cries of the pub turned to cheers.

His head throbbing, Patrick looked up at the rescuer. It was the stout Penn alumni from earlier who had insisted on buying him a drink.

"Admissions sure are getting sloppy," the man said, brandishing a smashed whiskey bottle. "How 'bout another pint?"

An hour later they were back at Ward's apartment.

Feeling sheepish about the sortie, Ward had apologized repeatedly to the bartender and other Kingdom locals. They had jovially shaken him off, already a drink and a laugh into stories over Phil's not-so-sprightly bar hop. It was the most action The Kingdom had seen in years.

"Ironic," said Ward, pulling a bag of frozen peas from the freezer in his kitchen.

"Makes for a good bookend," said Patrick, rubbing the back of his head. Ward handed him the bag of peas. "I didn't know it was Nickels and Baker that threw you out that night."

A toilet flushed and Alika joined Patrick and Ward in the kitchen.

"Yeah," said Ward, removing a contorted bag of frozen chicken wings to hold against his own head. "I never got their names."

Ward's apartment was tucked into a posh residential district along Pennsylvania Avenue, near the Art Museum. There was no doubt that Ward came from wealth and security. He possessed a financial confidence that must be nurtured from birth. Prices were not a variable in his decision-making. At restaurants, he ordered what he wanted. He only flew business class. His clothes were all designer brands. He drove a black Audi 400, leather interior. Out at night, his credit card could easily pass for a sixth digit. Yet despite the opulence of his lifestyle, he never acted superior to his two friends. It impressed Patrick and Alika, who had enjoyed a less material type of wealth during their own childhoods.

The kitchen was dimly lit by a soft set of track lights on the ceiling. Beyond the kitchen was the living room with its flat screen television, laptop computer desk, and two leather couches. Out of sight was Ward's bedroom, another flat screen, and a king size bed. Patrick and Alika had certainly gawked the first time they visited, but sensing that Ward did not want the attention, at least not from them, they had casually let slide their awe and settled into the provided comforts. In this way, they too felt the recline of privilege.

Ward never spoke about his parents, except to say that they worked in shipping and lived in San Francisco. They had come to graduation, but had to leave right after the ceremony. Patrick assumed it hurt Ward to see him and Alika surrounded by their families, abbreviated as they were.

Alika came around the kitchen counter and opened the freezer. "Here, Ward, trade ya." He handed Ward another bag of peas.

"Why?" Ward asked, exchanging the chicken wings.

"Some things just have a higher calling," Alika answered, pulling a pan from beneath the oven.

At midnight, ESPN's Sportscenter had ended and Alika lay asleep on the longer of the two couches. A few empty beer bottles huddled about a bone pile of devastated chicken wings. Ward clicked the TV off and with an audible wince the room went silent. Ward turned to Patrick. "Chess?"

Patrick ferried the food and drink remnants to the kitchen while Ward pulled up a chair to the opposite side of the coffee table. Alika rustled as Ward pulled the game from its place beneath the TV.

The three friends often played chess, all of them with varying styles and tendencies. Alika won the most, occasionally conceding a draw, but rarely showing any worry. Patrick grew incredibly meditative, often taking too long to make his moves. Ward was streaky, winning several games in a row before periodic meltdowns when he seemed to go strategically blind. Regardless of the outcome, they always enjoyed playing, and in cases where their numbers functionally decreased by one—such as when someone fell asleep—the remaining two would usually play chess.

Ward's set, an array of different safari animals, was a gift from Alika. *For the beast in you* had read the inscription on the birthday card. The set was carved from wood, with one side a shade darker than the other. Patrick took a pawn of each color and held them behind his back, shuffling them from hand to hand. The pawns were depicted as antelope. In silence, Ward arranged the pieces on the board.

A moment later, Patrick returned his clenched hands back into view. He held them out, and Ward reached forward a finger and tapped Patrick's left hand.

"Dark," Ward said.

Patrick turned his fist over and opened his fingers to reveal a dark brown antelope.

"Advantage?" Patrick whispered, raising an eyebrow.

"Hasn't been before," Ward sighed, turning the board so that the darker pieces were in front of him.

In regular chess, whoever plays as white, or the lighter shade, makes the first move. Alika proposed that instead of using this rule, which dubiously benefits white over black, the player must first guess the color before randomly selecting a pawn from their opponent's closed hand. Should the player guess the concealed color correctly, then they move first as that color—white or black, light or dark. Should the player guess incorrectly, then they also play as the color they picked but their opponent makes the opening move.

Having guessed correctly, Ward moved first, dragging forward his queen-side pawn. Patrick mirrored the same move. The knights were shaped as alligators, their heads protruding with closed snouts of teeth. Ward moved forward one such alligator to threaten Patrick's pawn. Patrick quickly defended by shifting forward his king -side pawn.

"The same old foreplay, I see" said Ward in response.

Patrick nodded.

The game continued, the men staring at the checkered board; the animal pieces, made by hand, stood still and stoic until ordered forth. The first casualty was Patrick's bishop, which he traded for a knight, denting Ward's line of pawns. The bishops were modeled as giraffes, their necks incredibly slender. Patrick had beheaded one earlier in the year after using a tad too much gusto to put Alika in check. "Was it really worth it," Alika had asked before casually moving his king to safety. The head had since been glued back to the body.

Ward castled his king to the opposite side of Patrick's attack. The castles, or rooks, were everyone's favorite. Not only for their use in the game, but because of the humorous-looking elephants that represented them. These were not intimidating pachyderms, as would be expected in battle, instead they were plump, smiley, and reminiscent of a loathed Thermodynamics professor.

The kings and queens were lions; the king with his magnificent mane and the queen with her posture and foreboding eyes.

Two hours passed. Ward stood to stretch while Patrick hovered over his army. They had traded pieces, but neither had won an outright advantage.

"Want anything to drink?" Ward asked.

"Um aw-rye," muffled Patrick, his hand pressed against his face in thought.

"Is that a yes?"

Patrick stared at the board.

"Pat?"

"Thanks, I'm fine."

Ward disappeared into the dark kitchen. Alika began to snore on the couch. Patrick looked intently at the board, searching for meaning in the order of the beasts. Ward had dug his pieces into a well-fortified position that Patrick was fearful to attack. Patrick played move after move in his head, scanning and sizing his options like pieces to a jigsaw puzzle; there seemed to be a billion and none were the right shape.

Patrick arched his back, sore from leaning over the coffee table. His neck felt like rubber that had hardened and cracked. Alika let out a big snore and rolled onto his side. A few breaths later the snoring was over. Patrick rubbed his eyes and looked at the clock on the DVD player. It was 2:35 a.m. He moaned and looked back at the board as Ward returned with a bottle of water.

"Give up?" Ward asked.

"Never."

Another hour later, just five pieces remained on the board. Ward had his king and queen lion-pair, while Patrick had his king, a rook, and a lone pawn. A great exchange had taken place when Patrick sacrificed his queen to break apart Ward's defenses. In a flurry of carved wood and hands, the board had grown desolate; only the fittest surviving. It was now Ward's turn and both players were fatigued.

"I know I've read somewhere about this scenario," said Ward. "Though I don't remember how it finishes."

"Good," said Patrick.

They laughed quietly. Both were tired. Silence lapsed back over the board.

"Patrick," Ward said after a time.

"Yeah?"

"I'm glad I met you and Alika."

Patrick looked up. Such comments were rare and Patrick grew wary. "Don't mess with me mid-game."

"No intention," said Ward. His face was genuine. "Just wanted to say that I've appreciated your friendship."

"Likewise," Patrick said, leaning back in his chair, expecting further elaboration.

Ward then moved his queen at a diagonal to put Patrick's king in check.

Patrick sat forward and returned his attention to the board. He blocked the check with his rook and Ward retreated. As Ward prepared for another attack, Patrick countered by checking Ward's king with his bishop. Ward moved his king to safety.

The checking, the jockeying, the threatening, and the retreating continued for another half hour.

At 4:00 a.m., without saying a word, Patrick moved his hand halfway across the board and held it there, palm open.

Ward considered the board one last time and shook his head. "Fine, fine," he said, taking Patrick's hand in a draw.

They both glanced at Alika.

"I'd rather not wake him," said Patrick. "Mostly for my own safety,"

"Agreed," said Ward. "You can take the other couch."

"Gladly."

"Then I'll see you in the morning," said Ward, yawning. He stood and walked with his water back into the kitchen.

Patrick stepped over the table, fell onto the couch and was asleep in a dozen breaths.

That night, Patrick dreamt he was running through a forest. He was lost and darkness was near. Every time he found a clearing, trees would spring up and fill the space, making his path denser than before. There was someone else running near him, but whether they were lost as well or chasing him, Patrick didn't know. He was afraid to call out. The night came in degrees and Patrick was still lost, still running. The other footsteps were getting louder, but Patrick was afraid to turn around. He kept running. Soon he could hear breathing, not his own, and he knew the other runner was just behind him. He tripped on a log and fell to the ground in a crash. Terrified, Patrick flipped over to face his pursuer. But there was no one, only the trees.

He awoke in a sweat, Alika shaking his arm. The shades were drawn, but at their outline, the light was bright and vivid. Patrick rubbed his eyes and sat up.

"Let's get breakfast," Alika said groggily, stepping into his shoes.

A week later, Ward moved back to California.

Chapter 6

September 2001
Boston, Massachusetts

The journey was not short or cheap, and yet by bus, train, and car, Patrick and Hadley made it happen. From Philadelphia to Boston, Boston to Philadelphia, like the soldiers of the Union; only with greater pace and less gangrene.

Hadley stood waiting at South Station. Travelers shuffled by at varying speeds with bags, backpacks, and papers. It was 6:30 p.m., Labor Day Weekend, and Patrick's bus was fifteen minutes past due.

The sun hung lazily over the Charles River as though just stirring from a nap. Boston seemed to feel the same. An afternoon thundershower had punctured the balloon of humidity that had enveloped the city for over a week. Cars passed by with the windows down instead of air conditioning up. The American flags set out especially for the holiday rippled without alarm in a whisper breeze. Cuts and dips from popular songs, old and new, dopplered against pedestrians out enjoying the brief reprieve.

From around the bend and out of sight, Hadley heard the downshifting gears of the Greyhound. She put a hand to her hair and patted at her denim skirt. Large, shiny, and rectangular, the bus came into sight. She cleared her throat, mummed her glossed lips, and felt at the silver necklace across her chest. The spectacled driver worked the bus up into his dock, catching a front tire on the curb.

It was not the final stop, but the driver would get out anyway, smoking a cigarette or making a phone call. Most of the passengers disembarked as well, the less-experienced ones clutching possessions and rubbing traveled eyes. Patrick came out in the middle of the pack, holding yellow flowers and open arms that Hadley rushed into. They hugged, kissed, stopped for Patrick to present the tulips, and then coiled back together.

"You're late," Hadley said, their foreheads touching and her arms about his neck, the tulips away from their press.

She felt warm from the glow behind his eyes, a shine that brightened in these moments of reunion. The weight of being apart had grown unexpectedly heavy on Hadley the past few weeks. It was hard to concentrate, and all things beautiful had found a means for dovetailing into thoughts of Patrick. This growing attachment bothered her at times, and once or twice she had nearly called everything off on account of her childlike dreaminess and distance from reality. Yet there was something gravitational about Patrick, even his faults and his shortcomings—the surprising history with alcohol, the more-expected obsession with the laboratory, the functional social awkwardness. Despite all of Patrick's attributes that she would have thought undesirable, an invisible cord had tethered him to Hadley, extending back nearly a year to the Boston Commons. He was not a man to be liked; he was a man to be loved.

Patrick pulled a hand from her waist to check his watch. "Twenty minutes? I'd call that early."

"Yeah? Well my parents won't. It's game time, Greyhound. Are you ready for the Hannigans?"

"Of course," he said, swallowing for effect. "Petrified."

She smiled and brushed the hair above his forehead. "As am I." She kissed him again, harder. "Because I'd hate having to sneak around."

They collected his bag and headed towards the T-Station, the sun drowsy and the bus driver still on his first cigarette.

Hadley and Patrick stood together in the full subway car hanging onto the green plastic handles. The courage that Patrick had pooled on the bus ride was beginning to ebb as the stops to Hadley's family home grew fewer. It had been nearly a year since The Jade and he was nervous about the approaching meeting with Hadley's parents. First impressions were not his strength.

In his mind, Patrick ran down the trunk of Hadley's family tree, remembering Alika's advice for each member. Mother and father—Rose and Anthony—be charming, polite, gain trust; no rude jokes. Older sister—Katie, lives in Cleveland—if home, be appraised as cute, a gentleman, funny. Two younger brothers—Wayne and Ian, both in high school—be cool, athletic, no science-talk. Younger sister—Stephanie, just a kid—be likeable, fun to play with. Nothing like being natural, Patrick thought to himself.

Hadley had met Patrick's father, George, on her third trip down. They had hit it off great and George had loved her. Patrick hoped this introduction would be just as easy. It was only the previous Monday, five days ago, when Hadley had invited Patrick for dinner at her home—not her apartment, her home. Hadley's parents were Boston-Irish, a definition that made Patrick unsure. Patrick had an Irish name, but it was an assumed name his French ancestors had taken when they emigrated. Hadley's family was the real deal. The Hannigans had crossed the Atlantic in the late 19th century, figuring prominently in Irish social politics and labor movements, even in prohibition bootlegging.

"You're all tense," she said, feeling his back. The steel wheels of the T screeched into their stop near Beacon Hill. "Relax."

"I am," Patrick insisted as Hadley led him off the shuttle and up a set of metal-plated stairs. "It's those Greyhound seats—they haven't gotten any softer." Beneath the surface, he was still trying to build himself up; his stomach alive with trepidation.

It was the same set of stairs that Hadley had climbed thousands of times. She had thought about this day often. Since elementary school, she had wondered about *The Someone* she would bring home to meet her parents, the one who stood out from the rest. Hadley had not told Patrick that she loved him, nor had he told her. There were other ways and words for showing compassion, Hadley argued. With her friends, even with Patrick, she poked fun at the ridiculous aura of the L-word. It was like the F-word; overused, misused, and misunderstood. Yet now, as she and Patrick emerged back into the sleepy Boston sunlight, she felt her criticisms starting to show holes. She almost said it right there, impromptu—*I love you.* Not provoked by all the usual clues of location, position, and time, but freely spoken upon emerging from a familiar subway, the wind at their back.

Patrick, oblivious to Hadley's internal dilemma, was talking at length about his research at Penn. Fortunate to have a trusting advisor during his undergraduate degree, Professor Martin Chester, Patrick had been invited to work on a new fuel cell study. The set-up catered well to Patrick's preferences of study, allowing him to do extensive research while taking the minimum number of classes to get his Master's degree. Alika would be working in the same lab as well, sweetening the deal.

Hadley, meanwhile, had taken a job with the Boston Globe, working in the marketing department. She had wanted a spot on the writing staff, but the Globe said it already had enough young writers. Determined, Hadley took the job in marketing, continuing to submit articles to local journals in her spare time. Gary Coulier, still lurking, had helped her get the job, or so he boasted. Hadley wanted to strangle the guy with a pack of floss.

"Alright," Hadley said, stopping along a busily advertised wall outside a pharmacy. "We're the first door around the corner."

Patrick nodded, saying nothing.

"You nervous?" she asked.

"No. I wasn't." His face tightened. "I mean—I might be."

Hadley came close and Patrick looked towards the corner.

"They can't see us here," she whispered, landing a quick peck. "Besides, you've got on fine with me, haven't you?"

"I suppose," Patrick said softly, relaxing somewhat.

"Exactly, and this apple didn't roll far."

"I don't know," Patrick said, creasing his forehead. "I'd peg you as more of a papaya."

Hadley laughed and pulled him up around the bend.

The house was on a slow side street, abutted on either side by similar brick three-story rises. The front porch was decorated with neatly arranged potted plants and diverse wind chimes. Cars were parked tightly along the sidewalk like books on a narrow shelf. A fire escape, painted green, crawled precariously up the side of the building. A Seminary student from Ghana rented the top floor.

They went right in without knocking, voices audible in the latter parts of the house. Apprehension returned to Patrick's gut. The home was well-worn and comfortable.

Hadley's father, Anthony, had been born in the living room to their left. Aside from a short stint abroad in Zurich, Anthony had lived in Boston all is life. When his father passed away, Anthony returned to Boston and met Rose Holley, the daughter of an insurance agent. They married, moved into his family home, and Anthony confided his dream of having their children born in the same room as him. Despite the plot's romance, Rose opted for the comforts of a Boston hospital.

Patrick and Hadley hovered in the small mud-room entrance. Ahead of them was a small front hall. To their left, lay the living room and a framed family portrait. Immediately to their right, a set of wooden stairs terraced sharply out of sight. They had yet to announce themselves. For a moment, Patrick weighed the option of ducking out. He could claim appendicitis or an ailing uncle in Cambridge.

Patrick turned to Hadley as a little girl came around the corner. She was all done up in pajamas, and from the clods of rice stuck to her front, it was clear that Hadley's baby sister had dined early. The girl paused when she saw Patrick, taking one small step back. Then, after a silent standoff, ran to Hadley without averting her eyes.

"Hey there Stuff!" Hadley said, kneeling to her level. Stuff was short for Stephanie. "You ready for bed already? Or have you been wearing these all day?"

Stephanie did not answer and continued to look at Patrick. It was a look of interest. Patrick smiled back, hoping she would like him. There was something holy about finding favor with a child, an unwritten litmus test that proved integrity. He stood tall and grinned wider.

Hadley followed Stephanie's gaze to Patrick, the object of attention. "Stuff this is—"

"AGAIN? THIS DAMN OVEN! TONY!"

The voice rocketed from the rear of the house like the backfire from a car. A woman of well-cured beauty with Hadley's hazel eyes came stressfully into the front hall.

"Oh. Hi Hadley, Patrick," she greeted, as though Patrick was a usual visitor. The smell of burnt potatoes reached out from the kitchen.

Rose leaned over the banister and yelled up the stories, "TONY!" She paused, looked back to Patrick. "How was your trip, hun?"

"Great, thanks," Patrick replied. He wanted to say more, but waited given the culinary circumstances.

No response came from upstairs. Rose yelled up again. Her hair was a curious dark amber, graying at the roots, and slightly frizzy. Rounder at the waist from five kids, she was still elegant in form. Her face was reddened about the cheeks and neck.

"Probably sleeping," Hadley said, trying to sound comfortable. "Can I help?"

"Well, as you can smell, the oven burned the potatoes again," Rose said, wiping her hands on the apron about her waist.

"Were you doing twice-baked?" Hadley asked.

"I was. But they're more like thrice baked now. Probably taste like charcoal." Rose turned to the suitor. "So Patrick! You're here." She came forward and gave him a friendly hug. "Sorry about this, I was hoping to put out a home-cooked meal, but it looks like we might just do take-out or pizza."

"Not a problem," Patrick said. "Are you sure we—"

Another voice came from upstairs, it was deep and slightly accented.

"Heyah Rosie, what is it?" Footsteps approached the landing. The father was coming down.

Hadley inched closer to Patrick. She could sense his angst.

"It's the oven again, scorching my food. Can you pop out and pick up something for dinner instead?"

"Of course, of course," the strong voice came again. Shoes met steps and down came Anthony Hannigan in khakis and a collared shirt. He came straight to Patrick and put out his hand. "Patrick, I presume."

"Yes," Patrick said, taking Anthony's hand in a firm shake. "Nice to meet you, Mr. Hannigan."

"Anthony is fine. Glad you could make it, how was the ride?" Anthony asked, stepping back to lean against the banister. He was tall and broad across the shoulders, hinting at his athletic career at Boston College. Hair, cut short and thinning, skin, loosening in select places, it was the eyes that made Anthony youthful. They were large and blue like oases.

"Not bad at all, slept for most of it." Patrick responded, wishing he had a post or table to lean on too. He was conscious of his arms. He folded them.

"Hadley tells us you're quite a swimmer," Anthony stated.

Patrick shifted and put his hands on his hips. "Certainly had my share of time in the pool."

"And you were at Penn right?"

"Yes, still there actually. Can't seem to get away…Have you been down to Philadelphia before?"

Anthony smiled. "I've spent some time there. Quite a city."

The two women and the young girl took in the patriarchal appraisal with subtle reverence.

"Well, it's nice to finally meet you all," Patrick said, facing four of the seven Hannigans.

"Oh, we're the nice ones," Anthony said, turning towards Rose knowingly. "We're still short the boys. They're the real trouble.

And Katie, she's alright, but as you know, she's out in Cleveland. Then, little Steph…she's alright too. Aren't you Steph?"

They all looked at Stephanie and she buried her head in Rose's apron.

There was something instantly admirable about Anthony, and Patrick respected him already. He was glad not to have to pretend.

"You alright with Italian?" Anthony asked Patrick.

"Sounds great," Patrick replied. "You need any help picking it up?"

"That'd be fine, I'll need the hands. Rose, you want to call it in? Patrick, come on in the kitchen and have a drink."

The question and invitation dispersed the mud room introduction. Stephanie pulled Hadley into the living room, Anthony walked towards the kitchen, and Rose went to the phone where she made what sounded like a three-word order. Patrick followed Anthony down the hall, taking an elbow turn and passing by the other door to the living room. He looked in to see Stephanie excitedly showing Hadley a new Celtics coloring book.

The Hannigan kitchen was out of a Dickens novel. Patrick paused after coming through its spry swinging door. An era, perhaps two, apart from the rest of the house, the kitchen boasted a high ceiling, corniced molding, and whitewashed walls. The floor was checkered with big square stone tiles. The oven was old, black, and sat like a gargoyle beneath one of two shutter windows that invited evening light from a small garden outside. Below the other window, and in contrast to the oven, was a great white sink, almost a bathtub in size, at which Anthony stood washing two glasses.

Between the sink and the oven ran a long wooden counter, worn so thin in places that new strips of wood had been glued in place. Carpentered cupboards were installed above, while over a dozen drawers of varying size were built into the space beneath the counter, creating a sense that counter and drawers were one continuous piece of wood. A round oak table, darkly furnished, but softening in spots, crouched to the left of the door. On the right stood a large refrigerator, metallic and spacey, the only element to assure visitors they had not suddenly time-traveled.

"Quite a kitchen, huh?" Anthony said, noticing Patrick's stare. "The folks that lived here before my parents put in a lot of money to re-furbish the original look. It was built back in the 1800's." He looked about thoughtfully. "This is one of the oldest quarters in Boston."

"It's beautiful," Patrick said, really meaning it.

"Beer, water, juice?" Anthony asked, starting for the fridge.

"Water would be great." Patrick was parched and he knew a beer would go right to his head.

Anthony didn't break stride. "Water it is." He opened the doors and pulled out a half-full jug.

"Thanks," said Patrick. He continued to look about the kitchen, but at nothing in detail.

Anthony returned to the counter and filled the two glasses. He handed one to Patrick, then stepped back to lean against the sink.

"So you're at Penn, and you're studying...chemical engineering. That right?"

"Yes," Patrick said, free-floating again in open space but happy to have a glass to hold. "Just starting my Masters and focusing on renewable energy—fuel cells in particular."

"Very good. And you're happy to stay in Philly?"

"I am," said Patrick, taking a drink. "It's not where I want to be forever, academia or Philadelphia, but at the moment I think it's the best place to be in such an evolving field."

"What made you choose energy? Chemical engineering is a wide field, at least the way I understand it. Pharmaceuticals, material science, biotechnology ..."

"True. I guess I've always had an interest in what makes things...go, work, have power to do the things they do."

"It's good timing for another big solution," Anthony said, finishing his glass of water. "Any others in your family go into engineering?"

"Not that I know of, but engineering does have a vast definition. I'm sure somewhere, someone was involved somehow." Patrick took another drink. "Hadley says you're in carbon fiber?"

"Yes," Anthony said, going to the fridge for more water. "I work in a small firm that puts together the drawings that eventually get sent to the engineers. I suppose I'm somewhat of a middle man. Most of our contracts are government—Navy, Air Force, NASA—so we've been growing ever so surely. The government is consistent, but rarely extravagant. Carbon fiber is still a little too pricey for most parts of the private sectors."

"I hear that's where the money is."

"The deep pockets that want to get deeper. You got it."

"How long have you been there?" Patrick asked.

"It'll be almost ten years. You know the whole business itself is pretty young just like your alternative energies. Being there from the ground up has been helpful. Makes it harder for them to fire an old man like me"

The conversation continued through the usual masculine topics—hometowns, sports, traveling, cars. Despite his father's profession, Patrick didn't know that much about cars, so he pushed the conversation forward to Boston, a topic that Anthony ran with for ten minutes. Watching Anthony, Patrick was impressed: the way Anthony spoke of Boston, his hometown, was passionate and loving; the way he spoke about his family was ten-fold. It reminded Patrick of his mother.

Rounding out his tribute, Anthony set his glass down with a soft thud on the counter. "I could go all day on this city. It's the best. But I'll stop before I knock you to sleep. I don't know how Hadley would feel about you cracking your head on these tiles."

"Probably not as poorly as my head," said Patrick.

Anthony laughed and Patrick sensed the end was near. He would be relieved when it was just Hadley and him; the audition over and her eyes buried in his.

"So any inclinations as to what it might be?" Anthony said, the question jostling Patrick. "The next energy source to drive our world that is."

"Great question," said Patrick, finishing his water. "There are a lot of possibilities. Some better than others at the moment—wind, solar, tidal, hydrogen, biomass, more nuclear—the list is ever growing, splitting, shrinking. In my opinion, will be a combination of several, with certain regions hand-picking the solution that's best for them. Whether that's economical, I'm not sure. I suppose the technical side of things has always been my focus."

"I agree," Anthony said, continuing to study Patrick. "You never know." Patrick had expected this sort of interview, but it had passed enjoyably, feeling less like an interrogation and more like a visit to the tailor.

Hadley came abruptly through the swinging door and went to the fridge. Patrick moved towards the table and placed a hand on the back of an old caned chair; stability at last.

"About five minutes and we'll head down, alright?" Anthony said to Hadley.

"Alright," she said, closing the fridge, a neon green sippy-cup in her hand.

"Any more to drink?" Anthony asked Patrick, reaching for his glass

"No thanks, I'm set."

"I think the boys just came back," Hadley said as she reached the door, pausing. "Hope you ordered enough food."

"Not a problem," Anthony assured with a wink, turning the water on at the sink. "If we run out, we'll give them the charcoal potatoes. They'll eat 'em."

As Anthony cleaned, Patrick faced Hadley at the door. She had stopped halfway out and was looking at him. The sound of rushing water at the sink was the only noise in the room. In later conversations they would playfully dispute who said it first, each one feeling responsible for the next three words soundlessly phrased to one another across the kitchen. It appeared to be simultaneous: a synchronization of the hearts, a silent mutual decree—*I love you*—a simple statement to ignite their own thundering, passionate, and unyielding tempest.

Chapter 7

January 2002
Interstate 95, New Jersey

Except for Hadley, the left-hand side of the bus was abandoned. A relentless evening sun beat against the oily, upholstered ranks of seats, forcing the rest of the passengers over the aisle away from the magnifying heat. Jostling along with the frost heaves, they were over halfway to Boston; four hours to go, with stops.

Hadley stared out the window at the snow-spotted highway median, patched by frosty islands. Hot licks of sunlight coursed through the glass, making her skin sticky and her shirt moist. Hadley hardly noticed. The events of the past few days consumed her entirely and she unabashedly allowed her countenance to rock like a seesaw; laughing, then crying, then humming. Hadley varied to such a degree that the elderly lady across the aisle could not be stayed. Cautiously, the woman stood and shimmied into the space between, lowering an aged hand onto Hadley's shoulder.

Hadley flinched, as if jerked awake. She looked up at the grandmother, the old woman's body shaking with the motion of the coach. She wore a gray sweater with beige suit pants, and the wrinkles on her face were well tended.

"My dear girl," the woman said quietly, a mix of care and Northern curiosity. "Is everything alright?" Her Long Island accent was hushed, but traceable.

Hadley hesitated, nodding as tears came to her eyes. The scene was garnering attention from other members of the bus. The elderly woman pulled a wrinkled Kleenex from her pocket. A girl from several rows ahead swiveled back to get better a view.

"There, there," the woman said, pressing the tissue into Hadley's hand.

Touching her eyes and nose, Hadley breathed deeply and smiled up at the elderly woman. "Thank you," she said, forcing a smile. "I'm okay, really."

"You sure?"

"Yes, thank you. It's just..."

The woman bent closer, willing to become a confidant. A man edged past her in the aisle on his way to the bathroom, glancing down at Hadley.

Hadley paused, dabbing at her eyes again. She gathered a stronger face. "I'm fine, really. This is very kind," indicating the tissue. "Thanks."

"Okay," said the woman, beginning to retreat back across the aisle. Maternal intuition told her it was emotions; love or lust or hate, plying the long, inner strings of the heart, conducting that exhausting symphony of feelings. "Just let me know if you need anything."

"Thank you," Hadley confirmed with a smile.

The woman waved kindly and settled back into her seat.

Hadley turned again to the window, feeling the eyes of the bus, pair by pair, begin to detach. She twisted the Kleenex over and around her hand, winding it up into a knot. She wore blue jeans and a light yellow top that masked the dampness of her sweat. Closing her eyes, Hadley placed left hand atop right in her lap, allowing the swaying sunlight to at once set afire, and at once extinguish, the diamond engagement ring freshly entrusted to her person.

Two days previous
Philadelphia, Pennsylvania

They were outside in a quad, eating and talking on a bench. Hadley was hungry from the trip down; three hundred and thirteen miles in nine numbing hours. Patrick had planned on taking her out to Pat's or Gino's for one of their famous cheesesteaks, but the bus was late.

They settled for take-away from the savory crepe stand outside the Penn student union. It was mild for January, hailed by weathermen as the annual mid-winter "thaw", but both Patrick and Hadley still wore thick coats. The hot food made their breath cloudy and thick in the lamp lights. It had been a month since Patrick's visit at Christmas, and though they had spent many hours on the phone, e -mailing often, the interim had felt eternal.

The crepes consumed, they snuggled together on the bench. It was Friday, Spring Term had begun, and the campus had a spirited sense of freedom.

They were quiet for a long time.

"You know?" Hadley broke. "I prefer when we're together."

Patrick didn't reply, the words settling.

"Whadda' ya think about that, Pat?" Hadley asked melodically.

Huddled beneath his chin, Hadley couldn't see a face, but could feel breathing and the steady rumble of a heart. Both quickened.

They ambled home, Patrick carrying her light duffel bag. Hadley was never sure how much to bring on these weekend trips. Packing too much made her feel funny, typically female, and she hated having to lug a large suitcase from the belly of the Greyhound. While packing too little left her occasionally unprepared and short-changed for the sudden adventures that Patrick was known to spin. In the end, she started leaving things at Patrick's, and he did likewise at her place; a large step that passed without discussion.

The stairs to Patrick and Alika's 4th-floor apartment were long and steep. The temptation to take them two at a time was always so strong that by the final landing, Patrick and Hadley, or practically anyone who visited, were breathing hard from the phantom haste. Only George, Patrick's father, took them one at a time, saying after each ascent that they were built for the impossible man: six feet tall, with the stride of a three-year old. Having raced up the final two flights, Hadley and Patrick fell onto the couch in tandem, where they happily remained for some time.

She had slept for almost half-an-hour when Patrick woke her with the smell of chocolate. He kneeled beside the couch, their heads level, a mug of hot cocoa wafting steam between their faces.

Alika had come home and Hadley could hear his humming in the kitchen as he cooked himself a late dinner, or perhaps a second. A pillow cushioned her head and a warm blanket lay across her knees and chest.

"Is that the illustrious Alika Tucker?" Hadley asked.

"In the flesh," said Patrick. "You still tired?" He placed the mug on the floor and touched his warm knuckles to Hadley's cheek.

"Not at all," she exclaimed with a stretch, throwing her hands and blanket skyward. "Wide awake!"

"Really?"

She reached for the mug, swinging her legs to the ground. "Really."

"You sure?" He stood.

She sipped gingerly. "Certain."

"Good," he said, beginning to backpedal. He left the room, returning seconds later with a box.

"What is it?" she asked, craning her head.

"Revenge," Patrick replied. With a rattle, the dog-eared Connect Four box fell to the dining room table. "Served best without warning."

"What a gentleman," Hadley sighed, rubbing at her eyes. "May I assume then that you've also *roofied* my cocoa?"

Patrick grinned and opened the box. "I think the evidence shows I don't require sedatives or relaxants to…"

"Have your way with me," Hadley suggested, stalking towards the table with her mug.

"What's going on in there?" a deep voice asked from the kitchen.

"Stay out of this Tucker!" Hadley warned, approaching Patrick.

Alika's lumbering laugh echoed from out of sight. "Planning on it."

"This is a new age," Patrick stated, snapping the long, hollow vertical stand into place. "Your disputed reign is coming to an end."

She came near and planted a long kiss on his neck.

"And your tricks will not help you either."

She put a hand on his chest, turned him and locked his lips to hers. The black and red chips clattered to the table. At parting, she took a chair and pulled the red chips towards her, flashing large brown eyes at Patrick.

He smiled and took a seat, "You know no bounds."

Hadley sipped playfully at her chocolate and popped the first chip into the rack.

The following morning, the air in the apartment was gelatinous; thick and humid. Hadley was first to discover the new climate brewing in the living room.

Patrick and Alika's other roommate, Sean, the one they hadn't known about when they signed the lease, had come in late and left a wet towel on the heater by the window. He had meant to open the window, remove the towel, or at least turn off the heater. Instead he fell asleep on the couch, spilling milk and Honey Nut Cheerios into the crevices of the cushions. Sean's testimony, given hastily to Hadley as he awoke and scurried to his room, was dubious at best.

The towel removed, the windows opened, and the couch given a loose detail, Hadley escaped into the kitchen for a cup of coffee. She made one for Patrick and took it back to the bedroom. She passed Alika coming from the shower. He wore nothing but a blue towel.

"You smell that?" he asked Hadley, sniffing the air with a slight grimace. "What did I tell you about making Irish food?"

"Very funny," she said, well acquainted now with Alika's dry humor. "No, you've got your buddy Sean to thank for this."

"Sean," he repeated, tweaking his lips and looking down at the floor. "Disappointing, but not surprising."

"He's working on an alternative habitat in the living room—kind of a marshy-honey-nut-wetland thing."

"Honey nut. That boy is going to get it," Alika said seriously. "How do you suppose we send him the right message, Hadley? What would your people do?"

"My people? Well..." She struggled to match his straight face. "Probably shouldn't get into that. Might keep you from sleeping. Us Irish, we're everywhere."

Alika shivered. "I'm scared already."

"As you should be." She arched an eyebrow. "Because it's also what we do to people who insult our cooking."

Alika didn't move. The towel was normal sized, but against his hulking frame looked more like a tea towel. He looked down at the mugs of coffee in Hadley's hands. "Oh, I see. You make them coffee." He looked back up at her, his face dead-pan and rigid. "That is terrifying.

Hadley broke into laughter. "Out of my way!" she yelled, sidling past him in the hallway.

He let her go, continuing on towards his room.

"And put some clothes on," she tutted. "It's almost ten o'clock."

"Here she comes," Alika rumbled, turning in at his door. "Visiting for a weekend and thinking she runs the show. Hadley, Hadley."

Still laughing, she pushed through the door into Patrick's room. He held the phone in his hand and a worried look on his face. There were no windows in Patrick's interior bedroom. At nearly all times, a halogen lamp in the corner coated the room with light and a soft buzzing.

"Yeah," Patrick said into the line. He glanced up at Hadley as she entered and gave a watery smile. "Of course."

A muffled female voice was audible as Hadley set his coffee on the bedside table. She sat down on the edge of the bed.

"Alright, thanks for the call," Patrick replied. "I'll see you then. Okay, bye." He hung up the phone and slumped onto his back

"What's up?" Hadley asked. "Everything alright?"

"A friend passed away last night," Patrick said, staring up at the ceiling.

Hadley paused. "I'm so sorry," she lay down across the bed and took his hand.

"Did you know him well?"

Patrick nodded, rubbing his forehead.

"Is the funeral today? I heard you say…"

"Yeah, at three this afternoon. I'm sorry, but—"

"You're going."

Patrick looked down and across the bed at Hadley, the artificial ambience reflecting off his glassy eyes. "Thanks, Hads," he said admiringly. "I should go tell Alika. It was John from the University."

Hadley nodded. Patrick had mentioned him often.

Over breakfast at a diner down the street, Patrick and Alika took turns telling stories about John Levine.

At least ten years their senior, John was a Post-Doctorate and trained ecologist in the Biology Department. He had been paired with Patrick for a University inter-disciplinary exchange program. The idea was to link together Masters, PhD, and Post-Doc students involved in similar work. The resulting dialogue was supposed to further student and researcher awareness of the available ties across different academic disciplines.

Patrick had first met John in October at an introductory luncheon. From their opening handshake, the two men formed a friendship that Patrick envisioned would last for decades. Patrick respected John dearly, and sought his counsel often, paying close attention to his refutes, applauds, and suggestions. Alika also began accompanying Patrick to see John, bringing ample questions about his own research into drug delivery. The man had a talent for understanding the links between chemistry and biology, and became an unofficial adviser to them both.

John was an academic; tall, casually dressed, mid-30's and always laughing. His work was on the relationship between ecosystems and climate change. To questions regarding his future, John would always say, "I've got enough to worry about today." When Patrick returned to Penn the week before, John had been in his office as usual, whistling Eagles tunes and looking through data. Patrick rehearsed in the coffee shop to Alika and Hadley what had been John's unforeseen farewell just days previous.

"Fossil fuels!" John had said to Patrick, catching him with these words at the door. "Have to find something else. The oceans, the forests, the mountains, and everything within and beneath them can't be sustained at our present rate of consumption. The shock from the changes in the atmosphere are going to be prolonged, rippling across generations. The planet will survive, yes, it has the reset buttons, but unless we also make a change, there's going to be an abundance of unnecessary suffering." John then paused and looked hard at Patrick. "I trust that you'll be part of our change."

John was Jewish and the funeral would be held within a day of his death. It had been his mother who had called, telling Patrick that John had left him a letter and requested that Patrick attend the memorial service. Patrick was so shocked that he sat silent for most of the call while John's mother answered his unasked questions. He sensed she had been on the phone all night.

"It was cancer," she said. "Don't worry honey that he didn't tell you. He didn't tell anyone. Only me and his father knew, and if he had things his way, we wouldn't have known either. It was advanced, Hun, tumored from head to foot he was. That hair he had wasn't real. Back in 1999 they gave him six months, but he pushed on. It was a matter of time."

"He mentioned you often Patrick," she said near the end of the call. "He was a good boy, my John. I know he appreciated you. Can you make it today? I know its short notice."

"Of course," Patrick had answered.

"Good boy. Then we'll see you at three."

Still in his suit, Patrick picked up Hadley at the Constitution Center after the funeral. He drove his old Subaru Legacy; blue and bought used his freshman year at Penn.

Hadley kissed him as she buckled in. It had just gone five o'clock and the seat was still warm from Alika's recently vacated frame. Patrick had dropped him back at the apartment.

"Everything go well?" Hadley asked. She wore jeans and a black wool coat.

"Yes," Patrick said, pulling away from the curb. "Great service, uplifting. I'm glad I went."

"A celebration of life?"

"It was," Patrick replied. "What an awesome family." His voice faded. The service had been pleasant, but its purpose was still strange. John's death had been so unexpected. His sudden departure would have been twistedly more acceptable as a heart attack. The secret terminal deterioration capped by a sudden case of pneumonia was harder to justify. Patrick thought of his mother, remembering his younger episodes of anger, sorrow, and humility. 'Death is hardest for the living,' his father often said.

"You enjoy some history?" Patrick asked.

"Just walked around mostly," she said, letting the subject change without protest.

"Mostly?"

"I might have gone to a gift shop."

"Oh?"

Hadley pulled a small Liberty Bell keychain from her coat pocket. "My sister collects them," Hadley explained, gently swinging her purchase.

"Any reason?" Patrick asked. He downshifted as the light changed ahead.

"For the crack in the bell?

"No, why your sister collects them."

"Not that I know of."

"She must have lots of keys," Patrick surmised.

"Perhaps."

The red light passed in silence.

"Hey Hadley," Patrick said, his eyes on the road as the light turned green.

"Yeah?"

"Can you open the glove compartment?"

"Okay," she said, slowly reaching forward. "And why's that?"

"You'll see," Patrick replied lightly.

Hadley stopped short of the latch and lashed a curious grin at Patrick. "I remember a similar invitation to this one…it didn't end well."

Patrick laughed. "I maintain I knew nothing about that."

"I bet," said Hadley sarcastically. Once, while at Patrick's family home in West Chester, Hadley had been directed to a drawer for matches. Alongside the large box of matches sat coiled an even larger black and yellow garter snake. Slamming the drawer, she had screamed and leapt onto the couch, crashing into George as he read the paper.

Hadley opened the glove compartment.

Into her lap fell a red rose and a black bandanna. She took the rose and held it thoughtfully, brought it to her nose. "Thank you," she said, leaning across the handbrake and placing a kiss on his cheek. She lifted the bandanna.

"I assume you know what to do with that," Patrick said, shifting and making a left turn.

"Hopefully nothing too kinky."

Patrick smiled. "Of course not."

"Man of mystery tonight."

Patrick shrugged.

"Fine, fine," she relented, pulling the black cloth up across her eyes. If she looked directly down she could just see the rose in her hands. Not that Hadley knew Philadelphia well, but after all the turns that Patrick made during the next ten minutes, she was clueless of their final destination.

"If this is the opening scene to a horror movie, I'm going to be very disappointed in you, Patrick."

In reply, he brought the car to a stop. "Sit tight and I'll come around to get you."

"You better."

She felt him leave. For a moment, the car was still. Blinded, Hadley knew Patrick was coming around the car on his way to open her door. He was known for surprises, but there was something different about this one. The silence remained, nudged occasionally by sounds of the city. Her door opened and she felt Patrick lean across and unbuckle the seatbelt. He kissed her as he guided the buckle back to the door.

"Easy down," said Patrick, taking her hand.

He guided her along, one hand at her back. They came to a door that was already open, and the heat of a building washed over them like a waterfall. Voices were audible. It felt hollow, like an atrium.

Hadley turned sheepishly into Patrick, squeezing his hand. "Where are we?"

"Hold on."

They crossed tile and carpet, stopping briefly before the sharp *ding* of an elevator presented an open door. Stepping inside, just the two of them, they began to ascend.

Ascending into the building, Hadley faced Patrick again. "I know you don't do hints, but will I be underdressed?"

"You'll be fine."

She exhaled in defeat. The elevator continued to rise.

"How high are we going?" Hadley asked. On cue, another bell announced they had reached their floor. Hadley felt the slight pressure of Patrick's hand on her back and followed it forward, trusting not to hear the *tink* of china and crystal.

"Good evening," welcomed a deep voice that made Hadley start.

"Good evening," Patrick replied. "Reservation for Simon."

"Patrick!" Hadley whispered anxiously.

"Of course sir, right this way," said the maître d'. Hadley turned to say something to Patrick, but was cut off. "Would the lady care to change?"

Hadley felt blood rushing to her face and she nearly tore off the bandanna.

"Yes," said Patrick. "I believe you have something for her."

"Yes sir," said the man. "Just through that door there."

Patrick led her off to the left and into another hollow sounding room where their shoes echoed like hoofs.

"No need for this anymore," said Patrick as he loosened the bandanna from her eyes.

Hadley gasped.

They stood in a bright, luxurious bathroom. The floors and walls were decked with blue and white tile. Silver taps shone at the sinks and bathtub, and gold-framed mirrors waited against all four walls. A blue dress hung softly on a hook. Hadley had bought the dress at a sale a few months previous. Leaving the article at Patrick's for a special occasion, she had forgotten it in his closet. Walking towards the dress now, Hadley wondered if maybe he had engineered it that way.

"Take as long as you like," Patrick said, retreating out the door.

Hadley showered and prepared within the reflective walls of the restroom. By the sink, she found her make-up and overnight bag. Tracing her lips and flushing her eyelashes, she glowed with anticipation. She slipped on a set of matching blue heels that she knew Patrick must have bought, only because she would have remembered them, and fastened on her favorite silver necklace. After a graceful final check in the mirror, Hadley walked to the door and pulled it open.

Patrick stood waiting with a bouquet of white roses. A long beige hallway stretched out behind him.

She walked towards him and wrapped her arms like a scarf about his neck. Patrick held her about the waist with the roses in one hand.

"Déjà vu?" he asked, recalling their first meeting at the Jade.

She kissed him. "With a few favorable differences."

The sound of a violin came from down the hall. Hadley cocked her head and smiled up at Patrick.

"I don't know what this is all about," she said. "But I love you."

Banks of clouds met and melted into one another as the Greyhound entered Massachusetts. The sun obstructed, several of Hadley's fellow travelers re-joined her on the left side of the bus. Hadley touched a hand to the window. The temperature was falling. In a few miles, they hit snow.

The flakes dashed past in a white rain. Hadley watched the ones that clung to the window. With their crystals dug into the glass, the flakes held tight until torn clear by the wind. Others melted into running beads and stormed off towards the back of the bus. It would soon be dark and Hadley thought about calling her mother for a ride from the station.

No, she would walk. Hadley longed for open air.

From her purse, she pulled the rose that had fallen from the glove box the night before. It had been an evening she had wondered about her entire life. Now it was past. The words had been said. The question had been asked. And she, Hadley, had said "Yes."

Several miles later, when the snow had grown heavy, she put the rose back in her purse and fell asleep.

Chapter 8

October 2002
Penn's Creek, Pennsylvania

A week before the marriage, George took Patrick fishing. They began each day at dawn, rising in the wood-smell of the single-room cabin lent to George by an old friend from high school. Mornings were crisp, and casting off their thick blankets required great might. They washed at a cold basin, ate, dressed, and then ferried their gear down a short path to the shore.

Flipped over near a small dock lay a weathered aluminum row boat and a sleek fiber-glass canoe. George and Patrick chose the row boat the first morning, speaking in whispers as they prepared the craft at a pebbled launch; isolated from civilization by miles. The autumn fog thinned to a feathery mist by mid-morning, exposing the red and yellow foliage blooming amidst the forest's proud pines.

The cabin was set in a small clearing up a steep bank from the river's edge,. Beyond the plot, and the rutted track that led back to a main road, the forest was thick and untamed. Either side of their dock, dense underbrush and towering trees bordered the river for several hundred feet, provoking the sensation of rowing about a moat. Further downstream, the riversides opened up to pastures and corn fields.

The first two days were father and son alone on the current. They caught and released until dusk. The light fading, they would reel in the lines, stow their poles, and paddle ashore for dinner. Their conversations over the water were boundless, and their trolling lapses of silence were equally deep. George spoke often of Mary. There was much that he wanted to say to Patrick about love and the way it moves. He believed that love was always changing, growing, retreating, shrinking. Paradoxically, it reminded him of his tours in

Vietnam. Who or what you were after was always in question; dipping beyond the next bend, eluding you into cavernous valleys, disappearing into thick webs of jungle. The flexing quiet was deceptive, lulling away awareness. Until, without warning, the bounty found you.

Patrick listened, asking questions that had lain dormant for years. It helped to speak about his mother. *Patrick had been sixteen when they lost her.*

"You can't let fear ruin your relationship," said George, on the evening of the first day. "You can't live every day afraid to get close." *George had been called to the scene by the police dispatcher, a close friend who had not known the identification of the drivers. The location of the accident was on a rural road that ran through a park. When he reached the wreckage, George had slowed and pulled his tow truck onto the shoulder about fifty yards away. It was a bad one, definitely a head-on. There were two squad cars, one on either side of the twisted metal. No flames as George could tell, but he could hear the scream of a fire engine not far away.*

Patrick nodded and watched his line. They sat in the aluminum row boat. Pine needles along its silver belly muffled the shifting of their feet. *The vice-principal had told him in the hall outside his 7th period U.S. History class.*

"Your mother," George continued. "I loved her so much. I want you to know that. I want you to know that if I had to lose her again, and re-live…everything…To have what I have now. I'd do it." *George had watched the officers move about the collision, there were three of them. One was helping two teenage-looking kids to the side of the road. They looked shaken but all right. The other two officers were trying to get at the other driver. Besides the calamity, the trees were the only other movement. They reverently nodded to one another and the victims. George studied the cars. They were both totaled. The kids had been driving a Dodge pick-up, rusting in all the usual places. The grill was grotesquely gnarled to one side. Glass had sprayed everywhere. George looked at the far vehicle, then looked closer. Its shape. Its color. Its crumpled frame. The fuzzy Sesame Street character atop the antenna. George blasted open his door and ran.*

Patrick observed the insects dart atop the water. *After the news, Patrick had collapsed in a heap against a wall of lockers, too shocked to cry.*

"The risk is worth the blessing," continued George, the line on his pole clicking. "I thank God for you and your sisters." *He had sprinted full speed at the crumpled heaps, which minutes before had been ferrying passengers. The two officers at the car faced to stop the charging man, but he was past their outstretched arms in two swings, running to the driver-side door that was bent painfully inward, deformed shut. The window was smashed. He reached in with trembling hands. The officers spun George away from the window. They had not known him as he tore past. They froze when they recognized him, seeing the fear on his face. George pushed past again, hurrying to the other side of the car where he climbed in the passenger window.*

Patrick looked up from the river. "You thank God?" he asked. God had been absent in their family since the funeral. *The hallway was vacant save for the vice-principal, a petite woman named Mrs. Lowe. She told Patrick that he could wait in her office until his father arrived. First, he had gone to find Kylie. His sister was taking notes in her freshman English class. The girl had wailed without restraint.*

"Yes," George replied. "Does that surprise you?" *He took Mary's hand, and she looked at him, unable to turn her head or squeeze back. Her eyes told him it would be okay. The steering wheel was pressed against her chest so tight she couldn't speak and her breath came in short trickles. Blood ran from her nose and a gash on her forehead. George wept, saying her name over and over. He kissed her hand, leant forward and gently kissed her forehead, her cheek, her eyes. Her jaw was broken, but she smiled anyhow.*

"I thought you didn't believe in God." *Before the bell rang, their father arrived, stains on his shirt, and they were on their way to the elementary school to collect young Colleen.*

"Why's that?" George asked. *An ambulance appeared and men in blue shirts rushed at the car. George remained where he was. The fire truck pulled up and men in yellow jackets shouted orders. George heard and saw none of it; all he saw was his wife. She smiled again, the pain fading.*

"You said so." *Patrick had scorned the sympathy from friends and family, becoming reclusive and bitter. He slid into depression, drinking alone in his room, sinking further from touch until a sudden rededication to swimming. The pool had brought him back.*

"And you believed me?" *George felt hands pulling him away. He fought them off and took Mary again by the hand. "I love you," he said. She nodded ever so slightly, closed her eyes, opened them, and mouthed a reply. 'I love you too.' Her eyes closed again. George waited for them to open. They never did.*

"So you've changed your mind?" Patrick asked, shifting in his seat.

The rod in George's hand bent forward into the water, the line growing taut. George placed a foot against the side of the boat and began to reel. He looked over at Patrick, eyebrows raised, "I get the occasional hunch."

The row boat had spiders. Neither man was afraid of spiders, but regardless, they flicked the arachnids into the water or hurled them ashore when one appeared.

"Tenacious little guys!" Patrick exclaimed on the morning of their second day. They had done a sweep the previous afternoon, evicting close to fifteen spiders from beneath the benches and the narrow gaps of the boat's aluminum rim. "They must have crawled back aboard last night," Patrick said, pinching one by the legs and tossing him onto the bank.

"They don't bother me, spiders," began George, organizing the position of the tackle boxes. "It's just the way they move…so unpredictable. Gets at my nerves." George stopped fiddling with the gear as another spider emerged from beneath his seat. He frowned at Patrick. "Let's take the canoe."

The morning air was sharp as George and Patrick paddled away from the dock. They glided quietly against the current. The tapping of paddles and the plop of the canoe's nose on the river surface mingled with the rush of water over exposed rocks. George's friend had told him about a small inlet a half-mile upriver; shallows where fish would congregate in the early morning and evening. That second morning, George and Patrick went in search of the inlet.

"Dad," said Patrick from the stern. They'd been on the water for over half an hour and the current had strengthened.

"Yes?"

"When you married Mom," Patrick began, "Did you stay in towing to support her, or because you wanted to?"

George paddled for a few lengths before answering. "My mother asked me that same question before you were born. Said I was capable of so much more—her way of saying I could do better for your Mom."

"And I suppose I could have," George went on, speaking in time with the dips of his paddle. "But I had little schooling, and the money I made was enough to keep us comfortable, especially after we moved from the city. And then you came along, and then your sisters, and you all grew up, and time just barreled on—it goes fast, Patrick, so fast..." George stopped paddling. "But to answer your question, I'd always thought about training to be a mechanic."

"And why didn't you?" Patrick asked quickly.

"Well...I knew enough about cars, had worked with them for long enough, and a few certification classes would have probably got me there. Your Mom would have supported me, I know. But taking the time and money out just never seemed to be an option. With Colleen gone to college now, I guess I could try. I'll certainly have the time. Not sure I could complete the license training though. Especially at my age."

George returned his paddle. "I'm rambling. The answer to both your questions is: yes. I drive a tow truck because I needed to support your mother, and then the same for you and your sisters. But having my own business, even if it was just towing cars, gave me time to be with you, my family. It didn't take me long to realize that was what I wanted most." George looked back at Patrick. "What's on your mind?" he asked. "I doubt it's towing."

Patrick stopped paddling. "It's about my career." His eyes patrolled the river edge. "My career and Hadley. I'm afraid the two won't...blend."

George stopped paddling as well. "How so?"

"Well, right now I can go two directions with my life," Patrick replied.

"Just two?"

"It feels that way," said Patrick. "I can continue to do research, stay at Penn or go elsewhere, and in four to five years wind up with a PhD..."

"But?"

"But they regulate what you can research, and usually you just assist other professors or doctorate students. Not that I don't respect what they're doing, but little of it interests me; none of it feels revolutionary." Unguided, the canoe had veered perpendicular to the shore. "And if I did get time to work on my own project then I'd just be writing grant applications all day to conduct studies that may already be behind schedule and possibly irrelevant by the time I finally get the money—technology advances so fast."

George waited for Patrick to continue.

"Research is what I've always thought I'd do," said Patrick. "But with Hadley, 'I' is someone I'm not so sure about. I've always planned for what I want to do with my life, not a life to be shared with someone else."

"Are you worried about providing for her?"

"That's part of it. The PhD stipend would be low at first, but once I moved on to a larger lab, the pay can actually be quite high."

"What's the other way you mentioned?" George asked. "You said there were two."

"I could forget research and go 'corporate'. Take work with a full-fledged company doing design work or consulting. I'd make good money on top of all the other perks."

"I sense that's not what you're after..."

"It's the lab, I'd miss it," Patrick confessed. "It's where I thrive. Like in swimming, but at a higher level."

"What does Hadley say?"

"Hadley's great. Too great. She tells me: 'Do what you like and we'll make it work.' Which is kind and supportive, but, I get misgivings. I don't thinks she understands what it might be like." Patrick paused before he spoke again. "I'm afraid I'll neglect her if I go into research."

Water was rippling up against the side of the canoe; pushing, pushing, and turning the craft around.

George eyed his son carefully. "What do you mean—neglect?"

Patrick waited a moment until replying. "I'm afraid I'll get so wrapped up in my lab work that even if I make ample time for her, that time will be tainted by my interest in a project. When we lived apart, cities apart, I would take time out for her when she visited, or drop everything and gladly go up to Boston. But once I was back in Philadelphia, alone, all my time was in the lab. Work just consumes me. It's always on my mind: the next possible solution, the proximity of a breakthrough, the answers to questions unformulated…it's a passion that I can't have competing with Hadley."

The canoe had now spun 180°, carrying them back downriver. Without warning, George stood slightly and drove his paddle at an angle into the river, striking the muddy bottom. He pushed down with great force, the veins on his forearms protruding. The current caught the stern, rotating the canoe, resetting it like an second hand on a watch. Facing upstream again, George sat down and began to paddle. Patrick followed suit.

"I don't like the phrase 'When I was your age'," George said levelly. "But at 23, I was an alcoholic. From when I woke up in the morning, to when I finally passed out, there was little else on my mind besides the next drink. It was terribly sad, and try as I might I couldn't give it up. What with the drink and my memories of Vietnam, I felt entirely powerless—I feared." George paused to clear his throat. "And to this day, I still get cravings, irrational as I know they are, but a weakness for alcohol is my burden to carry, I can't change that. And there are always moments of bitterness and anger over the things I saw and was made to do at war, but I can't change the past, the War happened. Some things we can change and other things just *are*—and the difference between the two is for each of us to figure out. You too have a taste for drink, like me and your grandmother, but here you are: paddling up Penn's Creek, almost through graduate school, engaged to a beautiful girl, still talking with your old man, and best of all, sober as a tree."

Patrick smiled and again stopped paddling.

"Respect the current," George said, turning around to face his son. "But never fear what you can change."

The excursion lasted three days. On the final day came Alika and Anthony, Hadley's father, to fill the remaining seats in the boat. They arrived in Patrick's Subaru, rumbling up the drive and parking next to George's truck in the mid-morning. Anthony emerged first, jumping free of his seat and bolting for the woods. Alika casually appeared from the driver-side. George and Patrick sat on folding chairs near the cabin having a late breakfast.

"You're on time!" shouted Patrick to Alika, who gave a tired wave, shut the door, and started towards the cabin. Anthony re-emerged from the trees, his face considerably more relaxed.

"Thank the Lord for that!" Anthony exclaimed. "Patrick, you sure picked a place where Hadley wouldn't find ya'."

They all came together and shook hands, hugged, and gave strong pats on the back. Pine needles and small twigs crunched and snapped beneath their feet.

"How did she drive?" Patrick asked Alika as the Polynesian enveloped him in a hold.

"Like a queen," said Alika, his eyes weary yet happy. "But I still think you're making the right choice with Hadley. That Subaru's a little old."

The men returned to where George and Patrick had been sitting. Two more chairs were produced from the shady interior of the cabin. Alika and Anthony sat, then stood to stretch, then sat again while Patrick went back to the car to get the extra food they had brought.

Taking the groceries from the car, Patrick stopped. The plastic bags were tight against his hands. He looked through the empty car and felt low whispers of the past running up through the faded interior and dented doors. The woods grew deep around him. The voices of the men by the cabin grew muffled and Patrick heard them as a child does his parents as he lays awake after bedtime. The air was chill and yet he was warm with assurance. He saw his mother, his sisters, his father—he saw Hadley.

After a brief lesson for Anthony, who had never fished, the rowboat was pulled down the bank and halfway into the water. A cooler with drinks and lunch was hoisted and placed snugly between two tackle boxes. After a quick sweep for spiders was conducted, the men climbed aboard. Patrick placed an oar against the soft mud of the bank and shoved the boat clear. There were ports for two oars, and after locking them in place, Patrick put the party in motion.

They set a return course for the shallows, the same destination where George and Patrick had gone the day before. The inlet was marked by a large birch tree that leant out from the bank, as if expecting company. Beyond the tree was a small lagoon where the water was tranquil, deep, and plentiful with fish.

Patrick rowed and dipped in silence for a space, everyone appreciating their surroundings. Anthony watched the shore, breathing in the rural air. George and Alika baited the hooks, masterfully knotting the worms and impaling them onto the sharp, shiny lures. Patrick just rowed.

The leaning birch came into sight and George hummed the opening chords to *Up Around the Bend*. Skirting the edge of the bank, Patrick maneuvered the boat into the shallows. The lagoon was fairly large, covering an area the size of a baseball diamond. Three small brooks fed into the pool, one of which was dry. The trees hung a little higher than the day before, the morning dew already melted away into river and sky. Patrick gave the oars two hard backward pulls and the slope of the soft bank just caught the belly of the boat, sending a scratchy reverberation throughout the lagoon.

"Well, now that we've woken all the fish," George said dryly.

They cast their rods into the water one at a time. Anthony went last under the tutelage of Alika, who had fished as a child in Samoa and then again in California. Despite the guidance, Anthony still managed to hook Patrick's windbreaker, tearing a gash in the light fabric.

"Trying to tell me something?" asked Patrick.

The bites came all at once, shortly after midday. Anthony landed the first catch, standing up and rocking the boat in great fervor as the tug on his line grew frantic. George helped him reel, while Alika gently dipped a net, returning to the surface with a thrashing brown trout.

"Must be at least 8 or 9 pounds," Alika guessed, bringing the net into the boat. "We keeping him?"

"Well," George said, knowing the laws. "What do you say, Anthony? He's your fish."

Anthony looked at the fish. It gasped for water, lurching in bursts, switched by an unseen tormenter.

"Nah, let's put him back," he said. "We've enough food in the coolers."

The next bite came before they had unhooked the first. It was George's line, and after a brief struggle the fish tore free, setting the line slack. A minute later, Alika pulled up a small catfish, his large arms ripping the fish from the water like a loose weed.

"Not much meat on him," said Patrick. "Give you a dollar to take a bite."

"Patrick," disapproved George. Anthony looked on, intrigued.

Alika took the fish off the line and held it in his hands, flopping. He considered it, gave the boat a grave look and then turned his back, the fish disappearing from view. He shifted, bent his head, and a hollow crunching noise echoed across the lagoon.

"No!" exclaimed Anthony and George together.

Alika continued to crunch.

"Oh Alika!" said Anthony. "The diseases!"

"Not so fast," said Patrick, reaching forward and pulling his friend around. Alika no longer held the fish, but his mouth was full. "Open wide."

Alika shook his head.

"Come on," prodded Patrick.

Alika smiled and spread his lips. Freshly chomped bits of carrot lay across his tongue. Anthony and George sighed in relief.

Just then the rod in Patrick's hand suddenly whipped forward, the reel whirring fast. Patrick pulled back hard on the lever and began to work the line.

"Saved the best for the groom," said Anthony, still beaming from Alika's trick.

The line grew tighter as Patrick pulled the fish towards the boat. The line was out towards the far end of the lagoon and Patrick stood to get leverage. He pulled and tugged, but the strain on the line was too much to wrap in any further. Patrick placed his foot against the rim of the boat, and Alika came around him to steady the other side. For five minutes, Patrick and what lay beneath battled in a dead heat. At times, Patrick could maneuver his position somewhat and make progress, but the quarry remained defiant.

"Might as well dig into lunch," said Patrick, flashing a tired smile towards the boat. "Could be awhile."

"Don't have to tell me twice," said Alika, and he popped open a cooler and began distributing sandwiches and fruit. Neither George nor Anthony opposed.

Patrick grew tired after a time and sat back down, allowing his Dad to feed him bites of sandwich.

"Fuel for Moby Dick!" Anthony declared, the whole experience a delight.

Thirty minutes later, the war still raged. The muscles on Patrick's arms ached and his legs were stiff. His eyes saw nothing but the break point of where the line met the water surface. Anthony ventured that perhaps it was a plant, a stick, or a boot. Patrick shook his head, he was sure it was a fish.

After his body, Patrick's mind grew strained; cinching like the line. He had been pulling, holding, releasing, and then pulling again for close to an hour. It was the back and forth motion that made it hard. The fish pulled, and Patrick pulled. 'If only,' Patrick thought. 'If I can only just wait him out, tire him out. Use up his strength. Then perhaps, in one great burst, in one great pull, I could…use him up…'

Patrick saw it.

The storm. The lightning shocked car. The spread of debris and charred lumber. The fish beneath the water – fighting. A flow of energy and resistance. A hook shining, sinking down in the open water. The snap of jaws about the lure. A rip of light and sound from the sky. The fish growing tired, its strength expended.

Lightning. Electrons. Energy.

Patrick released the rod and it shot out of his hands, hitting the side of the boat and then flipping into the water. Relieved, Patrick sat down and looked off into space.

No one spoke. The pole bobbed to the surface a few feet from the boat. Alika swallowed the food in his mouth and Anthony cleared his throat.

"Patrick?" George ventured, speaking for the boat. "You alright?"

He looked at them, confidence spread across his face. "We called it a draw."

Chapter 9

March 15th, 2028
Safehouse Five, New York City, New York
3:49 p.m.

I had been working with the police department for one week when I learned that people are critically different on paper.

Throughout my higher education I had read many files on atypical individuals, criminals usually, and made all the necessary credible assumptions, marking them down as hyper-this, deficient-who, manic-that, getting top grades for my analysis abilities. I remembered feeling substantially smug about the assessment for my first real case—a serial arsonist named James Boyle. My confidence was not to last long, evaporating as I entered the courtroom and actually met James; not the J. Boyle of the police reports and character sketches, but James the human being. No trial is 100% revelatory and no wrongdoer suddenly becomes forgivable after a personal introduction, but there is truly no substitution for living color. Arsonist James Boyle, now serving a 10-year stretch in Lewisburg, taught me that lesson.

Patrick Simon never had a trial, only sixteen years of speculation. The Media had a field day with his history with lightning. The tabloid titles were especially colorful: *Thunder and Simon, Zeus Strikes in Florida, Hydrogen Frankenstein.*

Regarding the things that Meredith told me about her father—relationships, family, friends, loves, fears—this is essentially all I had in my notes:

From Missing Persons File S-72612-1: Simon, Meredith…

- *George Arthur Simon: son of Sidney and Delia Simon (maiden: Tustin), born June 16th, 1950. US Army Vietnam Veteran, decorated with Bronze Star. Married Mary Shaw on August 21st, 1977.*

- *Patrick Hawkins Simon, son of George and Mary Simon (maiden: Shaw), born May 4th, 1979.*
- *Mary Simon, 43, dies in two-vehicle traffic accident, April 13th, 1996.*
- *Patrick Simon, BS Civil Engineering, summa cum laude, University of Pennsylvania, May 13th, 2001.*
- *Hadley Dyhan Hannigan, daughter of Anthony and Rose Hannigan (maiden: Holley), born March 3rd, 1977.*
- *Patrick Simon and Hadley Hannigan, married October 19th, 2002.*

Clearly, we are more than just a file.

And yet so fragile, so destructible—the human being, us, this incredibly detailed organism—perhaps, the universe's most complex—and entombed within, infused throughout, is a past, a present, a future; an unfathomable library of love, hate, fear, hope, memory, and thought, the likes of which man can only begin to comprehend. Even in the least developed, the unaccountable, there exists a gravity and depth that is worthier than all human advancement combined. And in an instant, all this, everything, is reduced to nothing; a mass of empty flesh, a fossil, a full donation to the earth.

I was seven when this reality was first revealed. It was winter time, shortly after New Year's, and my father and I were walking home from the supermarket. We passed a hardware store, our arms hung heavy with shopping. Seeing the shop reminded my father that we needed a new showerhead. The one at home was leaky. In an hour, the drip-drip-drip could fill a bucket.

Inside, I stood by the window, looking at a kids' playhouse. I wore a plump red jacket and held a bag of things like bread, cookies, and paper towels, but it still felt heavy. The little house was intended to be placed in a garden for someone my age; at least that's what the picture portrayed on the price tag. Lowering my head, I toddled inside while my father perused the plumbing section. The home was wooden, and a small counter by the window was meant to be the kitchen. There was a table and little stools to sit on. Against the wall was a carving of a cheery log fire. I set my groceries on the counter and went to the window. It was hinged and painted red. I pushed it open. The view looked out the real window into the street.

I watched for a minute, admiring the people walking by. Some were dressed well, others wore shabby clothes. Growing up in New York, I was used to watching people of different makes and models.

From my window, I observed an older gentleman cross the street. Stepping up onto the curb, something took hold of his face. I remember it vividly. It was not fright. It was not pain. It was not sorrow. It was a realization. It was like he'd just recalled where he left his keys. Except instead of turning around to get them, the man fell forward on the pavement.

A crowd gathered, people pulled cell phones from pockets, and two men tried giving CPR. I watched from my window. The first police car blazed up when my father came to get me. Looking over the roof of my house, he saw the scene. He told me he'd paid for the showerhead.

An ambulance arrived as we left the store and my father guided me on our way. I remember looking back to see the man hoisted onto a stretcher; they had closed his eyes.

While Meredith takes a bathroom break, I return to the observation room, accepting a checklist from Director Killian of items to discuss—places, names, events, discoveries. There's an understandable rise in anxiousness when names like Ward Prince start getting thrown around.

Meredith has returned to the room and is sipping from a bottle of water when I enter. She has declined lunch and my grumbling stomach wishes she would change her mind. I sit down and flip a sheet in my folder, looking down at Killian's conversation starters.

I ease back into the interview with some simple questions.

How old are you, Meredith?
I turned twenty-four in February.
Were you afraid to come back?
A little.

[Meredith points at my ream of notes.]

Why do you still use paper?
I just prefer it.
Me too.
...So you were 'a little' afraid to come back?
What do the monitors say?

[Meredith smiles and glances at the painting on the wall. We have medical scanners in the monitoring center that register changes in body temperature, heart rate, and brain activity—it's the ultimate lie detector test.]

Hanna, if you're worried I came here for the company, then you can relax.

[We stare at one another. I sense she has more to say.]

Have your colleagues examined the packet in my luggage?
I believe they've begun, yes.
Very shortly, if not already, you and your supervisors will be asked to release me, to suspend this interview.

["Pursue this," Killian says through my earpiece.]

What do you mean?
This material is too sensitive for certain individuals to stand by. They will want me let go. Permanently.
And who are these individuals?

'Who' is variable. What's important is the content of that packet and my testimony. We're through the family history and what follows is more potent. When they ask you to stop, we must continue.

That's hard to promise. I have superiors.

The power of this story kept my family from this country for sixteen years. There are many who wanted our absence to be indefinite.

But who exactly are these people?

Don't worry, they'll be in touch.

[Killian is breathing into my ear again; he's useless with a microphone. I leave the topic and Meredith seems satisfied to press on.]

Tell me more about your father's work at Penn.

Just at Penn?

Wherever's relevant. This is his trial.

And his personal life?

[The girl has an eerie sense of my thoughts. It is indeed Patrick's development that intrigues me more than the exact methods of his science. From simple observation, to general interest, to motivated idea—I wonder if Patrick himself could have foreseen the ensuing obsession.]

I'll leave that to your discretion.

Chapter 10

February 2003
Philadelphia, Pennsylvania

Patrick sat alone on a bench beneath a tree eating a sandwich. Snow had come early that winter, but never stayed more than a night. Traces remained on the edges of highways and along corners of alleys. Regardless, it remained cold; too cold, some said, to snow.

Although only four o'clock, shadows were already advancing across the quad behind the Van Pelt Library. Patrick finished his sandwich and crumpled the white greasy wrapper. This would be his final semester at Penn and his thesis was coming due in April. He stood and began heading across the grassy park, which felt crunchy and frigid beneath his shoes. The brick walks that typified the Ivy campus were slick and Patrick avoided them. He passed a garbage can and tossed the wrapper. It was a short walk to the Towne Building where Professor Martin Chester, Patrick's adviser, would be waiting.

Patrick loved and loathed these meetings. He loathed them because Professor Chester was so irritatingly difficult to please. No matter what Patrick brought to the table—be it a Nobel-worthy contribution—to Professor Chester, it was always lacking. This, too, was why Patrick loved these meetings, because they motivated him, and encouraged him not just to please his adviser, but confound him entirely.

Patrick ambled through the quad and into the cluster of engineering buildings where he had logged the occasional sleepless night during his undergraduate years. The area was quiet and shaded now, most of the students either in class, gone home for the evening, or hidden away and struggling over numbers and symbols. With all of the classes and requisites behind him, the trials of undergraduate life seemed a fond memory. There was less rigidity in his current world of academia and Patrick enjoyed it immensely. The hypotheses, the experiments, the analysis, even the grant-writing; he would surely miss doing research. After four months of marriage, Hadley had kindly talked him out of pursuing a PhD.

As he reached the outer door to the Towne Building, he felt the cellphone in his pocket begin to vibrate. Patrick checked the Caller ID and then his watch. If he answered, he would keep the Professor waiting. Patrick sent the call to voice mail and pushed through the door. He stopped again when he reached the first step of the stairwell, turning around and walking back out of the building into the cold. As the door shut behind him, he re-dialed Hadley.

"Sorry about that," he said when she answered.

"Not at all, catch you at a bad time?" she asked.

Patrick could hear the *rap-rap* of typing in the background. "No, just punched the wrong key."

"My little genius," she cooed.

He could tell by her voice that the phone was jammed between her ear and her shoulder. "You still at the office?"

"Yeah, just finishing up."

"Good day?"

"Meh, so-so."

"You want me to cook tonight?" he asked, his stomach still full from the sandwich.

"I believe that's a rhetorical question."

"Great. I should be home in an hour or so, I'm just going into my meeting with Chester."

"Do tell him 'hello.'"

"I would, but he'll just blush and start to stutter."

"Would he?" Hadley said, dropping her voice. "I confess. We're madly in love."

"I knew it."

"And running off to Honolulu."

"Oh?"

"We're adopting a child too."

"Really?"

"And starting a whaling company."

"Sounds delightful."

"We'll send you postcards."

"I knew you loved me."

They signed off and Patrick returned to the stairs. The railings had been worn smooth by years of traffic, while the stairs themselves had recently been replaced. Patrick was glad they'd left the railings.

At the third floor landing, Patrick could hear Tchaikovsky. Professor Chester was a man of taste, but not many flavors. He loved his Tchaikovsky, his Yo-Yo Ma, his John Williams, and his Guns and Roses.

The Professor had grown up on Walnut Street near campus. In any conversation with Patrick, he always worked in some anecdote about his childhood aspirations of becoming a professor at Penn. It was clear that Chester hoped Patrick would do likewise. The aging engineer had started out his career in mechanical engineering, only to go 'rogue' and join the ranks of chemical engineers. During Engineer's Week, when the different disciplines within the Engineering School competed against each other in a set of humorous tasks, the 'Chem-E's' always trotted out Professor Chester as their beacon of superiority.

Padding down the hallway, Patrick reached the open door to Chester's office. The music covered his approach and Patrick paused momentarily before entering. He had met with Chester on numerous occasions. This meeting should have been no different; the problem was that Patrick had never been entirely open with the Professor about his laboratory work habits. It was during this meeting that Patrick intended to come clean.

Patrick's thesis was a fuel cell study on methane collection from landfill sites. Methane created by natural decaying processes within the landfill was a harmful pollutant and greenhouse gas. Now, with capturing technologies, the Methane could be extracted, separated, and then burned for energy right away, or saved and superheated with steam. This latter process caused the Methane to split into its prime constituents: Carbon and Hydrogen. The Hydrogen emerges as a gas and is easily isolated from the Carbon. This gas can then be used to fill a fuel cell. Fuel cells are essentially batteries, using the flow of electrons to create a charge. A Hydrogen fuel cell can be re-filled by simply adding more Hydrogen. Patrick's thesis was a life-cycle analysis of the process, determining what would be needed to make it more efficient and applicable.

Patrick enjoyed the study. He could even bear to work with the "organic material" that smelled like an open sewer. Yet, in his deepest of intellectual capacities, he never committed to the project. The real work and science of the project had already been completed. Patrick's thesis was just a slight tweak to established technologies that were already well understood.

The replication reminded Patrick of his high-school chemistry labs, when the teacher would tell the students what was supposed to happen for that day's experiment. Patrick had raised his hand once and asked why the class was testing something that was already known. Why couldn't they work on something new? The teacher had smiled and condescendingly told Patrick that such work was "beyond the scope of the class." Patrick had since heard that statement dozens of times, especially throughout university; and how he hated it.

When Patrick settled on the topic of methane-sourced hydrogen fuel cells, or rather was assigned it by Professor Chester, he shortly began experiencing that same sensation from years previous. There was nothing new in what he was doing, nothing revolutionary. Fed up, Patrick decided on a bold course of action: he would conduct a second study in secret. For the past four months, since the fishing trip, he had done so.

Patrick took two steps to the heart of the doorway.

"Ah! Patrick," said Professor Chester from his desk, setting down an open manila folder. "Come in."

"As usual, everything appears on schedule. Data looks good. Hydrogen yield is stable. Carbon Monoxide levels aren't spiking."

Professor Chester was leaning back in an old leather desk chair, eyeing a progress report that Patrick had produced from his backpack. The leather on the chair was visibly splitting, collecting like loose skin about its creases and folds. Patrick sat across the desk from the Professor, staring politely into space.

The Professor was old. The pictures on his office wall held friends who were long retired or recently buried. Despite a medium height and build, the professor had played football at Penn and walked with a limp to prove it. His hair was light gray and faithfully combed back from his forehead. The grooming technique, students said, was what made Professor Chester such a good teacher—there was less interference between his brain and yours.

Regardless of the weather, Chester took walks every day at eleven and four. Several years prior, the registrar had mistakenly scheduled one of his lectures from 3:00 to 4:30 p.m. Patrick had taken that lecture. Each session, when the clock hit four, the entire class stood and accompanied the Professor for a walk.

"Getting along okay in the lab?" asked Chester.

"Yes, sir," replied Patrick. "It's like a second home."

"Ah?" the professor intoned. "Well, make sure it stays that way."

Patrick did not respond. He knew his hours in the lab were highest among his fellow graduate students.

Chester went back to the report, then stopped and removed his reading glasses. "You obviously missed my point."

Patrick perked. "Yes, Professor?"

The Professor focused on Patrick. The teacher's opal green eyes were sprinkled with faded brown freckles. "If the lab feels like a second home, make sure it stays second." He let the statement rest. "Understand?"

Reproved, Patrick nodded. The professor returned to the document.

After several minutes, Chester set the paper on his desk and looked up at the ceiling. "You're not enjoying this are you?"

Patrick had fallen into a daze and the question caught him off -guard. "Sorry?"

Professor Chester chuckled. "Patrick, I know your work. It's brilliant, it really is. You have a wonderful mind. We're lucky to have you. The sky's the limit—etcetera, etcetera. But …" he said, rubbing at his temples. "I can tell when a heart is not in the work. And right now, Patrick, yours is clearly elsewhere."

Patrick opened his mouth in defense.

"Hold on, hold on," said the Professor, anticipating a rebuttal. "I'm being honest with you." He leant across the desk, casting an invisible shadow. "Now, you be honest with me."

Patrick never had the chance to tell him everything. At first, the Professor was humored; amused that Patrick was doing small experiments on the side. When Patrick began to explain what the tests entailed, the delight faded. The sun dropped beyond Philadelphia and the room lost its cheer.

Sparked by the events on Penn's Creek, Patrick had become enamored with the concept of lightning energy. He maintained to Alika that he wasn't obsessed, just slightly overcurious. They constantly argued about it. The lab director was getting suspicious and the tests were blatantly dangerous. Alika told him to quit or talk to a professor. Patrick, not budging, continued to work.

Other scientists and engineers had explored lightning energy. After examination, the pursuit was always deemed primarily useless. In theory, there are massive amounts of energy in a lightning bolt. Every strike carries a potential difference of several million volts, with currents in the thousands of amperes. The problem exists in the storage and capture of the energy, not to mention the difficulty of predicting when and where a bolt will land. The energy comes in such a quick burst, and at such a high voltage, that harnessing a significant amount of the power is like using a fire hose to mix a glass of Kool-Aid.

Patrick had begun with calculations and rough sketches. His ideas had changed and morphed extensively before he brought his work into the lab. He realized it was risky to perform uncondoned experiments in the lab, but he felt stirred by the potential of his ideas. "Isn't that what labs are for?" Patrick had contended in a recent disagreement with Alika. "For theories and discoveries? Not repeat busy work."

For weeks, Patrick had been working late into the night, returning home to find Hadley asleep on the coach, or snoring with the lights on, a book across her chest. Patrick would tuck her in, turn off the lights and sit in the living room. He had told her about the project, the basics at least, and with fearless eyes she had encouraged him to continue. Patrick knew she didn't understand the risk and he had purposefully kept her in the dark over certain details. Carrying out personal experiments at an Ivy-League facility was not as commonplace as he had made out. The illusion made him feel unfaithful.

In confessing his work to Professor Chester, Patrick got as far as his atmospheric re-creation testing. Using a known concentration of gases, Patrick had mimicked an atmosphere within a closed system. Next, he had sent pulses of electricity through the concoction. Halfway through his description of the power source manipulation, Chester cut him off.

"Patrick! Please! Enough." The Professor looked unbalanced. "The more I know, the worse it is." He let out a long sigh. "Look, I appreciate your extended interest in this concept. And your dedication is remarkable, of course. But I'm sorry…this is ridiculous!"

"Professor—"

"I'm sorry, but I cannot allow you access to the lab if you continue to explore this…this…this entirely hopeless avenue. I respect you Patrick but these labs are for…"

"I know—"

"NO! You obviously don't know! And DON'T interrupt me," roared the Professor, pointing his finger like a dagger across the desk. "This is an institution for instruction and learning, not only is it an insult to me that you would go around completing some sort of supplementary project, but it is a taint on the University and the Department for you to be conducting such careless research."

The Professor's voice had grown rasp and trill, and he continued to punctuate with his finger, maiming the space between him and Patrick. "Believe me! I understand the desire to chase an idea, but there is a time and a place, and at the moment this school is not the place, and as a Master's student, now is not the time."

Patrick sat penitently across the desk. He had half-expected his adviser to be upset, but not this upset.

The Professor's voice grew labored, but he continued to point, to articulate, and to express his discontent. "So either you give this nonsense up immediately, OR, I will stand by as you are sorely prosecuted for gross misuse of University property!"

With the last stab of his finger, the Professor lapsed into a sudden round of deep coughs. He raised his wrist to cover his mouth, leaning back in his leather seat. No sooner had he reclined, when another surge of coughing grabbed at his chest. Small showers of phlegm sprayed across the desk.

Patrick stood sharply and went to the water cooler by the window to fill a cup for Chester. He stood by as the Professor drank and his breathing returned to normal. Nearly choking to death was not the reaction for which Patrick had been hoping.

"So how'd it go?" Hadley asked between spoonfuls of soup. "You're awful quiet."

"Went okay," Patrick said.

They sat at the kitchen table, newlyweds.

Alika still shared the apartment, but had been hunting for a new place. Although Hadley and Patrick wanted him to stay, Alika felt it was time to move on. Sean, the unfortunate roommate, had fortunately moved out after being bribed by Patrick with 76ers' season tickets. They had been a wedding present from Hadley's Uncle Pendleton, who called on occasion to get updates about the games, forcing Patrick and Hadley to constantly be checking highlights.

"He thinks I'm doing fine," added Patrick.

"Now, now," Hadley said playfully. "You hafta give me more than that."

"Well, it was pretty standard—"

"Come on. I know you guys have your science dialect and all, but..."

"Really, Hadley, it was normal and boring." He went back to his soup. "How was your day?"

Hadley lowered her spoon. "Well, to begin with, it was 'okay.' By midday, it was hovering around 'pretty standard.' But in a late surge, everything ended up 'normal'."

Patrick looked across the table at his wife. Her tone was warm and he knew she wasn't mad. She was making a point, and doing so with class. It was why he loved her.

Hadley looked back at her husband, knowing there was more. She had been a staff journalist with the Philadelphia Inquirer for only three months and already her questioning skills had grown noticeably more dexterous.

"You really are in the right profession," Patrick said. "I already feel sorry for our kids. They won't get away with anything."

"Don't change the subject," she said, returning to her soup. "Lay it on me. You're terrible at hiding things."

He had first mentioned his interest in lightning on their honeymoon to Martha's Vineyard. They had been sitting on a screened-in porch watching the waves. Patrick had watched in despair as his golden idea had passed over as a mere talking point, with Hadley making an abrupt segue into a story about her baby cousin, Thelma, who thought thunder was the sound of running angels.

Patrick hovered over Hadley's request. The last few months had been busy; Hadley with her journalism, Patrick with his lab work. Their waterways of communication had grown brackish.

"It didn't go well," he said at last.

"How so?" She had finished her soup.

"Well, the fuel cells project is going fine. Everything is on schedule and the results are what we'd hoped for…It's the…"

"Lightning?"

"Yeah, the lightning." Patrick said.

He stood, took his empty bowl and reached across the table for Hadley's. Patrick tended to multi-task when talking about something uncomfortable. Hadley let him take her dish, aware that an explanation was forthcoming. A large truck went by on the street below.

"Listen," Patrick began as he stood at the kitchen sink, running water into the bowls. "What with everything going on, both of us spending more time at work; you at the newspaper and me at school, I might have glossed over a few things. Nothing major really, but I guess I haven't been… entirely honest."

Hadley nodded patiently. "And does this mean that you're going to be honest now?"

Patrick came back to the table, still holding the dish rag. In fifteen minutes, he told her everything: the lightning-blasted tree of his youth, the fighting fish, his first experiments at Penn, the arguments with Alika, his discovery the day before, and the reaming by Chester that afternoon.

When he was through, Hadley frowned. Patrick was leaning forward on the table and she reached forward to tousle his hair. "Oh, Patrick. I'm sorry."

"No, I'm sorry. I was stupid. I should have told you when I first started. I just didn't want to worry you." Patrick took Hadley's hands. "It feels good to talk about it."

They both heard footsteps on the stairs.

"That'll be Alika," Hadley said.

Patrick kissed her.

"So that thing yesterday," she started. "With the magnets? Do you think…?"

"I don't know. I'll have to study it out."

He kissed her again.

"And these experiments," Hadley said finally, before Alika came in the door. "Are they dangerous?"

Patrick shrugged. "Not really."

One day previous

The impetus for Patrick's decision to divulge his experiments to Professor Chester was a curious incident that occurred the night before. The moment fulfilled that slip of serendipity which many breakthroughs seem to require; a divine intervention of sorts.

For months, Patrick had been sending large bursts of energy along a narrow wire, simulating a lightning strike. He performed most tests within a sealable fish tank, filling the space with an approximate atmospheric concentration of gases. He had tried various alterations for where the wire struck, the material of the wire, the size of the wire, the movement of the wire, the temperature of the wire, even the color of the wire—and nothing seemed to make a difference. He was becoming frustrated.

Lightning tends to have two strokes, one shooting down from the sky and the other blasting back up from the earth. Patrick's goal was to "capture" the remaining energy in the bolt after the down-stroke, hooking it like a fish. Nearly all of the energy generated by a bolt of lightning is spent on appearance: the 20,000°C heat of the bolt, the signature flash of jagged light seen overhead, and the propagating boom of thunder heard for miles. At the strike point, roughly 1% of the bolt's total energy is delivered. Patrick's hope was to grab the energy before it could dissipate. He wanted to blind and silence the sky.

While researching how to interject on the natural phenomenon, Patrick found that current science could explain relatively little about why lightning actually occurred. There were hosts of climatologists who could predict storms, safety specialists who could counsel on lightning survival and protection, and physicists that could estimate physical properties, but questions remained over the exact process by which lightning was formed. Most intriguing to Patrick were the scientists who had developed a strategy that could elicit a strike to a predetermined location—it was the lure he'd been looking for.

In his background reading, Patrick learned about the ICLRT—the International Center for Lightning Research and Testing—at Camp Blanding in northern Florida. Opened in 1994, the 100-acre Center was a joint project between the University of Florida and the Camp Blanding Florida Army National Guard. The Army had generously provided the 100-acre area for lightning research. Florida absorbs the highest number of lightning strikes per year for the United States, with over a half-million hits per annum. It was here, at Camp Blanding, that researchers had successfully triggered lightning strikes by shooting charged rockets into the belly of a thunderstorm.

The day he made his discovery, Patrick's frustrations were at a high. He'd just kicked a bucket the length of the lab, nearly clobbering a five-thousand dollar gas spectrometer. Despite the immense amount of time he was donating, his theories had made little headway; he had imagined being so much further along. Part of the problem was that he could never leave any trace of his tests. Alika had helped him create excuses or reasons for leaving certain things out or using a particular piece of equipment, but it was laborious and time-consuming for Patrick to set-up and break-down his experiments every time he conducted them. Despite his assistance, Alika was becoming increasingly intrusive as well, insisting that

Patrick exercise more caution. Just two weeks prior, Patrick had set fire to a lab bench when his electric charges sparked a nearby rack of paper towels. Patrick had not immediately recognized the blaze and for a week the lab smelled of scorched plastic.

The apparatus that Patrick used was primitive but effective. He could not, of course, simulate the full amperage and voltage delivered by a lightning strike, nor could he zip the blast down the wire at the near-instantaneous flash that constitutes a bolt—one ten thousandth of a second—but Patrick did manage to recreate one element of the process surprisingly well; something unexpected.

It was late, nearly midnight, and well past time for Patrick to be home. He decided to run one more test. The trial was nothing more than a fleeting stab, prompted by a bag of odds and ends that he'd found at the bottom of a drawer. Attaching his lightning leader wire to a unique series of batteries, he ran the test.

Whip!

A charge sucked down the wire and into the battery series. Nothing happened. Patrick attached a multi-meter across the batteries to measure the voltage. No change. Patrick sighed and began to unhook the batteries. The plastic bag that had held them was across the bench, and in reaching for it, Patrick suddenly stopped short.

In the bag were several small magnets, each the size of a domino. They were all arranged in the same direction. Curious, Patrick reached for the bag and pulled out the magnets. They were strong, made from Alnico. Feeling strangely calm, he arranged them at different angles around the strike point and re-hooked the leader wire to the battery series. The lab was quiet as Patrick generated the opposing charges at either end of the wire.

Whip!

The magnets shuffled on the table. Like rays extending from a sun, the magnets had aligned to the epicenter of the strike.

Patrick considered the sudden order, thinking.

Chapter 11

If a woman learns she is pregnant, then who does she tell first? It was a question that Patrick had never pondered until overhearing a telephone conversation between Hadley and her mother. It was the spring of 2003, they had been married for seven months and Patrick was set to graduate the following day with a Master's degree.

As Patrick understood it, the announcement of new life was meant to be an uproarious revelation, a celebratory event immediately followed by hugs, shouts, kisses, passion, and finally quiet whispers in the dark about heirs apparent. Hovering uncomfortably in the shadows of the hallway, holding two wine glasses, Patrick did not detect that same spirit of exhilaration in Hadley's voice—in fact, she was crying. Between sobs, Hadley kept saying the same words over and over: "We're not ready, Mom. We're not ready." Patrick returned to the living room, sat down, and promptly drank both glasses of wine.

Over the next month, Patrick withdrew all his applications for low-paying research jobs and took a job with a well-known oil company. The decision had been logistical: they needed money and the fossil fuel industry was going to provide them with plenty.

Patrick was assigned to a project team in Paulsboro, New Jersey, just over the state border, with the never-ending task of making oil derivatives more efficient. It was a good job; the pay and benefits were exceptional, his co-workers were friendly, and once focused, Patrick found his tasks engaging. Regardless, Patrick did struggle somewhat with the fact that he worked for an oil company. Only months previous he had been on the verge of pursuing a completely different source of energy; mining the potential of the skies, not the bowels of the earth.

For Hadley to bear a child at twenty-five was not unusual; far younger parents could be found anywhere. But to start a family at this point was becoming less common, almost old-fashioned. Women would ask Hadley about her career: how would she maintain it? Men would ask Patrick about his freedoms: could he bear to lose more? By the tone and gaze of their friends, pitiful at times, it was like Patrick and Hadley had been swindled into parenthood, as if in newlywed naïveté they had fallen in line with the Pied Piper of procreation. When she miscarried, some called it a blessing.

Patrick had panicked more than his wife that morning, waking to find their cream bed sheets crimson and embryonic. He had called the ambulance despite Hadley's protests. An hour later when the paramedics left them alone, they sat and cried together in the living room. They both acknowledged the pregnancy as an accident, they surely hadn't been trying for a child, and yet after the initial shock the couple had embraced their approaching offspring. Names were being considered, Patrick's old bedroom would be the baby's, Alika would be the Godfather, Hadley would begin maternity leave in October; their lives had already begun to bend around the fetus that had lifelessly flowed out between them that morning.

In the wake of these dashed expectations, they began anew to conceive a child, pressing forward undaunted for that boy or girl that neither had felt prepared to parent only a night before. A year later, a baby girl named Meredith would be the fruit of their determination.

December 2004
Mont Clare, Pennsylvania

It was Hanukkah and Patrick's family had been invited to a party at a co-worker's home. Although Patrick was not thrilled to be working in oil and gas, he enjoyed the people and was looking forward to the evening ahead; he now had few other friends besides work colleagues. Since graduation, Alika had moved to Washington D.C. to take a job as an engineering analyst for the Department of

Defense. He couldn't tell Patrick much about his work, only enough to say that he liked it and the government was forgiving his student loans. Ward, meanwhile, had remained largely incommunicado in California, returning e-mails and text messages at a decreasing rate.

The Jensen's lived north of Philadelphia, almost to Pottstown, in a town called Mont Clare. On the trip over, Hadley asked if the wife was Jewish, given that 'Jensen' didn't sound exceptionally Hebrew. Patrick said he wasn't sure. It was December and he was concentrating on the icy roads. Meredith, a few weeks over nine months, was harnessed into a car seat behind them.

The party was well-attended and Hadley mingled about, toting little Meredith, drawing all manner of coos. Patrick stood in a corner chatting with Reese Galloway, a colleague who worked in the Business Department on the floor above Patrick. Reese had also grown up near West Chester and swum competitively against Patrick in high school. Despite their history, they rarely spoke of swimming, and only if there was a lull in the conversation. Instead, they spoke about their wives.

Reese had married a girl he'd dated since high school, proposing after his freshmen year at Notre Dame. They had both been nineteen.

"Too young," Reese said to Patrick. "We were just kids." Then quickly, "But I love her to death. Wouldn't take it back for the world."

Patrick nodded along.

"Where'd you guys meet?" Reese asked.

"Hadley and I?"

"Yeah."

"In Boston during my senior year at Penn." Depending on the audience, Patrick adjusted the tale accordingly.

"Someone introduce you?"

"No," Patrick replied. "We met in a bathroom."

Reese chuckled, but stopped when he saw Patrick was serious.

The conversation skipped forward to work, to mutual colleagues, and then onto a story from high-school. As the talk expired, they just hung there against the wall. Their wives were about with the children and the men took long sips from their drinks.

"Well," said Reese, stepping into the room. "See you Monday." They shook hands and Patrick remained.

The house was well-adorned, comfortable, and Patrick thought about it being his own. He had a view of the whole living room, a fusion of talking and eating, which emptied into the kitchen where a growing group of children buzzed about a large island counter. The cake was soon to be served.

A set of stairs flowed into the far side of the living room, and on the near side an archway opened to a small foyer. An elder crowd of children raced up and down the stairs, chasing a leader whom Patrick recognized as the son of the evening's hosts.

Various groups of co-workers and guests, in twos, threes, and fives, huddled in brief conversations before breaking apart to reform again elsewhere; Patrick couldn't help making an comparison with splitting molecules. The ten-something bandits from the stairs were now zipping through this adult traffic like commuters on Interstate 76, while back in the kitchen the cake was being cut.

Patrick caught a glimpse of Meredith. The girl was dressed for the season in a black and red sweater, green skirt and white shoes. She was on Hadley's shoulder, wide awake and looking around the room. Hadley was talking to another woman who also held a baby.

Patrick broke from the wall just as the front doorbell rang. Everyone looked towards the foyer as Mrs. Jensen cried out from the kitchen for someone to answer the door. No one moved. The doorbell chimed again. Patrick, already several paces in motion, felt expectant glances from all around. With a nod to no one, he changed his course through the portal, crossed the foyer, and answered the door. In a bursting flurry of noise, a small army of kids poured into the Jensen home followed by two weary souls that Patrick presumed to be the parents. The kids instantly mixed with the other juvenile marauders and the adults collapsed into conversation with another couple.

Cake was being passed around, and a cooperating little girl brought a small paper plate to Patrick. "Thank you," he said especially. She shied away with a grin as Patrick continued on towards Hadley and Meredith.

Hadley was in mid-conversation as Patrick sidled up. In one motion, she shifted Meredith in her arms and passed her to Patrick. She was talking about what they had planned for the kitchen now that they had the money. Patrick took the child and moved away, understanding that he was no longer required.

Meredith looked up at her father, babbled something about "Keel Up In Potatoes," and then continued to look around the room. She was making a variety of sounds now, but no actual words. As a game, Hadley and Patrick would come up with phrases that sounded like her babbles. They both found it fun, but sophisticating Meredith's sputterings was fast becoming the bulk of their speech.

There was so much for Meredith to see at the party and Patrick aimlessly wandered the scene letting her take in the festivities. As they passed the coffee table, Meredith suddenly started to flap. He rolled her up into his chest, assuming she wanted a change of position, or maybe a change of something else. She struggled even more, waving her arms towards the coffee table. Patrick followed her eyes to a small group of guests playing with a dreidel. Patrick recognized the small four-sided piece from the desk of John Levine, his late friend from Penn. Levine had told him about the game, but never described the rules. Meredith calmed as Patrick moved closer to the game. There was a small space on a couch, but Patrick decided to stand and sway so that Meredith had a better view. An older man was explaining the rules, showing them how to spin the top.

"The dreidel," he began, rolling the piece over in his hands. "Has a letter on each side, forming a Hebrew acronym." He distinctly showed each letter, " נ ג ה ש. *Nun, Gimel, Hei, Shin*. Or when spelled out: *Nes Gadol Haya Sham*—'A great miracle happened there.'"

The man's countenance was wizened and placating, and his hair had separated into two wisps above the temples. There was no strain in his voice and he spoke slowly, mesmerizing two of the boys kneeling beside the table.

"This particular piece," he went on, "Is traditional, because it has the letter *Shin*. Most dreidels in Israel now bear the letter *Pei*, which changes the sentence to 'A great miracle happened here.'" The man hesitated briefly, part-presence and part-respect.

"Do you know the story of Moses?" he asked one of the boys.

The lad wiped his nose with his sleeve and nodded.

"Good!" the man cried. "Because now is no time for stories, but for gambling!"

The boys liked this.

Patrick continued to watch the dreidel lesson with Meredith, occasionally swinging large glances about the room, greeting people he knew. The old man went through the rules of Teetotum, the game of chance played with the dreidel, and the players each took turns spinning the wooden top. They played with pennies. Meredith was maintaining interest, more so than Patrick, and she struggled when he turned to leave.

"Alright, alright," he whispered.

"Such a beautiful girl!" said a shrill voice from across the table. The comment belonged to an older woman wearing a blue wool coat and frilly gray blouse. The attention of the game shifted up to Meredith and she shrunk slightly from the stares.

"Thank you," said Patrick, vicariously accepting the compliment. "She's really enjoying the game."

After a few polite nods and smiles, the remainder of the players turned their focus back to the dreidel and their volatile stacks of coppers. The woman from across the table spoke again. Her voice was wet and smacking.

"Would you like me to hold her for a bit?" she asked.

"You know, I'm just about to give her a change," Patrick lied, quite confident that Meredith would be fine with the lady, but reluctant to give her up all the same. "Perhaps when we come back?

She does seem to love the game." A few of the players looked up and smiled again at Meredith. Patrick felt awkward and wanted to leave.

The woman smiled and raised her eyebrows. Patrick shifted his weight to turn, but Meredith fussed again, waving at the board.

"Seems as though she wants to stay," said the woman proudly.

Patrick bobbed the child and was about to play the diaper card again when one of the children spun a *gimmel* to claim all the pennies in the pot. Everyone cheered.

"There we are!" said the older man as a boy gleefully raked a sizeable mound of pennies towards his chest. The shrill woman stood and walked into the kitchen.

Feeling safe, Patrick stayed as the next player spun the top, rotating it backward and then zipping it forward.

A two-piece action. Back a bit, then powering through, sending the dreidel spinning, spinning, spinning, fueled by that initial twist, wobbling here and there, influenced by the surface of the table, slowing down now, hindered by friction at every turn until the symbols set into the wood became more discernible, faltering finally, losing balance and toppling onto its side. And then another hand, reaching from above, repeating the action, flicking the dreidel back into flight…as if shocked into motion.

Patrick's jaw went slack and he nearly dropped Meredith.

He waited for the next player to roll, his heart beginning to race. Again, the player torqued their grip backwards before releasing forward to set the top spinning.

"Of course," Patrick mumbled. His mind was shuffling through scenes, pictures, figures, numbers, labs; settling finally on that perfect alignment of magnets at the Penn laboratory.

For nearly two years, Patrick had been thinking about how to utilize this interrupted finding. From his reading, which he often did during his lunch breaks, he had concluded that harvesting the energy of a lightning bolt was unlikely and impractical. It had been tried. Yet a lightning bolt does generate an incredibly short, but massive magnetic field. With the right configuration of magnets, perhaps the magnetic burst of a lightning bolt could spin a turbine like a dreidel.

Patrick beamed. His project was breathing again. He pulled Meredith close as they watched the players continue to try their luck. She wiggled around to look at him.

"Mush drop a lime tree," the girl said, drooling slightly.

"Whatever you say," Patrick whispered, kissing her on the forehead.

Chapter 12

November 2007
Philadelphia, Pennsylvania

Hadley finished her first novel the week before Meredith was born. It was only upon threat of being fired that she finally agreed to just stay home and be pregnant.

"For insurance reasons," Korey Devoir, the editor-in-chief of the Inquirer, had explained. "I can't have you giving birth on a desk of transcripts and grainy photographs of politicians."

He was standing at her cubicle, Hadley's feet propped up and her belly burgeoning. At eight months, she was still waddling into work, baby in the pouch, pounding out articles from the writer's 'courtyard'.

"Plus, you could use the vacation."

Relenting, Hadley went home and finished a novel.

She had started the book during her undergraduate studies at Boston College, crafting it as a short story for a writing competition. Finding the mornings to be her most productive moments for creativity, Hadley would rise an hour early in order to write. As the deadline approached, Hadley found that she had far surpassed the content limit for the competition. She slimmed the piece to within the specified limits and submitted the story.

The plot centered about a man named Nicholas Frost, a truck driver who spent his endless hours on the road listening to instructional tapes. The subjects ranged from Spanish, woodworking, the history of the Indian Ocean, material science, and beyond. Frost had driven trucks from the age of eighteen, and after two decades behind the wheel, possessed a vast amount of knowledge in an expansive array of topics, along with a warped set of social skills.

Hadley's original idea was to write Frost into a spy thriller. She imagined Frost picking up a stranded hitchhiker—an CIA operative escaping a botched mission—in the flats of West Texas. Driving to the next city, Frost and the operative get talking, and in the motion of discourse, Frost's identity as a savvy genius is revealed. Hadley imagined a wild mix of plots and adventures for Frost as he's recruited by the government as an undercover agent. She remembered growing giddy over the potential.

However, in drawing up an outline, Hadley found herself sidetracked from the super-spy conflicts. She narrowed, instead, on Frost's familial roots. Connecting someone to their present place in the sphere of imagination proved to be a tricky endeavor. Hadley continued to build the life of Nicholas Frost and soon abandoned her quest to write a thriller, choosing instead to focus on the relationship between Frost and his mother.

It was of little consequence that Hadley's amputated version of the Frost story did not win the writing competition, for she had found a passion. In the years that followed, Hadley thought often about Frost, slowly expanding his storyline, deepening his character, determining his hopes and fears, casting parts for his friends, family, and enemies. He became a part of her life, and semi-consciously to Hadley, a template of the man she wanted in her life. She had realized this when first meeting Patrick at the Jade in Boston, being instantly reminded of Nicholas. Patrick's social stutters, his brilliant mind, the conflicts over a deceased mother, his attractive demeanor and wry sense of humor, a few rural tendencies; it had felt right, and only fleetingly did she consider any danger in fusing fiction with reality.

Nine years later, pregnant and sitting at her kitchen table, she finally finished the novel. By definition, Hadley was already a Writer, posting articles on a daily basis for a nationally-renowned newspaper, but the title never felt right until that particular winter evening. She raised her fingers from the black keys of her Dell laptop, looking at the final words in the final chapter. There would be revisions, writing is in the editing, but the sculpture had been carved. She let out a yelp and threw her hands in the air.

When Hadley received the package from Doubleday Publishing, Meredith was eating Cheerios at the kitchen table. It was November, and the little girl with brown hair was three years old. She watched her mother stare at the tightly wrapped parcel.

Hadley Simon was inked in looping handwritten letters across a white label with the Doubleday logo imprinted at the top. Hadley had wondered about this moment. She had feared to dream about it, struggling to let this ultimate goal of publication pass by objectively in her subconscious.

Hadley lingered in the open doorway to the apartment, transfixed, the loveliest of smiles across her face. It couldn't be a rejection, she thought, it couldn't be. She wanted to jump, run, and scream; all at once. Nicholas Frost was to be real.

Rap, Rap, Rap, went Meredith's spoon against the side of her cereal bowl. The girl was looking at her mother in the doorway, unsure of what conclusions to draw.

Meredith was never an avid user of the word, *No,* even after learning what it meant. Other parents at her play group remarked on how little she used it, especially in a crowd of toddlers who seemed as addicted to the rejection as to their television shows. Meredith, however, had another habit, one which was wonderfully amusing at first, but had become less adorable to Patrick and Hadley with its exhaustive application.

"Who's that?" Meredith asked her mother. All day, the little girl asked questions, never waiting for an answer, but barreling onto another query. *How, What, Why* and *Who*; these were Meredith's four favorite words. "Momma, why's that?" She'd learned them from talking dinosaurs on an educational program, who, in their haste to improve the children, had failed to teach them to listen.

Hadley looked across the room at her daughter. Even Meredith's "who's and why's" couldn't rattle her elation. Closing the door and taking the package under her arm, Hadley returned to the table and sat down across from Meredith.

"Want to help Mommy open a present?" she asked.

Meredith stared at the brown wrapping and then back at Hadley. She shifted in her booster seat, mouth half-open.

Paulsboro, New Jersey

The elevator dinged as it reached the bottom floor of the Research and Engineering Branch. The smell of carpet and air freshener filled Patrick's nose as he stepped into the lobby. The receptionist had left for the night and the room was dimly lit. Patrick walked slowly through the center of the room and out the glass front doors, letting them close and lock behind him.

The winds had grown colder over the last few weeks and flurries that afternoon had dusted the cars in the parking lot. Behind the research labs and offices was an extensive network of oil silos and refinery equipment that bordered the Schuylkill River, across which waited Philadelphia, Hadley, and Meredith. On a good day, Patrick could make the drive in a half-hour. He brushed off his car, the newer model of his old Subaru, started the ignition, and drove from the lot.

It was six o'clock on a Friday, daylight savings was past and the sky was dark when Patrick crossed into Pennsylvania. It was discouraging to only see the sun from a window at work. Although never an outdoorsman or a creature of the forest, Patrick appreciated the time he spent outside; indeed, it had largely inspired his work indoors.

He hit traffic a few blocks from their apartment, the same home since college, but significantly remodeled. The car inched towards the first of several trafficked intersections between him and home. He considered calling Hadley to let her know his whereabouts.

She would have been at the apartment with Meredith for most of the day, taking her into work if necessary. Hadley's boss, Korey Devoir, had a soft spot for Meredith—Patrick figured it was more for Hadley—and gave Hadley leeway to work from home as much as possible. Whatever the motivation, it kept Meredith's growth with her mother.

Patrick thought about Meredith. She was three already. Patrick was twenty-eight, and Hadley, thirty. He remembered back to conversations with Alika and the times they had imagined their future families, careers, and geography; his current situation had never made the list. After a few weeks in Paulsboro, Patrick admitted to Alika that he had taken the ExxonMobil job out of panic. The miscarriage had been traumatic. Until Meredith's miraculous conception, home life had been gray. Alika and Patrick talked religiously on Sunday afternoons while Meredith napped and Hadley went to the office. Alika was still in D.C. with the Department of Defense and had been promoted to the role of Engineering Specialist, taking occasional trips to the Middle East where he supervised the transportation of sensitive physical materials, such as weapons, chemicals, fuels, and medicines. Patrick appreciated the chats and looked forward to them every weekend. The past year had been difficult.

Meredith was on the couch when Patrick came in the door. The Beatles were playing one of their Anthologies in the living room. The smell of cooked vegetables was heavy in the air.

"Vegetables!" Patrick cried out as he set down his bag. "A beautiful Irish woman must live here."

There was no answer from the kitchen.

Meredith stood up on the couch and clapped. "Daddy!" she yelled, slipping down to the ground. They met halfway across the rug, Patrick lifting her high into the air.

"And how is little Pony today?" he asked, planting a big kiss on her cheek.

"I'm gwate!" said Meredith, leaning forward to return the kiss. 'Mmwah,' went the smooch.

The sound of high-heels echoed off the kitchen's new tiling, and Hadley came around the corner into the living room.

After deciding to stay in the apartment, at least temporarily, Hadley and Patrick had made some improvements. They had taken up the living room carpet and re-finished the wood floor beneath, put in a new shower, painted all the walls, re-tiled the bathroom and kitchen, and installed a security system.

Hadley came near and Meredith swiveled around to face her mother, flashing a look of discovery.

"Who's this?" Hadley asked, extending over Meredith to kiss Patrick.

"Daddy!" Meredith cried, falling into his chest.

"Day go alright?" Patrick asked Hadley.

She nodded and smiled. "Yeah."

"Daddy!" Meredith yelled again.

"Dinner in a few," Hadley said, walking back to the kitchen, her heels punctuating against the new tile.

Meredith leaned forward and gave her father another kiss.

"What a lovely girl!" Patrick said, carrying her towards the couch. "But oh no!" he strained with alarm. "We might not make it! Meredith. Oh no!"

Simulating a crippled plane coming in for landing, Patrick weaved back and forth, lower and lower, towards a large leather couch that was another part of the apartment's reformation.

Meredith squealed with glee over the predicament, wriggling in Patrick's arms.

"Meredith, quick! Pull up on the controls! You have to save the plane. Meredith, it's almost too late!"

The living room was lit by two large lamps. Patrick careened in slow motion around the first and aligned for a crash landing on the nearby couch. The window shades were closed against the street and the new furnishings gave the room an amber glow.

"We're too low," Patrick said. "Meredith, pull up, pull up!"

"Yaha!" Meredith yelled, grabbing Patrick's arms and lifting with all the strength of a toddler.

At the last moment, and by an inch, Meredith landed in a heap on the couch, rolling across the fuzzy blanket she'd been sitting on before.

"Meredith, you saved us!"

The edges of the blanket caught on the girl's pajamas and curled around her. She looked up in delight at her father, satisfied with the flight.

Patrick cleared the table after dinner and waited for Hadley to join him in the kitchen. She did not. He finished washing the dishes, and set them to dry alongside the sink. They were using the dishwasher sparingly. Patrick checked the time on the oven, which was ceremoniously fifteen minutes fast. It read 8:30 p.m. He toweled off his hands and turned down the lights, walking out of the kitchen and down to Meredith's room. From outside the door he could hear Hadley's low voice reading a bedtime story. Patrick stopped short and listened from the hallway. It was Dr. Seuss, *Oh, the Places You'll Go.*

> *"**Fame!** You'll be famous as famous can be,*
> *with the whole wide world watching you win on TV.*
>
> *Except when they don't,*
> *Because, sometime they won't.*
>
> *I'm afraid that **some** times*
> *you'll play lonely games too.*
> *Games you can't win*
> *'cause you'll play against you."*

Patrick eavesdropped for a few pages longer then wandered back into the living room. He sat on the couch and stared into space. The Beatles had finished their set.

For weeks he had been trying to put his finger on what the problem was. It was elusive. He loved Hadley, he was sure of it. There was no doubt or regret over marrying her, but there was a lingering uneasiness. The limited amount of time they spent together, between his work schedule and her erratic hours at the Inquirer, magnified the divide.

With every encounter, a teething phoniness bit deeper into the limbs of their relationship. If Patrick gave Hadley a compliment, one that he meant, it had the resonance of something forced. When Hadley came close at night, running her hand down Patrick's back, the intimacy felt untrue, almost fake. Standing at the sink and brushing their teeth was a game of keeping one's mouth full of toothpaste until the other had come and gone. Before they were married, this had been one of their favorite times together: playing name-that-tune in gargling and sputtering voices, laughing until they choked and had to spit.

For over a year they had sat with arms crossed and eyes averted in the drab monotony of this waiting room. There had been no beginning that Patrick could remember, and yet the discomfort had gathered in volume over the past few months. Two people with the same secret; both want to share, but neither will be the first to break confidence.

The phone rang and Patrick snapped out of thought. Barely anyone called on the landline anymore. It was down to telemarketers and aging family members who only had room for one number per person in their fraying address books.

Patrick walked to the cordless phone mounted on the wall.

"Hello?"

"I'm very disappointed." It was Alika.

"Alika?"

"Surprised, as well."

"What's up? Why you calling on this phone?"

There was a pause from Alika. "You don't know why I'm calling?" he asked. "And your cell is off."

Patrick felt in his pocket for a phone. "What's going on?"

There was silence again on the other end.

Patrick found his phone and flipped it open. It was dead. "Alika, what are you playing at? Something happen?"

"Check your mail and call me back."

"Check my mail and call you back. Do you—?"

Alika hung up.

Patrick recoiled and looked at the phone, as if waiting for the receiver to explain.

He walked to the kitchen, checked the dining room table, scoured the living room, inspected their bedroom, he even looked through the bathroom—the mail was nowhere. From their bedroom, he heard Hadley walk back towards the living room. Patrick went to follow, but stopped short at Meredith's room. The door was open slightly and the low light of Meredith's night-lamp shone through the narrow gap. He peeked in.

Meredith was asleep in her crib, rolled to one side and cuddling with a purple horse named Drew. A stack of envelopes rested on the chair next to the crib. He ventured inside and crouched by the chair, taking the stack of papers in his hands.

Kneeling by his daughter, Patrick shuffled through the envelopes. Most of them were letter size, junk or bills. Nothing stuck out as the piece of mail that Alika had alluded to—then it occurred to him what post Alika had meant and he felt quite old for his mistake. He stood and looked down at his slumbering daughter, then bent to kiss her cheek.

He slipped back into the hall and went to their office, his old bedroom, and brought up his e-mail. Halfway down the Inbox, Patrick's heart suddenly began to race. The message was addressed to both Patrick and Alika from *The U.S. Department of Energy*.

The body of the e-mail was sparse on information: *Dear Mr. Simon…Regarding your funding request…from the many worthy applications considered…given the present financial circumstances…please find attached an explanation…Yours truly, Dr. Mitch Gower, U.S. DOE Administrator for Energy Research.*

Patrick downloaded and opened the document sent with the e -mail. A grand smile spread across his face when he reached the second line: *we congratulate you on your grant application, and invite you to a meeting on December 1st to discuss the terms of your funding moving forward…*Patrick leaned back in the chair and felt a tingling pulse from his core out to his extremities. They had done it.

Before reading any further, he printed the file and hurried down the hallway towards the living room. "Hadley!" he said, as loud as possible with a sleeping child in the vicinity.

"I can't hear you," said Hadley. She was sitting on the couch with a glass of red wine.

Patrick came into the room reading the contents of the letter.

"What is it?" she asked. He came and stood by the couch, still absorbed by the document.

"It's from the DOE," he said while reading. "They're going to fund us. Alika and I, they're going to fund the project!" He leaned over and smacked Hadley's forehead with a wet kiss. "Hadley!" he said again, as quiet as his excitement could muster. "This is it!"

Hadley looked up at her husband. She saw the rush of light to his eyes. He looked just like Nicholas.

Patrick ran from her towards the phone, picked it up, but hesitated. "Of course, I don't know his number!" He threw the phone back on the receiver and dug for his cell phone, walking towards the charger by the kitchen table.

Hadley, meanwhile, had come to stand by her husband. She wrapped him in a hug as the cell flashed to life and he scrolled for Alika's number. Patrick reached it and dialed. He put the phone to his ear and looked down at Hadley, pulling her in. "Ah, Hads. This is…Wow."

"Congratulations," she said, smiling. "You deserve this." She kissed him on the cheek, and then indicated to the phone. "Is that going to be Alika?"

"Yes." The sound of dialing grew from behind his ear. "Thanks," he said, kissing her again on the forehead.

The line connected and Hadley walked back to the bedroom.

"You read it?" asked Alika.

"Unbelievable!" bellowed Patrick.

Hadley changed with her glass of wine, preparing to go to the Inquirer. It was nearly 9:00 p.m. She would spend the next two hours making edits to the article she'd written that afternoon about the Governor's new family medical center. Apparently there had been some recent zoning developments that needed to be reflected in her entry. Hadley felt numb to the task.

Beneath the bed in a box, Hadley's returned package from Doubleday lay still alongside several other rejection letters and returned manuscripts. Hadley thought about the growing collection, refusing to cry as she pulled a clean top over her head. She decided not to tell Patrick. She would try again. Someone would take Nicholas Frost. Someone would take her.

Chapter 13

June 2008
Northern Florida

Patrick and Alika arrived at the Jacksonville airport shortly after midnight. Their flight had been delayed at Washington Dulles by a hurricane warning. It was early summer and the Florida storm season was hitting an early groove. For the final thirty minutes of the ride, Patrick had felt like an ice cube inside a blender.

As they passed by the airport's deserted gates and shuttered newsstands, Patrick felt full of energy. The freedom to walk and stand was gratifying, as much so as the weight of his shoulder bag, which held a thick manila folder of notes and documents from a week's worth of meetings in the Capital.

The funding that Patrick and Alika had been given was a joint grant to be shared between several other researchers, all of whom would be spending the next few months at the International Center for Lightning Research Technology—ICLRT—in Florida, the former military base Patrick had researched years previous, and a location that all participants agreed would be the best place for conducting further lightning research. Patrick had been impressed with how the different studies synched. There was a small team of physicists from the University of Michigan testing new lightning-triggering techniques, a pair of climatologists continuing a study of storm intensity, a Post-Doctoral student from MIT performing research on lightning safety, and two engineers—Patrick and Alika—conducting an exploratory study on "Magnetic Repulse Energy."

Alika had read the name over and over during his first look at Patrick's proposal. "Magnetic Repulse Energy, MRE…I think just the name might clinch it."

The grant request that Patrick had written was largely conjecture, and Alika was doubtful at first. For months, he had watched Patrick fiddle in the lab at Penn without success. It was the day after the magnet experiment that Professor Chester had forbidden Patrick to further utilize the lab "for personal ambitions." As a result, Alika had never actually seen this phenomenon of magnetic alignment. Patrick had planned to rig up the experiment in their apartment; that is, until Hadley got pregnant. After that, it was all theory.

Alika's skepticism of the project softened while he was working at the Department of Defense. It was the frustration of using the world's top technologies to bolster the world's most powerful army. Alika loved the United States; it had been his home since he was a child. Yet by entering the government structure, he had glimpsed the serious face that kept the American house in order. It reminded him of times in his childhood when he'd walk in on his father conducting business at the family shop in Samoa; Dad wasn't Dad just then, he was Mr. Aiono.

During his first assignment in Washington, Alika was put on a conceptual project to develop new applications for second-generation biofuels. Alika had been stunned by the breadth of possibilities that had already been suggested, even pursued. At lunch in the cafeteria, Alika had made a remark to a co-worker about the possibilities these technologies held for the rest of the world, especially developing nations. Alika's co-worker had shoveled down a mouthful of corn before setting aside his fork and looking at Alika with sharp eyes.

"I would avoid comments like that," he had said firmly.

"Why's that?" Alika asked, taken aback.

The co-worker gave him a bastion smile. "Take it from me, they don't take kindly to philanthropists around here."

In time, Alika learned that many of the technologies developed within the laboratories and workshops did eventually reach the "outside world." However, this overly acute and privileged application of his work was one reason that Alika decided to join Patrick in his funding proposal. The other reason was on account of Alika, himself. He felt as though he had more to offer.

It was a sensation he'd initially felt in high school in Salinas, California while writing an essay on how to improve the education system in Samoa. It was the first time that he felt the potential of applying his own knowledge to help another person, and though he knew that his suggestions on raising salaries and establishing a graduated training program for teachers in Apia would likely never be seen by anyone except his Contemporary Issues teacher, Alika held onto this belief.

Throughout university, this moral imperative to utilize his understanding grew and developed. He was never the one organizing demonstrations against child labor, crafting petitions to locally source the University's food, or leading panel discussions on ethics in the boardroom; Alika's stand was more subtle than that. It was manifest in the projects and assignments he selected, the questions he asked during lectures, and in the classes he chose to pursue. He was conscious of the magnitude of the world's problems, genuinely intimidated by them, and felt that he would only be suited to make an impact through proper preparation. After twenty years in the classroom and four years in the workplace, Alika felt it was time. He was ready to make a difference.

On a Friday afternoon in the summer of 2007, Alika called Patrick from his desk at work. "I'm coming up for the weekend," he'd said, his voice so baritone that Patrick's cellphone had rumbled in his hand.

"Alright," said Patrick, standing in the hallway outside his office. "To what do I owe the—"

"Lightning," said Alika. "And your magnets."

One month later, their funding proposal was ready.

A gray passenger van with *International Center for Lightning Research and Technology* emblazoned on the side idled at the curb as Patrick, Alika, and their fellow grant-mates emerged from the terminal in Florida. A young man jumped out and eagerly pried open the back doors for the plethora of bags being wheeled his way. Scientists do not travel light.

"This is gonna be tight," Alika whispered to Patrick.

"Stop complaining," returned Patrick. "You know you'll get the front."

Ten minutes later, Alika was riding shotgun and working the radio, while Patrick awkwardly balanced on the lap of a non-deodorized physicist in the crunched chaos of the darkened vehicle. The roads were fairly empty and the van roared along at top speed.

The driver's name was Raul. He'd come from Guadalajara in Mexico several years previous to study at the University of Florida in Gainesville. Raul and Alika quipped back and forth for most of the journey, as the remainder of the van either pretended to sleep or made jokes about government funding. Alika knew a good amount of Spanish from growing up in Salinas, so it was no trouble to talk at length with Raul about everything from soccer, strawberries, taquerias, and even magnetic repulse energy.

"Tell me about your project," said Raul in English. His accent was slight, and he reminded Alika of a good friend from his youth.

"Well," began Alika. "What we hope to do is learn more about generating energy with magnets. Though not really magnets themselves, but the magnetic field they produce."

"Sure," Raul replied.

"Lightning produces a very sudden and intense magnetic field. Our goal is to trigger a lightning strike to an array of magnets that will be propelled into a circular motion. You ever have a spinning top as a kid?"

"No, but I think I know. You take it and…" Raul made a twisting motion with his fingers.

"Exactly," said Alika.

"So the lightning becomes the hand that spins the top?"

"Basically, yes. But not so much the lightning as the magnetism from the lightning. The hope is that we can develop a technology that is applicable to other situations where there are high bursts of magnetic fields."

"Like, artificially?"

"Possibly," replied Alika.

"Why not just do that instead of all this?" Raul asked, waving his hands about the cabin.

"You mean a simulation in a lab?"

"Seems like a lot of extra work and danger to catch a lightning bolt."

"It's the money," said Alika, almost with a sigh. "Building something full-scale like that takes a lot of cash. They attached us to this project because these other guys will be triggering the lightning already. And for the most part, lightning's free."

"Very good," said Raul, nodding over the wheel. "I admire you guys. New energy would do a lot of good, no?"

"That's the hope."

The whole trip took under an hour. At its conclusion, the van rumbled into a dimly lit parking lot near a low-slung concrete building. They had passed several signs for the military base, each one offering a stern warning about the ills of trespassing.

As the van came to a stop, Patrick was first to the door handle, wrenching it open and leaping from the van. His leg had fallen asleep on the ride and he nearly collapsed on the pavement. One by one, some nimbler than others, the scientists and researchers emerged from the vehicle. Patrick respected these men and women, laughing and talking as they jumped to the ground. Most travelers would be exiting in a volley of curses and threats about the inhospitable, unbecoming, not to mention illegal, state of their transportation. But not these wanderers, they were here for something other than comfort.

A few dark trailers at the perimeter of the parking lot were visible in the scant light. Raul made a call on his cell phone and announced that the Director would be arriving soon. In the meantime, the van was gradually de-bagged and they stood in circles in the warm air, chatting and lighting cigarettes.

The group was mostly male, with the exception of the MIT Post-Doc, and two of the physicists from the University of Michigan. There were six researchers from Michigan, all of whom appeared to be young professors or older PhD students. The two climatologists were the elder statesmen of the group, and easily the most vocal. They both wore thin khaki trousers and fleece vests, and the loudest of the pair, a man named Joseph Undergram, wore a baby blue fanny pack. Altogether, there were eleven researchers; the makings for a curious soccer team, thought Patrick.

The project groups had six months to collect preliminary results on their individual experiments. At this point, their progress would be reviewed by an independent panel to determine if there was "a likelihood for results"; in other words, if it was still worth the government's money. Patrick and Alika had never done government-funded research, but apparently this procedure of combining grants was fairly new, as well as unpopular. The climatologists were borderline rebellious.

Alika came and stood by Patrick. "How do you feel?" he asked.

"Excited," Patrick said without delay.

"You call Hadley yet?"

"No. I should, but it's late."

"It's Hadley, she'll be up." Alika paused. "Now doing what, I don't know..."

Patrick sent a low check to Alika's ribs.

A counterattack was building when headlights spread themselves against the edge of the parking lot. An old Toyota Corolla came into view and cut across the lot, pulling up alongside the van. The crowd of travelers tightened. It was reminiscent of summer camp.

A crispy-haired man bounded from the car. "Welcome!" he boomed.

A hum of muttered responses followed and the crowd fiddled with their baggage. They were tired, and as domestic U.S. travel goes, it had been a long day.

The man moved forward and began shaking hands, introducing himself as "Manny Freedman, Director of the ICLRT." Patrick was surprised at his grip and charmed by his face. The man looked like a professor of some standing, probably at the University of Florida. He had the manner of a teacher.

"Now!" he yelled, "Raul, let's get these travelers to their quarters." He grabbed a random bag off the pavement as he spoke. "Over here we have your accommodation." Freedman turned and began walking towards the trailers. "The room assignments are posted on the door. It's three or four to a house. Any problems, there's a number in your welcome packet."

The researchers and Raul followed Freedman, the wheels on their bags grinding against the concrete. Freedman continued to shout announcements into the air, covering everything from bed linens, tomorrow's meeting, and the closest bar. Within minutes they had all found their lodgings and both Raul and Freedman bid them all a good rest until the morning.

There was little unpacking that first night. A rain swallowed the trailers in a tinny howl as raindrops pinged off the corrugated metal roofs. Alika and Patrick were assigned to a trailer with the MIT Post-Doc. Her name was Chloe, and the three of them chatted briefly in the kitchen before going to their separate rooms.

Patrick and Alika were at one end of the trailer, with Chloe and a spare bedroom at the other. Patrick pulled a few things from his suitcase, placing foremost a picture of Meredith and Hadley on the bedside table. They were in their winter coats, sitting on the steps outside the apartment. He held felt some guilt over leaving them for the next several months. Hadley assured him that they were both very proud of his efforts to "provide for the planet," as she put it. Except, for Patrick, it was this very assumption of well-doing that caused the most unease. Patrick loved the idea of helping other people with his work, but this had never been his prime motivation.

It was not glory, it was not money, it was not ethics—it was about the problem, the hunt for a solution. This had always been the reason.

Patrick brushed his teeth and dropped by Alika's room. "Alright?"

Alika faced away from Patrick, already unpacked; the man was notoriously organized. "Great," he replied, setting an alarm clock on a small bedside table. "These are some classy digs, eh? Glad we quit our day jobs." The floor creaked painfully as he stood and turned.

"Looks like you own the place," Patrick observed. "I'm heading to bed, you need anything?"

"You know," Alika started. "I might go snag that extra mattress in the spare room."

"One not enough?"

"It's just that when I lie down on this one…I get an unpleasant acupuncture treatment from the box springs."

"People pay a lot of money for that."

"True."

"Think we can get it through the trailer without making a racket?"

"Unlikely. This place is tighter than a submarine," replied Alika, placing a stoic hand on Patrick's shoulder. "But we can try."

Patrick smiled. He was out to bank as many funny stories as possible, anything to break the silences with Hadley.

Chapter 14

March 15th, 2028
Safehouse Five, New York City, New York
5:54 p.m.

Spindletop, Titusville, Signal Hill—none of these names have never really meant anything to me. Then again, I think most people wouldn't necessarily recognize these American heritage sites—only the black liquid gold they bled and the modern petroleum industry they spawned. It's the same with *West Chester, Penn's Creek, Camp Blanding*—if Meredith is telling the truth, these places in Patrick's past are to Hydrogen what the Spindletops and other historic wells were to oil. But I highly doubt this is why Meredith Simon has returned, to sort out historical discrepancies.

Whatever her intent, the way she has painted her father, clothed in his imperfections, is appealing and realistic. She has succeeded in showing him for the person he was, not the enigma he became. His search for answers had at this point led him unknowingly into the outer borders of obsession. For thirteen years he had parented his theories on lightning energy, and his time in Florida would allow him to finally venture into the heart of his desires. That his passions lay in a work that stood to benefit mankind masked the danger of his addiction, even justified its pursuit. Patrick would be his blindest and most vulnerable in the months to follow, surrounded by success, opportunity, and the rising potential that accompanies one's dream as it comes leaping and bounding within reach. His awareness of impending disaster would have been virtually nonexistent.

Back in the monitoring center, Killian says they're starting to get calls about Meredith. Nothing too mysterious, just other agencies curious about her name being flagged on the day's national security brief. I can tell its making Killian's anxious. He's practically quarantined the agents looking through Meredith's trove of documents and forbidden them from consulting with anyone outside our immediate section. Now he wants me to try a bluff on Meredith. I think it's foolish, but Killian wants to prove her conviction. We are fast approaching the point where records end and supposition, both official and conspiratorial, begin.

I watch as Meredith is given a bottle of water and led back into the interview room. She sits and waits for me, at least twice looking directly at the one-way painting mounted on the wall. I remove the bag from my mug of tea, drop it in the trash, and return to the room.

[I sit down, cross my legs and shoot straight into the false news.]

Meredith, I've been asked to end the interview.

Have you?

Yes, we've been advised to release you. Immediately.

Immediately…And what will you do?

[I sound robotic when I lie, and the act makes me uncomfortable. Meredith could not look calmer.]

Legally, we can't detain you any longer.

I see, and what makes you believe you're 'detaining' me?

I believe the setting speaks for itself.

So you're saying I'm free to leave?

Unfortunately, yes. I was hoping we could speak longer. We can return you to JFK or provide you with transportation to another location of your choice. It's up to you.

And under what conditions can I remain?

Well…if I deem your continued testimony to be a matter of protecting your or another's direct safety, then I can use discretion regarding your custody.

[For the first time, she appears to hesitate. I can't tell if this is real or for effect.]

If I leave this building, I won't be seen again. And not by choice.

[With statements like this, I usually wait for the technician in the monitoring room to validate with his equipment—but I know the result before his voice comes throatily through my microphone. "Vitals confirm."]

…Who is it? Who wants you out?
What's important is why.
Is it about some of the people you've mentioned?
Everything is relevant.
Clearly some parts of your story more than others.
That depends on who's judging.
Is that why you want to stay? To finish your account?

[She leans back, slipping into the same relaxed posture of before.]

I believe it was you who said this is a 'trial'. Shouldn't the witness finish their testimony?

["Forget it," says Killian suddenly into my ear. "She's not going to give any names. Move back to the list." Given the chance, I change the subject to something that more intimately interests me.]

I'll have to go speak with my supervisor. But in the meantime…are you hungry? We're past due for a lunch break.

I could eat.
Been craving anything in particular? New York has it all.
...American Chinese. Do they still do take-out?

[I smile and reach for a pen. An agent in the monitoring room could take care of the order, but appearance is everything.]

Thankfully, yes. Know what you'd like?
General Tso's chicken, fried rice, and an order of spring rolls.

[I return to the monitoring room and hand the sheet of paper to an agent, asking him to double the order. I flash a smile at Killian. "I see your multi-tasking again," he says. "If you can, try and come back to who she's afraid of. But don't interrupt too much; I'm interested to see where she's taking us." I agree and leave content knowing that nourishment is on its way.]

Do you mind if we continue?
Not at all.
Can you tell me more about how it ended?
By 'it', do you mean 'them' or 'the project'?
Both.

Chapter 15

July 2009
Boston, Massachusetts

Hadley took the phone call from the couch. Meredith sat below her on the carpet playing with a set of multi-colored blocks, making towers and watching them fall. The air conditioner hiccupped from the window. It was summer and Hadley had come home to Boston; the feel of the apartment in Philadelphia had grown stale.

"You're where?" she asked, propping up slightly. Hadley's parents and sister had gone out to a movie night at the local park. "When did you get in?"

Meredith pushed over another mound of blocks and screamed with delight. Hadley shushed her and set the phone on speaker. Patrick's voice filled the room and Meredith jumped to her feet, prepared to shout again. Hadley waved a finger at her and the five-year old reluctantly sat back down amongst her toys.

"I flew back in this afternoon," he said, pausing. "Was hoping to make it a surprise."

Hadley sat up and rubbed her eyes. Meredith had been ill during the night, requiring Hadley to hover by her bedside until dawn. The girl had since recovered, color returning to her cheeks, and now it was Hadley who felt rough.

"How long do you have?" she asked.

He hesitated again. "Did you just wake up?"

"Kind of," she replied, regretting her tone. She exhaled and swung her feet to the floor.

"Are you in Boston?"

"Yeah, we came up last week. Listen, I'll pack the car and we'll drive back tomorrow."

"Everything alright?"

She felt at her temples. "Yeah, I'm sorry. Meredith was sick last night—fever, sore throat, throwing up—the whole deal. We didn't get much sleep."

"Poor Pony. She feeling better?"

"A bit, she slept this morning. Just a stomach bug, I hope. Up and about now."

Meredith fumbled guiltily with the blocks.

"Good. Well, don't worry about rushing back," Patrick continued. "Rest up. Take a day or two, and I'll get things organized here."

"You sure?" she asked. "Not much in the way of food. Are you upstairs?" She paused. "Sounds like you're outside."

"I am," he explained. "Just on my way out to the store. Really, it's fine. I'm not in such a rush this time."

"Okay." She imagined him sneaking into the apartment, finding it bare. "Call me back later?"

"Sure," he said. "Love you."

"Love you too."

"Bye Dad!" Meredith yelled, but he'd already hung up

Hadley looked down at their daughter. "Feeling better, Pony?"

Meredith smiled. "Is Daddy going to be home?"

"He is," Hadley replied, rubbing again at her eyes. She had wanted more time.

Philadelphia

Patrick walked back to the locked door at their apartment building, no keys in his pocket. There were two other apartments that shared their outer door to the street, and Patrick hardly knew the residents of either. Dark windows and drawn shades were not the homecoming he was expecting. It was supposed to be a surprise; a knock at the door, gasps of joy, hugs and kisses for his family.

He pulled a cell phone from his belt, a new Blackberry for the project. A pair of college students walked past, talking about class. He dialed Alika. At a bus stop down the street, a mother smoked a cigarette while her daughter traced a finger along the graffiti of the plexi-glass bus shelter. The rings went to voice mail and Patrick ended the call. Ripples of tightness took hold across the length of his forehead as he sat down on the steps. The reason for being home in Philadelphia felt impossible, crushing. Three days previous, in the midst of their second summer at the ICLRT, everything had been progressing as planned.

Patrick's phone buzzed in his palm. He relaxed a little, assuming Alika was calling him back, but frowned when he saw the caller was Hadley.

"Hey."

"Hi," she replied.

"What's up?"

"Sorry to be so short."

Patrick nodded into the phone. "You didn't sound short—tired, maybe."

"Check," Hadley said.

"Like I said, get some rest and come back when you're both better."

"Ok, ok. Are you at the store?"

"Just about, yeah." The moving space of the street had quickened since their last call. Cars got in line for long waits. Foot traffic was heavier too. There was no need for Patrick to mime.

"We'll start down in the morning," she said. "Probably arrive around dinner."

"I'll order in Nutellia's. Alika's done most of the cooking down there.

"Business as usual then."

"I suppose."

They talked about Hadley's car and then hung up.

Patrick regretted the continued stalemate of their interactions. When he had first received the Department of Energy funding, the news had enlivened his spirits immensely. Hadley too, though she liked the steadiness of his previous oil job, also responded to Patrick's excitement. It was a brief reformation of the love they'd felt in their first year together. The intimacy, the jokes, the surprises; everything felt right for those few weeks after the grant letter arrived.

It was the ensuing decline that Patrick failed to prevent. As before, it had been when he spent the most time away from home. Upon proving the receipt of his funding to his old adviser, Professor Chester, Patrick had been permitted to use the labs at Penn to conduct some preliminary research. This preparation had turned into lengthy sessions apart from his family, a repetition of the devotion Patrick had shown for his work years previous when he had conducted his banned experiments. As Patrick returned home later and later, he and Hadley grew more and more distant. When the time came for Patrick to depart for Florida, Hadley coolly observed that he'd already left.

The distance of a second summer in Florida had only aggravated the strain. They'd held a few healthy discussions before he'd left in April, committing to more communication during his time away. It was a feat they had succeeded in before, living apart in Boston and Philadelphia for the entirety of their courtship. Patrick didn't understand why they couldn't still embrace one another at a distance. That they were no longer in love was absurd.

Aside from these struggles, the current round of research at Camp Blanding and the ICLRT was nothing like the first. Patrick and Alika now had full separate funding, a staff of three additional researchers, new equipment, and functioning air conditioning. By request, several of the original Michigan physicists had returned to help with the triggering events.

Not that sharing funds and facilities the year before had been so bad, but juggling the multiple agendas of the different studies had naturally created complications—the physicists, the engineers, the climatologists, the safety expert—accommodating everyone was difficult.

Leaning on his hands from the front stoop of his apartment building in Philadelphia, hunched against the din of mounting rush-hour traffic, Patrick thought back on that first summer in Florida, tracing the path that had led to catastrophe. Feeling at the cut on his forehead, he wondered how all this was fair; he questioned where he had gone wrong.

13 months previous
June 2008
Camp Blanding

All day they waited for storms. The downtime proved perfect for Patrick and Alika to tinker with the apparatus they had developed to test their theories. At first glance it looked like a skinny metal tire rotating about a thick, solid hubcap. "It's like a creepy merry-go-round," Joseph Undergram, the climatologist, had mused.

There were two work trailers, each set several hundred feet away from a platform-raised launching pad. Patrick and Alika shared with Undergram and Howard Booth, the other climatologist. The physicists and Chloe, the MIT Post-Doc were stationed in the other trailer. During their second week, the air conditioning went out, forcing the teams to work from their living quarters until evening.

At all hours, there was someone on storm watch; 'Showtime' tended to be daily at four in the afternoon. A sharp horn would blast if a weather system moved within a certain distance of the base. Then, like soldiers to their posts, the scientists would run from their living-room offices to the trailers near the launching pad. Instruments were checked, rockets were locked in place, wire leaders were run to measuring stations, pencils and keys flew into motion. The majority of potential storm events resulted in false alarms, sprints followed by slow walks to bedrooms for air-conditioned naps.

The most important measurement for provoking a controlled strike was the differential of magnetic charge in the air. Lightning is thought to be largely produced as a result of opposing positive and negative charges in a cloud. When this difference rose to a certain threshold on the monitoring equipment in the trailer, the Michigan physicists would all make solemn nods and signal the launch operator. The rocket would then be armed, aimed at the belly of the storm, and fired. This sudden projectile interruption, connected to the ground by a wire leader, was capable of coaxing a lightning strike down the wire.

From June to September, the team launched thirty-one rockets at $7,500 a shot. Six of them triggered a strike—an incredible success rate—and of their final ten rockets, four of them were hits. It was like playing Battleship, except on a much larger grid.

For Patrick and Alika, it was only these hits that produced usable data. A wire leader from the rocket ran directly through the platform and into a shallow enclosure below ground where their apparatus was installed. The leader, in length about 5,000 feet, passed directly through the center of the spinning wheel, which was made from a titanium alloy. The center block, or the "hubcap", was stationary and made of iron. The wheel was connected to the center block by carbon fiber spokes and a low-friction rotating gear. Both the wheel and the hubcap contained strong electromagnets made from an Aluminum-Nickel-Cobalt alloy—Alnico. The magnets were staggered along the wheel and hubcap, and looked like small discs set into the metal. At rest, both the hubcap and wheel were negatively charged, so there was always some jostling until a twitching magnetic standoff.

Machinists from the formal Camp Blanding military base had helped Patrick and Alika fashion and assemble the spinning magnet. It was incredibly heavy and required a helicopter to airlift into place. It was there at the machinist's shop that this contraption, Patrick's baby, first acquired a name. Before then, it had simply been "the apparatus", "the magnet", "the wheel", never anything familiar. Alika had been nudging Patrick for months to name it, providing friendly chastisement for Patrick's non-creative suggestions.

"Why not 'ERM'?" Patrick had protested after Alika had rejected another of his ideas. "It's an Electro-repulse magnet."

"Yeah, that's what it *is*, but not what you *call* it," replied Alika. "Meredith's a girl, but you don't call her Girl."

"Then why don't you name it?"

"For the same reason I didn't name Meredith," said Alika. "She's not mine."

On the day that the magnet was to be lifted into place at the test site, Patrick was speaking with a machinist from the shop. They were standing in a docking bay, admiring the first finished product. "So what exactly do you call this thing?" the man asked.

"An ERM," said Patrick.

The machinist grimaced. His cappuccino skin was spread finely over a thick muscular frame. He was over six feet, looked about forty, and the whites of his eyes were powerfully pronounced. The creases on his face were either scars or hardship. "ERM? Really?"

"Yeah," Patrick replied unsteadily. "An electro-repulse magnet."

"How long have you been working on this?" the machinist asked. He slowly wiped at a burst of grease on his hands.

"Quite a while."

"How long's a while?"

"From the beginning…" He thought back to the Penn's Creek fishing trip. "Almost seven years."

The worker stopped again. "Seven years?" he repeated. The machinist motioned to the wheel. "This supposed to make energy for the whole world someday?"

Such a destiny was indeed Patrick's dream. "It's possible," he replied.

"Then you need a better name," the worker explained.

Patrick looked at the man's name badge: *Darius*. The great emperor of Persia who defeated much of the known world. "Any ideas?" he asked, honestly. "Words aren't my strength."

"I dunno," the machinist said. "Not 'ERM' though, that's nothing to remember."

Patrick shrugged, mulling over what he remembered from history class. "What if I named it...'Darius'?"

The machinist looked at him warily.

"It's a strong name," Patrick replied quickly. "Darius the Great, he conquered Egypt and Greece back in the...thousands of years ago. Would seem appropriate."

The machinist softened and thoughtfully pursed his lips. "Well in that case, I think you're onto something."

One month later
July 2008

The leader snapped on the first rocket that triggered a strike. Severed as it was, the wire leader became something of an indiscriminate gun barrel; a lightning bolt its lone bullet. Due to the height of the break, the lightning's path angled several hundred yards north of the launch pad and struck an unused warehouse. The event was so instantaneous that no one knew the leader had failed until nearly a minute after impact.

"Did we get it?" someone yelled at last.

The trailers were connected through an intercom system during such "flash events". Patrick and Alika were checking their computer readout screens. There had been a flutter of magnetic activity, but nothing near the amplitudes they were expecting. A small webcam was set up on Darius, the magnet, and a counter was in place to count his rotations. The wheel was stone still. Patrick prayed it was another miss.

"Equipment malfunction," came the voice of Chad Juarez, the project leader for the Michigan physicists. "Looks like we had a break in the line."

"But we triggered it?" Alika asked through the radio.

There was a short silence. Juarez broke it. "It appears so."

"Where did it strike?" asked Chloe.

Another brief silence, flutters of paper, and then Juarez again. "Quite close."

There were ample questions in the wake of the mishap, particularly over the integrity of the triggering system. By nature of their joint grant, the group was required to consult after each working day. Although this seemed reasonable on paper, the actual execution became painstakingly monotonous. Within a few weeks someone started bringing beer and the meeting turned into more of an awkward tailgate. The mood was comparatively sober the night of the accident. The bolt had been leashed in so close, only to be let off its collar.

"You can't be lining us up for disaster like this!" said Undergram, easily the most vocal, at their nightly meeting.

"I assure you, it won't happen again," said Juarez, acting as spokesman and martyr for the Michigan team. He was balding, mid-50's, and possessed a rugged Latino charm that had earned him the nickname 'Don Juar'. "It was a bad line," Juarez continued. "We've contacted our supplier and they're sending us more reels. In the meantime, we're still confident about moving forward with our current equipment."

As the Michigan team constituted a majority of the room, it was Patrick, Alika, Chloe and the climatologists that he was addressing.

"Then answer me this," began Undergram. "How many successful triggers have you managed? Better yet, how many have you actually witnessed? Hate to think I was wasting my time here."

Juarez shifted. "I've been on-site for several. Three, I believe. As to myself, Dr. Undergram, I have yet to achieve a triggered strike until today. The fact that we were able to elicit a bolt was an important step."

"Dr. Juarez," said Howard Booth, leaning forward in his chair. His tone was even; the yin to Undergram's yang. "This isn't the evening news, this won't be publicized. Just speak candidly: Is the triggering system safe?"

During the late fall and winter of 2008, Alika and Patrick convinced Penn to allot them an old office space at the far edge of campus. It was chill, bleak, but in contrast to the heat of Florida, Alika and Patrick thrived. They paid no rent, but anything published was mandated to recognize the University as a sponsor. Patrick did not admit how much the Engineering Department had contributed already.

For months, all they did was compile data and target new energy grants. With two wars in the Middle East and the global economy in recession, government research funding had decreased dramatically, making the competition for funds tremendous. To their advantage, the preliminary findings were promising and they had documented their successes well. Of the six strikes, Darius had responded to all of them. This proved to be the main source of heat for Alika and Patrick that winter: videos of Darius zipping into motion, humming along after a direct delivery.

Alika and Patrick agreed with each other to downplay the apparent success of Darius. Their decision was based on the initial reactions of Undergram and Booth, who, upon viewing tapes of Darius, flew into wild prophecies about "saving the world," "preventing climate change," and "removing the filthy stain of fossil fuels from man's fingers." At which point, Alika locked the door and made them both promise to continue in confidence. They caught his drift.

Alika and Patrick knew the keys to more funding were reasonable applications for the technology. Obviously not everyone could have a rocket triggering crew on their front yard during stormy days to reel in bolts of lightning. However, if the same magnetic repulse that was produced by lightning could be mimicked, created in some other form, and if this could be used to start a generator or power a turbine—then perhaps Darius could become an Adam.

After much deliberation, Patrick and Alika focused in on three main areas of potential application for research and development—transportation, hydrogen production, and power generation. They initially included weapons development, but erased it, despite the inherent advantage.

Their conclusion after the first summer was that there appeared to be some sort of exploitable connection between the uncharacteristically large magnetic bursts of lightning and the proper placement of responding magnets. If the scale of the bursts could be controlled and simulated, then the possibilities for implementation piled up quickly. Alika and Patrick struggled to play it cool, trying to talk in "if's", not "when's." Yet as the data continued to shake down in their favor, they couldn't help but laugh across the dim light of their office at Penn; steam issuing from their mouths when the temperatures dropped below zero in January.

By Valentine's Day of 2009, all their grants were submitted and they took a much needed vacation. Patrick spent whole days with Meredith, playing on the floor with plastic horses while Hadley churned out articles for the Inquirer from the kitchen table. He felt guilty for spending so much time away, and when the funding calls began to ebb in around March, Patrick nearly persuaded Hadley to join them in Florida for the summer.

Nearly.

July 2009
Philadelphia

Tired of sitting and waiting for his neighbors, Patrick stood and took the small alleyway towards the back of the apartment building. He had long thought about the likelihood of someone breaking in through the fire-escape; so much as to install a security system after Meredith was born. Standing beneath the decrepit, black stairway, it looked more like a poorly laid trap than a path to safety. A few potted plants stood sentry outside the apartment below Patrick's, and on the floor beneath that lay the frame of a rusting road bike. The ladder, in need of a tetanus shot, was pulled up out of reach.

Two cars were parked behind the building, one was Patrick's Subaru. It hadn't been driven in a month and was in urgent need of a clean. Scratching beneath the wheel well, Patrick found the magnetic hide-a-key box. Too bad they didn't have one for the apartment.

Starting the Subaru, he pulled up just beneath the ladder. Climbing on top of the car, the ladder remained out of grasp. Patrick jumped down and rummaged around in his trunk, removing an old 7 -iron. Back on top, he hooked the golf club around the bottom rung of the ladder and began to slowly apply pressure. It wouldn't budge. The club kept slipping off the rung. Patrick figured it was rusted tight. "What fire code?" he muttered.

He considered throwing rocks at his neighbor's windows, or even just continuing to wait out front. It was pathetic, he thought, that he didn't even know his neighbors names, let alone how to contact them. There were people he could call, his sister Kylie for starters, but he was tired and just wanted the familiarity of his own home.

Patrick looked back up at the ladder. In frustration, he took a swing at it with the club. The metal-on-metal *Pong* reverberated against the building. For a moment, all was still. Then, with a crinkly crack, the ladder came alive and released straight down like a guillotine. Patrick leapt clear, and with a crunch, the ends impacted hard against the roof of the Subaru.

Cursing, Patrick jumped off the car to survey the damage. The roof was dented-in an inch or so, but no glass had broken. It would be a hard scrape to explain. He climbed back up and raised the ladder off the car, its mechanism actually locking in place. Patrick backed the car away and then gingerly made his way up the ladder, around the bike, over the plants, and up to his living-room window. The leaching structure swayed and moaned in the gathering twilight, and Patrick tried not to remember all the ways that metals can fail.

The curtains were drawn at his window, but Patrick could see the edge of the sensor that would supposedly trigger the alarm should the window unexpectedly open. Patrick hoped that Hadley hadn't changed the code on the control panel.

Expecting the window to be locked, Patrick was surprised when it gave smoothly at the first tug. After a brief hesitation, he raised the window fully and parted the curtains. The apartment was dark; empty, save for familiar outlines of tables and chairs, which refined as Patrick's eyes adjusted. Softly, he clambered into his living room.

He waited in silence for the alarm. It never rang.

Washington D.C.

The scars on his hands were blushing, but Alika knew the deeper shade of red was a good sign. The nurses had stitched him up well. He was sitting at the end of his bed looking at the new raises and bumps along his once-familiar skin. The lights were off, and the only noise came from his neighbor's TV through the wall. A game show.

Alika had arrived home several hours ago. After making dinner with the summer sunlight still pouring through the windows, he had lain down as the apartment was steadily overgrown by the evening. Sitting up, then lying down, then standing, then sitting again, he let the events of the past 72 hours sort. The sounds came back the strongest.

The howling roar of the explosion claiming the air, as if the tremor itself could breathe. The shockwave forcing anything and everything into a drumline of shattering, screaming, and coursing. The piercing tear of metal, yelping in fear, and the splash of glass and plastic. The thunder, loitering, ever-present. More screams, but human.

Alika got up and walked to the counter. A pad of paper was by the phone and he pulled it towards him. It bore the crest of the hospital he'd left last night. The top page held several phone numbers. Alika tore it off.

Deliberately, but without haste, he began to write, siphoning the thoughts of his mind onto the paper. When he filled a page, he ripped it clear and continued on the one beneath.

It was the afternoon. We were at the triggering trailer – George and Hal were tracking a storm moving north. It was moving fast, not a hurricane, but looked like one on the radar. We went to full alert, began monitoring the magnetic differential. Patrick was there, dozy as ever. He hadn't been sleeping much – Hadley. Chad was on his way back from lunch. He would have been there – had forgotten his cell phone in the car. The storm came up fast. I was doing pre-strike checks on Darius III – DIII is rigged for tests on hydrogen production. May be that magnetic bursts can strip hydrogen from water – similar to when superheated, knocking the hydrogen loose from its covalent bond with oxygen. We'd deliberated on safety of producing hydrogen – decided should be safe as long as H_2-gas produced was diverted directly to a remote storage tank. 'Remote' being relative – on a budget, could only pump the H_2 so far.

Storm came overhead and Chad still wasn't back. Mag-Diff had jumped just beneath the firing threshold. George and Hal said good to go. Patrick awake now – lazily watching webcam of Darius. Had been two weeks since our last hit. Beginning to wonder if DIII was ill-fated – something Divine. Pushed on. DIII had never been lightning-tested, needed the data. Mag-Diff crossed threshold – a bolt was building. Whether we fired or not, it was coming. Patrick OK'ed the launch.

Everything slowed.

George sent the rocket. I remember him looking at me after he pressed the button – expectancy in his face. And then the trailer erupted. The sound was awful. George and Hal disappeared. I was blown backwards against the wall, down to the ground. I saw Patrick thrown over the desk. I couldn't hear anything. I felt hot. Burning and tingling all around. Closed my eyes – thought I felt blood rush over them – it was sweat. Still couldn't hear. Another explosion went off, rolled over, covered my head. Sharp bursts of light and fire. A thickening smoky haze. I saw Patrick several feet away. He was in pain but moving. I reached for him but the sting w________

Alika twitched as the phone rang, making a deep gash across the page with his pen. The phone continued to buzz and chirp on the counter, dancing beyond his pages of scribbled handwriting.

Alika breathed and looked at the mess of words in front of him—hardly legible. He checked the caller ID and straightened.

"Hello?"

"Mr. Tucker, it's Mitch Gower," the caller said. Gower was the Department of Energy administrator for all alternative-energy funding. His voice was terse.

"Yes, Dr. Gower."

"I'm calling about Florida."

"Yes?" Alika knew what was coming.

"You doing alright?" Gower asked without emotion.

"Much better." Alika said, pushing the pad down the counter. "Thanks."

"Glad to hear it," Gower said unconvincingly. "I'm sorry to bother you so late in the evening, but I thought it'd be best to clear things up as soon as possible."

"Of course."

"Although this does appear to be a freak accident, I'm still going to have to put your study on hold. The committee will be in touch with you and Patrick in the next few weeks after an official review is held to determine if you will be permitted to proceed at Camp Blanding."

"Of course," Alika said. He knew what the run-around jargon boiled down to—they were finished. "Please let us know if we can assist."

"Have you heard anymore on—" Gower paused to check the names in front of him. "George and Hal? The technicians."

"I spoke with the hospital this afternoon. They're confident they'll make it. No internal bleeding, skin grafts were successful."

"That's great."

"Yes."

"Hope you recover well. I'll be in touch."

"Thank you. We'll look forward to your call."

Alika hung up and set down the phone. He sat there for a moment, the muffled applause from the game show mocking him through the wall.

He reached forward and pulled the pad back towards him. Printing slowly, he penciled a concluding sentence at the bottom of the page.

The hydrogen tanks – they were too close.

Philadelphia

The dream was nearly over when Patrick woke. The setting was the same forest. As usual, he ran, stumbled, and lunged towards a clearing that he knew was supposed to be there. He did not know his pursuer, he never saw their face, but their identity was familiar. He had been wounded somewhere in the abdomen and the pain was searing. The source of the wound was another mystery.

Of all the times he had endured this dream, there had never been a supporting cast. On this night, a small boy was running along with him, but unlike Patrick the boy was not afraid. His skin was dark, and if from anywhere, Patrick would have guessed South America or the Caribbean. Patrick wanted to stop and talk to the boy, even just yell to him, but the pain was too debilitating to do anything more than gasp. So he kept running, the boy keeping stride. They leapt over logs, dodged trees, and battered across streams. Then came the familiar footsteps, growing ever closer, clapping menacingly in his ear. Patrick tripped, turned around. The forest, the boy, the pursuer—all disappeared.

Opening his eyes, Patrick sat up and looked around. The curtains were drawn and the bedroom was dark save for the digital glow of the alarm clock. It read 2:02. He rolled over and clicked on the bedside lamp.

Patrick looked about, half-expecting the boy to be at the end of the bed. His clothes were slung on top of his travel bag. A toothbrush rested in a water stain on the bureau. Movement broke down the hall. Floorboards gave and voices collided in the living room. Patrick set the covers aside as footsteps ran towards the bedroom, except these weren't the feet from his dream, these were too close together. Patrick turned back towards the clock to see that he had considerably overslept—it was two in the afternoon. Meredith burst in the door.

"Daddy!" she screamed. The five-year old covered the room in a flurry, plastering her father with a strong hug.

Patrick winced as she pressed on several of his wounds from the explosion.

"Were you sleeping?" the girl asked, clasping her hands about his neck.

"Me? Sleeping so late. Never!" Patrick said, feigning embarrassment. "How could you think such a thing?"

Meredith giggled and gave him a look, one she must have seen on TV, or more likely, thought Patrick, from her mother.

"What!" Patrick went on. "You don't believe me?"

She shook her head.

"Really? Your own father?"

She shook her head again.

"Well, in that case," Patrick said, turning the girl into the covers. "I guess I have no choice then." Pillow by pillow, he began to bury her in a soft avalanche.

"No!" she laughed, kicking in vain.

"Are you going to tell anyone?"

"No!" she promised.

"You sure?" Patrick asked, flipping another pillow onto the pile.

"Yes!"

"Well, alright," Patrick said, pulling her free. "As long as you promise."

"Promise!"

"Is Mom here?" Patrick asked. "Or did you drive on your own?"

"She's in the kitchen," Meredith said, jumping to the floor.

The two of them walked down the hall. Patrick wore a long-sleeve shirt and a pair of Penn sweatpants to cover his legs.

"Mommy!" Meredith said as they reached the living room. "Daddy was still sleeping."

"Traitor," Patrick whispered as Meredith rushed off with her Dora the Explorer suitcase.

Hadley came out of the kitchen and Patrick did a double-take. She had changed her hair. The shoulder-length look had been lopped, leaving Hadley's locks to curl up business-like beneath her ears.

"Hadley," he said off-guard. "Hi." He met her midway for a hug and kiss.

"You just woke up?" she asked. She wore a dark blue blouse and a pair of white jeans.

"Yeah, I didn't set the alarm."

"Late night?"

"Not really. Must have needed the sleep."

She glanced at him as she walked to where her handbag sat atop a roller suitcase by the door. "And you still look tired."

"A bit." He wasn't sure when to tell her. She'd see the scars soon. "Speaking of which, how was the drive? You must have left early."

"Meredith woke me at five," Hadley moaned. "And I figured we might as well beat the morning traffic." She fished her phone out of the bag and checked for messages. She was avoiding looking at him directly.

"Smooth sailing?"

"Smooth."

"And she's feeling better?"

"Cured—the moment she heard you were home." Hadley finally looked at him, nearly speaking, but hesitating; something had happened. She stopped to consider a mark on his forehead when a look came over Patrick.

"Your hair!" he exclaimed, casually brushing his own down over the cut. "It looks great."

"Thanks," she replied, distracted. It had taken him this long to say anything.

"When did you change it?"

"Last week. My Dad thinks it's too short."

"Do you like it?"

She shrugged, "It's fine."

They ordered in Italian and watched Lady and the Tramp. It was a favorite of Meredith's, especially the part where the Tramp noses the final meatball across the plate for Lady. When the scene arrived, the girl artfully mimicked the motion, relishing the excuse to slurp individual spaghetti strands under the guise of true love.

They ate gelato and took a walk down to the park where Patrick and Hadley spent turns playing with Meredith on the swings. Patrick felt exhausted. He knew he was still recovering from the trauma, some of which the doctor said "might take time to get over." It was telling Hadley that troubled him most. Mitch Gower's call last night had been expected, but the weight now boring into Patrick's stomach had not. Essentially, he was unemployed. There would always be money in alternative-energy research, but details of the accident would eventually go public, and after that…funding would likely become scarce. At least Camp Blanding was keeping quiet with the media—explosions were nothing novel at military bases—and, as of that afternoon, George and Hal were in stable condition and holding. Alika would be fine, and he, Patrick, would live. The project, however, appeared terminal.

While they walked home, Patrick let Meredith skip between them. He wondered if the news might sound good to Hadley; if perhaps, this could be something to reverse their decline.

The July weather in Philadelphia was notoriously draining, but on occasion, the metropolis evenings arrived cool. This was one such night and Hadley threw all the windows open when they returned to the apartment.

Patrick commented on the alarm, how it did not go off. Hadley said she had disconnected the system a few weeks back. Patrick arched an eyebrow, but Hadley didn't feel the need to elaborate. She left him in the kitchen, walking down to Meredith's room to hasten along the girl's bedtime routine.

After a bath, a story, and a kiss, Hadley watched her daughter fall asleep. She sat beside the bed on a small blue stool with hoofs for legs. The breathing was the final result; the body taking over and reining the lungs into rhythm. Hadley watched her daughter's chest rise and fall, thinking about how beautiful she had become. The child looked so peaceful resting there in her first real bed.

Hadley stood and left the girl with one final peck before leaving the room. As she walked towards the living room and Patrick, Hadley muttered something of a prayer, or verse of self-propulsion, willing that what was to follow was best for everyone, best for Meredith.

He was in the kitchen, cleaning up, and Hadley could hear the stacking of plates. She stopped in the living room and set a course for the couch, where she sat. The sink splashed on and off, and she heard him take a towel from the rack to dry his hands. Patrick would have walked right on to the bedroom, when halfway across the living room, he noticed Hadley on the couch.

"Is she asleep already?" he asked.

Hadley nodded, not sure if she wanted him to join her yet. Patrick seemed to sense the same. He muttered something about luggage, laundry, and said he'd be back.

After a few minutes, she could hear him talking on his cell phone in the bedroom. Her own phone was on the coffee table and she reached forward to check it. She had opted for an iPhone over the Blackberry, feeling the former to be pleasantly less serious. She scrolled through her messages and e-mails, tapping a quick response to another writer at the Inquirer. Her nimble fingers padded across the screen until the e-mail was finished and sent away into space.

After nearly twenty minutes, Patrick returned to the room, asking Hadley if she'd like a drink.

"I'm fine, thanks."

Patrick remained standing, hands in his pockets. "Hadley, I need to tell you why I'm home."

Hadley had a slew of sarcastic responses for that remark.

Patrick came forward and sat next to her on the couch. He was clearly uncomfortable about something and Hadley found herself feeling slightly unnerved. She hadn't expected anything to have changed, nothing had in years, but the look on his face begged otherwise. "What's wrong?" she asked.

"It's the project in Florida," he began, speaking down to the leather cushion between them. "I'm sorry I didn't tell you sooner." He looked up. "There was an accident three days ago. Well, four days now."

"What happened?" She had to stop herself from moving closer.

"It's hard to explain, and we're still not sure exactly—"

"Are you okay?"

"Yeah, a little scratched up, but nothing serious or permanent." Only now did she notice the slight gash just beneath his hairline. She gasped as he rolled back his sleeves to reveal a potpourri of marks and bruises.

"Patrick!" She raised her hand gently to his forehead, then traced some of the wounds on his arms. "Where else?"

He raised his shirt to expose two big scars, one that ran down the left side of his ribs and another just beneath his left breast.

"Patrick!" she cried again, coiling. "They look treated, were you at the hospital?"

"For two days. They say there's nothing internal or serious."

"But—what?—I don't understand. How did this happen?" She was struggling to remain neutral. Another type of wound was soon to follow. "And Patrick! Why didn't you tell me?"

"I don't know. I'm sorry. I was just—I should have said something as soon as it happened."

"What is 'it'? How did this happen? Is Alika alright?"

Patrick told her everything. From the events leading up to the explosion, to the developments they'd made using magnetism to isolate Hydrogen from water. It was groundbreaking work, Patrick explained, possibly globe-changing. They just needed to confirm it with a strike. Or at least they wanted to, it might not have been necessary.

Hadley sensed a lot of doubt in Patrick's voice. She knew he was blaming himself. He carried on about the accident, describing the sudden terror of light and wind that seized their work trailer. He described the others involved, two technicians who were badly injured, still in hospital, and Alika, who escaped like Patrick without any major injuries. Alika was home in D.C. and they had both heard from their funding source the night before. "They're going to suspend the project," Patrick said.

He was devastated, Hadley knew it. She wanted to pity him so badly, but perhaps this was the best timing after all. Maybe changes are best made all at once, not gradually, one at a time.

"I'm so sorry," Patrick said in conclusion. "Hadley, I should have called you right away. This whole time—"

"It's okay," Hadley said. "I'm just relieved you're alright."

"I know, but…what with everything."

"It's okay."

The open windows ferried in the placid air from outside, and along with it, the sounds of the city. Patrick and Hadley sat suspended, hand-in-hand, in their living room.

"Patrick," Hadley said evenly. Harsh as it was, she had to push on. This was the right choice. Nothing was going to change, nothing would improve, they had tried—they would always be the same.

He looked at her, defeated.

"There're some things I've been meaning to say. For a while."

He nodded.

She fumbled with his hand. This was something she'd rehearsed. Saying it was merely a formality.

"I've been thinking this through for some time, and clearly I didn't know about the accident, but there's probably no point in waiting to talk about…this." She paused. "In fact, now's probably best."

Deep down, he braced

In three words, she set loose the landslide. "We're not working."

His chest locked.

"It's no secret to either of us," she went on. "We've been growing apart from the beginning. I know you feel it too. Seven years, Patrick. We've been married for seven years!" Her momentum was building; she would get through this.

His stomach tumbled.

"I can't speak for you, but it just feels like we're slowly dying, withering, spiraling into a mixed glob of mumbles, fake kisses, and uncomfortable silences. We fight over everything and then…you're never here! You're gone. I wonder if you were ever here. I know you love Meredith, and I know you would do anything for her, but..."

She anticipated him to enter at this point, to interject. But Patrick stayed silent, watching the floor, listening. They still held hands.

"By definition, we've practically been separated for the last two years. What with you in Florida all the time, or off in a lab. You have to admit it: we're never together, and when we are, well…it's miserable." She paused again, almost hoping he would say something. He did not.

"There's not much to it anymore, Patrick. There's not much more to 'us.' I'm tired of fighting, I'm sick of pretending everything's alright, I'm exhausted from being alone." She hesitated. "I want a divorce."

The dagger plunged into Patrick and the weight of the world tightened to a pin drop, cinching around Philadelphia, their apartment, the couch, them. She sensed him recoil.

He searched her face, her wrinkles, her eyes. Immensity canvased the room. Their feet were toe to toe.

For a moment, Hadley fleetingly wanted to take it all back, to try again. Perhaps this would do it. Maybe hope had not fled. But Patrick stood and let go of her hand. He looked about the apartment as her eyes dropped.

His silence was throwing her. "I didn't want this either," she said, focusing on the cushion. "God knows, no one wants this."

Patrick bent down towards her. She closed her eyes as his lips skimmed her cheek.

Without a word he left the living room and walked to Meredith's room. Hadley didn't move. A minute later, he emerged and walked to the door, unlocking the bolts.

Hadley stood. "Say something."

Patrick opened the door, and tried to smile. The fresh agony of his career being demolished mixed ruthlessly with this mighty aftershock; first the roof, now the foundation. He felt completely without hope, flattened and in shock. He was living his greatest fear.

"Patrick..." Hadley prompted.

When he did speak, his voice was quiet, subdued; a gazelle brought down by the lion. "Why today?" he asked.

The answer Hadley had rehearsed for this question was: Because things will only get worse. What she actually said emerged unexpected. "Because I don't love you anymore."

A strange surge of anger flared within Patrick, something ancient and territorial. Slews of rebuttals, vulgar and possessive, threatened at his lips. Void of all compassion, he thought even of striking her. A drink, he wanted a drink. This was still his house. This was his life. Who the hell was she?

But gripping the door handle, willing the monster and his devices to pass, Patrick's temperance won out. The rage drained. He breathed deeply, gazing one last time at Hadley, the woman he still loved. He saw the golden balcony of the Jade, walking in Boston Common, looking up at the autumn sky, the first kiss, holding her silently on the sidewalk of an unfamiliar street; and suddenly, he was alone, only dreaming, and these memories of his might never have been real at all.

Hadley began walking towards him, but Patrick put up his hand. He was afraid what he might do. She stopped, fifteen feet between them.

"I'll come round in the morning," he said, opening the door.

"But Patrick," Hadley protested. "Where—?" The door shut behind him before she could finish. "Where will you go?"

Hadley returned to the couch and sat down, studying her hands, her faded wedding band. The same sprite air and mottled sounds of Philadelphia rolled over the parking lot, the fire escape, and through the windows. She stood and walked to Meredith's room, tears gathering on the way.

Down on the street, Patrick let the door close and lock behind him.

Chapter 16

December 2009
Arlington, Virginia

It took Patrick an hour to find the bottle. The nook behind the washing machine made for an unusual liquor cabinet. It was a half-spent handle of whiskey, kept by Alika in the event of company, hidden on account of Patrick. Four months had passed since the split and Patrick was staying with Alika in Virginia.

Patrick walked back into the living room and stood at the window, parting the shades. The opposite apartment building was lit without pattern from top to bottom. Christmas lights ringed the railings and echoed from beyond blinds. A layer of snow remained from the last storm. The surface of the snowfall had hardened from the cold weather, caramelizing like sugar on a cake. In the small park between the buildings, Patrick could see where children had cut through the thin topping with their boots like steel hulls through an ice sheet. He felt the weight of the bottle in his hand.

Leaving the window, he went to the recliner and eased down. Alika was asleep through the wall. Patrick unscrewed the cap, placed it in his lap, and took the first pull.

The spirit thrashed at his throat and Patrick silently balled a fist against the darkness. He exhaled and flexed, coaxing himself onward. The last few times he had called his father, letting the veteran talk the son from the roof. There would be no phone calls tonight.

The morning after Hadley asked for a divorce, Patrick returned to the apartment as promised. He had not slept and they only talked for a few minutes. Hadley said much of the same and Patrick just shook his head, saying things would change. Although unfruitful, the encounter was less staged than their later talks, held primarily in coffee shops or parks, as though they needed a public area in which to destroy their most private relationship. Each time Patrick came expecting to turn the momentum, yet the harder he fought the further he sunk; Hadley was resolute. Unable to remain in the same apartment, Patrick had temporarily moved in with his sister, Kylie, just outside the city. Kylie taught elementary school history and lived with her fiancé, Henry, a professor at Swarthmore College.

For Patrick, it was the hugs that made it feel final. There was a difference in their touch. Worst of all was having Hadley delicately running him through with the barbed spear of separation while their daughter played on the jungle gym just thirty feet away. But if there was any agreement, it was over the girl. They vowed to be straight with her in the end, explaining everything. It was no secret that divorce could maim children.

From Alika's apartment, there were three bars that Patrick could reach on foot. Dozens by taxi. If he missed last call, there were always liquor stores. Carefully, he stood and went to the window, breaching the shades again. Snow was falling. The flakes drifted down, feathery and fleet. Crystal after crystal, a million parachutes.

"Beautiful," whispered Patrick, fogging the glass.

Memories threatened: Christmas in Boston…a sledding hill… laughter beneath blue covers…a purple snow jacket…

The window shades slipped back into place. He took another drink in the kitchen, wincing and setting the bottle down firmly on the counter. The green light on the microwave read 12:39. There were no sounds from Alika's bedroom.

Stoppering the bottle, Patrick took his coat and unlocked the door.

"Nope," said Alika. "He's still asleep."

"Still?"

"Uh-huh."

"Well, just tell him I called. Again."

"Will do." Alika paused. "Everything okay up there?"

Hadley sighed. "As well as it can be. Same old."

"Same old everywhere then."

"Yeah…I should go, I'm at work.

"Already?"

"I know, it's terrible."

"I'll pass on the message."

"Thanks."

Alika ended the call and looked across the kitchen. Patrick sat at the counter eating a bowl of cereal. "I can't keep lying for you buddy."

Patrick lowered his spoon. He had not shaved for two weeks. The athletic frame he had faithful preserved from his swimming days had withered and his eyes looked perpetually snuffed. He spent most of his days in front of his laptop and the television, looking at nothing in particular, applying half-heartedly to jobs and avoiding movies that discussed relationships. When Patrick told family and close friends that he felt obliterated, they believed him.

"You're calling her back, okay?" said Alika.

"Sure."

"Good," remarked Alika, watching him return to his cereal. "You going out today?"

"Maybe," Patrick replied into the bowl. "To the library."

"Ok, I'll see you tonight." Alika hated the sensation of speaking to his friend as he would a child.

"Bye," said Patrick without looking up.

Alika stopped at the door, several paces from the kitchen. He wore a gray suit, a white shirt, and a blue-striped tie. The shades had been drawn and morning sunlight bathed the room. "How long did it take to find?" he asked, his back to Patrick and the apartment.

Patrick focused on his cereal.

"Patrick." Alika turned.

There was no answer from the counter.

Alika stepped back towards the kitchen. "Where did you go last night?"

Patrick looked up, his mouth half-full. "Whadda ya mean?"

"The bottle."

"What bottle?"

Alika took another step. He stood by the refrigerator. "There was a puddle of piss and broken glass in the bathtub this morning."

Patrick set his spoon down in the milk.

"And you smell like a bar rag."

"I'm not sure what you're talking about."

"Come on Patrick!"

"What?"

"I'm not here to—"

Patrick picked up his bowl and smashed it down on the kitchen floor. The ceramic burst into pieces. "WHAT?" he demanded, glaring sideways at Alika. Patrick rarely yelled, let alone got mad.

Alika pursed his lips.

Patrick stumbled back off his stool into the room. "Help me? Is that what you feel like you have to do? You want to help me, Alika?" He began to tremble. "Well it's TOO LATE!" His eyes were tracks of red and his hands wretched from side to side. "Too late for that," he repeated aloud, and then again under his breath. "My wife. My daughter. My work. My career. Alika, I lost my own…I lost my own family…I've got NOTHING! AND IT'S MY FAULT!" His voice shuddered as he screamed.

Alika gently set his briefcase on the floor and came around the counter.

"It was me," Patrick went on, the alcohol still heavy on his breath. "I knew it would happen. I knew it." A pitiful smile picked at his lips, and he began to laugh, a slow, sorrowful chuckle. "We talked about it. Remember? You told me to be careful. To pay more attention to Hadley, my wife, Meredith, my daughter." Patrick pointed at the blowup mattress on the floor. "Always was a great listener."

Alika stepped closer until only a few paces separated the men. The clock read 8:35 a.m. Alika would be late for work.

"I made myself believe it was for them," Patrick said, shaking his head. "But it was a lie. A beautiful lie."

Alika took another step.

"Did I deserve this?" asked Patrick. "All these other guys, running around to make money…That wasn't me, right?….RIGHT?"

Alika continued forward.

"You know that, right?"

They were face to face.

"You know that," whispered Patrick. "Don't you?"

Alika nodded.

Patrick bowed his head. "Because I'm not so sure."

In one quick motion, Alika advanced and wrapped his arms around Patrick, tight as a cork.

As if set afire, Patrick erupted in a fury of screams and yells. The room shook with the roar of his suffering. Thrashing and spitting, he cursed Alika, Hadley, the lightning. With venomous fluidity, he cursed Hydrogen, energy, the world.

Alika just held him tighter, reeling Patrick in against his own chest as the neighbor next door muted his television.

When Patrick could struggle no longer, his strength extinguished, he went slack in Alika's arms. Gently, Alika set his friend down on the recliner and backed away. Patrick's breathing came in hesitant pulls and his body hung limp against the rocking chair.

Alika straightened his tie, collected his briefcase, and walked towards the door. Milk and soggy bits of Chex cereal pooled about the edges of the kitchen tile. The bar stool lay on its back. Light poured through the windows. And alone on his chair, Patrick bobbed back and forth like a fish in the patient current.

Interstate 95, Maryland

It was a three-hour drive to Philadelphia from Alika's apartment. Patrick much preferred his friend's living room to his sister's couch. The irony of living amidst Kylie and Henry's budding relationship while his own expired was less than ideal.

The call with Hadley had been short and to the point: she had the papers. Their signatures would begin the mandatory 90-day separation before the divorce could be legally finalized. Last month, Patrick had done a quick perusal of the divorce laws in Pennsylvania. The list of detailed classifications for the failure of a marriage was a depressing read. There were pages upon pages on various breaks, splits, and separations. Their situation was considered a "mutual consent no-fault divorce." Glossing through the marital offenses made him concede a tinge of gratitude that he and Hadley were at least parting amicably.

The afternoon roads were clear and the latest snowfall had long been plowed. The following afternoon he had a job interview in D.C. with a sustainable development think-tank. The group had a long name, something that ended in Institute. Alika had arranged it, and after their tussle, the whiskey, and the urine in the bathtub, Patrick felt he should at least give the job a look. The position paid little, but the hours were flexible and he could likely work from home, or even Philadelphia. Whatever the case, it would be better than sitting around an apartment.

He switched on the radio, fiddling until he found a steady signal from a classic rock station. The Who's *My Generation* was mid-chorus. Patrick looked at his reflection. He was thirty years old. His brown hair was receding on new fronts and his eyes had sunk further into their sockets. He did look better after a shave, but the stress showed.

Crosby, Stills, Nash, & Young followed The Who with *Teach your Children,* and another surge of dread funneled down Patrick's spine; less so for the marital death warrant on which he would shortly sign his name, but for the little girl's heart that they were surely about to break.

Philadelphia

"How'd it go?" asked Sheryl, Hadley's old roommate from Boston College. "She take it well?"

"She didn't have to," said Hadley, breathing deeply into the phone. "We didn't tell her."

Patrick had left an hour previous and Hadley had just put Meredith to bed. Although Patrick had sporadically traveled throughout much of her remembered life, Hadley knew young Meredith was getting wise about the odd proceedings of her father's recent comings and goings. She was midway through Kindergarten and already savvy to so much. Hadley's chief fear was that the other kids at school might piece together the actuality of the divorce for Meredith. She thought that surely this could only do harm, producing cancerous elements of distrust at the core of their relationship, festering to cause future fallout and a lifetime of poor relationships—at least these were Hadley's apprehensions.

"We were so close, but…"

"I know honey, I know. But remembah," said Sheryl, her Boston accent warping away her r's. "You got to push on now. No dallying, you hea'?" Sheryl had been through a divorce two years earlier and was sympathetic to the dilemma. Hers had unfortunately not been a 'no-fault.'

"I know," said Hadley. She was collapsed on her bed. "We did sign the papers though. That's a step, right?"

"Well, sure, but less so since yore' splitting everything, 50/50. Back when Chris and I were going over the fine print, ugh, it took weeks! Back and forth, back and forth. The man was a villain."

Sheryl rambled on as Hadley mulled over the botched attempt to tell Meredith about the divorce. Patrick said he would be up again soon to look for places. They could try again then. He had looked healthier this visit, even talking about a new job, but she knew he was still suffering, keeping up appearances solely for Meredith. He still loved her too, that was clear. Hadley thought of their daughter, sleeping through the wall, oblivious to this nightmare.

"I should get going," Hadley cut in at length. She loved talking to Sheryl, she had been a humongous help, but Hadley just wanted to think about something else, anything but the divorce.

"Okay honey, you'll call me?"

Arlington

When Patrick arrived back at Alika's, it was snowing again. The seasons had become unpredictable of late, an issue with many angles. Warming, now cooling, now changing. Patrick was not keen on getting into debates, despite the convincing studies he had read. It did, in fact, appear that a shift in the global climate was occurring. The recent ClimateGate, however, had shaken the public's faith and Patrick feared the associated skepticism might become rampant, halting further willingness to invest in renewable energies, a subject often lumped in with environmental stewardship. So far, the media storm was simply running its course. All the pundits were weighing in; reading and extrapolating wildly, likely from short briefs handed to them seconds before going live. Patrick tried not to blame them for their lacking commentaries and confused proportions.

Alika was watching the Eleven o'clock news when Patrick came in the door. The blowup mattress was propped up against the wall near the window.

"Anything good?" Patrick asked, sitting down next to Alika on the couch.

"Nuh sur ma hen rel fah." Alika replied through a mouthful of burrito. He was wearing big basketball shorts and a faded blue t-shirt for Pabst Blue Ribbon beer. There was something on the screen about a shooting near the Capitol building. "Nothing new," Alika said again after swallowing.

Two months prior, their project funding had been discontinued and their permission to utilize Camp Blanding revoked. Mitch Gower from the Department of Energy had hinted at a possible negligence law suit, but they had heard nothing in weeks. Solemnly, the pair had put Darius and their ERM work to rest. The decision should have carried more weight, but under Patrick's marital circumstances, the burial passed without feeling. Alika's new apartment was courtesy of his return to the Department of Defense, who, to his surprise, had quickly snatched him back.

"How'd it go?" Alika asked.

"We didn't tell her," Patrick said, staring at the TV.

Alika turned to look at Patrick

"We just froze."

Alika killed the TV.

Patrick continued to look at the black screen. "We were all at the kitchen table, kind of like we would be on any other night. The dinner was out, we were talking, eating, sometimes laughing…I'm sure to Meredith it seemed like a normal meal. It almost did for me." Patrick gave a weak smile. "Except for the divorce papers at the fourth setting."

Alika nodded.

"Hadley and I had hashed it all out beforehand: What we were going to explain, how it would sound, who would say what."

"Were you going to lead?" Alika asked.

"No," said Patrick. "She was."

"And she…"

"Meredith asked about Christmas at Grandpa George's."

"Curveball," said Alika.

A knock came at the door.

They shared looks.

"You order pizza?" Alika asked.

"No."

Alika stood and went to the door, looking through the peephole. As he did, the knocking came again. Whoever was knocking stood deliberately out of view. All Alika could see was a gloved hand.

"Who's there?" Alika called through the door.

There was no answer.

Alika repeated the question and the gloved hand knocked again.

Alika backed away from the door and moved slowly into the kitchen, opening a drawer.

"Who is it?" Patrick asked.

Alika put a finger to his lips for Patrick to be quiet. His hand emerged with a rolling pin. There had been a series of home invasions in the area, small-time robberies, and Alika was taking no chances.

Patrick gave him a sideways look. "What are you doing?" he mouthed.

Alika came to the side of the door, which was already unlocked. He motioned for Patrick to duck down out of sight.

"Alika!" Patrick whispered, pointing at the baking instrument.

Alika turned the door knob, and then pushed it forward, the pin held behind him.

The door opened inwards, and for a moment, there was just the sound of snow falling outside. Then, with a confident stride, a capped figure dressed in a heavy winter coat moved into the doorframe. Patrick noticed the shoes first, shiny as a new coin.

Alika pounced, pulling the suspect inside and throwing him to the floor in one motion. He kicked the door closed and locked it. Patrick yelled for order but Alika had already stopped. The face of their visitor had become visible. Lying on the floor, panting and smiling up at his old Samoan friend, was Ward Prince

"Ward?!" Alika and Patrick exclaimed at once.

"Not the homecoming I was expecting," Ward said as Alika threw the rolling pin on the floor and pulled him to his feet. "But at least you didn't leave me out in the cold."

"I could have—Why'd you—" sputtered Alika, looking incredulously from Ward to Patrick.

Ward shrugged and Patrick burst into laughter.

They went to Dave and Buster's, a nearby venue that Patrick found moderately disturbing, mainly in the way grown adults pounded away on video games like sugar-strung toddlers. Alika liked it for the appetizers. They took a booth and ordered a round of drinks.

"What are you doing, Ward?" Alika cried. "We don't hear from you in almost—when was graduation?—2001, so eight years! And now you're creeping at my door in the middle of the night?"

"He was waiting for his grand re-entrance," said Patrick, remembering the weighty check that Ward had sent to Hadley and him in lieu of his attendance at their wedding.

"A grand beating, is more like it," said Alika.

Ward laughed and took a drink. "What can I say? You know how things get." He waved his hands and they all agreed. "I do apologize. But, really, I was here in town for the night and remembered that you were in D.C., Alika. Thought I'd try and track you down. Didn't expect to get assaulted. Perhaps if you weren't there," he indicated to Patrick, "The Polynesian might have finished me off."

One by one, they caught up on their exploits since graduation. Alika and Patrick told him abridged versions of their respective career moves, as well as their recent venture together in Florida. Ward said he had heard snippets about it through the alumni newsletter. Alika went over their successes and failures, touching briefly on the accident that brought them back north.

At Ward's insistence, Alika spared some details on his developing relationship with a girl named Dolores. He had rarely talked about her around Patrick; never seeking high-fives after returning home the morning after with tie askew, not wanting to spark off further sorrow. Dolores worked in a CIA linguistics department at Langley, and the two had met through mutual friends. She hailed from a plethora of racial backgrounds, but mainly Haitian and Costa Rican. She was beautiful, Alika explained, funny, gentle, smart, and all-around lovely.

Ward too described himself as being lucky in love, although rarely with the same woman. It was a condition he had suffered, or enjoyed, at Penn as well, skipping from one willing girl to the next. He was not seditious or destructive, only quick to be bored, unlikely to linger. His most recent bite was a small-time television actress who he flew down to see on weekends in Los Angeles.

As for Patrick, Ward had seen the blowup mattress in Alika's living room, and assumed that something was amiss. Patrick explained his separation with Hadley, brushing over his dip into depression and drink, and focused mainly Meredith. The awkwardness was brief and the conversation easily changed course when the waiter arrived to check their table.

Ward seemed very much the same. He looked a bit more tan, a few years more mature, and his speech rang several syllables more fanciful. His dress was fine and fitting, he looked accomplished, and Patrick could not help but feel envy for his apparent progress in life. Ward explained how he left his first job in construction shortly after arriving. He explained that the people there were inept and fruitless, capable only of wasting his time—the judgment did not surprise the table. From there he had bounced around, working for various consulting firms until landing a spot with his current employer, REI. The name was familiar, but neither Patrick nor Alika could place it. Ward elaborated.

REI, or Real Energy Investments, was a budding venture capitalist network for those looking to invest in new forms of energy. Alika and Patrick vaguely recalled sending REI information during their massive mailing spree of grant and funding applications. Ward said he had never seen their application as he was more involved with finances than project selection.

REI had a formula similar to microfinance organizations that use multiple donations to fulfill small-sum loans, often in developing countries. At REI, accepted applications were filtered and highlighted according to future promise and submitter resolve. These projects were then strategically showcased to various investors, indicating a predicted return and risk. The difference between REI and microfinance initiatives was the general intent of the investor: profit-seeking versus welfare-seeking. Alika and Patrick were thoroughly impressed by their friend's ascension and they ordered another round as Ward explained how he was in D.C. to meet with a potential investor for a wind farm in Iowa.

They left the bar just before 2:00 a.m. The evening had been a needed reprieve for Patrick, a rewarding end to a hurricane of a week. At times, the comfort of being with his friends was such that it felt like they were back at their old regular, The Kingdom; a place where Patrick remembered life being so simple, shielded, full of promise.

After hugs, exchanged numbers, and agreements not to wield blunt objects or hide behind peepholes, Ward's cab arrived. As he opened the door, Ward stopped and turned back to Alika and Patrick.

"I might be able to help with your project," he said. "I can't promise anything. And if what happened in Florida does get out, well, you know it'll be challenging."

Alika and Patrick nodded in understanding.

"But let me talk to some people," Ward said effectively. "Maybe I can find a seam."

One week later
Philadelphia

Hadley took the call in bed around dawn. It came through the landline at the right side of the bed. She still slept on the left.

Reaching across, Hadley caught the phone on the last ring before the answering machine. The news caught her breath.

"When?" Hadley asked, sitting upright.

The female voice told her that he had gone during the night, a little after 9:00 p.m. He had been at the grocery store when someone saw him collapse. He was rushed to the hospital, but nothing could be done.

"What was the cause?"

The woman on the phone had been his doctor for the last twenty years. Heart attack, she explained, massive cardiac arrest. She asked if Patrick was home.

"He's—well, he's no longer at this number. This is his old one." Hadley explained softly. The doctor asked if Hadley was related to Patrick. "We're divorced." The woman understood and put the decision to Hadley over who would be best to tell Patrick the news.

"I'll tell him," Hadley said at once. "I'll call him." The doctor gave her a little more information about how the body could be identified and collected, as well as the likely steps for the funeral should the family choose to arrange one.

"Thank you. I'll let Patrick know. Have you called Kylie or Colleen?" The doctor said she had not. Patrick's old landline was George Simon's only Emergency Contact.

Hadley thanked her again and said goodbye. The woman expressed her condolences and hung up.

Hadley pulled up her knees and slumped against them. She allowed a few tears before gathering herself for the call to Patrick. George was fifty-nine.

When she told him, Patrick said he would handle it. He had returned to Philadelphia two days prior to look for apartments, finding one in Northern Philadelphia in a neighborhood near where George had grown up. His job interview at the Global Environmental Alliance Institute had been successful and he would be able to work from home. It was temporary, he told Hadley, the apartment and the job.

Several minutes after Hadley gave him the news, Patrick called back.

"Will you come with me?" he asked. "I know you have work."

Hadley hesitated—they were separated now and lines needed to be drawn. "I'll have to see about getting someone for Meredith..." she hinted. "Are you going now?"

"Probably too early...Maybe in about two hours?"

"Okay..." Then again, she did still care about him and George had been great to her.

"But look, if it's too much, I can just—"

"No," Hadley said, guilt or compassion winning over. "It's fine. Let me call Sheryl, she'll be around."

"Thanks," said Patrick. "I'll come by in a bit. We should tell her."

It was December 18th, one week until Christmas, and Meredith highly anticipated the days she had with Grandpa during their holiday visits. Meredith was playing in her room when Patrick and Hadley came in and sat beside her on the ground. Her pajamas were a colorful montage of Disney princesses. Patrick did the talking, his eyes growing glassy. Meredith just listened, letting her toys lay where they'd fallen on the ground.

Patrick explained that Grandpa was happy now, but that they wouldn't be able to visit him...this Christmas. He was unable to say *again*.

Meredith looked at her father and mother, both of whom were on the verge of tears. She came close and they hugged together. Her purple horse, Drew, sat reverently behind them.

"George?" she asked, looking up at her father.

"Yes," Patrick said. "Grandpa George."

Something about saying his name registered with the child and Patrick watched her eyes understand the loss. Her lower lip began to tremble, her face sorrowed, and her shoulders sunk. And then she cried.

West Chester, Pennsylvania

George's body had not been taken to the morgue when Patrick and Hadley arrived at Chester County Hospital to make the requisite identification. His body was being kept in the wing beneath the ward where Patrick and his two sisters were born. Patrick remembered coming there at age five when Colleen joined their family. She was in Chicago now, beginning a PhD in English at Northwestern. The Simon family was down to just the children.

A nurse led them to a corner area of the ward where the curtains were pulled tight. Guiding them to a specific bed, the nurse pulled a curtain aside to reveal a bed and a body covered by a sheet. She walked to the other side of the bed and asked if they were ready. Patrick nodded and she pulled back the sheet.

It was no surprise to see George, his eyes closed, and his face quiet. The surprise to Patrick was the peace he felt. It was like adrenaline, but soothing. For a time he just looked at his father, fighting tears and searching for meaning in the lifeless face. This was not the man that Patrick had known. There was something missing in the nose, the forehead, and the grayed hairs. He remembered a similar absence when saying goodbye to his mother.

After a nod to the nurse, the sheet was returned. Patrick felt down at his father's side, finding his hand. It was rigid and cold. Patrick gave it one last squeeze before being led out between the curtains.

"Go find Mom," he whispered.

After signing all the pertinent papers, Patrick and Hadley drove out to the family home. George had retired a year ago, his doctor finally convincing him to take some time away from work. George, however, had been determined to make retirement a temporary stand, refusing to sell his truck, which now sat in the deserted tow yard.

The house was in good order and Patrick could tell that George had spent much of the past year putting things in their place. The family had stayed in good touch over the years, getting together on holidays and sending cards on birthdays. He thought back to the last time he had seen his father alive. It was about two months previous in October. Patrick had come to talk, feeling ashamed that he had let his family separate at the expense of a science experiment. "It's in the striving," George had explained. "Happiness is in the striving."

Hadley made coffee and they sat at the table. A packet of Meredith's favorite cookies, Vienna Fingers, waited for Christmas on the kitchen counter. They would hold the funeral after Christmas, giving people time to gather after the holiday.

Hadley felt torn about the events of the morning and afternoon. Returning to all these familiar places with Patrick was playing with her convictions. She did not love this man anymore, she had decided that already. It felt unfair to spend time with him now, mere months since their split, but sitting together so comfortably like this was not supposed to happen yet. Hadley sipped faster at her coffee.

"I think he was ready," Patrick said, playing with the handle of his mug, unaware of Hadley's thoughts. "I think being here alone at the house this past year was too long for him. For the first time there was nothing to distract him. He must have thought of Mom everyday."

A clock clicked and chimed softly from the other room. A car went by on the street.

"I've never believed in a life after this, but there was something in the way he talked the last time I came here. Something that made me feel as though he did." Another clock rang down the hall.

"Did he talk about your mother?" Hadley asked.

"Not directly, no," said Patrick. "But he was terribly…at peace about everything. I'd never seen him so centered. I thought it was just to balance me out, or something. But I think he realized that he'd done what he could, the closest to what she would have, and now there was just the house. The past few months more than ever he must have—."

"Missed her," Hadley finished.

Patrick nodded and looked down at his mug.

They finished their coffee and Patrick drove Hadley home. He came upstairs to see Meredith and told her he would come back tomorrow.

Hadley caught him as he was leaving. There were tears in her eyes and she took him in a hug. It was late afternoon, but for the winter light it could have been evening.

"I'm so sorry," she said. He held her for a while, and then she reached up and kissed him on the cheek. Their eyes flitted over one another's and their breathing synched. Patrick wanted to kiss her; he wanted to feel something other than hurt, if only for a moment. As he lined up, Hadley pulled away.

Ten days later
West Chester, Pennsylvania

Patrick shut the door after his sisters and turned back to the empty living room. They had just finished holding a post-funeral reception at the family house. Having the service just after Christmas had been better than Patrick imagined. Everyone was still in good spirits from their yuletide celebrations and the funeral had felt more like a reunion than a farewell. The house was empty now, all the mourners gone home to prepare for New Year's Eve, the next party.

Patrick walked to the center of the kitchen. Hands in his pockets, he considered the cupboards, the counter, the stove; he walked over and looked down into the sink, out the kitchen window. His sisters and aunts had helped to clear up so there was little left to do. He opened a few drawers, poking in between the assortment of batteries, tools, spare parts, and rubber bands. In the final drawer, tucked in a sealed Ziploc bag, was the invitation to his and Hadley's wedding. He held it up, looking through the plastic at the promise of his former life.

Tears began to build behind his eyes and he swiftly replaced the photo and shut the drawer. The fridge was across the kitchen and he walked towards it. There were a few beers left in the meat drawer and no one else would be calling that evening.

Halfway across the kitchen, something suddenly grabbed Patrick's foot. He felt himself lifted up by one leg, and before he could realize he was slipping, he had landed flat on his back, slamming his head against the hard tile floor.

It was dark when Patrick regained consciousness. His hair was sodden and the kitchen tile felt slimy against his cheek. He had fallen a few feet from the edge of the fridge and his line of sight was aimed directly beneath the appliance. A tepid breeze from its compressor ruffled up against his face. A range of bits and pieces were strewn amongst the thick rug of accumulated dust beneath its frame. Bran flakes, milk tops, a piece of dull metal, receipts: nothing to be missed. It was an old fridge, and for years it had made the kitchen treacherous with its leaking and humid breath. "Stop running on the tile!" his parents had always warned.

Patrick sat up and checked his watch to make sure it was evening and not morning. It was still December 28th, meaning he had been out about two hours. He felt his head, finding a little bump where the tile had made impact. There was a light on in the living room and he half-expected his sister or Hadley to be leaning against the couch, watching him.

After turning on more lights throughout the house, Patrick came back to the kitchen and swallowed two aspirin with a glass of warm water. His head felt less shaky than he would have thought for a knockout. From the fridge he pulled some of the chicken that had been served at the reception and ate a few pieces with his fingers. He felt better, but restless. Wiping his hands on his jeans, he walked back into the living room towards the couch. He'd gone two steps when he stopped. "Could it be?" he said aloud.

He went back to the fridge, knelt down, and looked back into the forgotten space below. There it was, and not just *any* piece of dull metal. Patrick got up and grabbed the fly swatter from its hook by the cupboard. A few shimmies later, the lost key to George's tow truck sputtered across the tile.

It took close to thirty minutes to dig out the truck. A massive blizzard had hit the East Coast the day after George's death, leaving a foot of snow stacked atop and around everything. The weather had remained cold since the storm, so the snow was still fairly light and powdery. Nevertheless, by the time Patrick had hefted the last mound clear and sheathed the shovel into a bank of roiled snow, he had removed his jacket, his hat, his gloves, and he was still sweating.

Using an ice scrapper, Patrick cleared the front and back windshields, the side windows, the rearview mirrors, the headlights, and the door frame. The padlock on the gate looked like it hadn't been opened in months, but the mechanism still snapped open on the first jig. The town plow truck had already cleared the space at the front of the gate, leaving Patrick with an open path to the road. The final test was whether the great relic would start.

There were, of course, other sets of keys for the truck, but this particular key had been lost for as long as Patrick could remember. It had caused a few fights between his parents when it first went missing. At the time there had been no spare and George had gone tramping around the house turning over everything he could lift, which had apparently excluded the refrigerator, barking at Mary that the house was a thief. It was shortly after their move from the city and George was still adjusting to country life. Patrick had been a young boy at the time and overheard the disagreements relating to this mysterious missing key. He had hunted for hours trying to find it, imagining his father's pride when he solved the case. His mother would help him dress up as an inspector and he'd carry a notebook and a toy pipe, candy cigarettes if he could find any, and ask his father pressing questions. Then, at the end of the day, having fingerprinted the TV remote and his baby sister, cross-examined his mother on her alibi, young Patrick would regrettably hang up his inspector's jacket and go play something else.

Patrick smiled at the memory as he put the key in the ignition, his breath fogging in the frigid air of the dark cab. The engine sprung to life on the first try. After all its dormant years, the key was still to form. Patrick put the truck into first gear and eased the hulk forward through the snow towards the gate. Entering onto the main road, Patrick accelerated, listening to the healthy whine of the engine. George had done well to keep the truck in shape.

He did a lap through town, passing along the traditional Pennsylvanian high street, waving to a few faces that recognized the truck. Patrick figured they must have thought him recklessly nostalgic; and they would have been right. He traveled further along the outskirts of West Chester, going easy on the less traveled roads where the snow had been packed down into a slippery mat. The gas tank was full and he drove for an hour, passing familiar sights and historic landmarks of his youth. He kept the radio off, preferring the neutral silence to anything else. As he barreled along the local highway, his headlights illuminated an old faded sign that hung by a single nail. After passing the sign, Patrick immediately began to slow. He checked his mirrors at the next turnoff and then swung the truck around.

The road up to Pleasance Point had not been plowed, but Patrick could see several tire tracks leading up and around the winding hill. It was a foolish route to take in the snow, especially in a tow truck, but Patrick was soon treading up the slope in low gear. The engine roared as he struggled to keep the acceleration constant. On a few occasions the wheels slipped towards the outer edge, but each time Patrick managed to correct. The trees and underbrush were perfectly coated in snow and Patrick tried to avoid looking at their intriguing winter wear; he did not like the thought of having to call another tow truck.

Fourteen years had passed since he had climbed this same road with his father. He had returned a few times with friends in high school, once with a girl, and once after his mother died. He had told very few people about the tree; Alika, John Levine, Hadley. His father had known of course, although he spoke of it just once. It was shortly after the incident and George was telling the family over dinner how a crew of men from the nearby penitentiary had planted a new oak in place of the shattered old one. He had then looked to Patrick. "But I get the feeling the old oak didn't die for nothing," he'd said to all. "Of course not," Mary had said, "I heard they're keeping the wood for the bonfire on the Fourth." George then winked at Patrick and the meal went on.

The tires skidded close to the edge again as Patrick crested the top of the road and reached the top of the Point. The sky was grey and dark, but the glow of Philadelphia was as strong as ever. The tire marks that Patrick had followed up the drive disappeared now, erased by the sifting winter winds, and the truck made fresh tracks across the naked hilltop. He stopped near the middle and turned off the engine and headlights. Muted moonlight uncovered outlines and shadows made by the snow-weighted brush.

Leaving the keys in the ignition, he hopped out of the cab and into the snow. Patrick pulled a hat from his jacket pocket as he walked towards the shadowy branches of the oak. Its frame and presence were juvenile in the memory of its predecessor, still he felt a similar reverence upon reaching its trunk. Snow had drifted against the tree's Western face and Patrick leant on the opposite side looking out to the illuminated city.

Life had not gone as expected.

Patrick knew there was no one to blame for this besides himself, and introspection was not his strength. It was a fear he had expressed to his father on Penn's Creek; it was the fear of being helpless against his own inclinations, against something inside of him that seemed unchangeable. It was the terror that had been the final few years of his marriage as he felt Hadley slipping away, knew that Meredith would go with her, and yet felt powerless to stop such impending doom. "Don't fear what you can change," his father had told him that day on the river.

"Don't fear what you can change," he repeated, leaning against the young oak. His father was gone now, his mother too. He had lost his wife, his daughter in part. "What about the things I can't change?"

He stood there for a time; listening to the wind, not saying or thinking anything.

"What do you want to change?"

He remembered back to the mechanics shop at Camp Blanding, when the living Darius had asked him about the future of ERM technology: Was it going to supply energy to the whole world someday?

To change the world - that was what he wanted, and he did not fear it either. This sense of potential was why he had never shrunk to give himself entirely to his work, why he would never retire in the face of failure. It was a feeling that had stirred within him fourteen years previous—first at this very spot—and had frequented his life unpredictably ever since. It was the drive to innovate, to ride the frontier of understanding, to do something for the first time. This hunger for knowledge was not rooted in pride or ambition, neither selfishness nor greed. It was a passion of another glory; capable at once of immense power and dangerous vulnerability, often dismissed as naïveté. It was the genius that gave the world new light.

The wind continued to whisk across the hilltop, rattling the branches of the oak, coursing between the brush and layering the snow into restless and innumerable patterns. Patrick walked from the tree and came to stand at the edge of the Point, between the tree and the city. He brought his gloved hands together. The chill of the air was beginning to ebb through his jacket. His boots were buried up past the laces and he stamped them in his foot tracks.

Although he had never shied to the task of altering the world, he had long felt powerless to change himself. As he stood atop the hill that night, Patrick did not suddenly feel this fear lifted nor did he immediately recognize any novel global solutions, but in this brazing cold, Patrick felt hope for the first time in months. He felt he could change.

Chapter 17

April 2010
Bryn Mawr, Pennsylvania

Hadley looked up at the slight indentation in the car roof. She had never noticed it before. "Patrick," she said, turning to where he sat at the wheel. "Did something fall on your car?"

They were at a stoplight, on their way home from a parent's evening hosted by Meredith's kindergarten class. The event had started with a play performed by the students about a boy and girl who want to fix the Liberty Bell. The parents had applauded and stifled tears from the rows of abbreviated desks where their children sat during the school day. The room was brightly colored and lit, splashed with student artwork. After the performance, the parents were led by their children to the neighboring art room for a viewing of their most recent "pieces," followed by a trip to the cafeteria for cookies and juice.

"It's like someone tried to skewer you with a massive fondue fork," Hadley observed, running her hand over the damage. Meredith sat quietly in the backseat.

Patrick smiled. It was the remaining evidence of his forced entry into their old apartment last summer. While telling the story, Patrick realized the distance he'd traveled in a year. His conversations with Hadley no longer felt like a competition and they were starting to be able to laugh at themselves.

Shortly after New Year's, both Patrick and Hadley separately went suburban, abandoning their city roots. Hadley closed on a rich three-bedroom spread in a reasonably spaced neighborhood near Bryn Mawr College. Hadley especially liked it for the events held on campus. There was a backyard, bigger than some of the city parks, and Meredith made quick work of conquering the swing set left by the previous owners.

Patrick, meanwhile, moved into his father's home near West Chester. He was hesitant at first, aware of the medley of memories, both wonderful and tragic, that would no doubt be present. But in talks with his sisters, he agreed to it, hoping the return would be somewhat therapeutic. So far, it was working. Patrick was feeling better, enjoying work, socializing with old friends, and had begun work on a new Darius prototype in his spare time. Although the probability that any time spent on ERM research would be for naught, Patrick could not let it rest. The glimpse of potential he had seen in Florida was difficult to ignore.

The technicians, George and Hal, had since recovered and Patrick was in touch at least once a month. The government had covered their extensive medical bills and the media had miraculously been left out of the loop. Nevertheless, it was a skeleton, and if Patrick had learned anything through his think-tank new job at the Global Environmental Alliance Institute, it was that the world of power and energy was a sphere constantly at war.

Regarding domestic matters of diplomacy, the divorce had gone final. Hadley and Patrick told Meredith before the move to Bryn Mawr, and to mutual relief, the six-year old took the news surprisingly well. She told Hadley that her friend Lily's Mom and Dad also had different houses. Nevertheless, Hadley and Patrick were constantly anxious, and found the best way to allay their fears was through continuous contact. Patrick, therefore, would visit often, occasionally working weekends and afternoons out of the spare bedroom at Hadley's new home. They knew it was an unusual arrangement for a divorced couple, especially as they now spent more time in the same house than during their final years of marriage. Neither mentioned this anomaly, but the effort appeared to be having the desired effect on Meredith—she knew she was loved, and that her parents, despite differences, were happy too.

It was during one of his Saturday afternoon visits at Hadley's that Patrick heard again from Ward. The communication came through e-mail, received by Patrick on his phone as he sat on the back deck watching Meredith play on the swing set. The message was brief and had been sent to Alika as well.

P and A,

Good news about project. Will be in touch soon.

Keep phone on you.

-W

That was all. It was sent from his REI account and Patrick willed himself not to chase conclusions.

Meredith did a flying leap from her swing and ran up the slight grassy incline towards her father. "Daddy, are you hungry?" she asked.

"A little," Patrick humored. "Are you?"

"I could eat!" she exclaimed, shrugging her shoulders.

They went inside and Patrick began to fix them sandwiches with cold cuts from the fridge. Meredith managed her way onto a stool at the bar, propped her elbows on the counter and watched her father make lunch. Hadley was at work in the city.

"Mustard?" he asked, opening the fridge again.

Meredith shook her head.

"Mayo?"

She shook again.

"Grey Poupon?"

She hesitated, unsure.

Patrick laughed, "I don't think you'd like it."

They ate at the counter, Meredith telling Patrick about the field trip her class was scheduled to take the following week to the Franklin Institute in Philadelphia. She was excited about the oversized heart exhibit described by her teacher.

"You can even hear it beating!" She cried, nearly falling backwards off the stool.

Patrick's phone buzzed and Meredith mimicked it with a buzz of her own. "Daddy?" she asked. "When can I get a cell phone?"

"When your mother says so," he replied, looking at another e-mail from Ward. Again, it was short and to the point.

Tonight, 8:00pm EST.

Call in on the conference number below.

Use the Pin # to connect.

Will catch up then.

-W

Below the note was a forwarded e-mail from the REI Communications Department giving a phone number and 7-digit access code. The phone buzzed again—an incoming call from Alika. Patrick answered while Meredith reached laboriously for the bag of pretzels that lay clipped at the center of the counter.

"Maaahhh," she stretched.

Patrick nudged the bag into reach and stood to take the call. "Alika," he said.

"Who is this guy?" asked Alika, the sound of traffic in the background.

"Ward being Ward."

"You think he's actually found something for the project?" Alika posed. "Think it's legitimate? Conference call on a Saturday?"

"I don't know," Patrick said. "I'm not expecting anything."

In reality, Patrick's mind had become an autobahn of possibility. He assumed Alika was fighting similar considerations. They had loosely agreed that if another funding opportunity came around, and the numbers and conditions were right, they would give Darius another shot.

"I guess we'll find out tonight," Alika sighed. "I'm assuming you might drop in?"

"There's a chance," said Patrick. "Have to run now. I'm due to take Meredith to a matinee."

"Which one?"

"The new Alice in Wonderland."

"It's still in theatres?"

"It is here."

"I heard it can be a bit creepy."

"I'm thinking she'll be alright. Hadley caught her watching The Godfather the other night."

Alika laughed. "Hope she won't think any less of me."

They signed off and Patrick turned back towards the counter. Meredith was clipping up the pretzel bag, the news of Alice spurring her into action. She hopped off the stool and threw her hands in the air.

"I'm ready!"

Philadelphia

Hadley finished up the last round of corrections to her editorial for the Sunday edition. This was her first weekend editorial and she wanted it to be perfect. The afternoon had sped by and she guessed that Patrick and Meredith would be getting out of their movie date shortly. She was due to meet them for ice cream at four.

"Awfully close to dinner time," she'd argued with Patrick.

"It's a Saturday!" he'd protested. And won.

Their relationship had changed clothes since the divorce papers had come back that winter. The empty kettle had been lifted from the stove and Hadley quite liked it. She fancied their positive collaboration as a sign that she had done right, that a divorce was their best option. Still, at other hours, she doubted. Lying awake on her side of the bed, watching TV alone from the couch, eating a late dinner in her pajamas when Meredith was at Patrick's; she felt compelled to second-guess. Sheryl had told Hadley to start coming out with her, to start dating, or at least have a fling. "You have needs!" Sheryl claimed.

Hadley focused in on her editorial, making a final scan for errors or holes in her argument. The offices of the Inquirer were fairly derelict that afternoon. The spring weather outside was blue and beautiful, and Hadley tried to ignore the sunlight. She had chosen to write about the case recently upheld by the Supreme Court that would allow corporations or individuals to make unrestricted monetary contributions to political parties, candidates, and campaigns. The Supreme Court had ruled that the donations could legally be justified under the First Amendment, particularly by the "freedom of speech." In her piece, Hadley vehemently attacked the ruling, noting that the number of zeros imbedded in an account balance should not augment the voice of any one individual or group of citizens. The Supreme Court had ruled, she argued, with the assumption that the US had become an ideal society, overlooking the unfortunate reality that dollars and cents count for more than words and letters.

The editorial completed, Hadley made a print and walked the length of the writer's courtyard to Korey Devoir's office, her editor. A secretary walked by and told Hadley that he was upstairs in the Conference Room with the photo editor.

Hadley took the elevator and found Devoir alone in the Conference Room, his jacket removed and tie loosened. Windows opened to a view of the city skyline while a seasoned oval table dominated the floor space. He was looking at a few of the prints selected for Sunday's front cover, April 17th. It was undeniable that Devoir had something eternally handsome about his demeanor. He looked up as Hadley came in, flashing a smile before returning his gaze to the print in front of him. It was a picture of Corbin Thomas, the husband who had put a hit on his wife in the Wolfman murder fifteen years previous.

"Chilling, what people will do, isn't it?" said Devoir. His family was Swiss, and despite looking the part of an aristocratic European, his accent had a faint aura of Manhattan. Early-40's, late-30's on some days, he had dark brown hair that was graying just right. He was broad-shouldered, enjoyed racquetball, and drove a black Audi S4. In complement to everything else, it was traded among women that Devoir had the wealthiest of green eyes, and though Hadley had never tarried with them long, she knew that they had often tarried on her.

"This the Wolfman's master?" Hadley asked, coming around the table to take a look at the photo. It was an old shot of Thomas, and if anything, it was boyish. "The courts gave him life, right?"

"Not that prison is anything new—he's been away for a few years already."

"Just another paragraph to the resume."

Devoir laughed. "What have you got for me?" he asked, standing to look at Hadley, taking her in with such inspection that Hadley stood a little straighter as she handed him the editorial.

"It's very good," he said, scanning its content, gesturing for Hadley to sit. She did, crossing her legs as he paced in front of the windows. "Which of course is no surprise. In the years you've been here, we've seen little less than brilliance from your corner." He was all charm, with an exquisite habit for eliciting blushes, and as he lauded her writing, Hadley felt her cheeks involuntarily flush.

Devoir continued. "Which brings me to the point, Hadley, we want to promote you. We have for some time, and with the right pieces now in place, we'd like to offer you the position of associate editor of content." He let it hang in the air, studying her.

Hadley gave the appropriate smile and grace, muttering something humble; though a leaping fist pump would have felt more in order.

"Your editorials," he went on, "Have gained a reputation, and there is no doubt that other papers will soon come vying. But to be perfectly honest, even outright professionally candid, I do hope that you choose to stay with the Inquirer. We think that you'll help make this paper great."

Hadley gave another bow. "That's very kind of you Korey," she said, his first name sounding odd in her mouth. "I'm honored and surprised. Surprised and honored." Their eyes met and Hadley very much confirmed the rumors about Devoir's green eyes.

"Do you accept?" he asked, his tone so simple he could have been asking if she liked lemon with her water.

"How could I not?" Hadley said. "Thank you."

"Great, we'll meet on Monday with Human Resources to discuss the changes and announce to the company thereafter."

Hadley stood and they shook hands, their clasp longer than usual for a platonic agreement. She walked away, felt his green eyes on her retreating figure, took the elevator and returned to her desk in the courtyard. For all her years at the Inquirer, Hadley had always felt something between her and Devoir; an energy she had dismissed as a married woman. She logged off her computer and gathered together the notes that were spread around her keyboard. But she was no longer a married woman; she was a divorcee, a single mother, and thirty-one. Hadley knew Sheryl's insistence that she get back in the dating game was good counsel—if only for variety. Maybe she would go back to lawyers, her habit before she met Patrick.

"Hadley."

The papers rustled in her hands as Korey's voice called to her from the center of the room. He was walking towards her. "Yes?" she replied, turning to face him as he arrived at her desk.

"I didn't want to say this before," he began. The office was empty and quiet around them. He leant against a short bookshelf. "Given the circumstances with your promotion and all." They were a single pace apart. "But I've been meaning to ask for some time if you'd be interested in having dinner."

His phrasing was effortless, delivered with utmost confidence. Hadley struggled not to say 'Yes' too fast or to smile too widely.

"I know you're just coming out of a relationship, a marriage," he continued. "And not many people know it, but I too went through a divorce—it was many years ago now."

"Really?" she said. "You're right, I never knew."

"It's not something you really want to talk about, is it?"

"No," she agreed, feeling suddenly safer. "It's not."

"So what do you think?" he said with a pursed smile. "I know a few good places on the South Side."

Hadley thought of her ice cream appointment with Patrick and Meredith. No reason she couldn't also go to dinner after.

"If not tonight," said Devoir, sensing decision-making. "Always another evening."

"No," said Hadley quickly. "I would—I would love to, but my daughter, I have her for the evening, and—" she checked the clock on the wall, "I'm supposed to—"

"It's fine," said Devoir, putting up a hand, but not defeated. "Though she could always come with us."

Hadley felt her face reddening anew. He was inviting her six-year old daughter too! She was a writer and yet she couldn't think of any words. "Could we try for next week?" she managed.

"Of course," Devoir complied. "We can speak on Monday."

"Monday," she confirmed with a subtle nod.

A comfortable silence developed around them; Devoir not turning to leave immediately, and Hadley finally taking a full look at his eyes.

It started slow, Devoir standing up tall from where he'd leant, Hadley covering the short space between then. When they were inches apart, the room went quiet and cloud-like. He placed his hand against the small of her back, neither of them exchanging words as he drew her in. Hadley curled her arms up about his shoulders. Their bodies pressed as they came face to face. The first kiss was soft, short, and their eyes met intimately before a longer embrace.

Hadley felt a warming in her chest, a rushing in her head, and a stirring everywhere else. It was instant fulfillment, something that couldn't be wrong. But as her hands clung to Devoir, she felt herself pulling away, not so much physically, but deeper, in what some would call the heart. Painfully, she released her hold on Devoir's shoulder blades, undoing the bind of their lips.

"I'm sorry, Korey," she said, stepping backwards and fumbling for her pocketbook. Respectfully, he let her go. "I'm sorry," she repeated. Devoir looked at her with patient eyes and she questioned why she shouldn't just crumble back into him. "I should go," she said, avoiding his kind gaze.

"It's fine," he cut in. "Totally fine. I just hope this doesn't..."

"Of course not," she finished, touching her hair. "I'll see you Monday?"

"Monday," he confirmed, smiling and allowing her space.

Feeling a mix of foolish and thrilled, Hadley shouldered her bag and passed by his arms and frame, walking to the elevators without a turn.

Patrick and Meredith were sharing a sundae when Hadley arrived at the Dairy Queen. They sat outside at a picnic table, father on one bench, daughter on the other. From her appearance, it was clear that the lion's share of fudge topping had gone to Meredith.

"You been playing in the mud?" Hadley asked as she planted a large kiss on the child's cheek. "Mmm, chocolate?"

Meredith ignored the interruption and continued to sap the ice cream castle before her.

"How was the movie?" Hadley asked Patrick, sitting down next to Meredith.

"It was good. I liked it," he said between a spoonful of vanilla. "Meredith thought it was 'just alright'."

"Nothing like an original," said Hadley, trying not to look at Patrick's eyes, afraid she might see Korey's. On the drive over she had given herself a thorough interview about her behavior at the office, confused why she had resisted Korey. By the time she turned off the Interstate, huffing over a Colbie Caillat album, she had reasoned her actions to be evidence of wisdom, not stupidity—leave them wanting more.

"You have plans for the night?" Hadley asked, picking up a clean spoon resting on their table. "This mine?"

"Uh-huh," Patrick nodded over another bite. "Plans? Sort of, I guess." Hadley hesitated with her spoon, then dug in.

"It's not a date," Patrick countered, noting her body language.

"Who said anything about a date?" Hadley mumbled, mouth full.

"No one," Patrick said distractedly. He was still having trouble seeing other women. "Anyway, I got an e-mail from Ward today. Not sure I ever told you about the time—"

"Wait, Ward? As in…"

"From Penn, remember him? I never told you how he showed up at Alika's when I was down there this past winter." He told the story of Alika tossing Ward to the ground, rolling pin in hand, and then snippets of the conversation afterward.

"Weird," Hadley concluded.

"I know. Other news is that the company he's working for is a type of hub for venture capitalists, but specializing in energy investments."

"Oh?"

"He said he'd look around for Alika and me."

Hadley gave him a look. Unrelated, at her side, a spoonful of ice cream slipped down onto Meredith's front.

"And he knows about the accident," Patrick added.

Hadley pulled a sheaf of napkins from a tabletop dispenser and wiped up the avalanche on Meredith's shirt. "Are you talking tonight then?"

"At eight. We're having a conference call—me, Ward, and Alika. Maybe more, I'm not sure."

"That's great," she said, balling the napkins together. "Think there's something to it?"

"I hope. I don't think he's calling just to catch up."

She could see the excitement, the Nicholas, brimming in Patrick's eyes. "I can take Meredith now if you need to get going."

"It's okay," he said, shifting his attention to the ice-cream covered girl. "I can stay a bit longer."

West Chester, Pennsylvania

Patrick sat on the living room couch, a bottle of water by his side. The return to the family home had been a good idea, or so it felt when Patrick was active and busy; meeting friends, working from his study, hosting Meredith. It was when responsibilities waned and he sat indoors, stationary, watching TV, that the house felt too big and its chairs too empty. There were the shadows of his former life, the ghosts of his mother and father, and though he disbelieved it, the stigma of moving home—failure in the real world, a retreat to safety—still bothered him.

At exactly 7:58 p.m., Patrick began dialing. He'd written down the number and pin on a separate sheet of paper so he wouldn't have to toggle back and forth with his e-mail. From the coffee table, he pulled a pen and legal pad onto his lap, writing in large block letters across the top: *RELAX.*

He heard his call connect and an automated voice prompted him to enter his pin. Upon doing so, the robot-female told him that there was one other caller in the conversation.

"Hello?" a voice said. It was Alika.

"Alika, it's me."

"Bienvenido mi amigo."

"Just us so far?" Patrick asked.

"Just us."

"Hope it wasn't a joke."

"I'll be peeved."

A short silence fell between them.

"Probably at the beach," said Patrick.

A cosmic-sounding ding indicated that another caller had joined the conversation. Two more immediately followed.

"Patrick? Alika?" It was Ward.

"Hey Ward," they clumsily said in unison.

"Glad you could make it, sorry for the slim details. Everything alright?"

They small-talked briefly as papers shuffled on either end.

"I want to quickly introduce the two other people who will be in on this call," Ward continued. "First, there is Decklin Cross, head of project development for REI."

"Patrick, Alika," Cross said. "Good evening." His accent sounded British, maybe South African, Patrick couldn't quite place it.

"And to answer that question in both your heads," Ward digressed. "Decklin is from Australia." Polite laughter followed from all sides. "And second, Janine, my secretary, who will be recording the proceedings of the call." Janine gave a short greeting and the call turned to business.

Neither Patrick nor Alika still had any idea what this 'business' would entail, but both felt encouraged when Ward began the discussion with an explanation of the standard manner in which REI funded projects. He mentioned a few that were currently in process, several of which Patrick and Alika had heard of, one being a tower in London that had massive wind turbines built into the superstructure.

Ward then described how REI found funding for selected projects. Interested investors were presented with a project "package," which contained descriptions and analysis of REI-approved ventures. The package worked something like a stock portfolio. Instead of investing in just one endeavor, the investor could strategically allocate his money between different projects and mitigate risk. The projects were rated on their likelihood of success, just as stocks are rated on how reliable they are to provide a return on investment. It was REI's stance that money invested in this manner, especially in the uncertain realm of energy services and technology, would ensure greater and more consistent profits for the investor.

Cross then spoke briefly on how it works for the researchers, in this case, Patrick and Alika. He prefaced his part by indicating that their form of funding was very different than that of the US Government. With REI-sponsored initiatives, there were no caps to spending; within reason, of course. There would be standard audits and reviews of their work, but it was REI's philosophy that a bottomless source of funds removed "budgetary stress," as Cross put it, allowing the work to progress at a much faster pace—Patrick and Alika could relate. He finished with several points on compensation, discovery royalties, on-site accommodation, and insurance benefits. The locations of testing and development were usually at the discretion of the researchers.

Ward took over again and the fluidity of the transition gave Patrick the impression that Ward and Cross were in the same room. Patrick was surprised how much they knew about their project in Florida. REI had certainly done their research.

"Patrick, Alika, we've arranged for funding to be applied to your project."

Involuntarily and invisible to the conference, Patrick shot both arms silently into the air.

"However," Ward continued, "Due to the nature of recent events, specifically, the accident that occurred last August in Florida, we feel that further research and development should be conducted outside of the United States. This does not indicate that the technology is not safe, it is solely for logistical simplicity and swift commencement of your research."

Patrick and Alika were beyond words. They were back.

Ward carried on. "There are several firms and individuals that will have a stake in your research and a contract will be drafted which will indicate how the return will be distributed. This is primarily numbers and words, but also a nice assurance of the benefits from operating beneath REI's so-called 'umbrella'."

Patrick was now on his feet.

"We generally do not release the names of your sponsors, allowing them to remain anonymous. All communication, press releases, and financial issues are to be conducted through REI, leaving the donors out of the mix. We'll be in touch with more information in the following week, but for now, do either of you have any questions?"

The line hung in charged silence.

"When do we start?" Alika broke.

Chapter 18

June 2010
Washington D.C.

Returning on the Metro from lunch, Alika passed casually through security at the Pentagon's southeast entrance. The take-away Cobb salad had not been enough, and his stomach rumbled in protest as he traversed the hollow hallways. The afternoons were always hardest, Alika reasoned, avoiding a treacherous corner of vending machines. The consumption conditioning was all part of a recent effort to slim down and lose weight, just a few pounds here and there. He had started exercising more, joining a gym, playing pick-up basketball on Saturday mornings, and enrolling in the Department's self-defense seminar. Two months in, signs of progress were debatable, but Alika took solace in his motivation—Dolores. It had been six months, and in all ways wonderful, their relationship still felt like day one. Appetite panging, but mind at ease, Alika reached his desk and set to work.

Altogether, Alika had been with the Department of Defense for six years, working out of various offices throughout the Capital. Since returning from Florida, he had earned a permanent desk within the Pentagon. The re-entrance process had been unusually smooth; surprising his loyal co-workers who watched Alika quit and then return. He supposed it was partly on account of his work with Patrick. His superiors had questioned him extensively about his activities in Florida, any contacts or associations he had made there, but little about the actual nature of the work. He was certain they were aware of its unfortunate outcome, even if no one else was privy.

Alika was currently working on the Kajaki Dam project in Afghanistan. The US was spending vaults of money to restore various elements of the Afghan infrastructure, and Alika had been tasked with analyzing the transportation logistics for a new turbine that would need to reach the Kajaki construction site. The assignment belonged in the hands of a civil engineer, but Alika had completed similar projects in the Middle East for the transportation of volatile chemicals, thereby prompting faith in his capabilities. Involved in the design were not only engineering aspects, but defense issues, and Alika was meeting regularly with military tacticians who had experience maneuvering war zones. The Dam itself was located in the notoriously hostile Helmand province, adding a novel dimension to the engineering term *factor of safety*.

The project was pleasing to Alika, and far more rewarding than other jobs coursing through the DOD pipeline. The completed dam would supply nearly one million people with electricity. When Alika described it to Dolores she had been impressed; she adored his passion for making small improvements to the world.

Dolores had grown up in Miami, heading north after high school to attend Georgetown University, where she graduated *summa cum laude* in political science. Recruited immediately by Langley, she went to work in the CIA's Linguistics Unit, gradually working her way up the analyst ladder. Most days, Dolores split her time between analyzing information collected by Spanish-speaking operatives throughout Central and South America, and then sharing that analysis as appropriate with other agencies or organizations. It was the discretion part of the job that she enjoyed. As they were both under oath, talking about their work was comfortable for Alika and Dolores, and the normal elements of secrecy felt less binding. "If we wake up dead, we'll know we said too much," she joked.

Before Dolores, Alika's engagements with women had been flings and little more; ladies with whom he'd never connected beyond basic physical and conversational necessities. With Dolores, there was a footing he had yet to experience, an anchoring that left him neither fearing nor overconfident. He trusted her, and his feelings confirmed his decision not to travel with Patrick on this next round of lightning-chasing research.

Although he loved the project's element of exploration, Alika felt he was falling behind in helping Patrick with improvements to the models. They both agreed it was best for Alika to remain in the US and prepare for the next big step, continuing at the Department of Defense until the end of the year and then begin full-time in coordinating the development of a US test site, along with initiatives for implementation and application of the technology. The choice had settled fine with Patrick, who was adamant that Alika not fall folly to the forces that ultimately stripped him of Hadley. Nearly every time they spoke, Patrick would thank Alika for supporting him in those months after the divorce—the stability had enabled him to stand tall once more.

Back at his computer, Alika brought up an AutoCAD rendering of a road, thousands of miles away in Afghanistan. He tried to focus; there was much to be done. The following morning, he was scheduled to report on repairs for an important stretch of highway several miles outside of Kandahar. It would require extensive preparation, but Alika appreciated the evident concern that his collaborating military partners showed for the personnel that would ultimately drive these roads.

Settling into his drawings, Alika's phone buzzed. He checked it—an incoming e-mail from Patrick. The man had made great strides since those hazy days after the divorce.

Alika did not need to read the message to know its content. The subject line, an Otis Redding song, was a sufficient clue: *Sittin' On The Dock of the Bay.* They were going to California.

West Chester, Pennsylvania

Patrick pushed the cart to the final aisle and stopped, scanning the rows of various milks. He'd been a loyal 1% man for as long as he could remember. Pulling a fresh gallon from the cooler, he continued down the wall of refrigerated beverages until selecting a carton of low-pulp orange juice. His grocery store routine had become satisfyingly habitual. The next stop would be Dairy: cheeses and yoghurt.

As he placed the milk and OJ in the cart, a peculiar feeling passed over him—that bristly sensation of being watched. He turned around.

Along the shelves bobbed the usual pensive faces of shoppers, bending low or reaching high for an item on their list. Nothing, and no one, appeared extraordinary. Patrick wheeled on.

After selecting a sharp cheddar, Vermont-made, Patrick headed for the checkout. Nearing an open till, he suddenly hesitated. He stood at the mouth to the beer aisle. It had been a big day, worthy of celebration—he'd received their contract from REI, the research was set to go forward—and Patrick eyed the long, open shelves before him; every conceivable space consumed by a different brand of beer or spirit. He felt the lure brush his lip. It had been almost eight months since his last drink. There'd been a few beers out with Alika and other friends, but that wasn't drinking; real drinking for Patrick meant being alone.

He struggled with the temptation a little longer, hovering over the necessities in his basket, considering himself a case study for the curious onlooker; a son debating his inheritance. It had been weeks since his last A.A. meeting.

As Patrick turned the cart to take a gander down the aisle, that same feeling of being watched swept back over him. He knew he'd been acting odd, but the woman standing three aisles down was applying a different sort of observation. When Patrick looked up at her, she immediately ducked out of sight. Intrigued, Patrick released his interest in the case of Heineken and pushed his way through a group of teenagers to the aisle down which the woman had escaped. She had been wearing a green shirt and jeans, black hair and soft features. Reaching the aisle, Crackers and Drinks, he gave a casual glance up its length.

An older woman read the label on a juice bottle, and a mother, child in tow, hastened along a selection of cookies. The child pulled package after package off the shelf. There was no sign of the woman. Patrick pushed onto the next aisle, but again, saw no one of interest. Then he felt another tugging, this time a real one. He spun around.

"Pat!" the wizened lady cried. "I thought that was you."

It took Patrick a few seconds to remember her name. "Mrs. Galloway, Shona, how nice to see you." She was the mother of Reese Galloway, childhood swimming companion and former co-worker. Patrick glanced briefly over her shoulder for the off chance he might see the mystery woman again.

"You're looking wonderful," said Mrs. Galloway, snaring back his attention. "What brings you to town?" She gave a genuine smile and reached out to touch Patrick on the arm. It was evident she missed the old days of swim practice and high-school boys trouncing about her home. Despite a few gray hairs she had aged well.

"Well," he began. His life has been so unusual the past few years, it was always difficult to know how much to say. "I'm looking after my father's house for now, getting a few things in order."

"Of course," she lamented. "Oh I was so sorry to hear about your Dad." She reached out again, squeezing his wrist. She was an artist, a painter, and white flecks of Acrylic showed in the cracks of her hands.

Patrick thanked her, and by request, gave a well-worked abridgement of his life since working with her son in Paulsboro. He weaved through the peaks and valleys of the past few years. Reese had apparently mentioned to her that Patrick had suddenly up and quit.

Mrs. Galloway, like many old acquaintances, had seen and heard snippets of the work that Patrick was doing in Florida. There had been a few articles in the Penn newsletters, as well as in local newspapers. The Discovery Channel had even done a small piece at Camp Blanding during their first year. The story had focused mainly on the Michigan physicists, the ERM project passing with a mere mention.

"Oh Patrick," she said, "That's so wonderful. I do hope it works out. And as for relationships," she threw her hands up in the air. "You're not the first." Mrs. Galloway was also divorced, a bonding point that Patrick was still coming to understand. She was a dreamer, an eccentric, and he supposed she appreciated his desire to go outside the norm. Her boy Reese had chosen the more traditional route, perhaps inspired by the quirky finances and timetable of his artist-mother.

They chatted for a bit longer, interrupted at length by Patrick's cell phone. It was Alika. Patrick excused himself briefly, answering to tell Alika he would ring back.

After a hug-laden parting, Patrick got in line to pay. He dialed Alika and they agreed to meet on Friday evening to ride out to the airport for their flight out to San Francisco and the REI Headquarters.

His purchases made, Patrick coaxed the rattling wheels of his cart across the shabbily lit parking lot to his Subaru. After loading the bags, he returned the cart to one of the paddocks and started back to his car. The Subaru was developing a patch of rust above the driver-side wheel well. Patrick reminded himself as he got in and shut the door that he needed to address the decay sooner than later.

As he drove away, passing the long store windows, Patrick suddenly stopped the car. The same woman—black hair and green shirt—was standing at the shop window, watching him. Their eyes met and a faint chill stirred in Patrick's core. He opened the door and got out, scanning the storefront. The bone-white interior lights illuminated him against the stagger of cars in the lot. Inside, the usual mixing of shoppers and employees played out predictably. Again, the woman was gone.

Bryn Mawr, Pennsylvania

It was dinner time on Friday and Meredith was being fussy. Hadley had made her hot carrots and the child was refusing to eat them. She insisted they were too mushy.

Stoutly ignoring the protest, Hadley attended to her own food across the table. It was summer and the air conditioner bumbled away in the front room, straining to reach the rest of the house.

Hadley was having second thoughts about the size of the place. It was a bit big for two. Korey had given a similar opinion during his first visit the week before. They had been on several dates now—dinners out and dinners in—stretching the time they spent together, but never venturing further than their first kiss at Hadley's desk months previous. The controlled courtship was appealing to Hadley, and though she knew their encounters often left Korey blue, their situation was fast approaching the state of inevitability; just yesterday she had almost tackled him in the break room. She had yet to tell Patrick.

"How was camp?" Hadley asked, thinking to redirect both their attentions.

"I don't like the hot carrots," Meredith pouted.

She was attending a summer camp held on the Bryn Mawr campus by a group of local artists, professors, and teachers. It was two weeks long, and after five days, Meredith was already growing impatient with the earthy, holistic approach that the camp took towards teaching.

"Did you make anything today?" Hadley pressed on.

Meredith frowned. "Yes."

"What did you make?"

"We made a book," Meredith replied. "But we didn't finish. So we're going to keep working on it tomorrow."

"What is the book about?"

"There's this cat who—"

Hadley's phone went off loudly on the counter, making them both jump. Meredith's fork clanged onto her plate. Annoyed, Hadley stood and walked to the phone.

"Not supposed to talk on the phone while you're eating," Meredith chided from the table, biting into a carrot.

Hadley looked at the number. It was a New York area code. Against her own rules, she answered.

"Is this Hadley Hannigan?" a woman's voice asked. The accent was subtle Cape Cod.

"Yes, may I ask who's calling?" Hadley had always used her maiden name for work and writing, but of late it was all-purpose.

"Sorry to bother you so late, this is Carol Magnus."

Hadley nearly dropped the phone.

"I'm calling from New York."

Of course she was, thought Hadley. "Yes, hello Dr. Magnus."

There was a pause, and the voice returned a shade more candid, a touch more Cape. "So I guess it's fair to say you know who I am."

"I do."

"And I suppose the fact that I'm contacting you on a personal line, not at work, is also an indication for why I'm calling."

"I could venture some guesses."

"Perfect, then I'll cut to the chase. We're interested in offering you an editorial position here at the Times."

Meredith interrupted from the background. "Mommy, can—"

Hadley shushed her with a wave. "Wow, I…thank you," she replied, awkward and thrilled.

"We're not keen on poaching editors away from other newspapers, but we've been eyeing you for some time, and frankly, we're tired of waiting. That said, we understand that you'll probably need some time to think about it."

"Thank you, I—"

"Look for an e-mail from my office. It will have information about the usual questions: Money, benefits, schools, relocation—and if there's anything missing, just contact us. Alright?"

"Mommy," Meredith said again. She'd gotten up from the table and was holding out an empty cup.

"I'll let you go," Magnus said in omniscience. "Next step will be a meeting at our offices in Manhattan, but until then, look for the e-mail."

"Thanks, Dr. Magnus, I…appreciate the call."

"Hope to hear from you soon."

Before Hadley could respond, Carol Magnus, editor of The New York Times, hung up.

"Mom?" Meredith said, coming cautiously closer with her cup.

Hadley set her phone on the counter, staring out at the living room. Wrinkled paper, red pens, smudgy computer screens, green-blue linoleum carpet, stained coffee mugs, minutes, recording tapes, phone messages, blurry photos, big padded envelopes, boards and yellow tape, gray keyboards— 'Frankly, we're tired of waiting.'

"Mom?"

Snapped from her trance, Hadley swooped down to the child, aglow. "Meredith," she said, letting the interruptions slide. "What would you like?"

"More juice, please."

Taking the cup, Hadley went to the fridge. Her mind was in flux. She needed to call someone.

Washington D.C.

On Friday afternoon, Patrick and Alika stood outside their gate at Dulles International Airport. The plane was on time and their fellow travelers were forming tighter and tighter rings about the gate attendant. They were flying Virgin America direct to San Francisco; first-class. It was Patrick's first time sitting up front and he supposed the name of the airline was fitting to the experience.

The gate attendant, wearing an unusual beret, made the initial boarding call, including all first-class ticket holders.

Alika slapped Patrick's shoulder. "Shall we board then?"

Sitting in their comfy seats before take-off, the size of which was actually appropriate for Alika, a stewardess came around and offered drinks. Both men gladly accepted, avoiding the jealous looks from passengers seated in the first rows of coach. Patrick was tempted to turn around and explain their situation, to tell them that he usually flew Economy. Only after take-off, when the stewardess drew a set of curtains, could Patrick finally relax.

They talked for most of the five-hour trip, taking a break to watch a movie while dinner was served. With a mouthful of chicken and red peppers, Alika nudged Patrick. "This is living," he slurped. Patrick nodded, digging into a cod fillet.

Their discussions were over the details that REI had sent to Patrick. The thick envelope, reminiscent of a college acceptance packet, had included a formal approval for the project, a list of expectations for Patrick and Alika, a note on project confidentiality, a set of contact information for REI departments, some basic propaganda about other REI projects, and finally, two airline tickets for a set of briefing meetings in San Francisco.

The purpose of the visit was for Patrick and Alika to interface with REI executives, work out a concrete schedule, finalize a contract, and resolve any outstanding issues. As it stood on the legal pad that Patrick had tattooed with notes over the past few months, they would begin setting up the site and coordinating the purchase and transportation of materials immediately. A plot in Venezuela had been chosen by REI from the list of proposed locations that Patrick had provided. The preoperational logistics would require multiple visits and Patrick was expected to be doing most of the traveling. Already, dates were being budgeted in for Patrick to return regularly to Philadelphia. He had missed enough of Meredith's life.

The back and forth between continents would begin in February of 2011, with Patrick helping to organize and staff a team of in-country researchers and workers to run the operation, starting full-time in May. There would be three triggering platforms, helping to better manipulate test conditions, and their equipment would far exceed the aged instruments they had used at Camp Blanding. Additionally, a lab would be set up on site for developing simulations of the magnetic repulse from a lightning bolt; the main intention being to explore the possibility of creating artificial bursts for application. REI was most interested in the potential for large-scale Hydrogen production.

As the plane began to descend from its cruising altitude, Patrick and Alika wrapped up the issue of pay. As it stood, REI had negotiated salaries for both Patrick and Alika, as well as for the indicated staff positions that Patrick had requested in the application. The amount that both were set to make—deep into six figures—was certainly higher than their current salaries, and more than double what they were receiving at Camp Blanding. Although they were not about to haggle over extra income, there was curiosity over why REI would pay them so generously. Although Patrick had demonstrated on paper and with reports that ERM technology had a probable future, there was still a chance that nothing of worth would materialize. It was still a science experiment.

They agreed to consult privately with Ward about the large up-front salary. It was the only facet that made them wary, Alika especially.

At the gate, Patrick turned on his cell phone. He had two missed calls, one from a co-worker in D.C., probably wanting companionship at the bars, and another from Hadley. He dialed Hadley.

Bryn Mawr, Pennsylvania

Hadley felt the vibration of the phone against her feet. She leaned forward over the sleeping child on her lap to check the caller. It was Korey.

She held the phone, felt it pulse in her hand. Three rings, four rings, five rings—voice mail. Hadley set the phone back on the couch and waited to see if Korey left a message. He did.

She was a wreck. This was the chance that every journalist dreamed about. Hadley loved The New York Times. She would read its worst issue over any other paper. She questioned her hesitation. The decision should have been so easy. She could afford to wait for the house to sell. She loved New York. She loved the Times. She adored the image of taking Meredith to a private school in the city. And she could almost smell the fresh bagels that would accompany her morning commute; the pride of walking into the Times tower offices on Eighth Avenue.

The phone buzzed again, probably Korey. She let it buzz twice, three times, four times, she picked up the phone. It was Patrick. She answered.

"Patrick?"

"Yeah?" The echo of an air terminal resonated about his voice.

"I'll call you right back."

"OK."

She hung up. Meredith squirmed from the movement, dabbling Hadley's leg with a thread of drool.

She knew in her mind why she was stalling a decision. It was her men and Meredith. Of course she wanted to write for the Times; it was a goal, perhaps the reason she had started writing in the first place, but she could not see separating Patrick and Meredith, and she had clear feelings for Korey. She had to stop fretting. She had to stop questioning. For once, she had to make a decision for herself. She wanted to scream. Instead, she called Patrick.

They spoke briefly about his trip. He asked if she wanted anything from San Francisco. She said Ghirardelli chocolates if he got the chance. He inquired about Meredith's camp. She said it was going fine, explained the drool marks on her pant leg. He laughed and said he'd be there Monday morning to drive Meredith to camp.

"Patrick," she said, stopping the flow.

"Yeah? What is it? You sound stressed."

Hadley cringed at how well he knew her, something she had taken for granted. It was down to two things: tell him about Korey or tell him she was moving to New York.

"Hadley?"

"I was wondering about taking Meredith on vacation." Her free hand shot up, then down to the back of her neck in confusion. *What are you doing?* she thought, wrinkling her face.

"Oh?"

"And if you'd like to come?" She closed her eyes and shook her head. *What? What! What?!*

"When were you thinking?" he asked, shifting the shoulder strap on his bag. The question had taken him by surprise as well.

"Not sure," she replied, honestly. "Soon."

"Alright, can we talk about it when I get back?"

"Sure, I just know that you'll be getting busy with the project..."

"I'll make time," he replied.

They said goodbyes and Hadley plopped the phone on the couch. She sat there for a while, absently patting Meredith's thick brown hair. Hadley then picked up the phone and made another call.

San Francisco, California

The headquarters at REI were impressive; a tall, amber building with a shimmering marble façade. Inside, a lavish foyer and reception area greeted visitors and employees alike. After checking in, Alika and Patrick were ushered down a thickly carpeted corridor, oil paintings adorning the walls, into a leather-clad conference room complete with an awe-inspiring view of the Golden Gate Bridge. To their right, they could see the Giants baseball stadium. The secretary asked if they'd like anything to drink. Both took coffee.

"Mighty busy for a Saturday," Alika whispered.

"You can watch games from up here," a voice said from the doorway. They turned to see Ward, hands on hips, looking prim in a fitted gray suit.

After handshakes, Ward gestured for them to sit as the secretary returned with their coffee. The San Francisco Bay appeared to bloom from the windows behind them. Ward also sat, catching up on their trip while other REI executives and staff joined the room, Patrick and Alika repeatedly standing for introductions to each new arrival.

As Patrick watched the REI team settle in, he wondered who was in charge. Decklin Cross came in last, dressed as sharp as the others, and bowed slightly as he addressed Patrick and Alika. Cross was older and taller than Patrick expected, late-fifties maybe sixties, with a long weathered face that attached a subtle charisma to each of his expressions.

When the door shut at 10:00 a.m., there were fifteen people in the room. Each had come to get a look at Patrick and Alika's proposal, or more so, the minds behind it. As Ward brought the meeting to order, two more secretaries came through and placed water bottles around the great oval table.

The first item on the agenda was an overview of the project by Patrick. Cross would then describe the position of the Project Development department. Ward was to follow with insight into the project's involved financial commitments, as well as identified and targeted sources of future return. Alika would then present the project schedule and current plans for large-scale implementation, after which a question-and-answer period would be the final item before lunch. The afternoon was set aside for individual meetings and for performing the necessary paperwork. Everything, it seemed, would be neatly sorted in one day.

Patrick proceeded, plugging in his laptop to a podium at one end of the room and beginning with several slides from their previous study in Florida. He described the changes in approach and practice that had highlighted their two years of study. There were several shots of Darius, and a video of the device whirring into action after a bolt had been triggered through its center axis. Pens jotted notes at the table. The concepts were well above most heads in the room, but Patrick's hours and days of preparation and practice enabled him to present complexities as givens.

He moved on to a computer model of how they suspected a magnetic burst, applied in the right fashion, could potentially be used to strip water of its hydrogen constituents. In short, the vibrational disturbance created by the magnetic burst could be calibrated to break the bonds of a given water molecule; or so was the theory.

Patrick and Alika had produced hydrogen by using Darius as a turbine to superheat water, but they had never successfully proven in practice the dislodging powers of a magnetic burst.

The model showed a rendering of Darius IV, which Patrick was planning to assemble in Venezuela. The scale was much larger than the models designed in Florida, and the apparatus called for water to be circulated in thin membrane tubes around Darius as a strike was triggered. In this configuration, the simple rotation would not be splitting the water. Instead, the prolonged magnetic field created by the rotation of Darius and its magnets would be doing the work.

As Patrick finished and sat down, it appeared as though most everyone was content with the presentation. Cross spoke briefly and mechanically about how the project would proceed, conversing with an accent of protocol. There were no surprises to anyone. Ward was much of the same, showing several charts and graphs for expenditures and expected return on investment as a result of the project. The income was separated into percentages for Public, Private, and Government, but without actual dollar amounts.

Alika picked up where Ward left off, talking about the potential cooperation and collaboration that he would be working towards in D.C. as Patrick coordinated efforts in Venezuela. Already, he had plans for proposals to be sent to automotive companies for hydrogen vehicles, utility conglomerates that could provide small-scale test sites, and engineering firms that could design and build "hydrogen factories." In conclusion, Alika indicated that although much of their work was speculative, it was at the same time possibly just the low-hanging fruit. The floor then opened for questions.

A hand came up from a man sitting across from Patrick near the middle of the table. He was Asian, young, and looked highly Americanized.

"Yes, James Le," he said, introducing himself. "Patrick, you mentioned briefly that the project was shut down in Florida due to an accident. As far as I'm aware," he said, looking around the room to invite correction without expecting it. "We all know the details of the incident. My question is regarding how you plan to prevent a similar event from occurring again?"

Patrick leant forward on the table; it was a question he had pondered thousands of times. "Of course," he began. "The issue we faced before was a faulty leader. It was determined after the accident that the triggered lightning bolt never actually reached Darius, or in other words, hit the target point. The leader connected to the fired rocket failed at a height of roughly 1000 feet above the ground. The bolt then continued downwards, but strayed north, impacting almost exactly in the location where we were storing the hydrogen generated by our turbines. The lightning—"

"Thunderstruck," Le interrupted. Low laughs rose up around the room.

Patrick continued. "The lightning strike ignited the tank and caused the resulting catastrophic explosion—fortunately the hydrogen tanks were not full. To answer your question, the tank was vulnerable because it was not properly insulated. Precautions to be taken this time will guard against a similar comprise, even if the tank should receive a direct hit. Additionally, all hydrogen transport and production lines will be similarly insulated and safeguarded against electrical surges."

Patrick sat back gradually into his seat, hoping the response had not sounded too rehearsed. Le gave a nod to Ward.

"Any further questions?" Ward asked, looking around the table. No hands appeared. "Great, let's get lunch."

That evening, with their signatures on a myriad of dotted lines, Patrick and Alika drove south to visit Alika's parents in Salinas. They had rented a car, or rather, REI had rented them a car, a new Dodge Charger, which Alika powered down Highway 101.

They passed a wildfire on a nearby hill just south of San Jose. An unusually warm spring had dressed the grass in its brown, flammable summer attire several weeks ahead of schedule.

"Should we call somebody?" Patrick asked, pointing to the fire.

"Nah," Alika said. "They'll take care of it."

On cue, a white helicopter buzzed overhead towards the site of the blaze.

They drove through Morgan Hill, passed the potent garlic outpost of Gilroy, and then branched off onto Highway 25 towards the storied fields of Salinas, the final setting for Steinbeck's *Grapes of Wrath.*

Alika had not come to Salinas in an old jalopy, but in mourning nonetheless. At the age of six, his immediate family had been killed in a hurricane. The storm had come up fast, ripping ruthlessly through his native Samoa. Alika's family had been at the beach when the gathering clouds and merciless winds made landfall. Alika had stayed home with his grandmother that day, disciplined for having left the garden hose on overnight.

Alika had watched the storm approach from behind open windows and been happy that his brothers and sisters would likely be returning early because of the weather. Certainly they would see the dark skies and come home.

Though his father and mother, two brothers and two sisters, did see the storm and responsibly got in their car to drive to safety, a panic over a tsunami sent a surge of fear through the beaches' visitors, causing a few cars to zip away at high speeds. One such car, in an attempt to pass Alika's family, drove them off the road and down a small embankment. Out of control, the car careened into a bank of trees, killing all six inside. Alika had waited and waited, but his family never returned. They were found after the hurricane.

Alika moved in with his grandmother, who lived another seven months before succumbing to cancer. He drifted from aunt to uncle to cousin, until a conscious school teacher suggested that Alika apply to live with a foster family in the United States. It was a radical move, but she could see the life bleeding out of Alika; once a vibrant and brilliant boy. Alika consented, as did his cousin-guardian at the time, and Alika was placed with Marshall and Minnie Tucker of

Salinas, California, a couple that had never been able to have children.

Alika would be their first and only foster child. During high school they would legally adopt him as their own, loving him that way too, and Alika Aiono became Alika Tucker.

As Alika pulled into the driveway of the white-walled condo, the front door sprung open and out bounded Minnie. Despite standing half Alika's size, she still seemed to envelop him with her hugs. Marshall appeared next, shaking Patrick's hand while Minnie continued to hold her boy. Marshall Tucker was lean, gray, and perhaps the kindest man that Patrick had ever met. Minnie then came to Patrick, as Marshall took his turn embracing Alika. Minnie reminded Patrick of a kindergarten teacher, the type that you could never imagine being unhappy or saying a rude word. She was an icon of joy.

Hustling them into the house, Minnie sat them down to dinner, already kneading at a blushing Alika for details about this special someone named Dolores.

Chapter 19

Manchester, Vermont
October 2011

"It's like home," Kylie said to Patrick. "Only more beautiful."

They stood at a spindly black iron fence surveying a sweeping auburn valley. It was the heart of fall and the families were gathering in for the culmination of Kylie and Henry's mature engagement. The wedding ceremony and reception were to be held on the cultivated grounds of the mansion house of Hildene; the former summer home of Robert Todd Lincoln, son of America's 16th president.

Kylie's groom, Henry Trust, had grown up in Vermont and had family spread throughout nearly every county of the state. A true Green Mountain Boy, Henry's lean, muscular frame was accented by a burst of curly blond hair and two daring blue eyes. Henry loved reading, fishing, snowboarding, and now, Kylie.

The couple had met at a teacher's conference outside Philadelphia, just weeks before Henry finished his PhD and accepted a position at Swarthmore University. At the conference, Henry and Kylie were paired together for a breakout exercise, beginning their relationship with an argument about teacher-student ratios; Henry said there was an optimal balance for each teacher, Kylie said that lower was always better. By and by, the exercise ended and the conference broke for lunch. They followed one another into the banquet hall, around the buffet line, to a table by the window, then back into the conference, and finally out for drinks. A year later they were engaged, and three years further, Kylie stood with Patrick on the perch of an old observatory overlooking the confident foliage of the Equinox Valley.

Kylie watched her brother take in the view, tan and fresh off the plane from Venezuela. He had kept his life largely a secret during the past year, sparing only that he was working on an energy project in South America. Every one or two months he'd return for a week to visit Meredith, swinging by to see Kylie if there was time. To be truthful, she was afraid to ask. His life had been so stable until this obsession with lightning; or whatever it was he'd been working with in Florida. She had always hoped he would go back to his old oil job, convinced that his decision to quit was the spark to his divorce. Nevertheless, she loved him. When their mother died in high school, she had developed a strange responsibility for Patrick, a self-assigned feeling she sensed that Hadley, Alika, and others had also experienced. He had been different before their mother's accident, similar to herself and Colleen in confidence and spirit, happy and adventurous, less likely to want to be alone. Kylie saw flashes of this older brother at times, and more so recently since he had started working in Venezuela, but Patrick still appeared burdened and bent by his divorce and the death of their father. Though Kylie wished it wasn't true, she knew he was still in love with Hadley.

"I'm glad you could make it," said Kylie, leaning against his shoulder. "I know it's a long way."

"Wouldn't miss your day for anything," said Patrick, putting his arm around the bride. "Dad would be proud. Remember his reaction when you told him about the engagement?"

"Banging pots and pans," recalled Kylie. "Singing on the stairs, calling random relatives."

"I don't think he stopped smiling for a month."

Kylie grinned and tucked her chin. "Seems a lifetime ago."

They hung there together as a breeze crested the cliff across the fence and freshened their faces. The wedding party had been rehearsing for much of the afternoon, and all were taking a much needed break before dinner. The weather had been blessedly balmy for October, and the forecast showed no approach of winter for the following day.

"I wish he was here," said Kylie.

"I know."

"Mom too."

Patrick pulled her closer.

A path led from the observatory back down to the mansion house. Both Kylie and Patrick heard stones turning as someone approached. The way was sprinkled with leaves that had fallen that afternoon and they crinkled like wrapping paper under the girl's white shoes.

"I hope gals like her run in the family," said Kylie as they faced the path.

She was all in white, save for the pink on her cheeks from running about the window-pane gardens, around the ripe apple trees, and down to the secluded gazebo at the far end of the gargantuan front lawn. If not for the dress, she'd have long disappeared into the bordering forests as well. The grounds of Hildene were a magical place for a child with imagination.

Patrick smiled and welcomed Meredith forward as she reached the observatory. The girl stepped up to the fence and looked through its black iron bars, taking in the view as if it were a breath.

At dinner that night, Patrick took a call from Hadley. The families and friends were seated comfortably in an event room at a local restaurant called The Sirloin Saloon. Patrick was at a table with his sister Colleen, her boyfriend Troy, two of Henry's college roommates, and his Aunt Molly; Uncle Clyde, her husband, was on assignment in Cairo for the State Department. Their Surf and Turf dinners had been cleared and the party was preparing itself for dessert with satisfied stretches and belly pats. The wine had been flowing freely since before the appetizers and a selection of family members were already sufficiently sauced. Patrick stepped around one such uncle as he left the room and answered in a quiet alcove by the kitchen.

When Kylie had asked Patrick if she should invite Hadley to the wedding, he had not wanted to answer. The correct decision seemed obvious, as attending the wedding of your ex-husband's sister sounded strange in itself, let alone the memories it may stir for Patrick—but deep down he liked the thought of her being there. To break the stalemate, Patrick knowingly deferred to Meredith, causing Hadley's name to promptly be added to the guest list.

"Not interrupting, am I?" Hadley asked.

"Not at all," Patrick replied. "Just between courses."

"Great. The rehearsals go alright?"

"Yeah, Kylie picked an amazing place. Meredith can't wait to show you. Unbelievable gardens. Looks like the weather's going to hold too."

Hadley hesitated. "Meredith enjoying herself?"

"Of course," said Patrick. "I could hear her telling the horse and flour joke at the kids table."

"A crowd favorite."

"Where are you now?" asked Patrick. "We're putting a plate aside."

"That's why I called." She let out a sigh. "I feel really bad. I don't think I'm going to make it."

Patrick paused. "Are you still at home?"

"Still at the office. There's been some new developments in this Congress story—stupid reason, I know—but it means I can't really break away."

"I see," said Patrick, moving out of the way for a waiter to pass. He had a feeling she was not at the office.

"I really wanted to be there for Kylie," Hadley stressed. "Tell her I'll call once she's back from St. Bart's? I feel terrible for missing."

"It's okay," Patrick assured. He guessed she was with Korey.

"Think Meredith will be angry?"

"To be honest," he lied, "She's so deep into this group of wedding kids, I could be speaking Chinese and she wouldn't notice." Thoughts of his own wedding suddenly began to threaten. It had been this same season, nine years previous.

"How does she look in her dress?"

"Beautiful. I'll take plenty of pictures." Images of Hadley and Korey were now starting to crowd out the memories.

"Okay," Hadley conceded. "Well, give her a big hug and a kiss. And the same for Kylie. Wish I could be there!"

"I'll tell her you'll call."

"Thanks, please do." said Hadley. She paused. "Everything alright with you?"

"Great," Patrick replied. He wanted to hang up. "Nice to wear a coat again."

Hadley laughed. "The simple things."

"We'll give you a call tomorrow so Meredith can tell you about her 'flower girl' debut." A fresh wave of Hadley and Korey scenes attacked—beneath the sheets, in the shower, on the balcony. His imagination was turning against him.

"Or if she wants to call tonight…"

"We'll see how tired she is."

"Okay. Sorry again." Another pause from Hadley. "And then you'll both be back Sunday?"

"Uh-huh, the day after tomorrow." Her voice was only making the unexpected torture worse.

"Are Alika and Ward there yet?" she asked.

"Alika gets in tonight and—

"Give my plate to him!"

"Alika? He's on a diet." Patrick stepped aside for another waiter and his tray of dirty plates and cutlery.

"No!"

I know," said Patrick.

"For Dolores again?"

"Probably."

"And Ward?"

"Gets in tomorrow morning." He couldn't bare it any longer.

"How great. Well, give them my best too.

"Will do. Have to go."

"Okay, well..." The line chimed as Patrick hung up. "...Enjoy your meal," she wished quietly into the dead line.

Hadley hung up the phone and leaned back into the pillow; Patrick had known she was lying. She scrunched her eyes and rubbed them at the same time. Ever since the invitation came, Hadley had been oscillating between attending or not, going so far as to buy a dress. It had felt so odd though, and awkward—going to the wedding of your former sister-in-law. She was friends with Kylie, yes, but her conscious apprehension had kept her away. It was the same second-guessing that had stopped her from taking the New York Times position. Life seemed less certain than it once had. Her decisions felt more fragile to her own criticism; or was it her own wisdom?

With her eyes still shut, Hadley heard the lights go off in the hallway. There were footsteps then, bare feet on the carpet. She could hear a clock tick on the wall. And then Korey's lips touched down on her neck as his body pressed against hers in the bed.

The following day

In an afternoon glow, Kylie emerged from the mansion onto a set of marble steps. The wedding procession had already passed before her; down the same back steps, through the manicured gardens, past a four-piece string quartet, and down the aisle towards a majestic New England view.

Henry was waiting with the minister, his best men fanned out to his right, and Kylie's bridesmaids standing in support on the left. Meredith, the last flower girl, had just cast the final petals in anticipation of the bride. Kylie paused briefly. The quartet eased into Pachelbel's Canon and the gathered guests turned to watch her approach.

"Are you ready?" asked Patrick at her arm.

Kylie smiled and looked at her brother, the man she had chosen to give her away. His warm, familiar face was calming in the moment. She nodded and took the first step.

The guests stood in approving awe as she made her way to Henry and the overlook, its cliff guarded by a stone wall. As the aisle ended, Patrick left Kylie's side and Henry took her hand.

The minister, Henry's older cousin, proceeded with the ceremony. With local charm he weaved in stories, scripture, and Vermont anecdotes; reminiscing on tales from Henry's youth and the couple's engagement. He exhorted the pair to be unified in love, tenacious against obstacles, and patient in trial. He closed with a piece of storied advice for Henry, telling him to go out for walks when on the verge of an argument. "It's why I'm in such great health," the minister concluded.

After the first kiss, the guests rose to their feet, applauding as the newlyweds returned back up the aisle and stationed themselves in the gardens to receive the advancing tide of well-wishers.

They had invited 200 and prepared for 250. By Patrick's count, there would be just enough food. Under the auspices of a wedding gift left by Henry's late grandfather, Patrick had financed the whole wedding. He knew that Kylie wouldn't have approved, nor could he reasonably tell her where the money was coming from. She worried about him, and returning from South America with fists full of cash would only irritate her concern. Nevertheless, Patrick was confident that all the secrecy would soon be pleasant history, and ideally, front-page news.

While the guests made their way back up past the humming strings of the quartet, Patrick found Alika, Dolores and Ward sitting near the back.

"Gentlemen, Dolores," Patrick greeted, as they all stood for hugs and shakes.

"Such a beautiful place," Dolores admired. They all took another sweeping glance at the valley behind them, the rocky outcroppings, and the red-orange-yellow palettes that were every tree.

"I know," said Alika disapprovingly. "It's going to put certain ideas in certain people's heads." He nodded at Dolores.

Dolores turned to give him a sock on the arm. She wore an elegant yellow dress that matched Alika's tie.

"Really a nice service," said Ward, facing towards the house. "Never been to Vermont either. Quite an attractive little state. But the cell service..."

Although it had been months since they'd all been together in person, the three men kept nearly daily contact on operations and developments in both Americas—which, Dolores pointed out, should mean no business-talk at the wedding.

"Did you get a call back from Lockheed on that Darius part?"

"Ah, ah!" she interrupted.

Alika had been traveling throughout the country for most of the past year, working on contract frameworks for all the elements necessary to a nationwide rollout of Hydrogen fuel. Ward was involved with other projects simultaneously, but he was always in touch, providing the funds for their various activities. Patrick, meanwhile, was deep in the jungle, fine-tuning his most recent developments with Electro-Repulse Magnetism. The past few weeks had yielded a slew of results, the implications of which he still hadn't relayed to Ward or Alika. He hoped to do so before the evening was through.

Ward excused himself to get a drink and Dolores went forward to speak with the minister. Alika and Patrick talked about Meredith, who had scurried off again to play amongst the merry-making.

As they spoke, a man approached, whom Patrick recognized as one of the house's caretakers. He and his wife were around for the evening in case the wedding party required anything further of the mansion. The man had told Patrick earlier that his family used to actually live in the house, pointing out a row of windows, bordered by signature green shutters, which he said were the old servants' quarters. The trustees had since turned them into offices.

Catching the caretaker as he passed forward to help with the chairs, Patrick inquired about a particular tree that loomed alongside the overlook. It appeared to be wired into place, and concrete lined its insides like a spine.

"Excuse me," said Patrick. "This tree here. Is it dead?"

"Mostly, yes," said the caretaker. He was a short, handsome man, with features of a stage actor. "As you can see, they've tried to save it."

"And what happened?" Patrick asked. "Was it diseased?"

"It was struck by lightning," the man replied.

Alika slapped Patrick on the back. "That's our kind of tree."

The sunshine waned and left the guests crisp in the open air. Drinks substituted for overcoats and women shouldered men's suit jackets until the wedding dinner began in a permanent tent down a sloping hill to the side of the mansion. The elderly were escorted down first, trusting on the arms of teenage grandkids. The younger children followed, descending the hill in joyous pant-staining somersaults.

A band waited in the tent, playing melodic cover songs as the family and friends found their seats. Henry's brother and best man, Gordon, brought the group to order with a toast to the bride and groom. As the glasses fell, Gordon suddenly stepped back to join in on a surprise ballad with Henry's college friends, entitled: *Henry, Do We Have a Kylie for You*. The piano-accompanied piece left the tent in laughter and applause. Colleen followed, struggling for composure in reading a few words she'd prepared for Kylie. She pulled it together upon reaching a part about their parents, and the tables fell into polite silence as Colleen repeated Patrick's confirmation that George and Mary would have both been so proud. The two sisters hugged and Henry took over to express their thanks and love, and, to everyone's delight, announce that dinner was served.

Patrick sat at the head table with the immediate family, joining in the optimistic wedding talk. The appetizer was a fresh garden salad with local raspberry vinaigrette, or mozzarella sticks for the kids. Dinner was a choice of lemon chicken, New York Sirloin steak, or vegetarian baked ziti; of which Alika had a little of everything. Dessert was a selection of Ben and Jerry's ice cream, Vermont's own offspring, and the bride's favorite treat. "If she'd had her way," Henry said over dinner. "That's all we would have had—Cherry Garcia, five scoops each."

With the dinner accomplished, Kylie and Henry opened up the dance floor with their first two-step as husband and wife. Docile at first, the band played a few slow songs before mixing up the floor with a familiar medley of hits and grooves that had every generation on their feet.

Patrick took a few turns with Meredith until she got tired and wanted a rest. They found a table and Patrick poured a glass of water for them both. Two sips later, Colleen passed by and had Meredith skipping merrily back into the fray. Watching them go, Patrick let his eyes rest over the scene, his younger sister's wedding. She was 30, he was 32. The stirrings from his call with Hadley the night before had faded, but the setting naturally invited comparisons to his own marital status. He had not been entirely dormant since the divorce, going on a few dates arranged by Alika and Dolores, and then initiating several encounters of his own. There had been an old classmate from high school who still lived in West Chester and ran a clothing outlet, a colleague at the Global Environmental Alliance Institute who continued to call him, a lawyer from Pittsburgh who had helped with their REI contract; but the pleasures of their company had been purely physical, their touch failing to penetrate the skin. They all fell short of Hadley.

"Worn already?" asked a voice from behind him.

Patrick turned around as Ward's hand landed on his shoulder. Ward came and set his Jack and Coke next to Meredith's abandoned cup, unbuttoning his suit coat and pocketing a Blackberry as he sat.

"I would hope you're not on the phone at a time like this." said Patrick.

"Of course not," said Ward, taking a drink. "Just admiring the stars."

Patrick ignored the fib and put his hands out to the party. "So what do you think?"

"Looks great, my friend, looks great. Have you told Kylie where it all came from?"

"Not yet, no."

Ward smiled and gave Patrick another pat on the shoulder. "How long you back for this time?"

"Just the usual week." Patrick took a sip of water. "I leave again on Monday."

"Philadelphia to Caracas—what a commute. Still loving every minute?"

"I'm still there."

Ward looked Patrick over. He'd grown more social and comfortable since college, but not by much. "What you got there, water? How about something stiffer? It's on you anyway."

"I'm fine for now," Patrick replied. "I believe I accounted for at least two, maybe three, of the six bottles of wine at our table."

Ward took another drink and shrugged. "Fair enough."

"How was the food?" Patrick asked.

"Excellent. It was good to catch up with Alika too, feels like all we do is e-mail nowadays. Barely ever talk on the phone."

"The price of efficiency."

"Something like that."

They sat and watched the dresses and suits whip around the floor ahead of them. A few women sat at the adjacent table, and another man, who Patrick recognized as the minister, was on his phone at another. Ward took a deep drink from his glass.

"Ward," Patrick began, in a way that perked his friend's ears. "I think I've done it."

Ward set down his drink casually. "What do you mean?"

"Colombia—"

Ward cleared his throat.

"Venezuela," Patrick corrected. "I think I've worked out the regenerative bursts."

Ward leaned forward. "When did it happen?"

"Over the past few weeks," said Patrick, bearing a humble smile. "I haven't performed any full tests yet, but in theory, it should work."

"Did you tell Alika yet?"

"I haven't had the chance."

"And for the micro-generator too?" asked Ward hungrily.

"Both," Patrick confirmed, finishing his water. "Although the application for that one is still in question. It's the large power station prototypes that would come next, so that's where we're focusing."

"Amazing..." Ward looked momentarily off into space. "So would this mean...we could go public?"

Patrick suppressed another smile. "By my estimate, I'd say another month and I should have the necessary points ready."

"Patrick...that's brilliant!" Ward cried, a foxy curl on his lips. "Can I tell the Board?"

"Sure, I guess. But remember, I haven't confirmed with tests yet. The 'month' estimate is only a best guess."

"That's fine, totally fine. It's still really positive news." Ward raised his glass. "To Hydrogen."

Patrick raised his empty glass. "To Hydrogen."

Ward took a drink and let out a little whoop. "Whew! That's great."

Content, Patrick watched as Meredith spun around Colleen and then latched onto Alika and Dolores. *Jungle Boogie* rippled through the tent. "It'll be great to come home," he said.

"Surely." Ward was already playing at his Blackberry.

"Spend more time with Meredith," Patrick went on.

"Yup."

"Get healthy after a year in the jungle."

"Definitely."

"And then get going on the company."

"Of course," Ward said again absently. A few seconds later, he raised his eyes from the phone and looked over at Patrick, who watched with amusement as a dance circle formed around Alika. "Wait, say that again?"

"Huh?" said Patrick, distracted by Alika's unusual moonwalk.

"You mentioned a company," Ward said pointedly. "Your company?"

"Yeah, I'm going to start an energy company." Patrick turned back to Ward, whose face had frozen. "I told you about that in the beginning."

"Tell me again," said Ward, setting down his phone.

A group of teenage girls went chattering by with glasses of something other than soda.

"Well, once the technology is set, I'm going to start an energy company."

"Really? Like a joint venture?"

"Might be at first, but it should eventually be independent."

"Really?" Ward said again, looking impressed. "I didn't know you aspired to running a company."

"Ah, I won't run it," Patrick said, giving his attention back to Ward. "I'll just manage the energy production—the technical stuff."

"And will this be Hydrogen you're producing?"

"Of course." Patrick could see a slip of worry come over Ward. "Why? Are you concerned about the money?"

"Well," Ward began. "It's only, it's—"

"Obviously we're bound by contract to REI, so that will be first priority, but as we'll be the only one with this technology, the initial investors would receive a significant excess. This is your realm, but probably by at least…a few percentage points."

Ward looked at Patrick like he'd just thrown up in his drink. "Patrick…"

"It's going to be a non-profit energy company," Patrick went on, losing attentiveness. "Per barrel of oil equivalent, we'll charge as much as necessary to equalize the cost of production. A lot of the infrastructure will be profitable for other companies to build and service, so our role will be simply to produce the Hydrogen. As there are currently no competing technologies, we will have complete control of the market. Cheaper than coal, natural gas, and even nuclear, we could supply electricity at less than one cent per kilowatt hour. With the carbon price in Europe, it would be even cheaper—free, practically." Ward visibly gulped. "After retrofitting existing power stations, which will likely be the largest capital cost, we can then begin with vehicle fuels. As electrics are a good distance ahead, it may turn out that we apply the micro-generators as charging units instead, veering away from Hydrogen liquid fuels, but the power sector—that should be a sure conquest." Patrick stopped, turning back to Ward. "Sorry to ramble. I know you've heard this before. Alika used to talk about it back at Penn—it was originally his idea."

Ward had his hand on his glass. It was empty, but he took a drink anyway. A single mixed drop fell onto his tongue. He looked back at Patrick, his joy suddenly dissipated. The band transitioned into Billy Joel's *Piano Man.*

Patrick offered a loose smile without meaning to be deceptive. Free energy, not in the scientific definition, but in the monetary sense, was something he'd thought about extensively during the past few months in Venezuela. The ethics of energy had never been a motivator for Patrick, not like it was for Alika. He understood that there were those who stood to gain from his work—that would of course be changing the world—but it was seeing the true poverty in Venezuela and Colombia that stirred him; hearing the stories of those he worked with, and the way in which electricity and fuel could become saviors instead of dictators.

Ward then smiled too, a warped and incredulous grin that slipped manically into laughter. "Patrick!" He slapped the table. "Man, you gave me a scare! I thought you were serious."

Patrick had momentarily joined Ward in his laughter, but now became quiet.

"Whew! Don't go playing that to anyone else," said Ward. "We'd all get hung out to dry—a non-profit energy company." He wiped his face with his hand. "I can only imagine."

Confused, Patrick silently watched Ward as he stood up.

"I'm off to get another drink. You want one? Don't answer that—Yes, you do."

"Ward, I wasn't kidding," said Patrick. Except Ward seemed not to hear and proceeded to walk away, shaking his head at the apparent nonsense that Patrick had just spouted.

From his seat, Patrick followed Ward through the mix of bodies and music as he maneuvered the length of the tent to the bar. A seam of concern began working in Patrick's stomach. He rolled his empty water glass around on its heel—what had Ward meant by *hung out to dry*? The idea for a non-profit energy company had indeed been Alika's, but they hadn't discussed it in nearly ten years. Patrick decided to speak more with Alika and Ward about the details. Although the concept made sense to Patrick and felt feasible, perhaps there was some variable he was missing; an angle he could not see.

Before he could think long on the subject, Meredith appeared at his side and tugged him back onto the dance floor. The punching chords of CCR's *Proud Mary* filled the tent.

The night carried on for Patrick, spirits clouded his memory, social exchanges replaced others, and by and by, all worry over Ward's words was forgotten.

Chapter 20

March 15th, 2028
Safehouse Five, New York City, New York
7:40 p.m.

The wedding in Vermont was the final public sighting of Patrick Simon. Based on financial transactions, Patrick returned with Meredith to Pennsylvania and then flew out of Philadelphia to Caracas. It was not long thereafter that his face started appearing on the evening news. They said he'd lost his mind.

I've often been asked if there are patterns in the way that *normal* people *snap*; *normal*, as in your grocer, your barber, the father of your daughter's friend, those you wouldn't expect to *snap* and put a gun in their ear, endanger a child, burn down an office block, take advantage of their secretary, or lock themselves away in the attic.

Truth is—I have no idea why people do abnormal things. I can rattle off some trusted conclusions in the profession, describe the impact of chemical imbalances, personal tragedy, external stresses, buried appetites and addictions, suppressed emotions and feelings… But frankly, I try not to think too much about *the why*. I stay objective and just give an assessment on an individual's sanity. Because if I did care, if I tried to assign meaning to the acts of those select human beings I encounter, or the acts committed against them, I too would lose my mind—there is little room for empathy in the work of a criminal psychologist.

It's not just people either, its entire nations and countries. Ethnic cleansings, religious oppression, blatant corruption. Something happens, the rivers change direction and the rain rises, and I think that when people say—"Hanna, what was it? What drove them over the edge?"—what they're really want to know is—"Hanna, if it can happen to my neighbor, the one I've lived next to for fifteen years and occasional chat to at the fence, if they go nuts, then what's to stop it from happening to me? What's to stop my government from instituting legal segregation or glamourizing systematic genocide?"

Sometimes you can trace the break, the way firemen identify the source of a fire. But take Patrick Simon, if he were going to *snap*, logic would point to a breakdown occurring immediately after his divorce, the accident in Florida, and the death of his father. He did lose his bearings to a degree with his drinking and depression, but not to the magnitude of his later offenses—kidnapping, manslaughter, murder. Yet Patrick had righted himself in the months to follow, he had taken control of his life and stood on the brink of a major discovery…so why would he throw it all away? Perhaps it's because there's no shortage of demons, and after finally mastering his own ship, Patrick realized his dominion did not extend to the rolling seas into which he'd sailed, the deep waters of deep pockets. There was Korey Devoir as well.

We're taking another break and Meredith is alone in the room, calmly enjoying her Chinese take-away as if sitting at her own kitchen table. Killian meanwhile is pacing the monitoring room, debating whether or not to call the FBI Director. He believes we'll lose Meredith to another division or agency if too many details escape. It would clearly be frustrating, but I sense there's something that Killian's not telling me, perhaps about the contents of Meredith's luggage. I have yet to see one shred.

Meredith places the last empty container in a paper bag and I prepare to return. From this point on we have little official documentation to compare with Meredith's testimony. Killian's told me to have her be as detailed as possible. He knows as much as I do that Meredith has largely been steering the interview, yet she's also answering our questions before we ask them.

I step back into the room with another agent who removes the food containers. It's been over seven hours since I met Meredith at the airport.

How was the food?

Great, thanks. Local place?

Just down the road actually.

What's the name of it?

Baiji River.

Nice name. Did you grow up around here?

[The way she asks the question, I can tell she knows the answer. She is certainly one for assertion.]

I did, yes. Moved away some time ago though.

Well, welcome home.

[I nod and move on. This is not about my family.]

So before he took you in Florida, was your Aunt's wedding the last time you saw your father?

Yes, until Florida. We drove back to Philadelphia the day after the wedding. I was seven. He dropped me at my mother's and then came back the next day before his flight to South America.

What was he like?

Same as usual. He was Dad. If anything was amiss, I wouldn't have noticed.

So you remember the wedding, driving home, saying goodbye at your mother's…was Korey Devoir at your mother's when your father dropped in?

[The question is not treated as a surprise.]

He was.

And was there any confrontation between your father and Korey?

My father never got on well with Korey, he'd suspected him of having an affair with my mother, or at least wanting to. Yes, there was a confrontation at the house, but it never became violent…I know that's not what the reports say.

No, they don't.

[Meredith looks hard at me across the table. When she speaks, it's with the most emotion she's shown all day.]

My father is a good man. He wasn't the best husband or father, but he loved me and my mother. He was no murderer...he was the victim of circumstance, of the way things are.

What do you mean?

It was his focus and hope that made him so successful in his work, how he accomplished so much. My father trusted in a solution to everything, complete possibility...but this vision made him blind.

What happened in Venezuela?

Colombia...he didn't comprehend the power of greed.

Chapter 21

November 2011
Bryn Mawr, Pennsylvania

Hadley rubbed her eyes against sleep. She was sitting up in bed, laptop across her legs, midway through an unjustly long queue of articles that needed to be edited for the morning paper. Although as Editor of Content she rarely had to doctor the columns too much, the burden of holding the last red pen was heavy.

She glanced at the clock, startled to see it was already past 10:00 p.m. At least she could work from home instead of the office, electronically zipping submissions back and forth with the Inquirer's copy editors and layout team. She adjusted her reading glasses and focused in on a piece about ongoing talks between North and South Korea. It was rare for her to work so late; this particular session more the result of Meredith's ever-busy schedule than of procrastination or wordy writers.

On top of the after-school groups, sports teams, and music lessons, Meredith was becoming a high-demand play date. Her daughter's social aptitude comforted Hadley, knowing the rigors of adolescent acceptance that lay in wait as Meredith grew older, but it also meant that Hadley was playing taxi an extra two to three hours every afternoon. And those other mothers could talk.

It was a cooler evening, Halloween gone, and Hadley had even adjusted the thermostat. Nearing the end of the Korea article, her phone began to chirp from the bedside table.

She checked the number and was warmed to see Alika's name. It had been several weeks since they'd last spoke.

"Hey there Leak," she answered.

"Hads," came his voice, deep and tired. "I wake you?"

"I wish, just working from bed."

"Must be close to deadline."

"I try not to think about it."

"I'll be quick."

"No rush. It's been ages, how are you?"

"Fine, fine. Busy as usual. I'm up in the city for the night and Patrick wanted me to drop off some photos I developed—they're for Meredith."

"Very retro. Did you want to swing by tonight?"

"I know it's late…"

"Don't be silly, come over. Where are you staying tonight? You sound mobile. Are you driving?"

"Yeah, just coming out of a dinner." He stifled a burp. "Ate too much, I think. Meredith asleep already?"

"Yeah, she's zonked. You would not believe the timetable that girl keeps. You didn't answer me though, where are you staying?"

"I booked a place near the airport, my flight—."

"Nonsense," Hadley exclaimed. "Stay in our spare room. Meredith would love it! It's already made up, or just about, and we haven't seen you in ages."

"I don't want to hass—"

"Shut-up and come over."

"You sure?"

"You *are* the godfather."

Alika laughed, relented, and said he would be there in half an hour.

Hadley placed the phone down, happy to a distraction and the idea of a houseguest. She determined to work hard for another twenty minutes before taking a break to straighten up. Besides Meredith and Korey, she had very little company these days.

Meredith woke up in bed. The room was a soft dark by the nightlight. She sat up and looked around. All was still, her door barely ajar to the hallway. A glass of water was next to her bed. As she reached for it, a noise came from downstairs.

Thwack.

She froze. The moon-shaped clock on the nightstand showed it was nearly 10:30. Again, she heard sounds from downstairs, but more muffled and hollow.

Pom, pom, pom.

Then all was quiet.

Meredith swung her feet gently off the bed and tiptoed towards the door. She wore a light blue nightgown that came down to the knees and fluttered about her in the open air. Halfway to the door she heard another sound.

Creeeaak.

It sounded like the bottom step on the stairs. Meredith lost courage and turned back. A small tent was set up in the corner of her room, big enough just for her. At the moment it was full of stuffed animals, all of them busily crowded together, as though waiting out a storm.

She made for the tent, snuggling in between an old brown bear and a large Tweety Bird her Aunt Colleen had given her. It was cozy and warm, and she tried not to smoosh or disturb her tentmates. Her mother had bought the tent by request during the summer as Patrick sometimes spent the night outside in Venezuela. Erecting the tent helped to dampen the separation.

In between her furry friends, Meredith lay still, her head resting on her hands. She listened for more noises and tried not to imagine the faces and forms of the villains and monsters from the movies. For the next few minutes, everything was peaceful. Meredith grew sleepy in the security of the tent.

By and by, she fell asleep.

With a few articles left to proof, Hadley placed her laptop aside and headed to the linens closet in the hallway. She collected the appropriate sheets, blankets, and pillowcases, and then headed for the spare room at the far end of the landing. The stairwell opened up across a railing to her right, and the dark downstairs reminded Hadley to switch on the outside light for Alika.

In the room, she turned on a lamp and set to work. After too many hours in front of the computer screen, reading, for the most part, bad news, Hadley felt energized to be up and active. There was little furniture, just a bed, a chair, and an old chest of drawers. A few boxes were stacked in corners, as well as an unusual metal stork that a co-worker had given Hadley the previous Christmas. Its thin metallic limbs were unnerving and she'd sequestered it immediately.

The extra bed was a queen and had been left with the house. Hadley had thought about renting the room; her ideal tenant a tame college student, single librarian-type, someone interesting with whom to share an evening tea after the daily bustle. But her hours at the Inquirer, and Meredith's social calendar, delayed any coordinating, leaving the room at the command and disposal of the stork.

With the sheets fit tightly around the mattress, Hadley sheathed two pillows in matching blue cases and fluffed them into place. She picked up a folded blanket and was about to spread it across the bed when a sound came from the hallway. Footsteps on carpet.

"Meredith?" Hadley said towards the open doorway, the blanket still waiting in her arms. There was a painting on the wall in the corridor, a Monet print.

The footsteps stopped. It was not unusual for Meredith to be up and about. The child had imagination.

Hadley set the folded blanket on the bed and walked towards the door. Before she reached it, a large man stepped squarely into the frame. He was light-skinned, had short-cropped black hair, and his eyes made Hadley go rigid.

She let out a small scream and took a step backwards in surprise. The man moved quickly and grabbed Hadley by the throat, his other arm taking hers and twisting it. In a swift motion, he spun her around facedown onto the bed. She felt his hand clamp over her mouth.

Another man came in the door and went to the windows, drawing the shades and unplugging the lamp. He then moved to take hold of Hadley's legs, which she had started to thrash against the floor. This second man, Hadley could see from the corner of her eye, was thin, Asian, and wore a baseball cap.

"Stop moving," the first man commanded sharply. He continued to twist Hadley's arm.

The pain in her shoulder was piercing. Nausea and terror struggled for preference.

"Stop," he demanded, but Hadley continued to flail. The light from the hallway made horrific shadows of the men on the bedspread.

Seeing that she was destined to prove difficult, the man leaned closer to her ear. "Don't make things hard for Meredith," he whispered.

The words dug into Hadley like hooks. She went wide-eyed and bucked harder, the man at her feet struggling to hold on. She tried to bite, but the man's grip was too strong. The skin on his hands was greasy, like a slice of cheese left out in the humidity. Tears began to stream from her eyes, both from the pain and the fear. She felt herself flop against the bedside.

"You're not listening," the man said into her ear. He rested his knee against her rib cage and pressed.

Hadley stiffened and waited to pass out from the pain. It burned, it cut, it ripped, it stung, head to heart to toe. It was unlike anything, and she could only squirm for several seconds longer until slackening in exhaustion.

"That's it," the man said coolly, as if to a broken mare. She struggled to breathe through his cupped hand. He spoke slowly, his voice harsh, plain, and darkly satisfied. "Now, be still. I'll explain this once. If you listen, everything will be alright. Your daughter doesn't get hurt. But if you make things difficult, well…so can I."

Hadley strained her eyes and they found his. They were blue and empty.

"Do you understand?" he asked. "Nod, if you do."

She nodded. The sheet onto which she was pressed was growing sodden from her tears and running nose.

"Okay," he said. "Here's how it goes. I'm going to take my hand off your mouth. Don't bother screaming. There's no point. But, should you choose to, my friend here will scream back. And that can hurt."

Hadley heard the Asian man come forward, wincing as a hard metal object touched down against her spine and then tapped the back of her right knee.

The man at her ear continued with zero emotion. "We're going to tie your hands and place a blindfold on you. Once we have you both…"

The surprise of the attack was dissipating and Hadley was coming out of the initial shock. She struggled to place the men, what they could want, and how she might spare Meredith.

"…We're going to take you through the house to the garage," the man explained, going over the plan like a fire drill. "When we drive away, if you try to alert anyone, I will take off your blindfold and you will watch as we shoot your daughter. Is that understood?"

Hadley nodded again. Fears for herself were paling against these new threats on her child. Her fury was building to a boil.

The man was about to say something else, but suddenly paused. He had an ear piece of some sort, and he stopped to listen. Hadley heard a gargle of incoherent speech.

The man bent down slowly to Hadley's ear. "Where is your daughter?" he asked.

Hadley didn't move.

"She's not in her room," he continued.

Hadley had composed herself enough by this point to not react. Inside, she felt both hope and dread. On the one hand, Meredith was presently safe. On the other, there were more men in her home. She applied herself to think fast, or at least stall until Alika arrived.

"We're going to do what I said before, except I'm going to let you speak," the man said evenly. "If you say anything that I don't think is relevant, then, as promised, we'll put a hole in your leg." He took his hand off Hadley's mouth. "Now, where is your daughter?"

Hadley didn't speak immediately, catching her breath. The lack of oxygen had made her dizzy. "She's at her grandmother's," Hadley answered, still face down on the bed.

Immediately, the man whipped her around onto the floor. Twisting, he wound up to give her a kick, stopping short only when two more men came in the door. They wore faded hooded sweatshirts. The pair looked at Hadley lying on the ground against the bed, her face bloodied and full of fright. There was nothing to their eyes either, as if such a scene was commonplace.

"She's not there," one of them said, his accent untraceable. "Tossed the place good."

The pale man nodded and bent down towards Hadley. She couldn't help shrinking. He pulled her up onto the bed, allowing her to sit. The four men closed in around her, framed by light, the Asian man with his gun drawn. There were more sounds from downstairs. The men didn't react.

"We know she's here," he said. "And her closest grandmother, as you know, is in Boston. I doubt the seven-year old slipped up there for the night."

It was becoming clear to Hadley that these men were not your average intruders. A fresh round of tears issued slowly down her cheeks.

"We know if you're lying, Miss Hannigan," he prodded. "So, please, tell us where your daughter might be hiding. Now."

Hadley thought she knew. Meredith had a favorite hide-and-go-seek spot in her room.

"Just tell me what you want," she said, her body quivering.

"I did," said the man. He struck her hard across the face. "We want Meredith."

Recoiling from the blow, Hadley felt at her stinging cheek and wiped a trickle of blood from her nose. "What if she's not here?" she said quietly.

The man grinned viciously. "Glad you asked." He pulled a bronze-cased lighter from his pocket. He flicked off the cap and struck a flame. Staring at Hadley with the same acrid smile, he set the lighter to the edge of the bed sheet. "If she's not here…" The linen ignited instantly. "…well, then there's nothing to worry about."

Hadley watched in horror as the fresh sheet singed and charred, a small fire preparing to spread across the rest of the bed. The four men waited for her reaction as the smell of scorched cloth filled the room.

"Okay, okay," Hadley relented. She would not let her daughter burn. "I'll find her."

"Good," said the man, pocketing his lighter and smothering the sparks with a blanket. He gestured to the door. "Make it quick."

They marched her down the hall, past the master bedroom, bathroom, and to the top of the stairs. Meredith's room was down the adjacent hall. They stopped at the stairwell. Hadley looked around and could tell they were all listening again through their earpieces. She considered bolting for the stairs, but the Asian man's gun was jammed against her back. It would be futile.

The two hooded men suddenly headed down the steps, one of them peeking out the window by the front door. The other disappeared from sight. Hadley was spun around so she was facing the short-cropped man. His person was now better lit and she could see scars along his forehead and down his neck. His blue eyes should have been pretty, but they were lifeless and without feeling. He grabbed her by the arm.

"Is that Alika Tucker that just pulled up outside?" he asked, pronouncing the name incorrectly, *A-Like-Uh*. "Were you expecting him?"

"Yes," Hadley replied, stunned at the brute's knowledge, but also realizing the danger that Alika would now be in as well.

"Then this is your last chance," the man sneered. "Tell us where Meredith is—or she cooks."

Hadley considered the offer, nearly told him, and then spit in his face. He recoiled and Hadley lunged at him. As she did, the butt of a gun cracked down on her skull.

Hadley fell to the floor.

With his boot, the Asian man nudged at her ribs. She lay limp. "We leavin' her?" he asked, tucking the gun into his waistline.

"She's not important," said the pale, short-cropped man looking down on Hadley's still form.

"What about the girl?"

"It's too late, forget them both," commanded the pale man. "You get that room, I'll get this one. If the girl's smart, she'll make it out—and if not, well, this wasn't their first option anyway." He began walking towards the spare room. "Thirty seconds. And make it look amateur."

Satisfied, the Asian man stepped swiftly over Hadley's body and entered her bedroom, pulling another lighter from his pocket as he went.

Meredith listened to the sounds of the last footsteps descending into the living room. Prone in her hiding place, she could see very little.

Only minutes before, she had awoken to her mother's scream. Vaulting from the tent, Meredith had hurried to the door and seen the men coming. Without much thought, she'd run straight to her bureau, lifted a piece of fascia board at its side and slipped feet first into a small opening. Moments after lowering the board, the hooded men entered the room.

When Hadley and Meredith first moved into the house, Patrick had built a set of drawers for Meredith. When he was building them, he mistakenly cut the bottom drawer too short. "Standard error," he'd told them. With that drawer shortened, a snug little space was left along the bottom of the bureau. Patrick had fixed a sliding piece of fascia board along the side of the drawer to conceal the mistake, while also creating a secret hideaway. He had imagined that Meredith could stow her journals and such there as she grew older. Now the girl herself was lodged in the space.

From her refuge, Meredith never saw the men's faces, but the sounds of their search had been terrifying. As they began to ransack the room, her fear was so taut that she could not cry out. Instead, she just shut her eyes and prayed in the dark. The closest the intruders came to finding her was when they pulled out the bottom drawer. A wiry hand had come groping into the space, clawing at the opening; missing Meredith's trembling feet by inches. Her heart had leapt so loudly at her chest, she feared it might break.

Through the gap where the drawer had been removed, Meredith could see feet moving about, tearing the animals from their tent and tossing clothes from their hangers. She had shut her eyes again, covering her ears as well, trying in vain to block out the gruff breaths of the beasts beyond the bureau.

The men were now gone and she could hear nothing in the hallway upstairs, only a few creeps and snaps from distant parts of the house. Meredith slowly lifted the board, and slipped out into her room. It was as though a tornado had come and ripped everything from its home. Clothes, toys, books, pictures—nothing had been safe. She walked to the window, where her brown bear lay torn and upside down against the sill. As she picked him up, the first tear descended her cheek. She wanted her mother.

In the midst of the devastation, another loud noise came from downstairs.

Bam!

It was the front door, slamming shut. A loud deep voice followed the noise, bellowing through the house.

Clutching the bear, Meredith scampered towards her bed, the covers and sheets torn off. She heard more steps, heavy ones, covering the downstairs living room in a rush.

Fum, Fum, Fum.

And then the voice again, but more anxious, yelling. Meredith wanted to run for her mother, but she was too frightened to leave the room. What if the men were waiting for her? She started to cry, her entire body shaking.

Fum, Fum, Fum.

Dropping to the ground, Meredith began to inch beneath the bed, burrowing between the bedsprings and carpet until she was up against the wall. The big feet were soon ramping up the stairs, pounding like thunder.

BOOM! BOOM! BOOM!

And with this thunder, the smell of smoke.

Chapter 22

November 2011
Bryn Mawr, Pennsylvania

The front door was locked when Alika reached it. Drifts of smoke were starting to billow from all around the house. Without any hesitation, he reared back and lowered his shoulder. The frame splintered when he hit the door and Alika crashed into Hadley's front hall.

There were flames coming up at the back of the house, and ashy smoke was pouring into the living room and up the stairwell. Upstairs, there was fire already starting to lick out from one of the landings.

"Hadley!" he yelled. "Hadley!"

There was no reply, only the din of burning.

Alika started towards the downstairs kitchen, the apparent epicenter. A wall of red hot heat coursed from the back of the house, nearly flooring him. Through the haze, he could see the entire dining room and kitchen were already consumed. Releasing his extinguishing intentions, Alika switched to rescue mode—the house was going up.

"Hadley! Meredith!" Alika bellowed, now wondering if they were still in the house. 'Would they be standing on the back lawn?' he thought. 'Why weren't the smoke-alarms going off? Should he assume the worst and keep looking?'

Shoving thoughts aside, Alika remembered that Hadley had been working in her bedroom. As he hustled to the stairwell, the coffee table caught his shins and he went to the ground. Struggling back to his feet, Alika began to cough from breathing in so much air from the surprise. Growing light-headed, he lunged back to the front door, took a few deep breaths from outside and returned.

As Alika came up the stairs, the flames were growing stronger in the room off to his right, the wallpaper was threatening to curl in the hallway, and reaching the landing he nearly tripped over something in the darkness.

Alika bent down. It was Hadley.

Ten minutes earlier

As Alika pulled off the interstate towards Bryn Mawr, the roads, like Russian nesting dolls, became progressively smaller. At around 10:45 p.m., a half-hour since their call, he turned down Hadley's street. It was a one-way, more like a path, with a slight shoulder on either side. Although Alika had been here several times, he still needed his GPS on each occasion. The road only had houses down its left side, the right entirely dominated by a large untamed pasture holding strong against development. In the late evening as Alika drove past, the field was black as obsidian.

The traffic heading north that afternoon from Philadelphia had been barbaric, commuters fighting for every minute of the approaching weekend. The accordion pull-and-push had made Alika late for the dinner he had arranged in Allentown, a meeting with a state utility company. The discussion was over a test-scale hydrogen plant proposed for a rural Pennsylvania community. The representing executives had been concerned about the usual—safety, liability, exposure, cost. Despite the act, their eagerness to get involved was undeniable. Drilling in the local Marcellus Shale had been halted in several areas due to pending environmental action and rumors of a passable climate bill in Congress had the utilities scrambling for Alternatives.

Hadley's home sat just off the road, buffered by a short lawn and low iron fence. A driveway ran up the left side of the house to a garage at the rear. Parking on the shoulder, Alika turned off the car and gathered his Blackberry from the seat beside him. He quickly typed out two e-mails, managing the small keys with his disproportionally large fingers. One went to Patrick and Ward, detailing the meeting and some follow-up items, and the other went to Dolores, about nothing in particular, only that he'd had tiramisu that night and missed her.

As he breezed through his messages, Alika felt a twinge of exhilaration. The meeting with the utility execs had been a success, another pearl for their growing string. Patrick had been very busy the past few months in South America, making development after development. The business implications aside, Alika was grateful for his friend's triumphs. After the debacle in Florida, the meltdown of his marriage, and the loss of his father, Patrick was back on track. On the phone, and in person, he was a re-made man. The process had taken two years, but the healing was now advanced, sweetening Patrick's remarkable discoveries at their new facility. Most important was the successful simulation of a magnetic burst at the on-site lab, and more so, the nature of this burst. It was why Patrick was a week longer, and why Alika was delivering pictures for Meredith; a fatherly gesture in lieu of his presence.

Finished with his phone, Alika got out of the car. He tried to remember the last time he had seen Meredith. The late dinner in Allentown had dashed his hopes of catching her awake. He had a flight to Detroit at 6:45 the next morning, meaning an early rise. Any other weekend he would have stayed, but this meeting with General Motors was an important one.

A car started further up the road, its engine immediately roaring into motion. It sounded like a Suburban-sized SUV. Alika shut his door and watched as the taillights jostled and shrunk down the street. The nip in the air got him moving, and it was only now that he looked up at the house. It was a handsome home, white siding with blue trim, and certainly large enough. Alika had helped out with some of the moving. He walked to the front door, knowing Hadley was expecting him.

At the door, he heard another car start, this time from back down the road, along the way he'd came. The neighborhood was livelier than Hadley had described. He stepped up to the door as the car drove up and stopped at the foot of Hadley's driveway.

Surprised, Alika turned around. He wondered if the car was lost. It was a sleek black sedan, Mercedes. The windows were up and tinted, and in the darkness, Alika couldn't see the driver.

Stepping from the doorway, Alika intended to start towards the road. Instead, Bob Marley's *Buffalo Soldier* blared from his coat like a fog horn.

The volume on his phone was turned up loud, a setting Alika used when he drove. He jammed a hand into his pocket and answered. It was his mother.

"Hey," Alika said, a bit annoyed.

"Hi," Minnie said sweetly. "Did I wake you?"

The idling sedan picked up speed and drove away, turning some loose gravel as it went.

"Just the whole neighborhood," Alika replied, turning back to the house, expecting a startled Meredith to poke out through a curtain.

"The whole neighborhood, how could—?"

"Don't worry Ma, forget it. What's up? I'm here at Hadley's."

"Oh, I'm sorry. That's so nice of you to stop by. I was just calling about the wedding for Sylvia. You see, it's been moved slightly. A bit awkward…"

His mother carried on about a cousin's wedding, but Alika wasn't listening. He was smelling smoke, and immediately, he was seeing it too, wisps coming out a side window.

He dropped his phone and conversation in the grass and rushed at the front door.

"Hadley!" Alike yelled, kneeling at the top of the stairs over her unconscious body. Eyes closed, she didn't budge as he shook her arm. Like a towel, he threw her over his shoulder and began down the stairs. At the bottom, he stopped, Hadley still limp against his back.

"Meredith!" he screamed, straining his ears for a response. "Meredith!"

Alika heard nothing and continued out the front door. He spread Hadley on the cold front lawn and bent down close to her face. His hands were shaking too much to check her pulse.

"Hadley, wake up!" he pleaded. "Where's Meredith?"

Gathering that Hadley would not wake, Alika left her on the grass and charged back through the open door into the house. The blaze was gaining strength, the rear of the house tormented entirely by flame. Ash and heat made it near-impossible to see or stand. Alika battled back up of the stairs. Two of the rooms were filled with fire, but the last, and the one Alika remembered as Meredith's, the one he willed to be Meredith's, was still reachable. The roof was starting to cry out, the sound of cracking beams and columns wringing fear into Alika.

"Meredith!" he yelled again, skidding into her room. Even in the alarm, Alika still noticed the unusual disorder. The sound of the fire was reaching a crescendo. In the master bedroom, a rank of floorboards crashed into the kitchen, sending a shudder through the entire house.

"Meredith! It's Alika!"

By the racket of the blaze, he could barely hear himself, and the reality of not finding her was razor sharp. There were so many places she could hide. He tore through her closet, then the tent, and pressed himself to the ground, straining to see under the bed.

Alika seized when he saw her. The girl's face, stained with tears, looked out from beneath the far side of the bed. Although he couldn't hear her, he could see she was screaming for him.

Standing up, he threw the mattress across the room, ripped the box spring clear, and pulled Meredith from beneath the frame. No time for hugs, he slung her over his shoulder.

She clung tight, rigid and wailing, as Alika left the bedroom and entered a spark-wrought inferno on the landing. The flames picked at his every limb as they stumbled through the dark smoke that engulfed their path. He pressed on, trusting that the floor would hold.

The stairs appeared to be clear, but Alika's vision was beginning to blur. He leapt down them as fast as possible, praying his bulk wouldn't suddenly sink them into a pit of flames. Eight more steps, five more steps, three more steps…

Safely at the base of the stairs, Alika found he could no longer see; the smoke and ash had stung shut his eyes. Groping for the exit, he slipped. Meredith's scream was audible over the howl.

Frenzied, Alika scuffled to his feet. Meredith was alright, but with the fall, Alika had lost his bearings. He feared he might run the wrong way, carrying them into the flames instead of safety. One arm outstretched, he inched forward, feeling cautiously for heat, but hoping for the door. His fingers clasped on a knob. It was the banister, cloaked in soot.

Then Meredith was slipping. No, she was being pulled away. Alika whipped around, unable to see, yelling. Meredith was gone. He felt hands placed on his shoulders, gloved hands that began to pull him as well. In confusion, he tried to resist.

'Who was this?' Alika questioned, as a throbbing pain split into his head. The rising pressure in his chest reached a climax and he gulped deeply for air.

Instantly, Alika slumped, his body reduced to dead weight. The sounds of the fire ebbed away, the pain suspended, and as if by parachute he pitched further into the darkness.

Chapter 23

November 2011
Parque Nacional El Tama, Venezuela

A king, a castle, and a pawn—these were all Patrick had left. Losing appeared inevitable. Although he had never beaten Noé, the pair always played 'til the royal's death.

They sat on the porch of Patrick's small bungalow; the Venezuelan jungle entrenched round about. Noé was one of the guards assigned to protect Patrick and his staff of researchers. Thus far, their presence had seemed unwarranted, months passing without an incident. Patrick appreciated the common company nonetheless. Noé was from a neighboring province in Colombia, and played a ruthless game of chess.

Patrick surveyed his options, they were slim. Noé had him pinned in his own corner. The venue of their game and residence was an old tourist camp in a National Park south of San Cristóbal. REI had rented the plot for the study. There were mumbles at first about its suitability and safety. The camp consisted of a kitchen and dining room, a clubhouse-type pavilion, an empty pool, and an overgrown set of tennis courts. The members of Patrick's team, a mix of Americans from both continents, each had a one-room straw-thatched bungalow to themselves. The little huts formed a ring around the center pavilion and eating area. A low-slung fence made a perimeter about the camp, but it did little to hold back the wildlife. There'd been a scare just yesterday with a jaguar. Spiders were ever-present; massive ones the size of dinner plates. It was the way they moved that rattled Patrick, slowly mincing their pliable legs across his ceiling. Yet as the summer rainy season subsided, the insects became less prevalent, relenting perhaps for the heat. The Venezuelan sun packed a strong equatorial punch.

Despite the usual adjustments, physical and mental, to life in the jungle, the greatest surprise and concern for Patrick was the location of their testing facility. The test site was supposed to be built adjacent to the camp, but according to REI, the Venezuelan government was denying them permission. On top of continued governmental tension, it seemed that rumors had trickled down from the US that the testing to be conducted by Patrick was dangerous, possibly catastrophic. As a result, the facility was moved several miles away over the border into Colombia.

Bolstering his trepidation, Patrick learned from one of the local guards that the tourist camp had not been a victim of poor business, but had been deserted because of nearby fighting between drug cartels. He'd taken Patrick to see a twisted graveyard of bullet-tattered vehicles that had been towed from the road before the team's arrival. Though this made Patrick uneasy, Venezuela had supposedly clamped down on its borders, securing the jungle haven; at least that's what REI reported. Patrick was discovering that 'safe' in South America had a different definition than in the States.

To reach their facility, the team traveled down a rutted logging road to a bridge that marked the border between Colombia and Venezuela. Across the bridge, they continued for another few kilometers until reaching the site of an old military barracks. The former stronghold had also been riddled with bullet holes, as well as snakes and ambitious vines. The Colombian government had no problems with REI buying the land, and the whole structure was bulldozed and cleared. A hand-picked construction crew was trucked in from Caracas and within weeks the facility was complete. Fences and guard stations were erected to monitor and protect the rooms of absurdly expensive equipment. No one was taking any good faith chances.

With the lab up and running, Patrick set to work immediately, quickly training his team on procedures and methods. Since the accident in Florida, there had been ample time for Patrick to think about what could be done with the project. He felt at home within the lab's clean, mechanized setting, more so than outside in the hot, lethal rainforest, and this familiarity helped to boost Patrick's resolve. It was his first time outside of the United States, certainly to a developing country, and he'd initially found it difficult adapting to the unpredictable pace and state of this new environment. As the weeks wore on, however, Patrick found himself embracing his new surroundings, often pinching himself for the surreal situations that he would daily encounter. There were the nights going home to camp when the sky displayed its infinite jewel case of stars, evenings at the dinner table sharing a native dish with his diverse set of colleagues, occasional afternoons swimming in piranha-infested rivers, and mornings when heavenly sunrises bore his crew to work in a breath. Nothing in his old life compared to this setting, and it was in many ways a complete separation from the world he had inhabited over the last thirty years. After those first months abroad, Patrick not only felt rejuvenated, but renovated.

With his confidence blooming, he wasted no time in testing the scribbles and marks that constituted his notes from the past two years. By the end of August, six months after arrival, they had successfully triggered eighteen lightning strikes. Their success was unprecedented, and even with Patrick's most optimistic of theories, the data was synching neatly. Patrick realized the importance of the data, not just for his own ideas, but for the studies of other scientists. They were gaining insight into a substantial number of debated topics. Although he was eager to share, the REI confidentiality agreement bound him and his team from divulging details of their work. It was irksome, but Patrick abided, confident the day would soon come.

Throughout September, the lab team had consistently simulated lightning-like magnetic bursts, building assurance in their underlying project goal—simplify for application. This was cause for excitement, but the real leap had come in the past month after his return from America. Patrick had tried something new with the orientation of the testing apparatus and the material of the *cation* receptor. The resulting observations indicated that Patrick had discovered how to prompt highly-efficient regenerative magnetic bursts. If likened to a thermal engine, the efficiency of the system was staggeringly higher than previously believed possible. The difference was a squash ball to a racquet ball. The system would undoubtedly require further testing, but if the finding was legitimate, and Patrick had written to Ward that he felt it was, they could announce the breakthrough before the end of the year.

Noé gave Patrick a look across the board, the one that let Patrick know he was just about finished.

"How long do I have?" Patrick asked.

Noé smiled and shrugged. "Not long." His accent was heavy, but tender.

Three moves later, Patrick's king was mated and they shook hands over the board. Noé, Patrick knew, would not stray far. Oftentimes, the guard sat the whole night on the porch, a machine gun lying where their chess pieces now stood.

Patrick went inside and checked the time, it was nearly 10:00 p.m., the lights would go out soon and he was exhausted. The project team tended to rise early, around daybreak, and Patrick headed for the desk by his bed to enter the day's proceedings into a journal. It was both for scientific and personal reasons. Mostly he kept it for Meredith; for that someday when she wondered what her father had done in Colombia.

The camp was powered at night by a generator. During the evening it provided electricity and pumped water from a well into a raised cistern. Hot showers were only had on trips to the city. It was not luxurious, but they made do, and they spent the majority of their time across the border at the testing facility. A hired chef made them breakfast, lunch, and dinner—blending local cuisine with Western favorites for the North Americans. In his journal, Patrick penned a few lines about the day, highlighting in detail the dessert they'd been served that evening, *Postre de las Tres Leches*. Not going home for another week was the smart move. The video chats he had with Meredith were sustaining, but Patrick missed that extra dimension. It helped to think of Alika dropping off the pictures.

A few minutes later, the lights shut off for the night. Patrick lit a candle. By the quivering flame he brushed his teeth and ensured that his mosquito net had not been compromised. Satisfied, he pulled off his shirt and pants, and slipped into the small single bed. Sleeping beneath a mosquito net had taken some acclimation, but Patrick had come to enjoy the cocoon-like feeling. As he fell asleep, the rich smoke of Noé's tobacco permeated the hut.

It was still dark when he woke. A flashlight shone on the wall and something nudged at his arm. Turning over, Patrick saw the face of Noé hovering ethereally near the net.

"Dr. Simon," he said.

"Noé?" Despite Patrick's repeated protests, Noé still addressed him as *Doctor*. "What is it?"

"Dr. Simon, there is a call for you at the lab."

"What time is it, Noé?"

Half-asleep, Patrick flung aside the net and checked his watch. It was just past 1:00 a.m.

Noé waited outside while Patrick put on some clothes. There was no cell phone service at the camp and the closest signal was at the lab complex. A short-wave radio was set up in case of emergency, making walkie-talkies the prime tool of site communication.

"Do you know what it is?" Patrick asked Noé as he came outside, keen to go back to sleep.

"What it is," Noé repeated. "No sir. The lab call for you to come now."

"They say what it's about?"

"No," Noé said softly. "Just say urgent."

Patrick drove, familiar enough with the roads. He wanted to make this interruption short. It wasn't the first time he'd been summoned to the lab at such an hour. Usually the reason was trivial—calls from the States that should have been taken as messages, night-watchmen who grew wary about experiments running in the lab, and one guard who just liked to practice his English.

Before leaving, Noé convinced him to take two guards along in the open jeep. "Just in case," he reasoned. The guards smelled starkly of cigarette smoke and body odor, and Patrick waited with the engine running as they reluctantly climbed aboard. As fast as possible, he maneuvered out of camp and through the jungle night, down the logging road towards the bridge. It was admittedly a fun drive, especially at night, and more than once Patrick glanced up at the starry firmament above. He wondered what the crisis would be this time; the word *urgent* was a new addition to these midnight messages.

They reached the bridge, the guards absently bouncing along in the front and rear passenger seats. Patrick would have normally spoken with them, but he wanted to focus on the road, and they looked half-comatose anyway. Once across, they were just a few minutes from the lab and Patrick urged the jeep through the hardened ruts left over from the wet season. Despite his hurry, Patrick did not want to crash. A slight incline approached and he slowed to shift.

At first it sounded like raindrops, splatting down from the canopy overhead. Then Patrick saw the flashes along the road. Two sets of headlights flared up from the underbrush. Patrick slammed on the brakes and instinctively ducked his head as gunfire ripped open the windows of the jeep. He felt a hot flash on his left thigh and heard the screams of his passengers. He threw the jeep into reverse and punched the gas. The vehicle roared backwards.

The top of the jeep was open and the two guards were struggling to raise their guns. The one in the front took several bullets to the chest at once and slumped forward against the dash, his gun still on the floor. The guard in the back, already shot twice in the arm, stood in his seat to return fire. He never had a chance, taking a bullet to the neck and sputtering backwards across the roll bar. With his head down, Patrick kept his foot on the gas until the pop and clang of gunfire seemed to taper. Then, raising his head, he hit the brake and cranked the wheel.

The car spun on the gravel, nearly into the underbrush, gripping down just short. Machine gun fire picked up again from the scene of the ambush, and Patrick found himself broadside to the attack. The headlights were beginning to speed in his direction. The thwacking of gunfire pelted the doors and sides of the jeep. The rear-view mirror exploded in a mist of plastic and glass. Patrick shifted into drive, spinning his tires, steering the vehicle back towards the bridge. The border was still a few minutes away. If he reached it, then maybe he'd be safe.

For a few seconds, as Patrick dipped down a slight depression, his pursuers fell from sight. The gunfire stopped. His single remaining headlight traced the same road of minutes past. The sky was still full of stars and the jungle remained. He looked over and back at the dead guards, now bleeding dark red blood onto the floor. Their eyes were open and glazed with wonder. The pain in Patrick's thigh suddenly exploded, and he looked down at more blood, only his own. *What was going on?*

As fast as he could, Patrick barreled back down the road. The gunfire returned when the trucks came over the rise and found his tail lights. He could hear and feel the lead beat into the jeep. With every bump and jolt along the broken road, Patrick cringed. He questioned how far could he make it until they hit the engine, a tire, the gas tank, his head.

The gap between them was slimming, but the bridge was not far. Another volley of shots zipped into the jeep. Several impacted the guard beside him, several passed through the dashboard, and one caught Patrick in the right shoulder. He cried out through the howl of engines and rapping of reports.

Crouched low, his left hand guiding the wheel, his right foot hard on the pedal, Patrick could tell the lead truck was not far behind. He dared not raise his head. The bridge was around two more corners and a straightaway of about 500 yards. At the first corner, Patrick nearly lost control, his left arm not as savvy as his right. The pain in his shoulder was gouging, the nausea stifling. The second corner was slighter and he managed it more fluidly.

With the accelerator flattened to the ground, Patrick skidded onto the straightaway before the bridge, the border in sight. Except something was wrong—the bridge, it was...blocked. Two more sets of headlights sprang to life and illuminated the road in front of Patrick. The stationary pick-ups idled at the foot of the bridge. He was trapped.

Patrick kept his foot hard on the gas, rapidly approaching the roadblock. The lights at the bridge flashed, signaling his fate, while the gunfire from the trailing trucks stopped. Patrick glanced back to see his pursuers slowing to prevent a return into Colombia. Thick jungle rose up sharply on either side of the road and Patrick knew he had little chance of bushwhacking more than a few feet in the jeep. Lucid thoughts about Meredith, Hadley, and his family began to crowd his mind.

Gunfire from the trucks ahead checked his thinking. A few bullets picked through what remained of the front windshield. Patrick winced against the spitting glass. He imagined that there would be little to negotiate with these people, whoever they were. The jeep was just two hundred yards from the bridge and Patrick pressed harder on the accelerator. Perhaps equally irked about being shot up, the jeep responded, waxing higher. The trucks at the bridge were not budging, and several small arms reported from around their spotlights. Patrick held himself low below the dash as gunfire tore through the cab.

Feeling at the door, Patrick gripped the handle and waited. In his mind, he thought of the day Meredith first came home from the hospital. Then, with the lights growing brighter, he pulled the handle on the door and sprung from the speeding jeep.

Chapter 24

March 15th, 2028
Safehouse Five, New York City, New York
9:30 p.m.

They say that when the Devil wants to spread a lie, he'll start by telling a thousand truths. As I observe Meredith from across the table, I can't help wonder if there are comparisons to be made.

The accepted story of the Simon tragedy is fairly straightforward, twisted as any other crime of passion, but logical to follow. The same night as the arson at Hadley's, Korey Devoir was attacked in his home by an unknown number of assailants. After a short struggle, Devoir was overwhelmed, beaten, stabbed, and left to bleed out. A concerned neighbor stopped by to check on the noise and found him unconscious in the living room. Police and an ambulance arrived shortly to the bloody scene, pictures of which ran the following day in every national newspaper. Devoir, aged 40, would die on the ride to the hospital.

The same night in South America, Patrick disappeared from his lodgings at the REI camp. Early the following morning, the research group's personal security detail went searching for him and encountered a military roadblock at the bridge into Colombia. The Colombian officer in charge informed the guards that an attack had taken place on a border patrol unit after they attempted to detain a man driving alone in a jeep—three soldiers had been killed in the man's resulting resistance. The officer provided no further details, besides that the suspect—middle-aged and Caucasian—had eluded capture and was presently being sought.

A joint investigation was launched at the REI camp between the FBI and the Colombian military. Reports on the news showed footage of the research facility. Most of Patrick's colleagues described him as an ordinary, unassuming man: "a great scientist who loved his work"; "quiet and kind"; "kept to himself, but always cordial"; "definitely a thinker". Other reports were less flattering, painting Patrick as a consumed, erratic obsessive who cared only for his experiments. One of the guards said that Patrick had been drinking heavily since his return from the States, and an on-site housekeeper said she was constantly cleaning up liquor bottles and vomit from his bungalow.

Several days after the fire, with Hadley unconscious in hospital, two individuals came forward to the police saying that a week prior they'd been approached for a unique service by someone living abroad. The men, confirmed by authorities as known members of an East Coast crime ring, indicated that the caller had sought to hire them to kill his ex-wife and her lover. Although the men turned down the job and never learned the caller's identity, phone records showed that they had been contacted three times by a number in Colombia. The real aggressors were never found.

I remember the swing vote for me and everyone else was the girl, Meredith. Her story, related by police, was terrifying—hearing her mother's screams, hiding from the hunting intruders, frozen solid with fright beneath a bed as her home burned...who would cause such a thing? Despite the unlikelihood of a single scientist masterminding such a plot and disappearance, the evidence was nonetheless mounting and a warrant was issued for Patrick's immediate capture and detainment. The search for him intensified in Venezuela and Colombia, but it would be weeks before he was seen again.

I stare at Meredith as she takes a drink of water. She knows I'm skeptical, and I want her to believe that too. I want her to try harder to prove her story. In no account, theory, or even conspiracy, was Patrick's attempted assassination by an armed force considered. According to the record, Meredith has just told a lie, and lies in a story this complex are exhausting to maintain. She's jumped off the accepted track, created an alternate reality, and she must proceed to verify that her new detour ultimately, and legitimately, returns to this exact table where we now sit. There must be no loose ends, no historical inaccuracies, the laws of the universe must be completely obeyed, and there must be evidence to show that this new path is indeed the true path. She must show that the way things are has merely been a well-reasoned mirage.

I put my money on the record.

After the fire, did they take you to the same hospital where they took your mother…?

[I flip a page of the report in front of me, looking for the name.]

Hahnemann?

Yes, in Philadelphia. Alika and I had already been treated outside the house, but the paramedics still let both of us go in the helicopter.

Had you told Alika about the men?

I did at the hospital, while we sat in the corridor outside my mother's room. He was constantly dialing my father in South America.

Did he get through?

No.

Any visitors you remember?

A stream of people came throughout the day, although I was asleep for most of them. My grandparents arrived that evening. That's when I knew it was serious.

How did Alika react to your story?

He wasn't surprised. He seemed to know already.

What did he tell you?

The usual for a seven year old: that it was going to be alright, the bad guys wouldn't scare me anymore, not to worry, the police were on our side.

[Killian breathes a single name through my earpiece.]

Do you remember Mr. Prince coming to visit?

Not that first day, but several times after. He'd bring flowers, chat with Alika, give my Mom's hand a squeeze, talk with the doctors…but to be honest, I never really knew Ward. He was a man that always wore a suit—at seven, that was it.

Do you remember changes in your mother?

Nothing stark, but I could tell she wasn't getting better. I knew because the doctors became progressively more uncomfortable during their rounds. Soon after, Alika said we were going to a different hospital.

And your father, did he ever contact you?

All I saw or heard was what you did on the news—Patrick Simon: crazed scientist, jealous ex-husband, at large and afar, suspected of murder.

Chapter 25

December 2011
Washington D.C.

Alika's head rested against the fogged window of the taxi cab. They were idling outside an unassuming office building just north of DuPont Circle in the District. The driver fumbled and pecked at his phone, oblivious to the dilemma of his fare. Raindrops beaded together and made arbitrary road maps across the glass from Alika's face. The *pat-pat* of the rain on the roof had been steady for the twenty minutes they'd been waiting there. Alika bent his head to look at the meter: $24.25 and climbing. Extortion, but he'd allow it.

A pair of homeless men walked by the cab pushing shopping carts, and one of them looked in and winked at Alika. They then loped on down the street, stopping occasionally to peek in a garbage can or to consider an object lying along the ground. Alika watched them until they disappeared. Though the plight of the homeless was a different beast altogether, he could not help but relate his current predicament.

The enemies of the homeless were base, soulless, predictable—hunger, thirst, sickness, weather. Under the constant buffetings of these forces, the homeless learn how to hold their foes at bay, often remaining under siege until rescue or self-destruction. The consequences of defeat are final—death. By contrast, Alika wasn't sure who his enemy was, what they wanted, or if they even existed. Their motivation, his defense, their next move, his strategy, the consequences of failure—all of these were in doubt. What he did feel, fueled by the knot in his stomach, was that there was an adversary working somewhere. The sums weren't adding up, Patrick couldn't have done this.

It had been a month since Patrick's disappearance in Venezuela, Korey's murder, and the fire at Hadley's. Regarding

Patrick, Ward said that REI was doing everything they could to cooperate with the search. Similar to Alika, Ward was still in shock; neither of them could comprehend the sudden vilification of their friend. The media storm had been intense for the first two weeks of the investigation, and both Alika and Ward had regularly been sought for comments and questions. Meredith, too, had been forced to learn about public relations and spotlights. Cameramen waited everywhere, headlines rolled: *Hydrogen Hitmen, Local Editor Suspected Slain by Jealous Ex, Colombia to Philadelphia: Murder My Wife, A Child's Tale of Horror Revealed.*

Although there had been no trial, the circumstantial evidence was already convicting Patrick. Korey's funeral had been held a week after his death, prompting further malice from the public against this mysterious scientist hiding in the jungle. Interviews with former colleagues and friends showed loose proof of Patrick's history of drinking, a clear obsession with work, bitterness over Hadley's new love interest, and tales of a brief confrontation with Devoir before returning to Venezuela. In the eyes of the people, Patrick was a vengeful man, a criminal bent by aspirations to power the world, a menace stressed by his taste for alcohol, a bloodthirsty creature enraged by the broken marriage that he himself had destroyed.

Each rational explanation for Patrick's guilt was a fresh blow to Alika. He lay awake at night wondering what was true, split between accepting and rejecting his friend's authorship of such crimes, turning open questions around in his head—what warning signs had he missed, was it all a big misunderstanding, where would Patrick have gone…why had he snapped now. Alika began to avoid the morning papers and the evening news, focusing on Meredith instead, busying himself with other thoughts so that the possibility of Patrick's betrayal could rarely rest long enough to debate.

Hadley's condition was none better, worse even since the fire. During the past week, she'd been flown by helicopter from Hahnemann University Hospital in Philadelphia to Johns Hopkins in Baltimore. She was still in a coma. Meredith would be driving down from Philadelphia that evening with her Aunt Kylie. She'd be staying with Alika from now on, and he had made up a bed with the same comforter and sheets that she'd had before—navy blue sky with large sparkling stars. He'd perched a note on the pillow.

You must be the brightest star I've ever met.

For all the school that Meredith was missing, REI had arranged a private tutor. His name was Kyle and he was easily the most boring person Alika had ever met; like he'd been born to blend in, a throw pillow. Meredith seemed to feel likewise, but put up with him nonetheless. When he wasn't giving or preparing lessons, Kyle played video games on his computer. Meredith said that when Alika was away, he would shut himself in the bedroom and scream over a headset at the screen. Still, Alika appreciated his presence: he was a nice kid, treated Meredith with respect, and eased the load. At this point, any help was welcome.

Hadley's parents, meanwhile, were staying with friends outside of Baltimore. Anthony and Rose wanted to move Hadley up to a hospital near Boston. Alika understood and had asked them to wait just a few more days while the specialists at Johns Hopkins did what they could. Despite the divorce, Anthony and Rose had never stopped treating Patrick like a son-in-law; Rose especially. Thus they too were slow to judge Patrick as the means for bringing their daughter to the dark edge of mortality, arranging Korey's death, and nearly burning Meredith alive beneath her bed. Yet Alika could tell their fortitude against the adopted direction of the masses was waning. It seemed that one could only struggle so long against the state of affairs. Which was why Alika found himself waiting in a cab north of DuPont Circle, he needed to act fast.

The opposite passenger door opened and a slender, dark-skinned woman slipped in from the rain. She wore a beige coat over a blue blouse, black skirt and stockings. A brisk gust from outside momentarily relieved the cab from the stale scent of aging upholstery.

Alika looked over at her. "We set?" he asked.

Dolores nodded.

"How long?"

"They said about four hours, but give them five. After that, it's on your mark."

Alika checked his watch, considered the skin on his hands, and then leant forward. He gently rapped the interior plastic divider. The cab driver looked up. "DuPont Station," Alika said.

Placing his phone aside, the driver checked his mirrors and turned the car around.

Alika reached over and took Dolores' hand. "Thanks," he said.

They weren't giving up on Patrick yet.

Johns Hopkins Hospital
Baltimore, Maryland

It was dark when Ward arrived at the hospital wing. Stepping from the elevator, he walked a bleak, white hallway towards Hadley's room. Alika sat outside the door reading a book. He looked up as Ward approached.

"How is she?" Ward asked. He held a large bouquet of flowers. The gift shop tag dangled out from the packaging. It was his first visit to the new hospital.

"The same," Alika replied, closing his book. "The nurses said we can go in after they're done. Probably about five minutes." Ward nodded, looking about. He wore a blue pin-striped suit, no tie, shirt collar open.

There were no other chairs in the hallway, so Alika stood and set his book on the chair. "Take a walk?" he suggested. Ward set the flowers on top of the book, Umberto Eco's *The Name of the Rose*, and they set off down the hall. The wing, which formed a square, was quiet, frequented only by a few nurses and evening visitors. Meredith would be arriving shortly from Philadelphia.

Alika caught Ward up to speed on the plans for taking Hadley up to Boston. The specialists at Johns Hopkins had exhausted their techniques, concluding there was nothing more to be done except wait. Hadley had suffered severe head trauma and the doctors were uncertain how long it would take for her to regain consciousness, or if she would wake at all. Ward listened pensively, hands in his pockets.

Over the past month, Alika had done little else besides tend to Hadley, fend off the media bloodhounds, and coordinate with family. Above all, he tried to make life as normal as possible for Meredith. Given the loss of his own family, empathy came easy for Alika. He'd rented an apartment in Bryn Mawr near Meredith's school where Hadley's parents had stayed with her during those first few tempestuous weeks. Only returning to the way things were, even partly, would prove impossible. Meredith's classmates wouldn't stop asking her questions about Patrick, nosy parents buddied up to Anthony and Rose to confirm what they had seen on the news, and paparazzi waited behind mini-vans for when the final bell rang. After just two days, the Hannigans and Alika pulled Meredith back out of school. The girl was struggling to comprehend the degree to which this earthquake had shifted the features of her world. She was quieter than before, jumpy at night, and prone to spending long periods watching the driveway or the door, pretending to read.

"How you holding up?" Ward asked as they reached the end of the first hallway, the beginning of another.

"I'm fine," Alika answered, turning the corner. Outside of a bruise on his shin, he hadn't sustained any lasting injuries.

"Thank heavens for those firemen," Ward said wistfully. "And your mother."

"Yah," said Alika. "We'd have both been goners."

The night of the blaze, Bryn Mawr emergency dispatch received a frantic call from a woman in Salinas, California. She insisted that a particular address was in need of assistance. The fire department arrived at the location minutes later, saving two lives but not the house. Inspectors had promptly confirmed foul play.

"And Meredith, she's healthy and well?"

"On the surface, yeah, she's okay, puts on a strong face. But underneath, I don't know. It's been a nightmare. This is not the kind of shock that goes away overnight."

They walked and watched their shoes. Ward broke the silence.

"Who would take her if…?"

Alika smiled solemnly. "I would."

"You?"

"I'm named as guardian in their will."

"Whew. Did you know that?"

"Nope. It was mighty awkward to tell Hadley's family too. They want to take her up to Boston with Hadley."

"Don't blame them. Is that possible?"

"Sure, I could sign over custody. Probably makes sense."

Ward looked over at him. "But you're not, are you?"

Alika shoved his hands in his pockets and shrugged. They passed a nurse's station.

"You ready to be a father?" Ward asked, peering down what remained of the hallway.

Pulling a hand free from his pocket, Alika rustled at the collar of his shirt. "If it comes to that."

They walked the balance of the hall.

"No news on Patrick," Ward stated. "Beside the junk on the TV."

Alika frowned as they turned the next corner.

A week into the FBI investigation, REI decided that Patrick's project team could continue with their work. Alika had been in touch with Patrick's principal assistant, a Peruvian named Consuela Garcia. Garcia was smart, sassy, and brilliant. They had met at a function in San Francisco when the project first launched. Like most of the true scientists down there, Garcia was perplexed about the allegations against Patrick and eager to have him back. "We don't want to be Magellan's crew," she quipped.

Although they could consistently use magnetic calibrations to knock Hydrogen from its H_2O bond, Garcia and the other staff were having trouble repeating the experiments that Patrick had performed to create regenerating bursts; not quite perpetual energy, but just shy. They had enough evidence to prove that it was possible, but there seemed to be something missing in their procedures; some step that Patrick had performed without them knowing. This had leaked to the papers, prompting strenuous intrigue about the possible sale of technologies to terrorists and enemies of the West. Theories aside, the story had let loose a slew of details about the work Patrick was heading at the facility, and Alika had to admit, it had been healthy for business. The attention was gathering investors and collaborators from all over the world, each lining up for a piece of these semi-clandestine Hydrogen experiments in the jungle. Security was tightened at the lab, and arrangements were already in the works to move anything sensitive to another location, ideally back to the US.

Alika let his legs gradually come to a standstill, allowing Ward to pass. After a few paces, Ward slowed as well, turning back to Alika. They were alone. Windows offered a view of the parking lot to one side, while several propped doors, their occupants unknown, stood ajar on the other. Hadley's room was a hundred feet further on.

"Ward," Alika began. "I'm having trouble understanding."

Ward took a second before speaking, drawn in by Alika's frank expression. "Understanding what?"

"How things connect—the fire, Patrick, Hadley's coma, Korey's murder—I need you to be honest."

"What do you mean?" Ward asked, cocking his head. "Honest about what?

Alika glanced over Ward's shoulder. "About REI."

"REI?"

"REI."

"What about them?"

Alika said nothing.

"What about them?" Ward asked again, narrowing his eyes. Then, in a softer voice, "You think…REI had something to do with this?"

Alika shrugged.

"Come on." Ward set his face. "Really?"

Alika looked at him blankly. "You tell me."

The accusation hung between them. A medical student in scrubs passed by and popped into a nearby room. Ward's body flexed beneath his suit, and dropping his voice, he too stepped closer.

"You think this is some sort of set-up?" Ward asked delicately. "Hadley, Korey, Patrick's disappearance?"

Alika gently inclined his head.

Ward looked over his shoulder, thinking. "You know," he began, "I'll be honest, when I got the news I went straight to our research department. We keep pretty tight to the chatter around anything energy—and I mean anything. Not to ruffle the conspiracists, but people will go to extreme lengths to protect their investments." Ward began to pace. "And on top of that…it just didn't seem…like Patrick."

"No, it didn't," Alika replied, pocketing his hands. He waited for Ward to go on.

"Make no mistake, we're on an ancient battleground, you know that. It's a game of lords and subjects. The setting has moved from the fields and forests to the high-rises and boardrooms, and we wield pens instead of swords, but the primeval hunt for power remains." He paused for the sake of presence, his face forlorn. "This, however, this event with Hadley and Meredith was not a matter of war or battle. No, this was…something else entirely. And as much as I'd like a reason for it all, an explanation from Patrick himself…all these fallen dominoes, they trace a pretty convincing path." Ward unbuttoned his suit. "I just hope we find him soon."

An orderly went by with an empty gurney and asked Ward to keep his voice down. Smiling woefully, he stepped to Alika, placing his hands on the side of the Samoan's thick upper arms. "I suppose when Hadley comes around, we'll know more, but for now, I think we just have to be patient."

Alika stood without expression, breathing deeply. "Did he ever speak with you about his non-profit ideas? The energy company he planned to start."

Ward let go of Alika's arms. "He did, yes. At the wedding in October."

Alika looked hard at Ward. "As you said, this didn't feel right to begin with—the first and last time Patrick did anything even remotely violent was when he pulled Chase Baker off you at The Kingdom over ten years ago. He's not a killer, and never in a million years would he put Meredith in danger. Not to mention he was probably in the best state of his life over the past few months—he was in his element in that lab, he loved it."

"Alika—"

"Now I understand that maybe it's because we just don't want to believe that Patrick *could* do all this, let alone *did*, but what if, Ward, there really is something else going on? His idea for taking his work non-profit holds unprecedented financial implications for the energy world. You and I know the figures—there's trillions at stake here, trillions, rationality and reason shut down at those sums." Alika took a breath. "All I'm saying is that maybe Patrick was set-up, I don't know who or how, but it shouldn't be ruled out. He's not a killer. He wouldn't do this."

Ward took a step closer to Alika. "The non-profit thing, I was worried when I heard it too, but I never told anyone."

"Doesn't mean Patrick didn't. You know him, he doesn't always…"

A humble silence passed between them.

"Look," Ward said, putting a hand on Alika's arm. "I know things have been hectic. Can you get away for a bit this week? Take a break. You've been amazing with Meredith and the family. I'd say you deserve it. If not that, then you might just need it. Always good to get a little recharge. Maybe go somewhere with the Missus? Consider it on the company."

Alika looked down at his shoes, hunting composure. "I appreciate that Ward. I'll think about it."

"Alright," said Ward. "Just a suggestion."

Alika looked down the hallway. The nurses were coming out of Hadley's room. "We can see her now," he said. He went to start walking again, but Ward kept his grip on Alika's canon-sized arm. Alika stopped, considering the hand.

Ward studied him. "If you truly believe there's something else at play here…I can ask around quietly, check again with our analysts…could be that someone got wind of the non-profit idea and got spooked. I can check, but Alika…we may just have to accept and move on."

For an eternal moment, the two men stared at each other. Two nurses passed by in discussion and an elderly couple hobbled past. At length, with a pierced sigh, Alika broke the stare.

"You're right," Alika went on. "It's probably just the stress and, well, trying to make sense of everything—especially Patrick."

Ward nodded, buttoning his suit. "No, I know. I'm trying to figure it out too."

A family approached and the two men stepped aside.

When Meredith walked in the room with her Aunt Kylie, Ward was already gone. Alika sat beside the bed reading his book. Meredith came promptly forward and looked up at her mother, then over to Alika. Immediately after the accident, Meredith had been hesitant, the vessels and beeping monitors throwing a foreign aura about her mother. The cacophony of machinery and tubes could be so confusing. She knew it was Hadley, but there was something transplanted about the familiar face and body. Most distrusting was the large gauze wrap that turbaned the top of Hadley's head. The girl had since adapted and now enjoyed sitting with her on the bed.

This was Meredith's first trip to Johns Hopkins, and Kylie told Alika that she had liked all the brick buildings they had passed on the drive over. Kylie planned to drive home that evening and excused herself to go call Henry.

For the three weeks that Hadley was in Philadelphia, Alika or the Hannigans would bring Meredith into the city for the evening to be her mother. In the beginning it was hard to explain, but the girl now seemed to understand that Hadley was peacefully sleeping, be it a very deep sleep, and that she would soon return. Meredith's quiet spells would break during these sessions, and Alika marveled at how Hadley's presence alone brought her daughter so much peace.

The bed was tall, requiring Meredith to stand on tip-toes to get a good look at Hadley. Alika reached forward and boosted the child up onto the mattress. Meredith began to talk to her mother, telling her about the drive, and what they'd had for dinner at Aunt Kylie's house. She still wore her coat, a puffy yellow North Face that Patrick had bought her. Her hair was up in a ponytail and a few dark locks occasionally escaped down over her eyes. She brushed them away as she talked. There was plenty to catch up on.

Alika pretended to read his book, but thought of Ward and their discussion earlier. He'd been trying to feel Ward out and assess what he may know. The result had been disappointing; Ward was not a book opened at your choosing. Dolores had cautioned Alika against telling anyone else about his thoughts and plans. He supposed he could still change his mind, make a call and wait like Ward had suggested, but there was no denying the significance of his trip wires—two of seven doctors working in Hadley's new ward at Johns Hopkins had been approached by unknown sources seeking silent cooperation. Someone wanted to keep Hadley in a coma.

When Meredith stopped talking, he heard the rustle of her coat as she lay down. Alika looked up to see them; Meredith, huddled against her mother's arm, and Hadley, poised in a pure hush. To break such a sculpture would have been criminal.

"Alika?" Meredith said, her voice muffled by the coat.

"Yes?"

"Can you read to us?"

Alika swallowed. "Of course."

Arlington, Virginia

Alika took the call on his cell phone. He was sleeping on an inflatable mattress in the living room, his bed released to Meredith.

On the line was Hadley's father, Anthony. It was just past 6:00 a.m., and behind the curtains the skyline was brightening.

"Alika?" he said, his accent subdued. "We got a call from the hospital."

"Yeah?" The mattress squawked slightly beneath Alika's weight as he propped himself up.

"Hadley went in the night," said Anthony.

Alika paused, let it sink in. "I'm sorry." He glanced up at Meredith, sound asleep on the recliner. She had migrated there on tip -toes in the middle of the night. A blanket under her arm, thinking Alika asleep, she'd chosen the recliner over the abbreviated couch. It had creaked when she curled up between the worn arms. The recliner was fully extended now, her small blanket replaced with covers and a pillow beneath her head. It had been her father's chair.

Anthony agreed to talk more in person, and Alika suggested that he and Rose come to his place. Anthony said that they would be over as fast as they could. Alika put on a pot of coffee and checked his messages. For an hour he sent e-mails and made calls about Hadley.

At 7:30 a.m. when the Hannigans arrived, Meredith had since woken and fallen back to sleep in the bedroom. The grown-ups sat quietly over coffee in the living room. Anthony and Alika had spoken a lot over the past weeks, touching on terms rarely handled outside bloodlines or marriage. Alika respected Anthony, and Anthony trusted Alika. They decided to wait until after breakfast to tell Meredith.

The funeral, it was agreed, would be held the following weekend in Boston. Alika gently submitted that he would like to pay for the service and burial. The Hannigans were hesitant, but relented. Alika told them he would coordinate with the funeral parlor that Anthony suggested. They asked if there had been any word about Patrick. Alika shook his head.

Upon waking, Meredith was pleasantly surprised to find her grandparents in the living room. Busily, Rose made pancakes with Meredith, creating the batter from scratch. In dichotomy, the men retired with their phones to the bedroom. Standing on either side of the bed, they dialed various family members and friends, announcing the death. For Alika, it was the most conflicting moment of his life.

After Meredith had eaten, Rose brought her down from the kitchen counter to the couches in the living room. Anthony and Alika came through and sat with Meredith.

Alika would remember the moment in frames—Anthony telling Meredith that they all loved her very much—Rose holding Meredith and brushing her long brown hair—tears at the corners of Anthony's eyes—Meredith crying and searching Alika's face—the longing and sorrow painted on her eyes—tear-stained quivering cheeks—silence.

The tears marched for an hour; Anthony and Rose, the parents, grieving with young Meredith, the daughter.

Boston, Massachusetts

The December earth was too cold for a burial. Frozen ground supported the feet of Hadley's friends and family as they entered the church and filled the pews at St. Stephen's. It was where Hadley had been baptized, christened, and now, where she was mourned. The eulogies, given from a podium fronting the closed casket were reliant on hope.

Anthony spoke, as did Hadley's brothers and sisters, each sharing a short story about Hadley. The congregation was at the emotional beck and call of anyone who stood. There was the occasional whisper of Korey and Patrick, but neither were mentioned in the homages.

Meredith was the final speaker. As she walked to the podium, Rose at her side, tears overcame the assembled. Slowly, Meredith read a poem about her mother.

My mother loved me, and I know why.
She taught me to walk, to run, and to fly.

In summer, winter, fall or spring,
Her love would bloom and flowers bring.
By morning, afternoon, or tired night,
Her love would warm, comfort, and bury fright.

At home, at school, or at the park,
Her love gave light to fill the dark.

My mother loves me, and I know how.
Because I love her, and forever shall.

Alika bowed his head with the mourners and wept.

Chapter 26

March 15th, 2028
Safehouse Five, New York City, New York
10:25 p.m.

Conspiracies—I find them boring. I admit that everything is not always as it seems, that degrees of uncertainty exist, deception occurs…but there are limits to interpretation. Hollywood hasn't helped.

When I do come across one, I find myself focusing less on the tale than the individuals who tell it—the creators are what intrigue me. Some are delusional, overstressed by life. Others are chemically biased and perceive things that don't actually exist. Most are attention-seeking, posting stoic pictures of themselves alongside their theories. And sometimes the crafters are in denial, unable or not wanting to believe what lies before or behind them. But this doesn't mean they're quacks. Deciphering a sequence of events has a scientific feel; an allure of mystery that begins with curiosity, grows to interest, matures to passion, and results in obsession. I believe that Meredith, like her father, may have become entrapped within a similar spiral.

It's the same old villains that put me off—multi-national conglomerates, financial firms, "the government"—come on, be creative. In an energy setting such as this, I imagine it will be oil companies, banks, and Senators that made this lovable man disappear. Make no mistake, these theories can be striking—lifting you up by the scruff of your imagination. Indeed, the more interesting the conjured scenario, the more plausible it becomes.

Contrary to the theatrical attack on Patrick, Meredith's account of Hadley's death does not veer too extremely from the accepted truth. Except she's hinting at something beneath the surface, and by the pattern of her revelations, I sense that subtle suggestion will be as far as she goes. It's a smart strategy—letting the listener discover *the truth* on their own terms. That way the answer, right or wrong, becomes harder to wrest away.

Hadley's passing caused another heave of public interest in the Simon story. FBI and Colombian authorities began appearing on TV again to give updates on the fruitless search for Patrick. He had now become a fugitive. A bounty was offered for information leading to his arrest. Officials said that villages and cities alike were all being thoroughly combed. It was possible, they commented, that Patrick may already be dead—to survive this long in the Colombian jungle would require more than a cursory knowledge of the outdoors. REI, meanwhile, moved the ERM project back to the States, abandoning their foreign proving grounds for a growing facility not far from Camp Blanding in Florida. Rumors had begun to gain volume about the potential of this new Hydrogen technology, and although REI insisted that the innovation wasn't ready, public enthusiasm and interest swelled. Beyond the future of energy, this rise in REI's profile also gave the world its first look at Ward Prince. He was very likeable, attractive, and people agreed the spotlight suited him. It would still be another few years until he entered politics.

Back in the interview room, I sense Meredith wants to move on. I stall her instead, firing off a round of inane questions—if you want the truth, fluster the liar.

Are you suggesting that your mother was being sedated?

It would appear that way.

Who do you suppose it was?

Hard to say exactly.

Was she murdered then?

I believe that was everyone's conclusion.

Yes, but was it prompted by something other than complications?

Alika seemed to believe so.

And do you believe so?

Again, it would appear that way.

Have you been in contact with Alika?

From time to time.

Has he ever visited you?

Not recently.

Where is he now?

At the moment, I'm not sure.

[I should go on, but admittedly I'm curious as to what she'll say next. Where did Patrick go for all those months? I try another tactic.]

Would you like a break for the night? We can begin again in the morning.

I'd prefer to continue.

["We are certainly continuing," Killian assures through my earpiece. "Let's move on." I look past Meredith for a second, thinking. I then stand and leave the room. A minute later I return with two cups of coffee and set one down in front of Meredith.]

Sugar and milk?

Fine, thank you.

[We sip the hot coffee in silence. "Come on," says Killian. "This isn't tea time." He's paranoid that we'll lose Meredith if another agency or FBI unit gets word that we have fresh material on Patrick Simon. To be honest, I'm still not convinced that we've been hearing the truth. But *if*—and this is an *if* on a growth spurt—*if* it were to become clear that Meredith is a competent, highly-suggestive witness to her father's disappearance, and that she's hauled along a suitcase full of demonstrable evidence…Then yes, I may shortly be relieved of her care and off to visit my parents in Queens.]

Chapter 27

November 2011
Border of Colombia & Venezuela

Before first light, there was the darkness of the thicket, yet for its thousands of insects and living things, the bush may well have been a city. Local traffic picked up at dawn, rising in parallel with the vaulting sun. Massive thruways cropped up along the ground and numberless exit ramps branched skywards to leafy suburbs. Ants carried loads, spiders inspected leftovers, centipedes bristled along, and beetles scurried. It was a jungle morning, the movement of a single shrub sufficient to provoke years of academic study.

Obstructing the commuters that morning was a new and utterly obtrusive road block. The form, a man, was parked lifeless across all lanes. Unyielding, the versatile bugs simply adopted him into their routes; traveling down his back, over his legs and arms, through the holes in his clothes, and as they saw fit, sampling his fleshy surface.

Patrick awoke on fire. Sunlight clipped through the canopy overhead, illuminating the activity of his surroundings. Without much consideration, he frantically rolled clear of the bush, slapping away handfuls of bugs from his face, neck, and arms. For a few jerking seconds, he struggled and panted. His setting was irrelevant. Legs and miniscule teeth peppered him everywhere. Everywhere.

In the throes of his torment, Patrick suddenly went rigid, tranquilized by final memories of the jeep, sudden shooting pains in his leg, and a volley of voices. Patrick cocked his head against a fern as the ants crawled to safety and the voices came again—male and Spanish. Patrick hesitated to call out. He didn't know where he was.

Adrenaline failing, a deeper ache quickened throughout his every nook. Fighting preference, he hastened back into cover and lay prone.

The center of the bush was largely hollowed out, almost unnaturally. Patrick wondered if an animal lived there, and if so, when it would be home. The events of the previous night were returning and his thoughts zipped to and fro as bees to the hive—Noé at his net, an urgent call, driving down the logging road, flashbulb gunfire, the dead guards, headlights at the bridge…a crash?

Voices came again, this time more distant, and the pain in his left thigh flared like a stove. Starting at the hip, he felt down his sodden pant leg, wincing when he reached the wound. It was at the back of his mid-thigh. Patrick wondered if the bullet had just nicked; that always seemed to happen in the movies. Pricks of pain began to lick at his right shoulder, and tracing again with his left arm, he found the second hit. Both wounds luckily appeared to have clotted. Thinking about it made his head spin.

Rainforest morning choruses continued as Patrick finished his injury inventory, constantly swatting away insects of all shapes and sizes. The lightweight material of his thin khaki pants was shredded and torn every few centimeters, while the plain blue t-shirt he'd thrown on was also slashed and threading. There was another set of burns along his back, and his legs looked like the product of an infomercial knife demonstration. Tiny flies gathered in minute clouds about the drying blood. Patrick knew he needed help, but straying from the hideout meant exposure. 'What of the small army that had chased him the night before?' he questioned. 'Or could these voices be those of rescuers?'

The confusion of the episode and his body-wrenching pain made keeping still impossible. After one bug bite too many, Patrick again rolled clear of the bush. Tensed and alert, the rattle of the forest was deafening. Tall trees of differing species rose up all around, garnished by shrubby growth. Dirt tracks, similar to the one that Patrick now lay in, were unusually prevalent. The little paths wound about trees, bushes, and fallen trunks.

Ahead, fifty feet of embankment inclined towards a road. Patrick assumed it was the one he'd traversed in haste during the night, meaning he was still in Colombia. To his left, he could hear the river. He crawled forward a few feet and waited as more voices came from up the bank. Patrick marveled at how he had managed to get so far from the road. Beyond his final seconds in the jeep, he couldn't remember anything of the night before. There was a scratch of gravel and a truck started.

Patrick knew it would be safer in Venezuela, only if because he'd be closer to the camp. At this point in the year, the river would be low, perhaps fordable. Determining to make for the border, he angled quietly towards the sound of rushing waters, not yet wanting to be known. Although the terrain was navigable and the trees provided convenient cover, Patrick advanced slowly, hobbled by the exquisite pain of blood circulating through a damaged body.

The truck above locked into gear and began to move. Flush against a vine-throttled tree, Patrick peeked up toward the noise. Squinting through the leaves, he could just make out the vehicle's greater form. It was white and two men stood in the bed. Patrick stretched his neck a few inches higher.

A spray of gunfire from the river sent him straight to his knees, body bruised or not. Nearby underbrush gave at the intruding bullets, and the rattle of the emptying clip and chamber took command of the forest. Patrick nervously scanned the bushes and trees before him, shaking with fear. As quickly as it'd started, the shooting stopped. Voices from the road rose up to replace the racket. Patrick pressed himself harder against the base of the trunk, breathing heavy.

Another voice, closer than those from the road, answered the calls with a laugh and another burst of gunfire. Palm leaves cracked, birds lifted off from limbs, and tree trunks popped. Risking all, Patrick chanced a look around the vines to the sound of the smoking gun. There, in a clearing of waist-high ferns, stood a Colombian soldier, his weapon trained on a swath of adjacent jungle. Two other soldiers had come halfway down the embankment and were yelling at him. They too held machine guns. Patrick's Spanish skills were pathetic, but the soldier doing the firing was almost certainly mouthing off at the others, who shook their heads and turned back up towards the truck.

Transfixed by the presence of formal army personnel, Patrick felt momentary relief. These were men that he had associated with. Never on a personal level, but the army had been a great asset in securing arms for the REI guards. A few of them had even come to their 4th of July barbeque. Patrick hadn't given much thought yet to the identity of his attackers, but taking from the stories he'd heard from the guards, they must have been militia kidnappers or extremist rebels. Perhaps they'd even mistaken Patrick for someone else. Whatever the case, these soldiers themselves were obviously looking for him, and by blind reason, Patrick stood and prepared to hail his position.

As he stepped back from the tree, Patrick's pant leg caught on a batch of thorns. Stooping to free himself, he could see the solider a mere 100 feet away. At first, Patrick thought he was just fiddling with his gun, maybe checking its mechanisms; all Patrick's life, firearms had been largely a mystery. Plying away the last of the thorns, Patrick pushed himself up just as the soldier finished reloading his gun and set about releasing an entire clip into the surrounding jungle. Patrick dove back against the tree, several bullets exploding into its bark, the rest tearing through the forest in a terrifying racket.

His body and mind swirling with pain and puzzlement, Patrick wondered if this soldier was not here to rescue, but to hunt. 'Could those have been Colombian troops that attacked him?' If so, there must be some mistake. During the months that Patrick's team had been at the facility, the soldiers had been stand-offish, but responsive, dealing with the Americans when necessary. Patrick surmised that perhaps something diplomatic had happened between the two nations, or the soldiers had thought Patrick was part of FARC or someone illegally crossing the border. Whatever their current agenda, Patrick was not about to open negotiations.

His gun empty again, the soldier spit on the ground and climbed the rest of the incline back to the road. Deciding to keep his presence unknown, Patrick promptly headed for the base of the bridge. He needed to get out of Colombia.

The single span bridge into Venezuela was fairly new, re-built after the drug cartel battles of years past. It was steel framed, 100 yards long, and concrete slabs constituted the deck. Two large piers had been cast at either shore. Patrick aimed his gait toward Colombia's. Every movement felt like someone was jabbing a splintery stake into his leg. The soundtrack of the forest covered the balance of his disruption, and bush to bush, tree to tree, Patrick gimped onward.

After descending a slight depression, he was about fifty yards from the pier. His plan was to reach it, rest, then cross directly beneath the bridge. Once on the other side, he would skirt the road, watching for familiar vehicles to hail, ideally blue jeeps with the REI logo.

As covertly as possible, he continued on. Forty yards, thirty yards, twenty-five…

With no warning, two sets of hands pulled him sharply to the ground. Already void of breath, Patrick could not even cry out as he felt himself being dragged backwards off the trail. Despite the pain it caused, he started to thrash his arms and legs, resisting capture. He strained his eyes to catch the faces of his apprehenders, but twigs and sticks scratched at his face as he was hauled into yet another bush.

Released, Patrick spun around to face his captors. Two small men, one visibly older than the other, knelt before him. Their eyes worked over Patrick, taking in every detail. Their clothes were dark browns and greens, but not military fatigues. The sun had darkened and creased their faces, and Patrick reckoned they were from the more rural provinces. They had nothing except a small satchel, which the younger man wore over his shoulder.

Patrick sat there agape, taking in the two new characters and wondering if he'd wrongly assessed the actions of the army. Maybe that soldier from before had just been testing his weapon, maybe there was something else afoot, Patrick was far from knowing, but in any event he knew he'd rather take his chances with the military over this pair—with the authorities there would be a chance to explain himself. These guys had just dragged him into a bush; surely that was cause for alarm.

With all his remaining energy, Patrick reeled back and cried out. The younger of the two men leapt forward with surprising speed and slapped his palm over Patrick's mouth, stifling his scream. The older man deftly grabbed Patrick's leg at the wound, holding him fast to the ground. Shocked by the suppression, Patrick breathed deeply against the muzzle of the man's hand, feeling lightheaded from the pressure on his leg.

Footsteps intensified from beyond their cover as nearby soldiers responded to Patrick's cry. Voices approached until only paces away, speaking quickly to one another as they scanned the area, a mix of small trees and bushes that fronted the river. This particular bush, Patrick observed, was carved out in a similar fashion to the first and it dawned on him that these were actual hiding places, not animal burrows.

Sticks and twigs snapped as the soldiers approached and Patrick could see their uniforms through the leaves. As soon as they got close enough, he planned to make another effort for attention. Sensing this, the younger man leant forward to Patrick and said something softly in Spanish. Patrick shook his head. The man then tried again in English, saying just four words.

"They will kill you."

Immediately after the words had been spoken, there was a rustling in another bush just fifteen feet from theirs. In sync, two or three guns let loose on the sound, ripping mercilessly through the undergrowth. Another soldier then advanced and Patrick watched as he cautiously inspected the result of their firing. The soldier, short and young, chuckled as he pulled clear the bloodied corpse of a possum-like animal. The other soldiers laughed too as the animal was tossed lifeless onto the ground.

Patrick's heart rattled like a jackhammer.

After considering a few more bushes, the soldiers made their way back up the roadside embankment. Only once they had gone did the younger man remove his hand from Patrick's mouth, leaning back slowly with a look of offered trust. The older one peeked out through the thicket towards the fading voices, then turned and nodded to the other.

With the vicinity clear, Patrick was helped out of the bush. Shocked and unsure, he didn't move at first, lingering in the brush, eyeing the path he'd been taking before towards the bridge.

Sensing his apprehension, the younger man spoke again. His English sounded slightly schooled. "Go fast with us," he whispered. "Safety."

Patrick still didn't move. How could he be sure? Why would these strangers be helping him?

"No time," the man said, looking up at the bridge and the surrounding forest. "Have to go."

Heavily in doubt, Patrick signaled on that he would follow. He could always cross the river further along.

Moving swiftly, they herded him upstream, away from the bridge. After a few hundred yards, the pain in Patrick's leg grew too sharp and he had to stop. The throbbing had begun in the thigh, but now his ankle was producing the brunt of the discomfort. Patrick slumped down against a tree. Immediately, both men came to either side of him and lifted. Patrick cried out as they jostled his right shoulder. They spoke a few hushed words and the younger man ran ahead along the trail. The older man, whom Patrick put at 50, wrapped Patrick's left arm around his neck and insisted they keep moving.

"*Rapido, rapido,*" the older man kept saying.

Patrick, growing evermore weary and puzzled, obeyed. He kept saying they should cross the river here, then there, then over there.

A quarter mile later, the younger man suddenly appeared out of the brush with a wide-looking ladder, except it had crisscrossing rungs and was too short to be a real ladder. The old man brought Patrick alongside and signaled for him to lie down. Patrick, past the point of protest, followed orders, marveling at the convenience of such a readily-available stretcher. The rungs were made of rope, and the chords dug into his flesh as both men shouldered the frame and continued to walk. There was a strange stench to this new vehicle, a mix between rotten meat and salty fish, but the relief in Patrick's ankle made everything else bearable.

Just before he lost consciousness, swaying between the frames of these two anonymous allies, Patrick tried to ask their names. Drool substituted words, and giving up, he put his head back and melted into sleep.

The smell of smoke and dried leaves filled his nostrils. For the second time that day, Patrick woke. Opening his eyes, he saw a thatched roof, and for a moment, thought he was back in the bungalow. Raising himself up, Patrick looked around. The light was dim, but the majority of the room was yet perceptible. He was not in his bungalow.

There was a fire pit and grate in the far corner where a slender shaft of smoke wafted up through a narrow opening in the roof. A darkened light bulb hung bare above his head. The floor was tiled in spots, dirt in others. Several cloths and rags, which could have been clothing, hung on a makeshift drying rack near the fire. Several bags of rice were stowed in the other corner along with a dusty TV set, an empty hammock hung stationary behind him. At his feet, he saw his clothes, torn and bloodied, folded in a neat pile. Only then did he notice that he was naked, his body covered by a single sheet. Beneath him was a motley layer of blankets and woven mats.

Glancing beneath the sheet, happy to see everything in its place, Patrick inspected his thigh. It had been treated and the area was bandaged. His shoulder had also been wrapped, and along his back he felt more bandages, impact wounds from abandoning the kamikaze jeep. Patrick was bemused at his condition and curious about where he was. He thought about trying to get up, but felt his ankle twinge when he shifted; probably broken. He wanted to start piecing together what had happened, where he was, who had helped him, how he could contact the camp.

There was one door to the room; wooden, small, and cracked. It opened now, slowly, and an older woman bent down and came into the hut. Another fire burned beyond the threshold. Night had fallen and the flames were surrounded by several talking shadows. The woman shut the door and came towards Patrick, nonplussed to find him awake. Her skin was dark like the men's. Kneeling beside him, the singularity of the situation seemed to waver, as though Patrick had been her patient for years. Putting her hands up to show she was going to touch him, the woman felt his head and looked at his eyes. She smiled at him, a beautiful beam of security, and patted his forearm. Patrick opened his mouth to speak, but she was up and gone as fast as she'd arrived.

Before the door could shut behind her, the younger of the two men came in. Patrick felt sheepish about his starkness, but the man offered a smile as he knelt. It was like he'd come to visit a small child when their sick in bed. Patrick sat up and shook the man's outstretched hand.

"How are you?" The young man asked at first. He wore a shirt and dark jeans, and his hair was short on the sides, long on top. Apparently his apparel at the bridge was not his usual look.

"Better," Patrick responded, giving a thumbs-up. "Thank you."

The man nodded.

"What is your name?" Patrick asked.

"My name is Jorge," he replied, reaching forward to touch the bandage on Patrick's shoulder. There was a resemblance in his eyes that Patrick couldn't place. "And you are Patrick, Patrick Simon"

The address was unexpected and Patrick felt a chill of concern run through him. He faintly recoiled, fearing this to be a kidnapping. Although if it was, it seemed a very hospitable abduction. Perhaps he had said his name before passing out, he could not quite remember, or maybe there had been something in his pockets, but he'd forgotten his wallet, he had nothing but his clothes…

"How do you know my name?" Patrick asked guardedly

Jorge smiled again. "Noé, he is my brother."

"Your brother," Patrick repeated, absorbing this new information. He had yet to ponder on the role of Noé in this quandary. Patrick wanted to believe that Noé had nothing to do with it, but he wasn't sure—Noé had been the one to send him away unwarned into the dark. "Where is Noé now?"

Jorge checked a ragged Shark watch on his wrist. "He arrive tonight, three or four hours more."

Jorge went on to explain that the older man with him at the bridge was his and Noé's father, Sergio. Both knew little about what was going on, only that Noé had called early that morning to tell them to look for Patrick near the bridge. Noé had said to bring Patrick to safety and that he would come as soon as possible. As to why those soldiers were looking for Patrick, why they appeared so quick to the trigger, neither Jorge nor Sergio knew.

They were in a small village, Patrick learned, on the far outskirts of a city called Bucaramanga, the capital of the Colombian province of Santander. The entire community, Jorge told him, was about 200 strong and descendants of Amerindians. From the point where he collapsed, Jorge and Sergio had carried Patrick for another thirty minutes until they reached their truck. Patrick had slept the whole way back. They were now, Jorge said, about fifty miles from where they had first found him. Their mother, Magdalena, had tended to his ails, and Jorge gave Patrick a list of the injuries. He had been shot twice—once in the thigh, once in the shoulder—he had extensive cuts and scrapes on his back and legs, his ankle was broken, and he likely had a few broken ribs.

"You will be okay," Jorge affirmed. He was twenty-seven, five years younger than Patrick. "But you must rest. My mother will bring food and clothes."

"Do you have a phone that I could borrow?" Patrick asked as the door opened and the older man, Sergio came inside.

Gathering from his son that Patrick was well, Sergio reached into his pocket and pulled out what looked like a contorted button. He handed it to Patrick.

"The bullet in your leg," Jorge said with a grin. "For good luck."

After he'd eaten a bowl of rice and meat, the consistency of which was unusual—a seafood taste with the texture of chicken breast—Jorge returned with an old Nokia cell phone. As Patrick looked at the dialing pad, it occurred to him that he knew very few numbers by heart—there was Hadley's cell phone number, his own number, the number at the family house in West Chester, and a few landline numbers of his friends from when he was a boy. Upon arriving in South America, REI had given Patrick and his team a special distress number to call in the event they were in danger. Like everyone else, Patrick had saved the number into his phone, not thinking he'd ever need to memorize it.

Excluding the last batch from his childhood, Patrick called the first three remembered numbers in succession. Hadley's went straight to voice mail, as did his own. The house number just rang. He debated leaving a message for Hadley, but wasn't sure how to sum up what had happened. The spinning in his head had lessened, but he felt like he hadn't slept in days. When the beep came, he hung up, deciding to call back later that evening once Noé arrived. He assumed he would know more by then and perhaps even be able to go back to camp.

Patrick did not remember falling asleep, but when he next opened his eyes, Jorge had practically dragged him to his feet and out a small door near the back of the circular house. There were loud noises and shouting coming from beyond the walls

Jorge spoke harshly into his ear. "Have to go! Have to go!"

As Patrick began to limp along with Jorge, Magdalena entered in a hurry through the front door and began to put away Patrick's bed and clear away his clothes. The sound of trucks and the flash of lights worked their way through cracks in the roof and along the walls. Exiting through the small door, Patrick turned back to see Magdalena burying scraps of his old clothes in a bag of rice.

Entering into the cool night, Patrick got a brief look at the village, a series of small concrete huts and thatched homes, some with corrugated metal roofs. Power lines spindled and wound from one house to the next and there were some lights on. He and Jorge weaved around one or two such homes until reaching an open field that looked lightly cultivated. Across the field, the jungle rose up like a wall. The throbbing in his ankle was returning with haste. He wore a pair of old jeans and a thin green t-shirt.

Stopping briefly to look around, Jorge pulled Patrick into the open, nipping at him with bits of spirited Spanish and English to move faster. There was more shouting and a single shot was fired into the air as they reached the tree line and Jorge yanked Patrick down a slim path into the darkness of the forest. Noises of nocturnal life picked up to cover the retreating yells and flashes of light at the village. Patrick winced from the pain in his ankle, thigh, and ribs. Damp ferns and leaves brushed at his body as Jorge led him deeper. The reality that he was awake and being spirited away again landed on him suddenly. Questions about where he was and how he could trust Jorge circled in his head. Certainly the lights and shouting at the village had been about Patrick.

As Patrick made to stop and ask Jorge what was going on, Jorge pulled him sharply off the trail and down a less traveled route that opened up to a small clearing and another hut, less adorned than the others from before and with no windows. Without hesitation, Jorge threw open the door and pulled Patrick inside. As they entered, Patrick doubled over, not from any pain to his body, but from the smell. It was one of the most pungent odors he had ever encountered; the musk of death, rotting, salt, and age pooled together.

"Over here," Jorge commanded. "Lie down."

"Where are we?" Patrick hissed back, not moving immediately. He wanted to know where the smell was coming from, what it was. With no windows, the hut was completely dark.

"No time," Jorge said again in a whisper. "You must hide."

"But where are—."

"Shoosh!" Jorge said, putting a hand through the blackness to grab Patrick's arm. The sound of dogs barking began low and grew louder from outside the hut. "Hurry," Jorge said again quietly, pulling Patrick deeper into the hut. "Lie down here."

"I don't—"

"Shoosh!" Voices were joining the approaching dogs in their proximity.

Jorge then grabbed Patrick, swept a leg against his ankles and dropped Patrick to the ground. As Patrick went to stand, he felt something heavy land on top of him, pressing his body down to the wooden-planked floor. The stench magnified ten-fold as Patrick felt Jorge wrapping this mass around him as if it were a rigid, thick coat. Nausea roared in his stomach as Patrick felt another weight come down on him. He was pinned inside something, the inside of which was dry against the back of his neck. His breath came in gasps, burdened by his trap and the odor.

Patrick heard Jorge go to the door and open it. The dog barks were now very near, but muffled by his covering. Light shone into the hut and with his head so close to the floorboards Patrick could distinguish several sets of feet enter the hut and begin talking loudly with Jorge, the scratch of paws was evident too, and now the dogs were howling, even pushing at whatever it was that blanketed Patrick. The flashlights gave a slight glow to where Patrick lay, but the ambience did nothing to indicate where he was, and what was giving off that crooked smell.

Patrick thought about crying out. He was so bewildered. He had never functioned under such circumstances. There was no doubt this search was over him and it was likely the army again. He thought back to the soldiers' actions at the bridge, blowing away the possum in the adjacent bush. Perhaps that was explainable and this was REI stepping in to help him.

As Patrick prepared to make his presence known, another set of feet entered the scene. The shouting stopped and the dogs left the hut. Barely perceptible, Patrick could just make out voices speaking. There was then a shuffle of feet, the lights fell away, and Patrick felt himself being left alone in the dark, dreadful hut.

Dizzy with exhaustion, sickness, and pain, Patrick pushed with all his might against the weights on top of him, thrusting his back into the air. He could feel the cuts on his back re-open and grow wet with blood against his shirt. The intermittent piercing in his shoulder and legs was now constant, as if his flesh were being ripped from the wound. Swaying slightly, Patrick managed to achieve some back-and-forth momentum in the weight, and with an applied pressure that brought him to the brink of consciousness, he felt the mass begin to slide clear, tumbling to the side. Shrugging off the last of these repugnant duvets, Patrick pulled himself clear and staggered towards where he thought the door was, his arms out in front of him. Several steps into the darkness, he fell to his knees and began to retch, heaving clear what little rice and beans he'd managed to consume earlier.

Convinced that this was the end and that he could withstand not another prick of pain, Patrick made a final effort to find the door, crawling forward through his vomit. As he did so, he felt a rush of air on his face. The door had opened. A flashlight shone in through the space, illuminating Patrick's sorry state. Above him, the man with the light, Noé, stood aghast in the doorway.

Before passing out, Patrick did two things: he looked at Noé, grateful and afraid, and then turned back to face the depths of the hut. Patrick then reeled in horror, crying out at the display—dozens of crocodiles, empty and hollow, stacked on shelves and on the floor, all of them staring lifelessly forward.

There was a lot of explaining when Patrick returned to consciousness.

After Jorge had buried Patrick beneath a mound of curing crocodile skins, the soldiers had tracked Patrick with the dogs, using the scent of clothes recovered from his REI bungalow. Jorge had held them at the door, saying that the dogs were merely attracted to the smell of the crocodiles. The soldiers may well have found Patrick if Noé had not arrived to intervene with several bank notes.

He had since been brought to another hut, one where Noé, his family, and other men from the village used to dry their crocodile skins—which operation had since been relocated to where Patrick had been hidden. There were still remnants of a smell, but nothing to the extent of what Patrick had just experienced. For the balance of the night, Patrick and Noé sat at a fire outside the hut and discussed what they knew. Noé went first.

Shortly before the ambush, Noé said he had been radioed at his post about a call for Patrick. Once seeing him off, Noé had gone about his duties as usual. When Patrick failed to return, Noé said he'd grown wary and radioed the guard in charge of camp-to-lab communication. This guard contacted the lab and learned that Patrick had never arrived. Noé immediately took a jeep to look for Patrick, trying in vain to reach the radios of the two ride-along guards. This was around 3:00 a.m.—almost two hours after Patrick's departure.

In the morning dark, military trucks blocked the bridge. They told Noé there had been an accident and that he could not cross. When Noé demanded to be let through, the military backed him down at gunpoint. Radioing back to the camp, Noé asked the on-site lab guards to begin down the road from the opposite direction. They too were met shortly before the bridge by another blockade of military personnel.

When Noé asked how long the road block had been up, the officer in charge replied that the bridge had been blocked for nearly four hours, and that no one had been allowed to cross during that time. Noé had racked his brain about other routes that Patrick might have taken, but not knowing any, drove deeper into Venezuela until he could get cell phone service. At around 4:00 a.m., he called his brother and asked for someone to go look for Patrick. He was certain that something was wrong.

Morning came and a full search began all along the road throughout Venezuela. When they tried to expand their investigation into Colombia, the military prevented them, saying that they would be leading the investigation. This was when Noé learned that three border patrol soldiers had been killed and that the suspect at large was a middle-aged white man. The Venezuelan National Guard had been asked to join the search as well, and roadblocks were already being set up on both sides of the border.

"They think I killed three men?" Patrick interrupted. "But how? They were the ones shooting." The likely answer, however, soon occurred to him—the collision of the speeding jeep.

Patrick then re-told his version of the story, from the attack to the crocodile hut. As he spoke, Patrick felt a taut tension building between his temples. He wondered for the first time if perhaps the situation was not just a misunderstanding, if it had been deliberate.

Along with Noé, most of the REI guards were participating in the search. He said the military had requested him to meet in the city of Bucaramanga the next morning—most likely on account of his closeness to Patrick.

"What about the guards?" Patrick asked, describing how they'd been slaughtered alongside him.

"Both are missing," said Noé, concerned. "But those two go missing a lot. One of them…he is trouble."

Patrick rubbed at his eyes. He was exhausted and overwhelmed, and his mind felt like it was slowing down.

"I must go soon," said Noé, dawn approaching. "Like I said, they are expecting me."

"When will you come back?" asked Patrick.

"I don't know. Soon. Have you used a phone?"

"Yes," Patrick said. "I tried to call my…family. But didn't get through, why?"

"I think this is why we came here."

"The call? No, I doubt the Army could do that…I mean I don't know, but it seems…unlikely."

"I don't know why we came here," said Noé, shaking his head. "Maybe someone see you."

"What will they do if they find me, the Army?" Patrick asked. "I'm not Colombian, can they...?"

"I don't know," said Noé. "I have not been back to the camp, but I hear that more Americans coming. If they are here to help, I tell them about you."

"But the guards and the operator can show how I left the camp for the phone call," said Patrick with a look of hope. "If you think it's safe, you can tell them where I am."

Noé nodded. "Okay, I will."

A silence passed, the red coals in the fire pulsing like organs. Patrick looked back at the hut and then to Noé. "What's with the... alligators?"

Noé smiled. "They are crocodile."

Noé had once told Patrick that the men of his village worked 'in the fields.' Patrick reasonably assumed this meant they were farmers of some sort, and given the cash crop of the region, he figured they grew coca or poppies. He never asked.

"It is what we do," Noé explained. "We hunt crocodile."

They were poachers, hunting caiman crocodiles in the nearby marshes and rivers. For many years, Noé's village had survived under this trade. They made their living by selling the skins over the border in Venezuela. Noé said he never told Patrick because he feared his misgivings, his Western opinions. Patrick admitted that he had been raised to think of poachers as evil men stalking the woods, plundering the animal kingdom. The way Noé put it: they worked just like farmers, tending their quarry like a herd of cattle.

The demand for skins had always been healthy and had hit a peak in the 1960's. But over the past few decades, it had become harder to find buyers. They were all being shut down. Furthermore, when crocodile hunting had been made illegal, men were hired to poach the poachers. Noé and Jorge had lost an elder brother this way.

Noé said he understood that people were afraid the crocodiles would disappear, and he admired that some would care so much about something they would probably never see. But Noé did not understand why his village would allow the crocodiles to be pushed into extinction. The caimans were their livelihood, and besides, they weren't always hunting. The village kept crop fields as well; these serving a dual purpose—part-subsistence, part-alibi.

Before Noé left, it was determined that Patrick would wait there at the hut for his return. Noé was cautious about taking Patrick back to the camp, he said that Colombian soldiers were swarmed along the border, Venezuelan troops were in the camp and it would be pointless to take him back there. Their best chance was to let someone at REI know what had happened and trust they would come to his rescue.

What made Patrick most uncomfortable was if the Colombian soldiers had found him based on the calls he had made with Jorge's cell phone. Surely their investigation did not extend to tracing calls made to specific numbers outside their territory. As far as Patrick knew, this required advanced technology and intelligence, meaning that there would have to be cooperation in the States as well...It seemed like a reach, but Patrick nonetheless agreed with Noé to stay put and off the airwaves until the picture became clearer. Patrick injuries were still severe enough to limit him from traveling long distances, and it would be several weeks until his ankles and ribs healed sufficiently. If Americans were arriving at the camp, Patrick expected that more rational interventions could be made, and with Noé on the case it would surely be a matter of days.

Two weeks later

Patrick sat alone by a small fire outside his hut. It was not dark and there was time yet to watch the sky turn into a starry looking-glass. There was a narrow opening of canopy overhead, created Patrick assumed when this humble plot had been cleared. He scratched at the thickening stubble on his face and prodded at the coals with a stick. A high-pitched howl from the dense forest around him, perhaps the scream of a monkey, prompted Patrick to stand and begin to smother the fire before him. It was time to go inside.

During his first few days outside the village, Patrick had been desperate to leave, fearing every minute for his safety and his families' peace of mind, watching and waiting for Noé's return. After his old bodyguard failed to return, Jorge came to Patrick with a cryptic message from Noé –*be patient, let pieces develop*. It was a chess metaphor, one that Noé had told him often during their matches, and Patrick could only assume that more time was required. That had been ten days ago.

When the delay stretched on, Patrick's fear turned to frustration. He slept a lot, his body requiring the rest to achieve the right degree of healing. His bed was either in a hammock or on the floor with an arrangement of blankets and thin mattresses. He was given a wooden crutch to get around. By its height, it had clearly been custom made for him. Three times a day, Magdalena brought him a basket of food and a jug of boiled water. His bathroom was around the back of the hut, a hole he had dug at the woods' edge with his crutch.

As he recovered, Patrick never strayed far from the hut. The jungle was not a safe place to stroll and the constant sense that he was being watched or stalked reminded him of his father's stories about Vietnam. Given the time of year and shade of the canopy, the temperature never grew too hot, but if it rained, the humidity and mosquitoes raged. Jorge brought out an old can of bug repellent that Patrick guessed was at least fifteen years old.

In the scramble after the ambush, Noé had been able to bring only one of Patrick's possessions, his journal. He'd taken it from the bungalow just before a Venezuelan police unit had arrived to assist with the search effort. Patrick was grateful for the distraction, as writing enabled him to flee his present setting. Given that his whole day was downtime, he spent many hours recalling the details of his afflictions. As Patrick was very much a technical writer, he crafted the record like a report; objective, third-person, structured. He did not begin with the events of the ambush, nor his arrival in South America, but returned instead to the source of his work—the lightning-blasted tree on Pleasance Point. Noting feelings and opinions where he could, Patrick traced the switch-points of life, from his youth and on to that very hut. It was a detached autobiography.

In the mornings, Magdalena would usually wake him, sneaking up with his breakfast and water. Patrick would then write until midday, when more food would be brought. In the early afternoon, he would enjoy inspecting the nearby plant and animal life. It was like living amongst a zoo exhibit, immersed in plenteous biodiversity. Occasionally, he'd hobble back inside to safety if he sensed anything large approaching. Though he had survived much, the beauty around him was not free of danger. Spiders and insects occasionally managed to breach the hut, and more than once, Patrick lay awake in the darkness as intimidating hooves and paws paced around his walls; comfort did not come easy.

Jorge would visit in the evenings, sometimes with Sergio too, ever-cautious that Patrick not be discovered. They would bring a bucket of water for Patrick to use for bathing. The company was relieving to Patrick's solitude. More than once he feared that his relative isolation, the infected feeling of his living conditions, was going to his head; how could he judge his own sanity without a reference point?

After he was left alone for the night, the English lessons for Jorge over, Patrick would retire into the hut, reclining on the hammock and continuing to write by candlelight. He never went to the village, never left the plot of the hut, and never saw or heard anyone but Noé's family and the non-human residents of the jungle.

As time passed, Patrick grew more comfortable with this remote routine. Still, the thought often crossed his mind that Noé and his family had ulterior motives for keeping him stowed away like this. The suspicions came ashamedly in the night as he lay on his mat listening to the sounds of the forest; it was when he did the bulk of his thinking. Above all, he feared the puzzle of his attack. He agonized over Meredith, Hadley, and Alika; they would naturally be concerned over his sudden disappearance and unusual accusations. He regretted not leaving Hadley a message to explain everything.

Patrick knew that if he decided to contact REI, they would instantly be able to find him. He wondered as to why Noé was taking so long, if he'd been unable to find someone to tell about Patrick or if Noé was actually on his side at all. His speculations knew no bounds, revolving often about the credibility of his employer—could REI have been involved? It was the issue of motives that Patrick couldn't determine—if this was a setup, what was the play? The obvious answer was that someone wanted to take his technologies. Except the technology was not finished, and there were elements of the design that only Patrick knew. He was not demanding large sums of money for his discoveries either, nor had he ever shown a desire to become a Rockefeller. If anything, he would be aiming to make less money through his own energy company, the non-profit outfit.

Whoever the enemy, or whatever the mistake, the military was out to find him. Patrick knew nothing of extradition laws, but by common sense, it made sense that if he was convicted for the killing of Colombians, then the Colombians could choose his fate. Thus if he was to leave Colombia, it would have to be in secret.

Three weeks later
New Year's Eve, 2011

Patrick sat by another fire, plotting.

It had been over a month since the attack and his seclusion—his beard was full and his hair the longest it had ever been. Noé had sent several more messages, as cryptic as the first— *will continue our game soon – must protect pieces still left – the king is best held back.* From Noé's brevity and indirectness, Patrick took little comfort, growing distrustful and distant from Jorge and Magdalena. Was it all an act? Were they keeping him alive and hidden for other reasons? Why were they helping him, a man they'd never met?

The waiting had gone on too long. He was tired of staying hidden, surely his disappearance could do little for his case of innocence—this had not occurred to him immediately. Noé soon became the blame for all of Patrick's woes; it was his bodyguard's fault, all of this. If he'd just hailed the soldier peacefully by the bridge, if he'd managed to cry out when they came searching for him there, if he'd decided to leave this hut sooner...

His journal was full now, front and back, overflowing with extra pieces of paper that Jorge had brought him in supplement. He'd burned through over a dozen pens. He was exhausted by the absolute ignorance of his situation and had decided not to stay. The next day, after Magdalena had brought him his lunch, he planned to follow her back and make his escape. The men would be gone and Jorge had described how most of the village slept during the high heat of the afternoon.

Stoking the fire, preparing to put it out again, Patrick heard something moving along the path. Jorge had already come and gone for the night, and no one ever visited him this late. Patrick usually would have retreated to the hut, or dashed around to wait in the bushes, but he waited instead. He was tired of hiding, whoever it was, he would meet them. His ears were now well-tuned to the difference in the steps of a human and the stride of an animal, and the sound approaching was undoubtedly human.

Patrick stood, no longer needing a crutch, the fire glowing at his feet. If it was a foe, he had nothing to defend himself, only hands and a suppressed sense of freedom—and he was half-hoping to employ both. As the form of a man cleared the jungle path and entered the clearing, Patrick still wasn't sure if he should attack. It was Noé.

They stared at one another, both with set faces. Patrick had imagined Noé's return in a hundred ways, but never had he imagined Noé to carry a face so grave.

"Where have you been?" Patrick asked, almost in accusation.

"I am sorry," said Noé. He hadn't moved from the spot where he'd entered the clearing. "I was kept away."

"Yes, I know."

Noé noticed the fists in Patrick's hands. "You must let me tell why. I know it was long. But…I could not return."

Broken as he was by the experience, Patrick wanted to both repudiate and believe the old guard. He was so tired. "How can I trust you? How can I trust you when you left for me so long out here? You sent nothing but short messages that said nothing."

"I know," said Noé, taking a few steps closer. "Please, I explain." He held up his hands for Patrick, his face straining with honesty. "Please, Patrick, listen." Noé's look was one Patrick had seen before. It was a countenance of sincerity, the one Noé held every time he beat Patrick in chess, as though handing him a bough of respect.

Patrick relaxed slightly and sat down, pointing rudely to the rock where Jorge had sat earlier that evening.

Noé sat, pulling several sheets of newspaper from his pocket and holding them in his lap. He looked across the fire at Patrick, their faces sparked by the dance of flames.

After Noé had left Patrick, he had gone to Bucaramanga to meet with the army. There he met the same border patrol unit that had been at the bridge the morning Patrick went missing. No other REI personnel were present. Noé was taken to a small interview room at a local barracks and told to wait. After an hour, two men entered and sat down. They were Colombian, but not military. Without showing any identification, they asked Noé why his brother had made three phone calls to the United States the night before. The two men were dressed in casual clothes, loose-fitting, and spoke with neutral accents; little about them was distinguishing.

With his best chess face, Noé took a deep breath and confessed that he had asked Jorge, his brother, to make the calls. Noé explained that Patrick was his friend and he had worried for his safety. Having Patrick's mobile at the REI camp, Noé had picked several numbers to call, all of which his brother dialed.

Noé never knew who the two men were, as they left the room immediately after he gave his answer. Later, one of the soldiers told

Noé that the men were American spies. Noé was never sure; there were a lot of American spies in his country.

Patrick sat wide-eyed across the fire listening.

With the first interview over, the Lieutenant responsible for the border patrol unit entered the room. His name was Luis Escobar, and Noé had seen him several times at the bridge and the REI lab. He was a handsome man, clean shaven, and kept a silver-plated pistol in a well-displayed holster. Escobar asked Noé to relate his story about how Patrick had disappeared. Once Noé had finished, Escobar leaned back in his chair and lit a cigarette. He smoked it to the smallest of butts and then flicked it on the concrete floor.

"Do you love your family?" Escobar asked in Spanish.

"Of course," Noé replied.

"What would you do for them?"

Noé shifted in his seat, sweat building at his collar like water behind a dam. "Anything."

Escobar stood and straightened his uniform. "Good, then you will never repeat your story again. Is this understood?"

Noé swallowed.

The Lieutenant looked down at him with determined eyes. "Have I been clear?"

Noé nodded. "Yes."

Escobar then left and Noé was escorted back to the bridge to continue with the search. From then on, members of the border patrol unit were never far away. FBI investigation teams soon arrived at the camp. News cameramen and journalists appeared in vans and jeeps to document the story. All the REI guards, even the operator that had sent the *urgent* message for Patrick, changed their stories to match an official version of events—Patrick had left in the middle of the night, been hailed by a Colombian border patrol unit, and his attempt to escape detainment had resulted in the death of three soldiers. The two guards reported missing on the same night as Patrick were found dead in an unrelated dispute outside the city of Cucuta; an apparent drug deal gone sour. There were the stories coming from the US too—Patrick's ex-wife and daughter had been attacked in their home, rendering the ex-wife in a coma, and her present lover had been stabbed to death at his own home—foul play was suspected. Noé could only stand by and watch. In this hurricane of stories, who could be trusted?

After one month of searching, the accepted conclusion was that the jungle had executed her own justice on Patrick. The setting was too remote, too unforgiving, too untamed for the common man to survive. Without their project leader, REI packed up the lab after Christmas and moved the operation back to the United States. The journalists had left long before, as well as the FBI teams, and the guards and staff members were allowed to go home with their final wages—Noé included.

Patrick sat on the rock with his mouth open, shoulders hunched, his hands clasped and dangling between his knees. When he spoke, his voice was low and weak. "What about my family? What happened to Hadley?"

Noé paused and looked at the fire, aware that he would be the first to tell Patrick.

"Have you heard anything of them?" Patrick asked again, his volume rising.

Again, Noé hesitated.

Patrick saw it. "Tell me, Noé! What happened to Hadley!" he demanded, apprehension mounting.

"I'm sorry," the guard said.

"What is it?"

"Hadley, she is passed."

Patrick's soul wrenched. "How?"

"They say you did it," explained Noé, the reluctant messenger. "You organize murder."

"How long ago?"

"I don't know, not long, a few days. There was a fire."

"A fire…" Patrick said with horror. "And Meredith, my daughter?"

"I think she is okay, I don't know much more. But Americans look for you too—say you kill wife and her lover. Here..." Noé handed him the clippings, all from English newspapers. *Simon Family Tragedy; Editor Dies of Stab Wounds; Hydrogen Zealot Still At Large in Jungle; Simon: "He was an angry drunk"; A Little Girl's Worst Nightmare; Simon Death-Toll Rising.*

For all the numbness that Patrick had felt living in a remote Colombian village with gunshot wounds, broken bones, and tortuous uncertainty, nothing compared to the shock and torment that encased him over the next few hours. Hadley was dead, Korey was too, and Meredith…he just wanted to be with her. Though he had run scenario after scenario through his mind, this was bitter magnitudes worse than any of his myriad imaginings. Hadley was gone and he was being blamed. The entire night, he read the newspaper clippings, examining every word. Poison though it was, he could not remove the cup from his lips—over and over he read the crude depictions of himself, studied the horrifying ordeals, and stared into the crinkled photos of those he loved most. Anger swelled with tsunami-like stature in his breast and tears escaped his eyes in droves. He did not sleep a single minute.

The following morning, New Year's Day, Patrick left the crocodile hut. Bidding farewell to Magdalena, Jorge, and Sergio, he hugged them all tightly before jumping in Noé's truck. There would be no more waiting; he would swim the Gulf of Mexico if it meant being with Meredith.

Within three hours, he and Noé reached Bucaramanga. They drove straight to the bus station, arriving around midday. Bucaramanga was much like other places Patrick had visited in South America; low-slung in height, terraced windows, a pitter-patter of nice tiled homes between rotting colonial-era tinder boxes. Noé said the region was known for its petroleum companies. They hadn't spoken much on the drive, Patrick lost in thought about Hadley and Meredith. Noé had few more details.

From Bucaramanga, Patrick's plan was to get a bus to Bogotá and head straight for the US Embassy. If they arrested him, then at least he would have a chance to give his story.

At the station, Noé paid for Patrick's ticket, giving him more money for food and lodging in Bogotá. He gave Patrick his cell phone number and waited with him until the bus came. They sat in Noé's truck and ate warm *arepas* from a food stand near the station.

Various tourists busied themselves about the city and Patrick found it odd to think that people vacationed there. He still had a limp and wore a pair of Jorge's clothes—denim jeans and a tight green FCUK t-shirt beneath a gray hooded sweatshirt. Over his left shoulder he carried a small brown backpack with some food and his journal. They had passed few army vehicles during the trip, and here as well, it seemed as though there would be little problem for Patrick to reach the capital. A report on the radio briefly mentioned that Patrick had yet to be found and was suspected to have perished in the wild. Noé told Patrick not to worry, just to get to the Embassy—if he was to be caught by anyone, let it be his own countrymen.

Walking to the bus, Patrick caught his reflection in the shiny metal of its siding. The rough beard, the scruffy hair, and foremost, the trial and heartache had rendered him a new man.

Before boarding, he turned and thanked Noé, embracing his guard.

"Vaya con Dios," Noé wished.

As he climbed the steps, avoiding eye contact with the bus driver, Patrick fumbled with the bullet in his pocket.

Chapter 28

January 2012
Arlington, Virginia

Alika waited in line for his coffee. The shop was a busy place at that hour of the morning, just before nine. Many of the faces were familiar to Alika, but only a handful ever made small talk. Most were keen to a perception, their morning-business aura. Obviously they were up to something important that day, as the only words they spared were for the barista.

The offices rented by REI for Alika and his growing staff were on the 15th floor of a high-rise office tower in Arlington. The coffee shop was in the atrium, allowing Alika to avoid a return into the January frost. Holiday decorations still hung around the building, and a large Christmas tree sat merrily at the center of the hall; it was a Monday, the second day of the new year.

After leaving the shop with his Regular Tall, Alika crossed the tiled floors, stepped alone into the elevator, and whistled upwards. There were a few calls that needed attention and a staff meeting to lead at ten, but little else remained for Alika to think about besides the Seven Energy deal. The paperwork had been examined down to the watermark and was to be signed in two days. Alika would be representing a small company named Green Equator, an entity that was little more than a name for the ERM technology to be sold under. At the outset, Alika and Patrick had acted as independent contractors receiving funding from REI. Green Equator was created to be a middle man for the middle man, channeling money back to REI and its investors.

Seven Energy was also a relatively new member of the world energy court. With headquarters in Singapore, Seven was a true multi -national company, with no fixed ties to any particular country or government. Their founding capital had been pooled in the late 1980's, consisting of investors from all over the world. With the fall of the Soviet Union, Seven made its first windfall with contracts for Russian pipelines and natural gas, and in the mid-90's, their Initial Public Offering for stock was the largest in over a decade. From there, they branched out in several different directions, operating offshore oil rigs along the coast of West Africa, working in the Canadian tar sands, drilling for gas in the Marcellus Shale, and cashing in on renewable energy tariffs across the European Union with wind and solar projects. Their portfolio was almost more diverse than REI's, and although Seven was known to take risks, the winning horse didn't always return to their stables. There were failed investments on geothermal and marine energy start-ups, as well as oil fields in the Middle East that had become battlefields instead, but with Seven's size, it could almost afford these hiccups. This deal with REI and Green Equator would be their first foray into Hydrogen energy, and with Seven's reputation, it was likely that more firms would soon follow.

The suite for Alika's Green Equator team in Arlington had four offices, a lounge, and a conference room. In the year that they'd been there, it had rapidly become too small for Alika and his recruits. There was an office for him and an office for Patrick. Another office was filled with a pair of full-time marketing graduates, whom Alika had hired straight from an employee expo down at Georgetown. Then there was the small army of receptionists that were camped in the largest office, the lounge, and occasionally the conference room. Except these weren't your run-of-the-mill secretaries; Alika had a way of meeting unemployed savants. These "receptionists" ranged from disillusioned law school grads, aspiring actresses with accounting degrees, even a bartender with contract writing experience. Thus, by karma, or simply good conversation-making, Alika had acquired an oddly elite office.

With his calls returned and coffee drained, Alika turned towards the daily assault on his Inbox. It took surprisingly long to reply to e-mails, even the ones that required just a few sentences.

Sunk in an automated zone of coordinating and answering questions, Alika's eyes were still fixated on the screen when his secretary, a Davidson grad with flawless writing skills and a dry humor to match Alika's, popped in to say he was late for his own staff meeting. Alika checked the time, it was 10:10. He promised to be right there. The secretary said she'd stall his audience.

As he was leaving the room, Alika's phone buzzed on his hip. The number was long, but without much thought, Alika knew it was Colombian. He'd grown used to the country code. Alika shut the door and answered.

"Alika?" The familiar voice said.

Alika's heart began to thump, but he followed script. "Hey, Phil Beam, right? From the contracting place in Bogotá? Yeah, don't say a word, I'll get right back to you when I have those figures. Just about to step into a meeting and I know these calls cost you a bundle. Can I call you back at this number?"

After a short pause, Patrick answered. "Yes."

"Great, thanks Phil, take care. Will call you back as soon as possible."

Alika hung up the phone and leaned against his desk. He breathed deeply, closing his eyes. Soundlessly, an almighty burden slipped from his shoulders to the ground—Patrick was alive. Where he was, who was with him, what he knew; Alika would have to wait just a few hours longer to hear.

Stoppering at the emotion bursting within, he opened the door of his office and walked briskly to the conference room to begin his meeting. As the marketing guys gave an update on the infrastructure talks with General Electric, Alika finally let himself smile. Though he knew Patrick must be somewhat confused, Alika found pure comfort in knowing that his friend was indeed alive.

On his way home that evening, Alika stopped at a gas station and headed straight for the bathroom.

There'd been surveillance and phone tapping during the first weeks after the fire, and it took only one visit by a friend of Dolores' to confirm that Alika's home and phones were being monitored. Further digging showed that the cover was private and not omnipresent, though it was likely that Alika's call records were being reviewed. It was unnerving and infuriating, this phantom in the dark, never being sure if the stalker was real or chimera. At times, Alika had felt like going to the police. Yet he feared the repercussions and who was actually involved. Dolores suggested he wait. With Patrick in such public tatters, Alika's cries of intrigue might only aggravate matters. There was Meredith too, and with the plans Alika had put in motion, he needed to be around to supervise orbits.

Once inside the station bathroom, immersed in the smells of lemon and vinegar, Alika pulled a prepaid cell phone from his pocket and dialed back the number Patrick had used earlier. A deep sounding voice picked up after five rings. Alika asked for Patrick.

The voice said there was no Patrick at that number. Alika gave his name. There was a long break and Alika heard the phone shuffle between hands.

"Phil Beam..." answered Patrick. "The bartender at The Kingdom, right?"

"The very Phil," confirmed Alika.

"We free to talk?"

"For about ten minutes."

"Good," Patrick sighed. "Nice to hear a familiar voice again."

"Glad to know you're still with us," replied Alika. He could sense the tribulation in Patrick's tone.

"Phil Beam," Patrick repeated, tinny over the cheap cell. He then paused for so long that Alika thought they'd lost their connection.

"Patrick?" Alika probed. "You still there?"

"Tell me about Hadley," replied Patrick with evenness.

Alika gave him the details, sparing little, sensing that Patrick's malnourished mind was devouring every available bit of information. Five minutes later, when Alika finished, there was again quiet.

"You've been busy," remarked Patrick, several octaves more relaxed. "I...never would have thought...and they're safe, both of them?"

"Both safe."

Silence once more from Patrick's end. "How did it come to this? Who would—I wasn't sure if it was just me going loony in the jungle—but why go after me?"

"Still working on that, as well as the *who*?"

"Yeah," said Patrick thoughtfully. "Is it money? Is it the non-profit idea?"

"I wouldn't count it out."

"Damn."

The enormity of the predicament swelled on the line.

"So where are you?" asked Alika.

Patrick gave Alika a quick synopsis of his journeys in the jungle, from the bridge to the hut to the Colombian capital. "Still here in Bogota, trying to figure this all out. It's not like I can just hop on a plane, can I?"

"No, definitely not," Alika replied.

"Should I turn myself in? Would that help anything?"

Alika hesitated. "I don't know Patrick, I guess it's your decision. If you're tired of running, then by all means stop...but there's a pretty tight case against you. They even had me doubting. Might be best to prepare a defense."

Patrick went quiet again. "Damn."

They concluded that Patrick would sit tight and begin to plan his re-entry while Alika continued to gather and pass information. With what Patrick had learned from Alika, his haste to return to the States had eased somewhat. Yet as Alika described the ups and downs of Meredith's winter, the unjust separation from two parents and the lingering trauma of the fire, Patrick yearned to be with her.

After setting up another time to speak, they hung up and Alika stepped from the bathroom, apologizing to the boy anxiously waiting by the door.

San Francisco, California

Straight off the plane, Alika was collected by the driver of a black Town Car. The middle-eastern fellow wore musty cologne and had an affinity for acceleration. Zipping through late afternoon traffic, they arrived shortly at the Fairmont Hotel. Alika's room had a view to the Bay, and the porter brought his bags in through the door. Leaving them unpacked, Alika stood at the window, looking out over the tumbling water.

Meredith was up in Boston for the week, staying with Hadley's parents. In a bloodless custody battle, Meredith had decided that she would rather stay with Alika instead of the Hannigans. Already having legal guardianship, Alika was not required to offer Meredith a choice, but in good faith to Anthony and Rose, it was made clear that she could go with whomever she wanted. To Alika's relief, she chose him. The girl was no longer in danger, but for what he'd done, Alika preferred that the responsibility fell to him.

After collecting Meredith in Boston, they would spend a few weeks in Arlington while Alika and his staff shut down the Green Equator office for the move south to the new facility opening in Florida. REI's tutor, Kyle, would accompany them as well. Meredith still tolerated him, but out of kindness, not academic respect.

As the water darkened in the dusk, Alika thought back to the day that he and Patrick had signed a different contract. They'd been looking out on these same waves, but from the REI Headquarters. Alika's apprehensions about the approaching contract were even greater. REI had scheduled interviews with several major networks and periodicals for the following day. Alika, Ward had prophesied, would become a world figure overnight. Oil barons would fear him, eco-proponents would canonize him, and children would one day learn about him in text books. Alika exhaled at the thought.

For him, this had started as a quest to help mankind; a labor for the general good, a scheme hatched with Patrick in that frigid Penn office space after their first summer at Camp Blanding. For Patrick, it had always been about the solution, his drive to conclude on something unknown. Therefore, without consideration or agreement of motivation, they had prepared to change the world, moving forward with ideas that progressively became more feasible with each passing day—Hydrogen, they proposed, could replace petroleum and coal within twenty years. They'd set out to make it happen, starting down this frightful gauntlet upon which commitment and good intentions had enhanced their vulnerability.

Alika questioned what he had contributed, what he had sacrificed. Nothing, by comparison, and yet here he stood, hours from signing a gargantuan energy contract that would undoubtedly change the future of millions, if not billions of lives. Patrick had done it, he had found the answer. There were creases to smooth and improvements to make, but the fundamentals had been pronounced. And Patrick's reward? His family's? Patrick's mere consideration of Alika's half-baked humanitarian proposition for "free energy", to not fully monetize his discovery, had presumably been the catalyst of this disaster.

Yet the question remained—who had gotten spooked? Ward had known, so by association it was likely that other REI partners knew as well, but from there the investment-venture capitalist network separated out by a hundred degrees—the number and power of suspects was staggering. Amidst these shadows, however, Alika took strength from the things he knew. Knowledge, he'd once been told, is the most powerful leverage.

The Bay boiled in the evening wind while Alika looked over the final elements of the contract from his hotel room. The exact dollar amount on the deal was unspecified, as there were provisions for royalties and bonuses to be paid to Green Equator/REI should associated revenues for Seven Energy reach a certain threshold. It was, "the contract that kept paying," and Alika had to admire REI's negotiation team. The upfront total to be paid through Green Equator was $5.2 billion, a number that Alika found hard to fathom. It was too large, but according to Ward it was an average-sized investment for a contending energy company. They were buying a technology, a very good one, plus the nearly completed facility in Florida. Shell and ExxonMobil also had made bids, some larger than $5.2 billion, but Seven's was the most hospitable to reoccurring income.

Up front, Alika would receive $100 million. This too was staggering, and Alika had no idea what he would do with such a sum. Again, he didn't feel as though he deserved it. His position at the new test facility and lab site in Florida would be interesting, and perhaps he was worthy for that task, but he was only taking it as a means to stay close to the action. Everything had happened so quickly, and he'd barely stopped to think about what was best for him. Although he wanted to be close to Dolores, he felt an unyielding desire to ensure Meredith's well-being, and thus Hadley's and Patrick's as well.

The facility in Florida, a space-age version of the lab in Colombia, was ahead of schedule and set to open in March. It had been rudimentary designed by Patrick over a year ago, and REI had broken ground in October with the expectation that they could sell it in a package deal. The risk was yielding dividends, and many of the team members from Colombia were being flown in to continue their work, landing as valuable new employees of Seven Energy. The site was being modeled into something of a compound, in anticipation, Alika assumed, of becoming a full-blown power hub. Officially titled the 'Eco-Energy Center,' the project was known more intimately as *The Eco*. Due to its fairly remote location, close to half-an-hour from the next town, there were plans to build a school on-site with classes beginning in the fall. A housing complex was also nearly finished, complete with a market and restaurants. Meredith was sold on the swimming pool.

Over the course of the contract negotiations, Alika had been afforded little input, disabled by the puppet hands from San Francisco. The only section of the agreement that he had maneuvered was for Meredith to receive Patrick's $100 million. The amount was to be set aside in a trust fund. As Alika had described to Patrick, life for Meredith had been tumultuous. The days after her mother departed had been sullen, and Alika had feared that the girl's brightness would continue to wane in the winds of their dilemma. Despite Alika's attempts to protect her, Meredith was privy to what the world made of her father. There were the news stories, the magazines, and her old playmates from school. At night she often came running into Alika's bedroom, afraid of noises and whispers in the dark. Christmas, however, brought more than presents. Meredith grew more talkative, embracing the season's buoyant feeling, laughing more than she had in weeks. Alika marveled at the turnaround. It was almost as if the girl perceived that things were not as they appeared.

The meeting with Seven Energy was hosted at REI's headquarters in San Francisco. Ward and Decklin Cross were present, as was James Le and a few other REI wigs. Several executives for Seven Energy entered the room at precisely 11:00 a.m. and business was conducted in short order. There would be no bartering or negotiating at this gathering. The skirmishes had been fought; all that remained was the treaty.

Ward sat down next to Alika, asking him about Meredith and Dolores, chatting about developments at The Eco. Alika carried along, acting his usual self as Ward opened up a leather folder to go over the final details of the contract. Alika was still unsure how much Ward knew about the attacks, and he had not spoken candidly with him since their walk at Johns Hopkins. While Ward rattled on, Alika mused at the irony of returning to this room without Patrick; as if they'd gone to war, won the battle, and then left their General alone to die in the trenches. Today they would celebrate their victory and

Patrick would not be invited to the feast. Alika considered the men in the room, wondering how close he might be to the orchestrator.

For all documents, Alika was the chief signatory. It marveled him that a few papers symbolized such a gross amount of money. As the proceedings progressed, he was called forward to finalize the transfer of rights and privileges. The amount of the sale was being kept quiet from the media, although a small brief had been leaked to stir stock activity.

Pen in hand, Alika leant forward on the desk to make the first signature. As he did so, his own views and leading questions on life and work came haunting back in waves.

Alika Tucker.

"The amount of social conflict caused by the oil trade is staggering. How many lives would be spared or improved through a wise replacement?"

Alika Tucker.

"The environmental implications related to the extraction, refining, and burning of fossil fuels are immense. What will we sacrifice to provide a stable earth for coming generations?"

Alika Tucker.

"Money. It has always driven the trade and development of energy. And, in part, it has worked; many presently have abundant energy. But at what cost? And how would delivery of energy to poverty-stricken regions change their condition?"

Alika Tucker.

"Think about what problems we could focus on if we reduced the geopolitical resource struggle over spark and flame. How bare would the slate stand? There's clean water, sanitation, food production, medicine, AIDS, climate change…think of the number of people, even just engineers, who would be freed to work on these challenges."

Alika Tucker.

"There is no doubt that we must have energy. It is no longer a want, but a demand. Fossil fuels have served us well, but we now must find a new way to fuel our needs. And this path should not compromise the future of our children."

Alika Tucker.

Chapter 29

She sat comfortably on a picnic blanket of grass. All around was farmland, brown and churned, and she waited patiently for the crops. The weather was dry, cloudless. The terrain rolled off in every direction, running headlong into banks of mountains at the nethermost reach of sight. She had watched the planting season, the Farmer and his workers busy along the raised rows of earth; they had even let her help. That had been a long time ago, she knew, but surely the seeds would soon spring.

The sun shone on her shoulders and she wiggled her toes. She crossed her legs in the way young women do and wondered if anything would grow that day. It had been a good while since the Farmer's last visit and the ground had kept quiet. But as she sat there thinking, something strange happened—she saw a shadow. It was far off in the distance, but stretched the width of the valley. It was moving towards her, ever so evenly. She was worried. How would the plants grow in a shadow? The shade grew closer, enveloping the land, plunging it into relative darkness. She thought to run, but where?

When she looked up to see the shadow's source, the sun-stroked plain was all but swept. The sight was magnificent. A wave, taller than the mountains, was descending with its peaks down to meet her. Coursing and blue, the waters held a perfect form, soaring into the midst of the valley, aiming to break directly where she lay. Closer and closer; and the shadows were forgotten for what cast them. The smell of salt and sea landed first, swelling her off the grass and diluting her fear. The wave did not check, and she inhaled as water met earth.

She opened her eyes. There was nothing at first, only light, brilliant white light. Then there were forms, hazy and rough, slowly gathering detail.

She felt wet all over. A few drops of sweat ran over her eyelids and down to her lips.

She closed her eyes and felt the touch of linen on her fingertips.

The darkness was softer this time, as though a lamp had been switched on in the hallway outside her bedroom.

In time, the light came back stronger, and she felt her feet rub against one another. Then she turned her hands over. Something moved in the blur of color in front of her. She opened her mouth, but no noise emerged. She felt a hand take hers, and then another touch her shoulder. Exhausted, Hadley squeezed back.

April 2012
Bethesda, Maryland

Over the first two days, Hadley gradually regained consciousness. It was not a sudden bursting from slumber, but a delicate emergence. Her first coherent word was "Meredith."

Through those initial hours of waking, the world was fitful and jumbled. Its edges sharpened by degrees, revealing depth and movement. The veil between dreams and cognizance, with its threads of silk, steel, and gold, released and absorbed her all at once. Thirst lapped intensely at her lips and currents of nausea beat about the spectrum of her frame. Indeed, the sensation was that of overcoming the harangue of addiction; neither body, soul, nor mind was spared.

By the evening of the second day, Hadley could talk to the nurses and doctors. They communicated in slow gulps, connecting enough for Hadley to learn that she had been in a coma for six months and outside it was April. As per her family, no one knew them and could offer no news. Hadley's strength was so sapped that she barely stayed awake for more than thirty minutes at a stretch. Each time she woke, without exception, she asked for her family; daughter, husband, mother, father.

Although limited physically, Hadley's mind promptly regained its vigor. The last event she could remember was standing at the top of the stairs, her thoughts and emotions a woven thatch of fear, maternal protection, and suspicion. Resultantly, she also treated the nurses and doctors with apprehension, asking pointed questions over her arrival, her identity and condition, and the causes behind her recent tenancy within unconsciousness. Their apparent ignorance over who she was and how she got there was unnervingly legitimate—to the extent of doubting sanity. They didn't even call her Hadley. Her chart read Gloria Fisher.

The bed was corralled by a white curtain, similar to the one she had passed through with Patrick to see George. Through the window behind her bed she could see blossom buds on the trees. The bed curtains were opened most of the time and Hadley found herself in a wing with at least a dozen other women. The majority had suffered serious injuries or also lay unconscious. None looked too available for a chat. Hadley wondered into what sort of hospital she had been admitted.

The doctor, in good practice, said that Hadley was mighty lucky. The only permanent damage was to her right eardrum, and it was likely that her hearing on that side would be permanently weaker. Physical rehabilitation was prescribed as she had gone so many months without proper movement, but her brain activity, motor and communication skills, all appeared in full order.

Despite her relief for the doctor's optimism, the swirl of confusion surrounding the state of her family, the care of her daughter, and her exact whereabouts made Hadley permanently restless and irritated. The nurses and doctors refused to tell her anything more than it was April. It wasn't really imprisonment, as the care of the nurses was still requisite to survival, but when the head nurse again denied Hadley permission to phone her parents, she tried to escape.

The attempt came on the third day, proving the doctor's suggestion for rehab. Slipping from the bed, Hadley's legs gave out immediately and she landed with a painful thud on the floor. The head nurse, Rosa, came and helped her back onto the bed. Rosa was black, echoed of Southern Virginia, and kept her hair knotted tightly in a bun. Her disposition was imposing for the ripple of muscles along her arms, but the tickle of her laugh was irresistible and could be heard as far as the parking lot. As Hadley's head rested back on the pillow, she began to sob. She just wanted to see her daughter.

On the morning of the fourth day, with her vision strong enough, Hadley was handed a letter. Rosa brought it with a glass of water and medicine. Without hesitation, Hadley ripped open the envelope. The note was handwritten.

December 16th, 2011

Hadley-
You will no doubt have many questions. I'll try to answer as many as I can. First off, Meredith is safe and with me. For now we are at my apartment in Arlington.
As of today's date, Patrick is missing in Colombia. The details are hazy and we've still heard nothing. Search teams are looking for him. But the fact that he has not been found leads me to believe that he's alive.
You are in Bethesda, MD, at the US Naval Hospital. You're in a special wing for Witness Protection patients. None of the doctors or nurses know your real identity, but they will if you talk enough about yourself. You were attacked Hadley, you may not remember. The resulting fallout was highly publicized.
It appears that someone tried to kidnap Meredith, but panicked when I arrived and decided to burn the house. This was likely to get to Patrick. Shortly after the fire broke out, he disappeared. There's mixed reports as to why. It has all been very confusing.
It would be best for us to talk soon, much might have changed. There are directions on the back for reaching me. Follow them carefully.
No one knows you're alive except myself, Dolores, and a handful of Witness Protection agents.

We had a funeral for you – the world thinks you're dead, even Meredith, even you're family. I'm sorry. I had to make a decision – someone wanted to keep you asleep.

Contact me right away. Don't call anyone else.

Love,

-Alika

PS: Go easy on the nurses

Hadley read the letter twice more and hailed Rosa. Before anything, she gave the nurse a sudden hug.

"My, my. What's this for?" asked Rosa with a laugh, patting Hadley on the back.

"For putting up with me," Hadley replied, her grip still weak.

"Ah, Hun, it's okay. I know this isn't easy."

On the back of the paper, scrawled in Alika's cursive, was the promised set of instructions.

-Call Dolores at this number

-If she answers, speak freely. She knows everything.

-If it goes to voicemail, ask one of the nurses to leave the following message:

"Hi, Dolores, this is (name of nurse) at the Hospital in Bethesda. Just calling to let you know that Gloria is doing better and would love to hear from you. Thanks."

-Wait for my call

Rosa brought a cordless phone from the nurses' station outside and sat next to Hadley on the bed. She placed the call and set the phone to speaker.

As the number dialed, Hadley asked Rosa how quickly she could leave.

"Whenever you want, this isn't jail," she whispered. "But I'd advise you stay and get that rehab. Probably about two months."

"Two months!"

The call went to voicemail and Dolores' recording invited them to leave a message. Rosa read the script and hung up.

Hadley thanked her and collapsed in relief and concern on the bed—Meredith was alive, Patrick was missing, she was dead to the world.

Alika never rang. He came in person.

Hadley was propped up in bed reading a John le Carré novel when the door opened to his figure. The book fell from her hands and she immediately began to cry. There were no words. She held up her arms as he crossed the room.

Alika moved to the side of the bed and wrapped her in a hug. As strong as she could, Hadley clung to her friend and mediator, the closest link to her scattered family. The collar of Alika's shirt was soon sodden from her tears and running nose.

"Patrick?" she asked, voice wavering.

"Alive," Alika assured. "For certain."

For a few minutes, Hadley just cried into his shoulder.

Alika pulled up a chair and sat beside the bed. Rosa came by with tissues and water as he proceeded to outline and color-in the past six months. The last thing Hadley remembered was lunging for the man at the stairwell. Alika was the first to hear what terror she had endured. He listened carefully, made a few notes on his phone as she described the pale-skinned man with the bronze-cased lighter, and then carried on chronologically with details about the fire and their rescue. Hadley had guessed the girl was behind the dresser. She laughed in relief about Minnie Tucker's intercessory call to the fire department.

From the front lawn, and before the smoked carcass of her home, Hadley was taken by ambulance and helicopter to Hahnemann Hospital in Philadelphia. After being stabilized she recovered healthily, showing signs of regaining consciousness. Until, almost overnight, she warped into a sudden and curious deterioration. Alika grew curious over the decline, as well as the change in persona of her caretaker. After cornering one of the doctors, he discovered that Hadley was being set into an induced coma—someone wanted her to keep quiet, assumedly until a certain time, perhaps when Patrick was finally found.

The sedative doses, a drug called Propofol, the nervous physician revealed, were being applied gradually so as not to incite suspicion. Medically induced comas were a risky practice, and used only in select circumstances to help speed recovery in the brain after severe trauma. The doctor told Alika that he wasn't given a choice—they'd threatened his family. Exactly who *they* were, the doctor wasn't sure. The contact was all done by phone—except once, when a light-skinned man caught him by the arm outside a supermarket to confirm his cooperation.

Under the auspices of seeing a specialist, Alika had Hadley transferred down to Johns Hopkins. Prior to her arrival, Alika made contact with every doctor at Hopkins that might have access to Hadley. They promised to indicate if they were approached. It didn't take long. Of the seven doctors, two were contacted on the day Hadley arrived. It was done by phone, anonymous calls made to their personal lines. Male voice, same message: we need your cooperation, matter of government security, imperative, we will contact you with more details.

Her coma, they explained at Hopkins, was advanced; little could be done besides wait. The prognosis meant a likely transfer up to Boston, closer to the Hannigans, but farther from Alika. Fearing that in her slumber she would never be safe, subject to the will of suspect antagonists, Alika made the decision for Hadley to disappear. It was not a rash choice entirely, but calculated based on a contact that Dolores had within the U.S. Marshals Service. The Witness Protection Program would be capable of hiding Hadley until she recovered. Dolores' contact, whom they met several times near DuPont Circle, said that they could assist in a "consulting capacity" for Hadley's extraction and subsequent admittance to a special witness ward at the Naval Hospital in Bethesda. If Alika was willing to finance the expenses, a place could be arranged for Hadley. As she was not an official witness in a federal case, the operation would never be documented, only executed.

On the night of Hadley's supposed death, Dolores' contact and a pair of off-duty agents infiltrated the hospital. They first altered the vitals monitoring system, showing an expected list in brain activity and pulse. As alarms signaled the night nurses, the first one to Hadley was a substitute from "another ward." The visiting nurse struggled in vain with the others to bring Hadley around, but the coma patient was fading fast. At seven minutes past four in the morning, Hadley was pronounced dead. When the Hannigans and Alika came to view the body, the agents delivered a neurotoxin—*tetrodotoxin*, or TTX—that made Hadley appear convincingly deceased. In transit to the morgue, her body was replaced with another, a victim of a car crash who had indicated on her driver's license that she would like her body donated to science. The undertakers had never met Hadley, so her replacement might well have been anyone. The closed casket funeral happened to be family tradition, and with the bells at St. Stephen's tolling, Hadley arrived at this particular wing in the United States Naval Hospital.

Alika retrieved a copy of the funeral program from his briefcase, along with several newspaper clippings that he had set aside for this moment. In humble silence, Hadley read Meredith's poem. She wore a grey t-shirt and blue pajama bottoms. Her tears drenched her top like sweat from a run. Rosa returned with more tissues.

Next it was the print, Hadley's own domain, where there was no shortage of shocks. In those recent months, Alika had grown optimistic over Patrick's and Meredith's progress, marking their advances. For Hadley, the personal injustice of it all was bitterly fresh. Before handing her the sheaf of periodicals, Alika ran over the more tender items in person—the terror of the fire for Meredith, the supposed jealous rage of Patrick, and most delicate, Korey's murder. Hadley threw her hands up over her mouth with a slight shriek, tears streaming as she hunched in the bed weeping.

Still struggling with the brutality of this dam break, Hadley clutched at the crinkly newspapers, running over the accused deceit again and again with the same treatment that Patrick had in his hut. She continued to cry, clenching her teeth over this assault on her loves and her life.

"Tell me what really happened," she said at length, her lip shaking.

Alika began with Meredith, watching Hadley's eyes yearn to behold more than his memories. They talked about the weeks after the fire, her hills and troughs, and their recent move to "The Eco" in Florida. He then described Patrick, all that he knew, from the coordinated ambush at the bridge to his current situation along the Mexican border. Since January, he and Alika had been in constant contact, with Alika aiding where possible. Patrick had acquired a powerful ally at the equator, enabling him to get as far as he had without detection. It would not be long before he crossed back into the States.

"Why us?" Hadley asked, staring absently at the pattern of the tiles on the floor. The stories made her anxious and angry. "Is it Patrick? Did he discover something worth killing for?"

"Likely," said Alika. He described Patrick's loose idea to start a non-profit energy company and then the size of the Seven Energy deal signed in January.

"So billions..." Hadley concluded. "And then on from there—because the coal, oil, and gas industry...we're talking trillions now. And Patrick...he was going to rob them of that."

Alika nodded.

"But who?" Hadley said in frustration. "Is it REI?"

Alika and Dolores had done extensive research on the depth of REI's connections. The findings were inconclusive. REI had opened shop in 2004, growing quietly with the support of private equity and various entrepreneurs, some of whom Alika had met. The group did link to a vaster consortium of investors, banks, and lenders, and indeed, their fingerprints could be lifted from many a money jar and government checkbook around the globe, but so could the indices of many legitimate corporations—global acquaintance did not imply general corruption. In their hunt through records and data, they found nothing even remotely sinister. In fact, the nature of their work was quite the opposite, creating jobs and promoting clean energy.

"I can't be sure," Alika answered. "But it doesn't seem like it."

"And Ward?"

"Same. Another question mark."

She threw a glance around the room. "Then who are we hiding from?"

"For now, everyone."

Hadley tapped her fingers against the bedspread, her eyes falling ponderously into the space between. Roundabout, the room absorbed the final light of the day. Central cooling breezed down from vents overhead and medical monitors chirped and puttered from wall to wall. A delivery truck in the parking lot reversed in a drone of beeps and gas. Alika had been there four hours and would need to be going.

"Did you tell him yet?" she asked. Her hands had folded themselves across her lap. "That I'm awake."

Alika shook his head, smiled, and pulled another cell phone from his pocket. "I thought you could."

He gave her Patrick's number and a set time to call. Alika was returning to Florida the following day and would be in contact soon. His cover for the visit had been a 'last-minute meeting'—translated by his staff as 'I'm going to see Dolores.'

Hadley asked about the relationship and Alika explained how they were still together. They had decided to keep things in neutral until everything was sorted with Meredith.

"You cease not to astound," said Hadley, emotional, but out of tears.

"She's been great," said Alika. "I'd have gone off the edge without her."

"Wedding bells?" Hadley pitched.

Alika blushed and cleared his throat.

"You're going to see her tonight. Aren't you?"

"Well," he shrugged. "It's on the way."

Circumstances were unlikely to allow another rendezvous until Hadley was mobile. They had gone over the plan for her rehabilitation and eventual travel to Florida, but for now, Hadley needed to heal. She was in good hands with the nurses and doctors of the ward, who knew that identity and business were not to be discussed.

As Alika stood to leave, Hadley squeezed him around the torso as hard as she could. "I can't believe you killed me."

He looked down through weathered eyes, straight-faced as in younger, sweeter times. "It was personal."

That night, as Hadley lay awake looking at the shapes of the shadows cast along the wall by the lights outside, she thought about the last time she had seen Patrick.

Her cheeks were still damp from fresh tears shed over Korey. Their romance had kindled in haste, conflagrating to a height that soon became known to all. And though Hadley had been content with Korey, it was not happiness. Such joy was possible, she had thought, for Korey was more like her than Patrick, but some barricade prevented them. Korey said he felt it too. She had questioned what the bulwark was, whether it was the heaped rubble of Meredith's hope, or a haze of her misplaced pity for Patrick. No material made sense. The ultimate decline began after Kylie's wedding, starting with this "confrontation" at her home that the newspapers had snapped so dramatically about.

Patrick's flight had been that evening, and though he had already said goodbye to Meredith the night before, Patrick made the drive once more to again bid adieu. Hadley remembered being so stiff, avoiding his eyes, and disputing the visit; Meredith had homework and Korey was over. Whenever they met, she threw her coat on him like a rack, covering his face from view. Part of her felt this treatment was guilt, another a manifestation that she still loved him, a part further that she loathed Patrick for stealing her twenties. With stubborn indifference, she had busied herself in the kitchen with dinner while Patrick talked with Meredith at the dining room table.

The issue began when Korey came in from the back deck, where he'd gone to sit while Patrick visited. Meredith ran past him on her way upstairs to collect a new book for Patrick to see. Korey had been drinking, not heavily, but two beers on the deck and he was slightly buzzed. The two men shook hands cordially and chatted about Patrick's time in South America. Hadley stood away from them at the counter, watching the exchange—it had been one of their better conversations…until Korey made a genuine comment that was better left unsaid.

"Thanks for letting me take care of your family."

Hadley had watched in trepidation as she saw Patrick wince and turn his head. He'd never been great in social situations, worse still when something upset him. "I can take care of my daughter," he had said firmly.

Korey shrugged. "For now, sure."

Hadley had frozen, wanting to intervene, but Patrick had diffused the situation himself, walking up the stairs to see his daughter. It was one of Korey's less pleasant displays of pride and she snapped at him until Patrick returned.

Korey was still acting cavalier and held out a hand in assertive apology. Patrick pushed past the hand, at which point Korey grabbed his shoulder. In a semi-scuffle, Patrick shoved off Korey's grip and bumped him away as Hadley raised her voice. Although his athletic frame had withered somewhat in the years since Penn, Patrick was still an agile man and Korey stumbled backwards several feet into the edge of the counter. She remembered shouting at them to stop, hoping Meredith wouldn't come downstairs. Water was boiling over from the pot of pasta on the stovetop.

Holding up his hands, Patrick began to back away, apologizing under his breath. Korey took several steps forward, as if he wanted to continue, but Patrick was going. Without further aggression, he said goodbye to Hadley and left through the front door. No one knew that he was walking from one conflict straight into another.

Now, lying alone without strength in this crowded room, her fiction snapped and Hadley finally knew. The truth let her sleep the rest of the night, on until breakfast, when she woke to Rosa's shake, seeing first the phone beside her bed.

Next to God, there was no one she would rather talk to.

Chapter 30

March 15th, 2028
Safehouse Five, New York City, New York
12:02 a.m.

Hadley, alive. Of all the fantastic history that Meredith has unraveled, this gem is really stretching it. Killian tells me to come out to the monitoring center, and as I stand to leave, Meredith asks for a sheet of paper. When I challenged her to uphold the lie about the attack on Patrick, this is not what I expected, all these wild stories—it's late and I'm going to ask Killian to suspend questioning until the morning. There's an apartment upstairs where Meredith can stay and maybe my parents are still up.

I rip a sheet of paper from my pad, toss my pen on the table and walk to the door…ambushed by a corrupt Army division in the jungle—saved by poachers—Hadley drugged into a coma and then sedated further—a US Marshal extraction…has to be fiction.

When I enter the monitoring center, there are phones ringing and agents scrambling. It seems that despite Killian's order to keep the case quiet, some details have escaped—even to the media. What a storm this story would be…and we're not even to the end. Killian stands quietly in the middle of all the disorder, rubbing the back of his neck. "It's all verifiable," he says as I approach, "Everything." Killian explains that our team has finally gotten through the last of the documents in Meredith's luggage. I've yet to see any of the contents and Killian points to a pile of papers on the nearest desk. I leaf through the stack; affidavits from a man named Noé Moreno, dated transcripts of Colombian Army communications, a patient description of Gloria Fisher from the Naval Hospital, pictures of a ratty wooden hut.

"And yes," Killian says, "I'm aware you can put a story to anything, but this all checks out. Comparing the order of the paper evidence with Meredith's verbal testimony, they are perfectly in sync." Killian's cellphone rings and he checks the number before letting it go to voicemail.

I ask why I wasn't informed before.

Killian smiles and I can see his hunger for a result. What it must mean to get answers after all these years—might even make you vulnerable. "I needed you to stay skeptical," he says.

Fed up and tired, I swear and throw the papers back on the table. This is a not a bedtime story. Twelve hours we've been at this, twelve.

Killian looks at me condescendingly. "I couldn't tell you," he says, not amused by my tone. "You're an interrogator, not a counselor. We both know that you're at your best when you're critical, and today I needed your best." Killian receives a message on his phone. He reads it and then looks back at me. "So get back in there before we lose her. You're wasting time."

With my face blended in a mixture of confusion and frustration, I turn and leave the monitoring center. I dislike compliments.

Entering the interview room, I don't sit down immediately—I pace instead. It's not for presence, but because I've got a cramp in my leg. Meredith is carefully writing something on the scrap of paper. From where I'm standing, it looks like random shapes.

What's that?

The Eco. It'll be easier to visualize what I'm going to tell you.

[I nod and Killian barks at me to hurry up. If Killian is anxious about losing Meredith, then it must mean that there's someone outside the FBI vying for her. I'm still not sure where Meredith is going with her tale—she's yet to accuse anyone directly…and maybe that's what has people nervous.]

You'll forgive me if I don't immediately accept your version of events.

I understand that it sounds unlikely—if that's what you mean.

[My pacing continues. It's helping with the stitch.]

What mystifies me is how Alika was doing everything by himself. He had some help from Dolores, you say, and some of her conveniently placed "colleagues" with the US Marshals, but besides that, did he act alone?

Nearly.

Then how did your father get out of Colombia?

Chapter 31

April 2012
Mexicali, Mexico

The clang of metal pans was subtle that morning, and for the first time in a month it was the smell that roused him; a baritone scent of grease and fat that carried through his window, saturating the room. Patrick rolled over and checked his watch, a fake Timex from the vendor outside. Alika would be calling in an hour—frustrating, because Patrick had accomplished little. Progress is difficult when hiding in Mexico.

He popped from the bed and moseyed to the bathroom. His room was above an aging Chinese restaurant in the upper part of Mexicali, one of several famed border towns beneath California. Patrick spent most days down at the local library, battling for internet time with gamers and kids wanting to do homework. He was trying to gather information on the identity and motive of his enemy, but this was not the place to do it.

Supposedly, the truck to take him across the border would be ready that night and he could leave the following morning. Patrick strived to stay optimistic as he passed beneath the cold shower. They'd been delayed three weeks already. It was torture being so close to America, to Meredith.

Showered and dressed in plain clothes, Patrick headed downstairs into the kitchen. Jimmy and Li Wan were busy at their woks and large pots catering to the morning crowd. Patrick gave the pair a quick wave before slipping out the backdoor into the morning heat; during the past month, he had eaten more noodles than any man should. He ordered coffee and *pan* from the breakfast-stand a block away. Although he kept his appearance as nondescript as possible—sunglasses, hat, beard—no one was looking for him here, and he felt fairly anonymous in public.

Food in hand, Patrick walked a few more streets until he reached the park, a dusty plain of baseball diamonds, graffiti-slashed trees, and rusting municipal effort. It had the best service for cell phones, and the wide open space allowed him to speak without fear. The city was modernizing, in the way that pleases Americans, attracting chain franchises and building large parking lots. With the usual exceptions, the streets were fairly safe. Mexicali's drug trade was controlled by one specific group, sparing the city from the indiscriminate gang violence that continued to torture many of the other Northern provinces of Mexico. Patrick usually stayed inside at night, reading books from the library and making notes about the research of the day. It was difficult to know what to focus on—avenging his family or refining his work; from the room above Jimmy's *Wok of the Town* restaurant, neither seemed possible.

The phone rang at exactly 9:00 a.m. It was an old Nokia that Patrick had bought from a run-down electronics store. Sitting on a bench, he took one final sip of coffee. It had been four months since he had broken free of the jungle and first contacted Alika.

"Good morning America," Patrick said, answering the phone.

There was no answer.

"Alika, you there?"

Nothing, just the sound of open line.

He figured it was a dropped call. They happened all the time. "I'll hang up... okay?"

Still no response.

"Call back."

The voice came low and soft, barely audible. "Patrick."

The coffee cup slipped from his hand. The lid burst at the ground, flooding the dirt at Patrick's sandaled feet. "Hadley?"

Breathing and the sound of muffled tears rolled into his ears.

"Hadley?"

"Yes."

For a moment, neither of them said anything; the contact casting away the fear and anxiety that had loitered out of reach.

"Where are—?" They both said at once, emotion building in the connection. Patrick stood up and began to pace around the bench.

"I'm in Bethesda," Hadley said. "At the Naval Hospital."

"You're awake," Patrick stated.

"I'm awake."

"How long have you been…out?"

"About six days now," she said. "Alika came to visit yesterday."

"And you're…healthy?"

"I'm going to be fine," she assured.

Hadley told Patrick everything she knew about her condition and how long it would be until her rehabilitation was complete. She recapped Alika's visit, rehearsing what she knew about Patrick and Meredith. They talked about Korey too, the bitterness of his collateral death, pausing for Hadley to collect herself at times. Patrick knew that Hadley had cared for him, loved him maybe. He had to constantly remind himself of the gauntlet of shock that Hadley was passing through, recalling the hours and days following his own exposure to the transformed landscape of their world. They had been left in the path of a 100-year storm, abandoned to sputter and gasp unprotected in its swirling winds of power and wealth, allowed to flail in what polluting refuse it willed to deposit; Patrick had been condemned, Hadley, pronounced dead, and Meredith, orphaned. It was waking from a bad dream, only to find a nightmare.

Patrick listened in concentration to Hadley, continuing to pace without regard as she talked about her options. Hadley was skeptical as to why she couldn't announce herself to the world. Aside from allowing Meredith to be with her, Hadley also felt this would help expose the people who had wanted to keep her quiet; investigations would have to be made. Patrick explained that he'd felt likewise at first, having regular arguments with Alika about turning himself in. The risks to going public had convinced Patrick to stay hidden, mainly the uncertainty of their adversary—if they were willing and capable to have committed all that they had, then what else could they accomplish? The case against Patrick was tight, Alika would lose credibility if foul play could not be shown for Hadley's coma, and the perpetrators could always strike again. Although Hadley was not entirely convinced, she let the matter rest.

"What about you?" she asked. "Patrick this is all so..." her voice caught. "The explanation from Alika combined with all the newspaper stories...it feels so convoluted. The drugs can't be helping."

"Nor will six months of sleep."

Hadley laughed softly through her stuffy nose. "Yeah."

"How long do you have to speak?"

"I think the card said something like three hours," she replied. "Tell me about Mexico—Alika said something about smuggling?"

Patrick cleared his throat. "I'm just the driver."

January 2012
Four months earlier

The bus from Bucaramanga arrived late to Bogotá. There had been a flat tire minutes short of the capital and many of the riders disembarked, catching other buses or walking off knowingly into the night. Thankful to rest on a comfortable seat, Patrick stayed with the bus, listening to the frantic radio and trying not to mourn. At the station, he walked to a local information board and found a map for nearby hotels. What he would do for a shower.

After studying the area, Patrick walked from memory down a busy street that reported to have several '1 Star' hotels. It was almost midnight and the city bustled with carnal activity. Lazy-eyed women purred seekingly from the entrances of bars and clubs. Territorial men with gelled hair, smoked and stared. Cars and trucks juiced their engines, windows down to the streets, while hatchback taxis zipped their fares in and out of traffic. Patrick was numb to any threat. Hood up, his mind had become a stir-pot of darkness and thunder. Hadley was dead, Meredith was in limbo, they'd been betrayed—vengeance never felt so justified. He pitied the man who might impede.

Just past a closed grocery store, Patrick saw a sign for a hostel. He had never stayed in a hostel, though he knew they were cheap, despite the extra consonant, and his funds were limited. The building was painted baby blue and looked reputable. He assumed the clientele would be student-age, international, and he debated the wisdom of staying in such a crowded place; perhaps it was wiser to get lodging at an out of the way hotel. As he pondered what to do, Patrick noticed his reflection again in the shop window of a clothing store. He looked like a backpacker; no one was going to recognize him.

The entrance to the hostel was a caged metal door. Instructions were tacked next to an intercom button, which Patrick followed until a voice came over the line.

"Yes?" answered an accented female.

"I'd like to see about a room."

The door buzzed. "Turn the handle and push."

Patrick heaved his way through and found a set of cement stairs that led up into a well-lit reception area. Everything was incredibly chic, except they'd gone overboard with the neon. An adjacent lounge buzzed with youthful jabber, none of it English.

"Yes?" the same voice came again. A young Latina girl sat in front of a bright computer screen, looking impatiently at Patrick.

"Hi," replied Patrick, approaching the desk. "Do you have any available rooms?"

"We have beds only," she informed him. Her tone was not rude, just matter-of-fact.

"Great, I'll take one."

"Mixed guys and girls, ok?"

"Not a problem," Patrick said, pulling a few thousand pesos from his pocket. She told him the cost and he paid, using the name of his old roommate at Penn.

Handing him a towel, a room key, and a packet of sheets, she told him the room number and pointed down the hall. Before Patrick could gather his things, the girl was already back to her computer screen. She never asked for ID.

"Gracias," Patrick muttered, shuffling off.

The hostel was fairly full, milling with twenty-something's from all over the world. In the common room, a group of Europeans ate at a large table, while a few Asian guys huddled around a soccer match on TV. In the kitchen, a pair of girls stirred a potent brew, and along the wall a mishmash of young persons used a bank of computers. With his hood up, Patrick passed nonchalantly through the room and found his quarters. There were five bunk beds spaced throughout the room, and he found an open mattress on which to spread his sheets. Taking off his shirt, he spread it on the bed to mark his territory and headed off to find the bathroom.

After a divine shower, Patrick puttered back through the narrow corridors. Though there were belongings everywhere and it was 1:00 a.m., the room sat empty. There could have been a frat party for all Patrick cared. He slipped beneath the sheets, turned to face the wall, and instantly fell asleep.

As had been his jungle custom, Patrick woke shortly after dawn. The room was heavy with the smell of sleeping humans. Little did the bunkmates know, there was a famous felon in their midst. Dressing quickly in the same clothes, Patrick quietly shut the door behind him and deposited his key at the front desk. Outside, the virgin light welcomed a pleasant Bogotá morning.

At a one-shingle leather shoe store, jammed between two office buildings, Patrick inquired in basic Spanish about the location of the US Embassy. The shopkeeper, busying himself with the display of merchandise, looked Patrick over and asked if he spoke English. Patrick admitted he knew a little. Pleased by a chance to practice, the man took Patrick by the shoulder and pointed down the road. With a thick animated accent, he proceeded to describe the way.

"You go down straight, straight down! Then you see a big... uh...hotel! Fountain, boosh!" His arms made bursts in the air. "Go right, follow road. When see a...uh...uh..." He went on for another minute, and by the time he was done, Patrick knew he'd need another source. Biding the shopkeeper thanks and good luck, Patrick headed off towards the hotel, the fountain, and the 'boosh.' In front of the hotel, a lavish-looking spread, Patrick decided to hail a taxi. His ankle and thigh were starting to throb with the walking.

At the Embassy, essentially an American fortress, Patrick was directed by a guard to a set of waiting lines at the far side of the building. With its strong columns and chariot-capped statue, the front of the structure looked Roman and mighty. The formidable feel of the compound alerted Patrick to the meaning of his visit. As soon as he passed through the doors of the building he would be standing on American soil. It was then his intent to announce himself, trusting in his country to give him fair treatment and trial. Unsure of the protocol and doubting there was a form he could fill out, Patrick had decided to turn himself in via the standard issue of having lost his passport—the truth seemed innocent enough.

As he approached the lines, Patrick saw there was one queue for *Citizens* and another for *Non-Citizens*. The lines funneled down to a single security point with a body scanner, which then led into the Embassy where there were undoubtedly more lines. Patrick went through the Citizens line first, which held only a dozen or so people. His stomach turned over several times as he explained to the soldier at security why he couldn't provide identification.

"There's a number on the website or you can wait in the other line," the soldier said curtly. Patrick looked over at the Non-Citizens line, stretching back half a city block, and considered revealing his identity. Before Patrick could respond, the soldier told him to please step back and go to the end of the line. Hands up, Patrick obeyed.

Two hours later, Patrick made it back to the exact same soldier. The sun had since risen to reign and beat down on the shuffling crowd. Everyone sweated and fanned themselves with documents.

After passing through the rotating full-body scan, which was custom now at all airports and government buildings, he was admitted to the Embassy. Patrick had been right about the existence of more lines; they snaked like an intestine throughout the low-ceilinged hall. There was a separate line for citizens, which again had no wait. A woman was checking ID's as he approached and explained his situation, mustering back his most American of accents. The woman was Colombian and without much thought nodded for Patrick to pass.

There was a wall of windows, the clerks behind them slowly digesting the never-shrinking crowd. Feeling spoiled, Patrick was gestured forward after just a three-person delay.

"Passport or identification, please," the clerk said. She was young, pretty, and weary.

"Sorry," he replied. "That's actually why I'm here. I lost my passport when my luggage was stolen." The legitimacy of the statement was calming. He had nothing to hide. He hadn't murdered anyone.

"No driver's license or other identification?" It was clear she'd already had a long day.

"Sorry, no. All stolen."

"Alright, sir." Her voice was nasally through the speaker. "I'm going to slip a form through the window, please give your full name, date of birth, and social security number."

A short yellow form came beneath the window and Patrick filled in the requested information.

"Thanks," he said, sliding the paper back. She appeared not to hear him. Patrick looked down the hall at the painstaking wait of the non-citizens. It would take them hours, maybe all day. He turned back to the window, just in time to see the look on the girl's face as she punched in Patrick's final information. It was a look of recognition, and something else—fear.

Patrick studied her. She glanced at him, then focused back on the screen, as if to take refuge. Fright had chased the beauty from her face. Patrick stayed himself to be calm, but his heart thumped in his chest regardless.

"Mr. Simon," she said. Her voice was a touch strained. "I've never done a temporary passport before, it may take a few minutes. If you'd like, you can sit over there in the lobby while I process your information."

The failing of her composure, from slack to rigid, rattled Patrick further. "Sure," he said, pretending not to notice. "Take your time, I'll wait." She gave him an unnatural smile as he turned to leave.

The lobby was a few chairs squared around a low table. Patrick slowly walked towards them from the counter. The seats were wooden with red cushions and on the table were pamphlets about America, freedom, and citizenship. Patrick felt uneasy. He looked back at the window, the girl was gone.

Get out. The sudden upwelling was almost audible. *Get out,* the feeling warned again. Patrick stopped, and waited. A third time, *Get out.*

He immediately changed his course towards the exit. There were no guards there, only the soldiers back at the checkpoint. The hall scratched and chirped at the sound of voices and shoes scuffing the tile floor. Patrick half-expected someone to yell after him, but he reached the exit and pushed through into the light. The doors vacuumed shut.

In the open air there was still a good distance until he'd be out of sight. People passed by, heading into the Embassy. The sun had gone behind a cloud, but Patrick was sweating profusely. His heart rumbled. Part of him wanted to stay. What was the worst that could happen? He had done nothing wrong. Then, in a nauseating flash, he remembered snippets from the headlines—*Crazed, At-Large, Deranged, Murderer.*

There was a one-way rotating gate to exit at the security point, and a family ahead of Patrick passed through it playfully. His pulse thundering, Patrick looked at the guards. They were going about their business without concern. Patrick reached the gate and pressed his hip against it. The lock slipped open and Patrick swiveled through. Two paces further, Patrick heard the radios explode in a crackle of chatter. The message came first in Spanish, then in English. Fortunate for Patrick, his language skills had improved.

"Man in gray hooded sweatshirt, backpack, leaving East Exit. Apprehend at once. Priority."

Patrick plunged through the thickening line of Colombians and ran. After only ten yards, he could hear the yells and footsteps of the guards behind him. His lead was substantial, but already, a siren was whining up from the front side of the Embassy.

Dashing along the line, Patrick cringed from the burn in his thigh and wrenching at his ankle. People looked at him with confused looks, but no one stepped to block his path, neither did they make room for the pursuing Americans. Patrick looked back to see both soldiers closing in. Their gear chinked and rustled as they pushed past the last fragments of the line and accelerated into a sprint. Patrick avoided their eyes and dug harder, angling for the mix of buildings rising up to his right.

He broke across an unused security road, entering open space for the first time. If anyone wanted a clear shot, now was the time. Pushing, pushing, Patrick tensed for the bullet, expecting that same shocking tear; the sniper on the roof, the side arm of the guard. The siren droned louder, but no one fired.

Adrenaline pulsing, he crossed into an alley and out of sight of the Embassy. Bolting down the small path, Patrick ducked left down a larger street, and then right again up an alleyway, distancing himself from the edifice as much as possible. A fruit stand blocked the end of the alley. To the surprise of the salesman, Patrick burst sloppily over the table, sending produce in all directions. Before the vendor could cry out in disgust, Patrick was past and struggling into stopped traffic.

It was a main roadway of sorts, and Patrick dodged and threaded between cars, trucks, and motorcycles, crossing over a grass median. Glancing behind, he saw a guard emerge at the fruit stand and a set of flashing lights burst out at the intersection two hundred yards to his right. Patrick felt warm blood on his thigh and knew he didn't have much left.

Crouching as low as he could, Patrick skirted a few cars as traffic began to pick up. The police vehicle weaved closer and closer. His foot caught on a drain in the road and Patrick crashed to the ground, rolling over against the back wheel of a stopped truck.

Exhausted, Patrick lifted his eyes to see three soldiers entering traffic not far ahead, weapons trained. If he stood, they would see him. Back the other way, another set of soldiers hopped out of the police vehicle. The traffic was still stationary, but the accordion pull of movement would soon leave him exposed. His leg felt like it was coated in lava. It would be so easy just to stay.

The soldiers were surrounding the traffic column, aware that he was crouched somewhere in its midst. The truck against which Patrick leant, locked gears and fixed to move. Rocking forward and bringing his hands up, he prepared to surrender, feeling sick to his life's inevitability. The injustice made him tremor. The tremors made him ball his fists. The fists made his arms drop back to the ground. The ground felt hard again beneath his feet. And it was then that his feet made a decision.

He lunged forward, grabbing the back door of the nearest car, a red Toyota—it was locked. Crouching down he moved on to the next car, a white Ford—also locked. He heard more shouts from the soldiers, English, trying to stop the traffic from moving. The next car, a black Mercedes, Patrick pulled the back handle—locked. He slumped, sure of being caught. His struggle would soon be over.

Then, with a sharp *thop*, the doors to the Mercedes unlocked. Snapping up, Patrick eyed the door, as if it had spoken. Grabbing the handle again, he eased the door open and leaped inside.

On the opposite side of the car, behind the driver, sat a large black man wearing a beige suit. "Can I help you?" the man asked. His accent was American, a tinge Southern.

Patrick pulled the door shut, breathing hard, half-standing half-sitting, unsure what to do or say.

The cars all around them were starting to move.

"Sir?" said the driver, eyeing the intruder with distrust. Patrick saw his hand come off the wheel and drop out of sight to the center console.

"Drive on, Lou," said the man in beige.

Lou nodded and the car kept pace with the surrounding traffic. Patrick watched as the soldiers passed by outside the tinted windows. The Mercedes was soon through the next intersection and barreling into the city.

"Sit back," the man said, his voice deep and relaxed. "Looks like you could do with a rest."

Patrick opened his mouth to speak, but fell short. No breath. He felt his sweaty arms and neck sticking to the fine leather.

The man smiled. "You're not here to rob me, I know that." Beneath his suit he wore a tight knit shirt, a set of sunglasses nestled in his breast pocket. "But you look familiar…have we met before?" His face was full and long, and his eyes thundered with confidence. "Under different circumstances, of course."

Patrick looked back up at Lou, who also bore a grin. "I don't believe so."

"What's your name?" the man asked.

Fearing that he may have got in the wrong car, Patrick hesitated. There was still a reward out for his capture. He again second-guessed whether he should have let himself be apprehended—this time by American soldiers.

"I'm Mars," the man returned. "Mars Bellefonte." He raised his right hand to shake Patrick's.

Winded from the chase, Patrick struggled to invent a reason for his pursuit. He felt too tired to lie, too frustrated to create a new story. "I'm Patrick," he said with admission, reaching over. "Patrick Simon."

Mars smiled and squeezed Patrick's hand. "That's right!" he exclaimed. "I know you—mad scientist from the jungle. Hey Lou, we got a fugitive on board."

Lou glanced back at Patrick as Mars let loose a thundering laugh. The car was moving quite fast and the doors had relocked, nevertheless, Patrick was heavily considering bailing out.

"Looks like the G.I.'s gave you quite a chase," Mars said. He furrowed his brow, as if to better read Patrick's mind. "They'll be hunting for you on the streets."

Patrick stifled a gulp. "Could you take me to the nearest bus station?"

Mars winced. "Bus station? That's where they'll look first."

There was little Patrick could say to that, so he said nothing, avoiding Mars' gaze.

"I bet you're hungry," he said, growing more serious. "I'm on my way to lunch. Come with me."

Food was the last thing on Patrick's mind. The preceding five minutes had dramatically thrust his whole plan, his whole world, into uncertainty—again. Now he was speeding through Bogota in the back of an S-Class, about to lunch with a stranger in a beige suit.

"Unless you have other plans," the man offered, sensing Patrick's hesitance.

Ten minutes later, they pulled up to a large hotel fronted by blue fountains and greenery. Patrick felt out of place in his jeans and hoodie. Taking no notice, Mars ushered him in through the automatic front doors and back into a restaurant that overlooked a decadent pool at the rear of the hotel. The lobby was all glass, frosted and sparkling, christened by large paintings of mountain ranges and valleys. The concierge and reception counters were a soft-green marble. Shining steel elevators opened and closed beyond a modern lounge fit with an ebony piano. Guests and residents mingled in the foyer, their suitcases ferried back and forth by smartly-dressed bellhops.

At the entrance to the restaurant, *The Mabel at Las Colinas,* people waited for tables. Mars strode past, acknowledged by the maitre'd, attracting not a few stares from the crowd. Patrick followed him to a large open booth by the window. On his feet, Mars grew. Built like a rugby player, with large wide shoulders and an imposing torso, he walked like the hotel was his home, stopping at tables to greet people, shaking hands, and bending to kiss ladies on the cheek.

At the booth, a waiter came immediately for their order. "Mr. Bellefonte, what will it be?"

"Carlos, I'll take the club on rye, no tomatoes, Swiss cheese, mustard. My friend here..." Mars studied Patrick: still out of his senses, a little boy at the parents table. "He'll take a bacon cheeseburger, with everything."

"And to drink, sir?" the waiter asked, writing down the order.

His English was reminiscent of Jorge. Patrick imagined the phone call to his friends back at the village. Noé would go ballistic.

"I think we'll just be having water today," said Mars. "Patrick, here, went for a jog in the heat."

The waiter gone, Mars turned his attention to Patrick, as though he'd suddenly fallen from the sky. "Now, let's back up a bit. I've read about you, I've seen grainy pictures of you in newspapers," Mars touched at the silverware on the table. "But it's been awhile, and all I remember is: Colombia, mad scientist, and you're American—right?"

Patrick looked across the table at his host, still dazed.

Mars smiled. "Patrick, I'm not going to turn you in."

"How can I trust you?" Patrick asked, taking a peek at the tables behind them.

"You can't," said Mars. "Not yet at least." He then leaned in close. "But I'll tell you something now—the situation you're in at the moment, on the run...I've dealt with similar issues."

Patrick nodded, beginning his story, indulging Mars over lunch in the harrows of the past few months. The burger was exquisite, and Patrick would have licked the grease from the plate had he been alone. Mars listened intently, asking questions about REI, Patrick's family, and the Hydrogen technology. It was the first time that Patrick had divulged certain details of his work, previously bound by REI's confidentiality agreement. Unconcerned about any contracts, or if Mars would believe him, Patrick experienced some catharsis in releasing his burden. He still felt blindfolded to the chessboard in front of him, the battlefield of this predicament, but he was gaining a clearer sense of where the pieces stood and where he might move next.

"So you think you were set up?" Mars asked seriously.

"I don't know," Patrick said. "It seems that way."

"And they went after your daughter?"

Patrick bit his lip. "Yes."

Mars ran his hands over his chin. "Sounds like you're a victim of circumstance, Patrick. A victim of being you."

Patrick shrugged. "It's my family and friends who are the victims."

Mars nodded. "Do you trust this…Alika?"

"I do."

Mars examined Patrick, weighing him on an invisible scale. He stood from the table, "Let's go."

Patrick set down his water, fearing that perhaps he'd said too much. He followed Mars back through the restaurant and across the lobby to the elevators beyond the lounge. As they passed the front doors, Patrick considered bolting, but the burger felt heavy in his stomach. He was still unsure about trusting this new acquaintance.

"We're going to call your friend," Mars informed him, ringing for the elevator.

"Alika?"

"Yeah."

There was a silence as they waited for the lift. Patrick moved to break it.

"So, do you—?"

"This is my hotel," Mars anticipated, the doors opening with a chime.

"Ah," nodded Patrick.

They stepped into the elevator.

Mexicali, Mexico

"How long were you there?" asked Hadley.

Patrick sat back down on the bench, shaded by the noonday sun. "With Mars? January to the end of March, about three months."

Patrick described the apartment that Mars had given him, along with the medical help for his gunshot wounds and ankle. His stitches had torn open in the chase and his ankle had never set properly. Mars demanded he get surgery to have it re-broken and put right; he was not a man to whom you easily said 'No'.

Hadley laughed. "Living ritzy for three months, I'd say you deserved it."

"It was nice."

"So this *job* in Mexico, for which you've been recruited for your driving skills," Hadley began. "Is this for Mars?"

"It's for a friend of his," said Patrick. "It was supposed to be a one-day layover, one-week at the most."

"But it's turned into a month?"

"Mars is furious. He said I could leave if I want—I have all the right fake documentation—but I feel like I owe it to him."

"To break the law?"

"Sure. The man saved my life." Based on past experience, Mars had urged Patrick to enter the US at a physical border, not by air.

"How does he know all this anyway?"

Patrick smiled to himself. "He's a fellow victim of circumstance."

Mars Bellefonte had grown up near Dallas in the city of Irving. He had played football and earned a scholarship to play at TCU, explaining his size. After college, he considered trying for the NFL and even went to the Combine, except his mother got sick before the Draft and Mars went home. Unable to keep up with medical bills and other family finances, Mars needed another source of cash flow. Like many before him, Mars turned to the narcotics trade.

His mother passed in the late-90's, and on a whim Mars ventured to Colombia. Still young, he had ended up under the wing of a Caribbean businessman. Through extensive bartering, and a measure of intimidation, Mars established a trafficking route into the US through offshore oil rigs. The racket made him incredibly wealthy and he quickly outgrew his apprenticeship. Demand was strong, his supply was steady, the smuggling uncontested, and his margins were enormous. Things were so good that Mars was thinking of expanding to other services—until he met Ramira. A local beauty, Ramira tamed Mars and his powerful ambitions, prompting him to rethink his employ. The day she told him they were pregnant, Mars quit the business. Instead of cartel infrastructure, he pooled his assets into other enterprises—hotels, museums, casinos, hospitals. *The Mabel* was named for his mother.

"And why all the help for you?" Hadley asked. "Does he recognize a kindred spirit?"

"He's never said," Patrick admitted. "But I trust him."

Hadley breathed out deeply. "In times like these—a rare luxury."

Patrick leaned back on the bench, angling his head up to watch the leaves on the tree above him. He'd looked at them before, those same dusty flags, carried away in countless discussions on matters that despite their reality still sounded crazy.

"Are you going to be able to cope?" Patrick asked Hadley. "Not seeing her."

The question ushered in a short silence.

"I'll do my best," said Hadley. "Doesn't feel like I have much of a choice."

"It's been the hardest part."

"How have you managed?"

He let out a sigh. "It's been some consolation to know she's with Alika. He sends pictures from time to time."

"He brought me some too."

"She's grown hasn't she?"

"She has," said Hadley, audibly flipping through several shots. "Her hair…"

Through the line, Patrick could hear a struggle for composure. "It won't be long," he promised.

"How have you done it?" she asked again. "And with everything else..."

"As hard as it is," said Patrick, "And I think about it day and night, I'd either be putting her in more danger or giving up a chance to be with her."

Hadley lost it all over. For a solid minute, she bawled uncontrollably into the phone. Patrick heard a nurse approach to comfort. Tragic as it was, the sounds of her anguish stirred remnants of long-dormant resolve. He felt the redemptive feeling of renewed responsibility, and with it, a surge of love.

One week later

Patrick was delayed another week until the first of May. Idling in the mild dawn, the engine of the stolen Mexican soda truck breathed fumes into the air and around through the open windows of the cab. At quarter to five, his uniform and hat on straight, Patrick received a text message to proceed. Shifting the heavy beast into first gear, he began the two-mile drive to the border. In the rearview mirror, he looked back at the unlit sign for Jimmy's restaurant. The decaying building slept on in the hum of the decrepit fluorescent street lighting, the smell of noodles yet unleashed.

Patrick had to be timely; the soldiers at the border posts would reach the end of their shifts in fifteen minutes. He angled the large truck about the street corners and through the green lights that dominated his path. Traffic was building from people already on their way to work. There was no one else in the truck but Patrick.

What exactly the cargo was, he didn't know. Patrick had purposefully never asked.

At 4:50 a.m., he neared the entrance to the United States of America. Patrick had rehearsed this moment since Colombia. He had all the appropriate documentation and ID to make the crossing. There were several checkpoint lanes, and at this hour only two lanes would be in use. Directions in Spanish and English began to show up along the side of the road, instructing the traffic how to approach. Patrick eyed the armed soldiers on the ground and in the newly-built towers. He hoped none of them had been transferred from the Embassy in Colombia.

On cue, two cars zipped from a side street in front of the truck. Patrick laid on his horn as rehearsed. Some people were likely returning home now, partly sobered from wild nights at the local bars, clubs, or casinos. With a drinking age of 18, Patrick regularly saw packs of American high-school seniors prowling outside the liquor stores and then stumbling down the street an hour later.

The cars ahead of him wheeled and curved characteristically along the slow ramp towards the border. When it was their turn, they revved their engines and jerkily pulled up to the booths at the same time. Without hesitation, both border patrol officers came around and began to question the drivers. Patrick knew that neither driver was intoxicated and that they had proper identification. They would have to be let through. It was all part of the rouse.

At 4:55, with just five minutes remaining on the shift, Patrick inched his soda truck to the window.

"Heya pard," Patrick said with a practiced drawl.

The officer, clearly exhausted, flashed a loose smile.

"Guessin' you'll be needin' 'dees." Patrick handed out a set of border documents for the truck, all of them craftily counterfeited. "Keepin' dem illegals out okay?" he asked in feigned disgust.

"Just doing our job," the officer replied, skipping down through the papers.

"Good. Family and me, we from Texas—we 'preciate it."

The officer stopped reading and glanced up at Patrick, then shot a curious eye down the body of the truck. For a long breath, Patrick thought he had blown it, but the officer's fatigue was on his side.

"Thanks," said the officer belatedly. "I need to ask what you're carrying in there?"

"I think you prolly read jus' fine," Patrick said, bobbing his head at the big cursive letters.

"That's what I thought," the officer said. "Your ID?"

Patrick passed it down.

"Well, Mr. Joyce," the guard said after a check. "I have just one question."

Patrick raised his eyebrows, uncertain. "Sir?"

"You wouldn't happen to have a loose soda rolling around in there would you?"

Patrick gave a wink and bent down to his right. "Well, you in luck sir." He pulled a half-spent six pack from the floor of the cab. "I jus' happen to be packin'."

It was the only soda in the truck.

Twenty miles north, in Brawley, California, Patrick parked the truck outside a deserted loading dock.

Hopping down from the cab in the morning sunlight, he shouldered a new backpack and walked out to the street. As promised, a dark green BMW 550i ED was parked a block away.

Mars sure had class.

Chapter 32

June 2012
The Eco, Florida

It was an evening for milkshakes. Alika ordered strawberry and Meredith chose a chocolate-vanilla twist. They were sitting outside, the heat of the day dissipating in the early June dark. Overhead, the flaps of the table umbrella shuddered from the occasional dance of wind. Maxwell's was the first of three eateries built within The Eco, and easily Meredith's favorite. It had been two months since their arrival; Alika starting his new role as Director of Lab Studies, and Meredith continuing, to the best of her knowledge, as an orphan.

The facility, west of Camp Blanding by about an hour, was astounding, a place of discovery. Indeed, no expense had been spared. The exterior of the buildings were all marble, white and gray, with blue and black blotches thrown arbitrarily about in neo-artistic array. Landscaped berms nestled and fell up against the walls, cupping outward into sparkling fountains and ponds. Battlement green-works ringed the roof to create pleasant terraces with soft grass and seasonal flowers. True to the overall mission, the whole Eco was powered entirely by prototype ERM Hydrogen fuel cells.

By design, the complex was separated into Work and Home, connected by several paths. On the *Life* side, there were apartments and condos, a small shopping mall, restaurants, and a large exercise center with saunas, tennis courts, and a pool that bore the zigzag of a massive lightning bolt across its bottom. The *Work* zone was no less impressive. Together with the mesmerizing domes, light-capturing windows, and comfortable interior design, the lab spaces were first-class and equipped with every conceivable piece of equipment.

The research teams were stellar, hand-selected from the top labs and programs throughout the world. Morale was high, and using an array of languages, the chemists, engineers, and physicists worked collectively, forging new ideas in the wake of Patrick's discoveries. Media coverage had been favorable, rousing interest in various sectors and sending Seven Energy stock prices to all-time highs. Proposals for collaboration from other industries were in abundance and external job inquiries flooded Human Resources daily. The buzz about the globe, from academics to pundits to scientists to politicians to celebrities, was that Seven had done it—they had discovered the successor to oil. Naturally, there were skeptics, but the technology was so shrouded in mystery that the naysayers had little to attack.

Away from the spin and flash, Alika knew the sheer side of the mountain. Although advancements in Hydrogen technology were occurring at a relatively rapid pace, there had been setbacks. In Patrick's absence, development had slowed. His former team members were struggling to reproduce the groundbreaking results from his final weeks with the lab in Colombia. The discontinuity was troubling, especially to Seven executives. "What?" they would ask Alika, "What did your colleague do?"

The milkshakes arrived, thick and too viscous for a straw.

Meredith dipped her spoon in and out of the glass like a candlemaker, the ice cream clinging to the utensil. Meredith loved ice cream, and without regard she began to devour the treat. In time, she looked up at Alika. He had not touched his shake.

"You don't like it?" she asked.

"No, I like it" replied Alika. "I'm just waiting."

"Why?"

"It's too thick."

Meredith made a face, holding her spoon in the air. "Ice cream is never too thick."

"This is a milkshake. I'm waiting until I can use the straw."

Meredith leaned across the table and looked into Alika's glass. "That might take a while," she observed, returning to her twist. "I'll be on my second by then."

Alika plied at the shake with his straw. The solution was softer now, and the ice cream bobbed like a buoy. He glanced back at Meredith. She was watching. Alika ducked his head and gave a tug at the straw. After a moment of fabricated suspense, he smacked his lips.

"Ready?" she asked.

"It's perfect," Alika said.

In a few weeks, Hadley would arrive on a Greyhound from Bethesda. She had been delayed by yet another battle, one unrelated to Hydrogen, a bittersweet discovery. Patrick was already near, hiding at a motel in Tallahassee, preparing for the next big move. Plans were clicking forward like teeth on a gear, yet each advance only added further variables, complicating life for Alika. The stress was regularly overwhelming. With his directorship at the lab, the covert orchestrations for Hadley and Patrick, his parental duties to Meredith, and the long-distance relationship with Dolores—there was legitimately too much.

Meredith's straw hit air at the bottom of her glass. She reached for the stainless steel mixing cup, a quarter-full with leftover shake. "Reload!"

The umbrella quivered under another breeze. A bus boy came to clear a neighboring table. Inside, there was the sound of waitresses singing Happy Birthday. A family walked around the patio to their car. There was a rumble of thunder.

Alika watched Meredith over his straw, reminded that 'too much' was relative.

The next morning, Alika's office phone rang and rang. Seven was conducting their quarterly research assessments, gradually burying Alika in paperwork and sticky notes. As the intermediary for all lab work, Alika was required to report on the measured progress of each lab division. The stack of paperwork was all due to Seven; the sticky notes, less so.

Alika's secretary, Claudia Schuh, had a penchant for Post-Its. They were everywhere. The little yellow notes had become so excessive that Alika bought an especial board on which to place them. It was meant to be a gentle way of showing the practice's absurdity. Claudia took it as a compliment and scribbled even more.

Alika plucked three notes from his inbox. Two were inspirational quotes that Claudia had found online, and the third was a copied Snapple Cap Fact.

"Claudia!" he yelled from his office.

"Yes, Mr. Tucker," she said, breezing into the room. She was tall, willowy, and small-town Georgia. Meredith called her Boots. "How can I help?"

Alika still couldn't gather the heart. "Could you...could you call over to Consuela and ask her to come up?"

"Why sure," she said. When Alika traveled, Claudia would stay with Meredith and the two would sit up half the night playing games and giggling. "Anything else?"

"No, that's all. Thanks."

She curtsied and left.

Alika let out a deep sigh as he considered the expectations lying on his desk. Seven was pushing to have a mass-market prototype for regional Hydrogen production centers before 2013. Electricity generation would be their first campaign. The goal was to begin full-scale production by 2016, ramping up operations domestically in parallel to growing demand. They would build Hydrogen factories throughout the country, similar in geography to powerplants and oil refineries that perch on the edge of large cities. Infrastructure contracts were in their final stages and corollary investment would ideally blow through the roof once the deals went public. Under the auspices of Green Stimulus, the government was taking a strong role in the process, offering to subsidize the cost of

the projects in return for partial ownership of the p
power stations. This was national energy security at i
type of decision that could determine an election.

When approached, the utility companies had been hesitant, balking over the riskiness of emerging technologies and Hydrogen. Yet as money began to move, the utilities pulled up their chairs. Coal lobbies and certain state politicians were striking hard at the Capitol, but had thus far met tough resistance from old allies like BP, Shell, Chevron, and ExxonMobil. Alika had suspected that these other petroleum powers might try to hinder Seven's lead into the Hydrogen market. Instead, they were preparing for Hydrogen developments of their own. Alika learned offhandedly that licensing bargains had been struck in return for political teamwork. The status quo was to continue to exploit oil as long as it remained profitable, but with carbon sanctions looming, the barons wanted to be ready.

Consuela Garcia poked her head around the corner. "Hey there," she said, swinging her body into the room. Even in a lab coat, she was curvy. "May I come in?"

Alika always kept it business with Consuela. No games. She was too smart, too good at what she did, and too attractive. "Did you get that message I forwarded from the corporate office?"

She sat down and crossed her legs. "The one about the mass-market apparatus?"

Alika nodded.

"Yes, I got it."

"And…"

She re-crossed her legs. "And I don't understand what they're thinking." With her soft features and hazel eyes, Consuela looked more like a Miss Universe contestant than a laboratory brain trust. Since Patrick's disappearance, she had carried on his work, assuming Seven's public face for their new Hydrogen technology. She was becoming the new image of energy—youthful, intelligent, beautiful.

"I don't think Seven is *thinking*," said Alika, rotating in his chair. "I think they're panicking. They want their Hydrogen."

"And they can't have it—the prototype just isn't there," Consuela explained. "We're testing the environmental impacts, but what we're testing isn't even what the prototype would be anyway! Some pieces are still missing."

"We're going to have to give them a reason."

"Ok," she said, putting her hands together and leaning forward. "How about…We need Patrick."

Alika left the office around 6:00 p.m. It was a novelty to live so close to work. Door to door, the walk was less than five minutes; too short on some days. Meredith would be waiting for him. It was Tuesday, which meant her night to pick a movie.

From Alika's office above the laboratories, his path home led overtop of the Magnetics Lab. The walkway was a showcase corridor for visitors, windows looking down on both sides. Protective blinds came up when testing was in-progress, giving the avenue a retro-futuristic vibe. Researchers were usually present at all hours and Alika liked to stop and look down through the glass at their work. Today the lab was empty. Alika halted anyway to observe the black countertops and shiny instruments. Part of him wanted to be down there in the action where the developments were made. It was empowering to stand on frontiers.

"Nice view," a voice said from down the hall. A man approached.

Alika didn't have to see a face to know who it was. "Hey Ward."

"Good to see you," he said, coming forward with a smile. Ward wore a crisp suit, one hand couched in his pocket. Alika had seen less of him recently with REI's role fulfilled.

"Yeah, same," said Alika. He stepped up to shake hands. "What brings you through?"

Low light from either window illuminated their faces.

"Did you get the e-mail?"

Alika shook his head in sincerity. "No, must have missed it."

"Huh." Ward settled his shoulders and opened his hands. "I've joined Seven."

Alika's face alone showed his surprise. "Wow…Great!"

Ward worked a smile. He looked down at the lab below. "It's exciting. Never thought I'd end up hawking Hydrogen from rural Florida. I suppose you know the feeling."

"Life has its surprises."

Ward nodded, still examining the space below.

"What will you be doing?" asked Alika.

"My official title is *Director of Energy Development*." He turned back to Alika. "Which boils down to: make Hydrogen the new oil."

Alika cleared his throat. "And are you working out of The Eco?"

"I'll be all over, but my main office will be here. I've been taking a closer look around, it's an impressive place."

"Best there is."

"I don't doubt it."

Alika looked at his watch. "Hey, have to run, but we should catch up this week."

"That'd be great. Tomorrow?"

"Yeah, give me a call. Maybe around ten? We can grab a drink. Meredith should be asleep by then."

"How is she?" Ward asked.

"Great, but waiting on me." Alika slapped Ward on the back. "Good to see you."

"Likewise."

Alika carried on down the corridor, leaving Ward alone above the labs. Patrick had long fallen out of conversation.

Meredith was sitting in the living room with a stack of DVD's. "So many choices!" she said as Alika came in the door. Kyle closed a book and stood up from the couch. The teacher wore his usual khaki pants and loose button-down shirt.

"All set, Mr. Tucker?"

"Kyle—for the hundredth time—call me Alika. And yes, all set. You're welcome to stay if—"

"Nope, it's fine. Gotta run." Grabbing a backpack, Kyle skirted awkwardly around Alika and out the front door. Alika knew he was off to play video games. That's all the kid did.

"Alika," Meredith said seriously, pointing to the tower of movies. "I think I'm going to need some help."

Patrick told Alika to relax.

"I don't like it, Patrick. Not at all."

"So he got a new job, good for him."

"Something's up. They know you're alive. He knows you're alive."

"Ward? Might be good if he did. Anyway, I thought we'd ruled him out?"

"No one's out. Remember your visit to our nation's Embassy?"

Working with Mars, it was agreed that Patrick's presence in Bogota had been known. The security cameras at the Embassy and the handwriting on his information form would be conclusive. Surprisingly, nothing ever reached the media, and any knowledge of Patrick's erratic visit must have been kept internally. None of the men knew how to take the silence. It was yet another variable.

"Alika—"

"It feels wrong."

"What do you want to do?" asked Patrick. He was aware of Alika's stress levels. They had a habit of spiking and provoking sudden outbursts. Patrick experienced similar highs and lows, and the two played a rotating game of neutralization.

"I say we jet soon. Get Meredith out of here."

"We can't," said Patrick. "It'll be too complicated."

"And things aren't already? Ward is here! I know he was our buddy back at school, but to be honest, I'm not sure we ever knew the guy."

More than anything, Patrick wanted to grab his daughter and flee. The motels of Tallahassee were not growing on him, but the risk of rushing their plan was too great. It would be impulsive to flinch now, after all the waiting. As to Ward, Patrick wasn't sure; reading people was not a personal forte.

"Forget it," said Alika in frustration.

"Okay. Let's say *they* do know I'm alive—assuming that *they* is still an unknown entity with a stake in Hydrogen—what then? What does that change?"

"Then they'll be waiting for you here."

"The Embassy was five months ago. In a different country. I could be dead."

"You were at Mars' hotel for months. Someone could have said something. I'm sure plenty of people knew."

"There're countless possibilities," admitted Patrick.

"I have to go," Alika said, frustrated. He was at a gas station a few miles from the complex.

"Relax," said Patrick.

The day after Ward returned, Claudia left the office early for a doctor's appointment. Alika was putting a dent in the Seven reports, and with his secretary gone he was relieved of any extra notes. She had started to buy different colors and the Post-It board was rapidly becoming a Jackson Pollock.

Ward called around five to confirm drinks. Alika found it so hard to gauge the man. He had never understood Ward in college and nothing had changed in the intervening decade. Alika did feel that Ward was not a killer. Alika had known killers in Salinas. There was a wily, rabid switch about them. Some had been his classmates in high school. Initiations for the Norteño or Sureño gangs occasionally required the pledges to jump someone or be jumped themselves. On occasion, the entrance exam ended fatally; Alika had lost a good friend to that mess. Although Ward was something else, maybe there was a difference when you end a life with words or on paper. Governments and generals had done it through the ages, especially kings.

That night, as Alika walked to Maxwell's, he vowed to keep his guard up. His acceptance of Ward's arrival had not been reversed by the call to Patrick. As brilliant as he was, Patrick had a limit for character analysis. Alika himself was admittedly no seer, but the past eight months had taught him that there was some wisdom in paranoia.

"Alika! Over here!" Ward cried, already at the bar and several drinks in. "Andrew, I want you to meet Alika Tucker," slurred Ward. Behind him a TV showed highlights from a Florida Marlins game.

Alika shook hands with Andrew Tuttle, one of their top physicists. "Hi Andrew, good to see you." He was a nice enough fellow, tall and lean, a little creepy—occasionally offering to crack your back.

"Oh you know each other," Ward said disappointedly. "I'm beginning to realize how small this place is."

The bar was full for a weekday, and various members of staff sat at tables and leant against chairs. Outside of the scientists, there was a sizeable administrative staff, as well as various maintenance, custodial, and technical positions. Seven had made a PR point of employing local people.

The three of them talked for a few minutes, speaking over the din. Ward indulged Andrew with a few undergrad stories; including the one about Alika breaking up his bar fight.

"And I started that, didn't I?" said Ward, tottering on his stool. "Awful bad move."

Andrew sidled off shortly, leaving Alika and Ward alone.

"And then there were two," said Ward. "It's a nice night. Let's go outside."

They sat at a table, not far from where Alika and Meredith had ordered their milkshakes.

"Alika Tucker, can you believe we're sitting here?"

Alika took a drink in place of answering.

"It's amazing," Ward repeated. "Right?"

"It's something else," replied Alika.

"When I think back to Penn and The Kingdom—The Kingdom! Remember that place?" They'd been talking about it for ten minutes with Andrew. "Damn. Time sure does get a move on."

Alika took another drink and nodded. It gave him confidence that Ward was drunk. "You going to be able to beat this heat?" he asked, changing to a simpler subject.

Ward shrugged. "I don't know, we'll have to see." His sleeves were rolled up and he waved his tan forearms about in the air. "There's just so much going on."

Alika almost pressed him to elaborate. If Ward was drunk enough, perhaps he could learn something. If there was anything to be learned.

"Hydrogen," Ward continued. "It's a beautiful word. A beautiful thing. Amazing to think that this all started from Patrick. 'Ol Patrick, thinking he could control the sky."

"Amazing," echoed Alika. He wondered if it was best to allow Ward to just jabber on; this was his first non-business mention of Patrick in weeks.

"Did you know, Alika, that in some medieval villages, they believed that ringing the church bells would prevent a strike to the steeple?"

"I did. Patrick told me once."

"It's funny how our minds work in the presence of a greater power. We get this foolish hope of control." Ward paused, and then chuckled. "Like my liver before a bottle of McCallan's."

Alika cracked a smile.

"Wish he was here to celebrate with us—Patrick. Perhaps a toast?" Ward sloppily raised his glass. "To Patrick. And the fire of heaven."

Alika also raised his glass, Ward rushing forward to meet it. Beer spilled onto the table as their glasses clinked. "To Patrick," Alika said.

"You know, it's very interesting to me," said Ward, settling back in his seat. "How the progression of discovery works. It's such an iterative process. Little contributions, minor fixes, delicate bumps, here and there, all add up to this magnificent creation. It's artistic, really: Progress. It's almost like…almost like…a beautiful mosaic."

Alika rubbed at his chin. "That's well put. I suppose it is."

"I've often wondered what piece I might be in such a picture," said Ward. "Perhaps in this very scene before us." He set his beer on the table. "Alika, have you ever wondered that? What piece you are?"

The question was phrased a smidge too clearly. Alika looked at Ward, but his face was pointed up to the sky.

"I haven't," said Alika, feeling the world begin to melt away. "Have you?"

"I have."

"And?"

Ward brought his gaze down to meet Alika's. The man looked sober as a priest. "I'm not any of them at all."

In complete stillness, they stared directly at each other, faces fixed.

"Alika," Ward said at last. "I'm the guy that sees the mosaic. Every piece for what it is. I notice what it looks like. I'm the one that points it out. I understand that if you trim it just right, I mean, just right—this edge to that one, one corner to the other—how perfectly it would fit in with everything else—the rest of the gallery."

Alika said nothing.

A waiter came to the table and asked if they'd like to see a menu. Neither of them said anything, ignoring the invitation. Casting a strange look, the waiter backed away and left the table.

"That's a lot of pressure," Alika said. "Being a curator."

Ward shrugged. "I'm no curator. The world takes care of that."

"Then what would you call yourself?"

"I guess you could say—I'm more of an art dealer."

"And what's in it for the art dealer?"

Ward looked back up into the sky, tracing lines between the stars and their constellations. "Everything."

They sat silently for a time. Alika struggled to compute the full meaning of this encounter, debating whether or not Ward was in a state to be taken seriously. "And Patrick?" he asked, piercing the quiet of the patio.

Ward returned his gaze to the earth, the weight of mountains hanging behind his eyes. He held out his hands and smiled convincingly at Alika. "When fires start in forests, they don't just pick on trees."

Alika immediately stood, pushing his chair back with a screech. He hung over the table like an umbrella, locked in a riveting stare with Ward, seething from the statement. Having cared so much for Patrick and his family, with all the sacrifice, after numberless nights of doubt and nerves, it infuriated him to hear Ward comment so glibly on Patrick's travail. Alika wanted to get violent, he wanted to strike; he wished he could get answers, take Ward someplace where no one would hear his cries, find out *who*, *why*, *how much*; he longed for truth, for a release. More than anything, he desired the power to go back in time and eliminate his idea for non-profit energy—it had brought nothing but sorrow.

Instead, Alika severed the tension with a grin. "Good to see you Ward, have to be off."

Ward loosened his shoulders. "Leaving so soon?" he asked.

"I should go," Alika said, draining his beer. "It's late."

"Late, schmate!"

"I have a sitter for Meredith," Alika explained, walking away. "I said I'd be back."

"I'll be gone in Chicago through the weekend," Ward yelled after him. "Maybe some golf when I get back?"

Alika pretended not to hear.

Chapter 33

July 2012
Jacksonville, Florida

The bus ride provoked reflection. It was not so much the vehicle, the Greyhound clientele, or the potato-chip smell of the seats, but Hadley's last comparable trip—the weekend Patrick had proposed. Ten years and she had come completely about-face. Travelling south, not north; experiencing warmth, not chill; divorced, not engaged; presumed dead, still Hadley.

The bus pulled into Jacksonville around 10:00 p.m. The steps down to the curb were an estuary of humidity and conditioned air. Hadley descended in a gray hooded sweatshirt and walked to the open cargo doors to retrieve her bags. She had a small duffel and a suitcase on rollers. Wheeling over the pebbly pavement, she claimed the first idling taxi at the stand.

The driver hoisted her suitcase into the trunk. "Where to ma'am?"

"The Hertz on Cassat," Hadley replied, relishing the human contact.

Thirty minutes later, Hadley pulled out of the car rental lot in a white 2012 Ford Fusion. The new car had a built-in GPS and estimated the drive to The Eco at two hours and fifteen minutes. Listening to the automated directions, Hadley maneuvered out of Jacksonville and began driving west.

She messed with the radio, tuning until she found *Florida's best soft hits of the 80's, 90's, and Today.* The fluffy chords made her pensive. She thought of Patrick and Meredith, feeling weak to their proximity, and wondered what they would think of her new black hair, freshly dyed by Rosa. She pondered on her parents and siblings, imagining with humility the toll that her loss might have taken. There was solace in knowing that she would be reborn to them soon. Toiling through this induced ordeal she had yearned for their support, especially that of her mother. The two months of rehabilitation had been unforeseeably lengthened to three.

In their thorough examinations of Hadley, the doctors found a lump in her left breast. Further tests exposed it as a cancerous tumor. The invader was the size of a sunflower seed. Rosa told her its discovery was fortuitous. The cancer was Stage 1 and could be treated through minor surgery. The procedure to remove the lump was performed promptly and the specialist deemed soon after that no radiation or further treatment would be necessary. As she had yet to begin her physical rehab sessions, Hadley's doctor estimated it would add another two weeks to her recovery time.

Despite the staff's optimism, the cancer was an emotional tipping point for Hadley. From her bed in Bethesda, she recalled Life as an ally always working the grain in her favor—now everything was splintered. Mired secretly beneath hospital sheets, unable to walk, mourned by her daughter and family, Patrick a fugitive, strangers burning her home, Korey murdered—the weight was too much. Hadley began to sift into depression and bitterness. She skipped meals, snapped at other patients, and fitfully destroyed newspapers if the writing was poor. On some days she just lay lifeless on the bed, refusing to be comforted. Rosa would try and cheer her to no avail. Hadley even stopped her calls with Patrick and Alika, keeping the curtains drawn.

After two weeks of misery, a letter arrived. Inside was a picture that Meredith had drawn for school. It was from when she had briefly gone back to Bryn Mawr, after the fire and before the funeral. The class was studying the Revolutionary War, in particular the letters that had been sent to soldiers from their homes. The assignment had been to display something that gave you hope. Meredith had drawn the living room in their old Philadelphia apartment. She was a handy artist and the resemblance was clear. Sitting on the couch were Hadley and Patrick, and on the floor leaning up against their legs was Meredith. Alika was drawn behind the couch with his arms folded. “I think she still remembers The Godfather.” Alika had scrawled on a green Post-It. The picture was drawn in colored pencil, dated December 1st, 2011.

Hadley stared at the picture for the remainder of the day, intermittently laughing, sobbing, and whispering to herself.

The next morning when Rosa arrived at the ward, Hadley was lying on the ground, her head laid on her arm and feet splayed in either direction.

“Hadley!” Rosa cried, rushing to her side.

Stirring, Hadley looked up. “Rosa?” she asked blearily, “Been expecting you.”

“Sweet Helen! What happened?” A few neighboring patients woke to take notice.

Hadley winced, rolling over. “I’ve been practicing.”

Rosa looked at her sideways. “Practicing what? Playing dead? Nearly scared the breakfast out of me.”

“Walking,” Hadley explained, smiling for the first time in days. She looked disappointedly down at her legs, “I might need some help.”

Two months later, the day after Independence Day, Hadley walked out of the hospital and caught a taxi for the bus station.

The Eco, Florida

There was a gate at the complex, manned at all hours by armed security guards. It was past midnight, balmy and clear, when Hadley pulled up to the booth. A short sunburnt man with a blue cap approached her window.

“Yes?”

“Hi. I’m a new employee, just arriving.”

“Name?” From his side, the man pulled a clipboard into sight. He was 30-ish with a drowsy complexion and stocky legs.

"Clara Fox," she said, swinging a slight drawl. Off the books, the Witness Protection agents had helped set up a new identification and background portfolio for Hadley.

He scanned down a list. "Ah, here you are Ms. Fox. I-D?"

"I have the name badge right here," she said sweetly, retrieving an employee card on a lanyard from the front seat. "Of course, I can get my driver's license too if—"

"No, that'll do," he said quickly, finding her attractive. "You new here?"

"Yes, actually," Hadley replied. "Starting tomorrow. Nothing much, just cleaning."

"Good job," he said, getting comfortable. "Where ya' from?"

"Jacksonville."

"Yeah?"

Hadley feared the conversation might break into local knowledge. "Not much of a drive, but tired anyway. Probably should get moved in. I'll be seeing you though?"

"'Course," he said proudly. "I'm Ben. Work nights mostly."

"Well," Hadley said, putting an end to the chat. "Thanks for the help."

The guard raised the gate and Hadley drove on. She didn't recognize the other man in the booth. He planted a cigarette between his lips as she passed, lighting it slowly with a bronze-cased lighter. They had not been this close since the fire.

The road forked ahead, one branch leading to the lab and test areas, the other towards the residences and local amenities. Hadley followed Alika's directions past several restaurants and darkened stores until she found the apartments. The flats were sharply built, reminding Hadley of a wealthy retirement neighborhood outside of Boston. She found *Building 5* and parked out front. Crickets chirped as she stood from the car. Sounds of living ebbed out of windows and screened porches. Stars blinked knowingly. She felt like she had arrived late to summer camp, when everyone is already zipped up in their tents.

Hadley quickly retrieved her belongings and shuffled down to Apartment #2, her new home. Using the badge ID, she beeped open the door. Lights came on as she entered, revealing a combination kitchen, dining room, and living room. It was tastefully furnished and looked much like a hotel extended-stay suite. There was a packet on the counter with welcome information for new employees, garnished by two bottles of water and a basket of candy and fruits.

Too excited to rest, Hadley polished an apple and busied herself with unpacking and exploring the apartment. She called Patrick and told him that she had arrived safe. He was still in a motel near Tallahassee. The plans for their departure were almost set—two more weeks.

The envelope from Alika was in the nightstand. Inside was a picture of him and Meredith. It was one of those your-head-on-their-body shots. Alika was an eye-patched swashbuckling pirate, and Meredith was the parrot on his shoulder. On the back was penned a single sentence.

Even if we don't all realize it, we're excited you're here!

The next afternoon, Hadley attended an orientation session at the Human Resources office. She wore blue jeans and a black shirt. The fake resume that Alika had pushed through HR showed Hadley as a seasoned custodian. Outside of the standard household duties, however, she was far from a janitorial wonder.

With her new style, Rosa agreed that Hadley looked little like her formal self. It would take a close examination to decode Miss Clara Fox. Regardless, Hadley felt edgy at being so exposed. Alika assured Hadley that Ward would be overseas for a few weeks, so there was no need to worry about bumping into him.

Hadley's supervisor was a lean, grouchy woman named Hazel. With little variation, she smoked Virginia Slims every forty minutes. After meeting briefly with a chirpy HR member, Hadley was released into her care. At a runner's pace, Hazel played tour guide, showing Hadley the break room, the bathroom, the smoker's corral—which Hazel utilized—the cafeteria, Hazel's office, and the mail room. The rooms were pleasantly decorated and abundantly equipped. Green, in all its verdant cloaks, was a definite motif.

The Eco complex itself was entirely interconnected, with separate arms dedicated to specific areas of research and development. From the sky, it looked like a sun with orbs at the end of each ray. The building they had first toured was the 'human needs' center; officially, the Resource Wing. North of the complex were the lightning fields.

"You punch-in down at the break room," Hazel said over her shoulder as they walked. She had a labored gait and her voice was coarse. "You saw the little machine, right? It's there on the wall by the Cokes."

Hadley had not, but she nodded anyway.

Hazel was leading her into the heart of the complex. Weaving through bunches of scientists with lab coats, and men and women dressed in office attire, Hadley tried to shield her awe. Down every hallway there was some interesting lab, new-age workspace, or impressively configured conference room. The center of the building was dominated by a glass dome, which at this daylight hour seemed to shatter into a million pieces of shimmering light. Hadley hoped Patrick would have a chance to see it. Alika had not exaggerated when he said the complex was something of a small city.

To her relief, none of the employees seemed to notice her or Hazel; they passed through like ghosts.

"Ya got offices here," Hazel said as they reached Hadley's assignment. "Vacuum, empty trash, wipe surfaces—the usual drill, nothing you haven't done."

"Uh-huh," went Hadley, unconvinced by her supervisor's confidence.

"Next, you got the bathrooms. Again, no surprises. Here's your closet." Hazel leant down and pressed her badge to a pad by a door. On the wall was a sign that read *Custodian*. The lock popped open. The room was like others Hadley had seen, but only in passing; shelves with toiletry items, rolls of garbage bags, a mug filled with pencils. "You got your chart on the back of the door. Just go down when you're done and check through. Yadda yadda, same old deal."

Hazel shut the door and looked at Hadley. "You sure you don't smoke?"

Hadley left Hazel's care for her apartment around 5:00 p.m. Upon walking outdoors, she knew a storm was shortly to strike. Palm fronds rapped against one another and the sky was steel blue. Car windows went up and seasoned employees lengthened their stride. Hadley mimicked their brisk pace down the sidewalk. Raindrops arrived, plump as grapes. She began to trot, the warm water making dots on her jeans. As the downpour commenced, Hadley skidded beneath the awning of her building.

It was less of a yell, than a shout. It was swifter than a glance, only a blink. It happened as Hadley turned to go inside—Meredith running full tilt through the rain.

Hadley froze.

The girl was a football field away on the other side of the parking lot, speeding to reach the safety of cover. An awkward young man with a backpack gave chase. They found shelter and began to shake the water off their clothes. Meredith beamed at her soaked attire, brushing knots of rain from her forehead and cheeks. Her brown hair was down, wavy in the wet air.

Hadley walked forward a few steps into the rain.

She had anticipated this moment like no other. In her mind, there had been differing circumstances, alternating settings, but always the same outcome. A hug of remedy; stretched long enough to begin to cure the cavernous wounds of separation and misery. There would be kisses and more hugs, but this first embrace would commence the healing.

Hadley hung in the deluge, as though transfixed at a disappearing oasis, quenching what maternal yearnings she could. It was Meredith, her daughter, smiling within a voices' call. Part of her wanted to run and abscond with the child now. The way seemed so unfettered. The teacher could be dealt with, and then there was just her car and the beckoning road towards Patrick. They could be halfway through Louisiana before Hadley's shift that night.

Instead, with the deepest of loves, Hadley rooted her feet to the ground. And as quickly as she'd flitted into frame, the torrent subsided and little Meredith bounded off stage.

The mother waited another few minutes, drenched, wondering at the shockwaves of resurrection.

Hadley's first night at work was a release. She'd crossed over enemy lines and the apartment had become her foxhole. The solitude was foreign. At the ward there had been other patients and nurses, people buzzing about. In Apartment 502, Hadley was alone, pinned down to ask the internal questions that respectable distractions had thus far excused. The torture of the inquiry was the emerging limitations on her agency. Everything about the future felt rhetorical.

It was therefore liberating to wander about the quiet office space, steadily ticking her way down the task sheet. There was something familiar about cleaning. She reckoned it was the likeness to editing; always polishing.

Besides a few other custodians, she saw no one during her eight-hour shift. It truly was the perfect cover. Hazel came through at 5:00 a.m. as Hadley was finishing with the men's bathroom. They exchanged good-mornings.

"David told me you came down and ate with them during their 3 o'clock break," Hazel said, half-asleep. "In the cafeteria."

"Yes," Hadley replied, unsure if this was an accusation. "They invited me." It had been a lovely time too, a half-dozen janitors raiding the fridges.

"Good, they're a nice bunch," Hazel yawned. She leant up against the wall in a pair of black jeans, watching Hadley as she squeezed out the mop. "You about done?"

Hadley stopped to wipe her face. "About, yeah, just have to vacuum the second and third floor hallways."

"Nah," Hazel said, shaking her head. "Forget that, no one will notice. Do it every three days or so."

"Really?"

"Yeah, take it easy and clock-out on time," the supervisor egged. "Those hallways will run you at least another hour. Truth is, no matter how spotless, nobody's gonna know the wiser."

After a few more questions about the night, Hazel slid off to have a smoke. Hadley tidied her cart, consolidating the trash, and cleaning the mops and buckets. The work had been exhausting, but weighing in her recent exit from rehab, Hadley assured herself that the required exertion would decrease.

Alika had called earlier that morning, keeping the chat short. More than ever he was paranoid about communication. Visiting Hadley at work or at home might arouse suspicion, he said, so they'd agreed to meet at a bar outside the complex in two days. Hadley could hear the stress in his voice. The man had endured and given much, and she knew she'd forever be aware of only a fraction.

The sun split through a space in the blinds, waking Hadley as the light came to rest on her face. She started when she woke, lying on the couch with her feet up.

After coming home from her first shift, Hadley had made dinner-breakfast and collapsed. As doors clicked above and around, people going to work, Hadley had let her eyes close in nocturnal peace. She had drifted to sleep in the living room, hidden cozily away from the marching footsteps, jangling keys, and morning salutes.

She rolled over onto her side now, comfortable and set to return to slumber. But something caught her eye, a form out of place.

Without looking, Hadley knew it was a person. Like a tripped switch, she was suddenly at full alert, her back to the trespasser.

The sensation was horrible. It was not Alika and she questioned who else it could be. Hazel? As if the answer lay within the white-blue checkers of the sofa, Hadley stared wide-eyed into the cover, struggling to control the trigger of trauma.

The suspect's breathing became audible, low like a man's. Whoever it was, they were not moving. They were waiting.

Outlining a plan of escape, Hadley considered flipping over and flinging the coffee table in that general direction. Having the advantage of surprise, she could then bolt for the door. The strategy was shallow at best and she tensed at the realization that there might be more than one intruder. There had been last time.

Not willing to be dialed into another coma, Hadley decided to risk it. In one motion, she spun her feet to the ground and grabbed the edges of the coffee table. The man was sitting on an ottoman by the TV. He stood as Hadley let out a cry and hurled the table into the air. It hit him square in the chest and he fell backwards over the ottoman and into the curtain blinds of the sliding glass door.

The plan was perfect, only Hadley never turned to run. With the furniture in flight, she had seen his face. Instead of fleeing, she clambered forward.

Before Patrick could say a word, she was kissing him.

Chapter 34

March 15th, 2028
Safehouse Five, New York City, New York
1:35 a.m.

It's an election year and my first chance to vote for Ward Prince.

After several years at Seven Energy in Florida, Prince returned to California a very connected man. He married the daughter of a steel magnate, settled in Sacramento, and became a father. While still at Seven, Prince had been a key player in the sale of ERM Hydrogen technology to other companies, spreading its use around the world. With his handsome face, agreeable disposition, and wide reputation for reducing global dependence on fossil fuels, Prince easily cruised to victory in his 2018 bid for State Representative of California. Two years later, with his state emerging from serious debt, Prince moved successfully from the House to the Senate, where he spearheaded the Energy Interdependence Act of 2023 and several Greenhouse Gas Reduction bills. In November, he'll be running for President, favored for the Republican Nomination.

Throughout the books and movies that have involved Patrick Simon, there are often ties to the rise of Ward Prince. Except there was never any clear motive, no argument that could clear up why Patrick would need to be eliminated, no evidence that could disprove the cases built against him. And how could Ward have predicted the success of Patrick's Hydrogen technology—the wealth, the power, the control? What crystal ball would have shown him a path to the Resolute desk?

Bringing in Meredith's story, I still don't think Ward could have foreseen the result of deleting an idea such as *non-profit energy*. But if not Ward, then perhaps someone else.

Are you suggesting that Ward Prince – the presidential candidate – set-up your father?

I'm just telling you what happened.

When was the last time you saw Ward?

At the Eco. Just before we left.

What happened?

I was out by myself for a walk. On this path, here.

[Meredith makes a mark on the map that she drew earlier, indicating one of the paths between the Home and Work sections of the complex.]

It was the Fourth of July and there were going to be fireworks that evening. I had already passed the field where the men were setting up, watching them as they tied the rockets in place.

[She traces a line near a central open area.]

Nearing the laboratories, here, which emerged from this central building like spokes on a bicycle wheel, I met Ward coming the other way. He was wearing shorts.

Shorts?

Yes. The tennis racket in his hand explained the attire, but he looked odd out of a suit. He reintroduced himself politely, shook my hand and asked where I was going. I told him that I was on a walk. He asked to join and I agreed. It was the first time we'd ever been alone. He asked me all sorts of questions as we ambled, though nothing out of the ordinary.

[Meredith continues to trace their path, and though the map does help me picture them, I don't really understand its purpose.]

We looped about the entire lab complex, passing the lightning fields, until we'd arrived back where we started, here, at the fireworks.

And that was it?

Not quite. Before going our separate ways, Ward knelt down on the stones. Face to face, he said he was sorry about my parents.

What did you say?

I don't remember.

[I pause, looking again at the drawing.]

Was this why you wanted to draw the map?

No. The map's for what I'm going to tell you next.

[I don't say anything. She adds a car to the drawing.]

At which point I will be finished.

[Meredith looks back up and gives another one of her arrow-point stares. Then, visible only to me, she taps the piece of paper in front of her.]

And it will be your move.

Chapter 35

July 2012
The Eco, Florida

"You realize how strange this is?"

"Very strange."

Patrick and Alika sat in a parked car, watching as men in orange jumpsuits scurried around the field in front of them. The parking lot was especially elevated for viewing, but far enough away to inspire safety. Sounds of the storm echoed like artillery in the distance.

Patrick looked up at the sky. "How's their trigger rate?" he asked.

"One in three."

"One in three?"

"Yeah."

"Do they have a Darius down there?"

"No," Alika replied with a grin. "They re-named it Alexander."

Alika's silver Acura was the only vehicle on the platform, which was large enough to fit a score of Suburbans. The President of the United States and several other national dignitaries had been parked in the same spot just the week before, watching the show. The President had given a press conference at the center of The Eco dome, extolling the efforts of the individual scientists, and declaring the center "a massive step forward in the bid for domestic energy security". Patrick had watched the broadcast from his motel room.

"Then again," said Alika, "They aren't shooting at every storm anymore. I think it's down to five tries a week."

"I'm surprised they're shooting at all. We were past lightning in Colombia."

"No, *you* were past lightning. And they're still trying to catch up."

Patrick gave a forlorn smile. He missed his work. "I didn't ask to leave."

A wind rushed up over the lot and prodded the car. The orange jumpsuits were finished with the leaders and jogging back inside.

"Do you think it was Ward all along?" asked Patrick, staring out at the expanse. He had posed the question before. "That night at Maxwell's, did it make you think all this was his idea?

"I think he knew," said Alika. "But the plan wasn't his."

"He never struck me as a follower."

Alika glanced at Patrick. "In this game, we're all followers."

The men had disappeared from the field. There were five platforms equally spaced in a circular array. A bunker-type structure with windows was off to their right. A medley of weather utensils spun and gyrated on the roof. This was the command station; a distant cry from the old trailers at Camp Blanding.

"The platforms are configured for different storm heights," Alika said. A final siren, muffled through the car windows, shook the air to indicate the field was live. "Chad's idea."

"Juarez?"

"Yeah, he came down from Michigan for a few weeks during construction."

"How's he doing?"

Two sharp whoops went up from a loudspeaker. At the far end of the field, a rocket launched skyward. A shuddering crack followed immediately, snapping down the line. The flash split the early evening. Thunder dissipated over the complex.

"Got her," Alika said mildly. "Chad's good. Still doing his thing up north." The orange jumpsuits were surfacing again on the field. Alika started the car and turned to Patrick. "Disguise."

Patrick pulled the hat and aviators from his lap and put them on. "Everything set with Consuela?"

"Operation Peru is a Go."

An invitation had been extended for Consuela to have dinner that evening with Alika and 'a married couple from Switzerland,' a set of supposed recruits. Such introductions were common and the meal would be served at Hadley's.

"I appreciate this," Patrick said.

"What are friends for?"

"Usually?" Patrick replied, securing his glasses. "Not this much."

They drove in silence, Alika ferrying Patrick back through the complex to Hadley's apartment. For the past week, she and Patrick had visited often, mostly outside The Eco. Hadley was adjusting to a routine of working nights, sleeping mornings, and finding Patrick during the evening. Day by day, they carried the weakened coals of their marriage back to the hearth, building a brighter, warmer glow to lift them in the misery of their adversity and prepare for the obscurity that lay ahead. Sometimes they would return to her place at The Eco, Patrick hiding in the backseat, and then spy for Meredith. Twice, they had seen her.

Alika slowed the car as they approached the apartment block. "That's Kyle," he pointed. The young man was off to their left, walking in the direction of the shopping center.

Patrick nodded, watching Meredith's teacher lope down the street. He wore a green polo shirt tucked into khaki trousers with no belt. Over his left shoulder hung a bulbous black backpack. "I see what you're talking about. A little awkward, isn't he?"

"Just a smidge." Alika said. Kyle spotted the car and gave a quick wave. "But altogether harmless."

Hadley was chopping zucchini at the counter when Patrick knocked at the door. After a glance through the peephole, she let him in.

"Smells great," Patrick said, taking off his sunglasses and cap. "Need any help?"

Hadley walked back around into the kitchen. "You? Help?" She wore a khaki skirt beneath a plain white apron.

"Of course," he said, coming around the counter. "The jungle made me domestic."

They were hip to hip.

"Who said there was anything tame about cooking?" The tail of the zucchini disappeared as Hadley made several final cuts. The even slices collapsed into one another like limp dominoes.

A few carrots sat on deck beside the cutting board. "Could I cut those?" Patrick asked.

"Sure," she said. "But only those. No fingers." She moved away and cracked two eggs into a cup, mixing the yolks before pouring the beaten contents into a bowl. "How's Alika?"

"Okay," Patrick said, peeling the skin off the carrots. "We saw Kyle on the way back."

On a plate, Hadley mixed a heaping bed of parmesan cheese and breadcrumbs. "Awkward, right?"

Patrick began to chop. "My exact words."

One by one, Hadley dipped the zucchini slices in the egg, coated them in crumbs and cheese, and then placed them on a frying pan. "See any fireworks?" she asked, focusing on the task.

"Just one."

"Impressed?"

"Very. It was surreal to sit there and watch from a distance."

"See, that's what I don't get."

"What?"

"The lightning, that's not how they're getting the Hydrogen, right?"

"Not the amount they want, no. They're studying the process."

"To find…?"

"How to calibrate and set the magnets so they most efficiently strip water of its Hydrogen—do you remember Ward's analogy?"

Hadley smiled. "Like a speaker in the middle of a room that blows women's clothes off."

"That's what we found in Colombia."

"You mean: what you found in Colombia," she corrected, emphasizing Patrick.

"It was a team effort."

"Of course," she said suspiciously, bending to open the oven for inspection. The smell of chicken and melting cheese escaped into the kitchen. Hadley shut the oven and began to tidy the countertop. The instruments of the kitchen filled the following silence; the sound of the frying zucchini, the chop of the knife, and the hum of the oven.

"Hadley," Patrick said at last.

"Yes?" She faced him, prongs in hand. Immediately, she knew he was hiding something. His countenance betrayed him. "What is it? Did you cut yourself?"

Patrick shook his head.

Hadley took a step towards him, taking his hand in hers. "Then what is it?"

He shrugged and threw his eyes toward the cutting board.

On the counter were the carrots, diced and separated. Hadley looked closer and saw that they were especially arranged. She mouthed what they spelled.

"*Will you*" she said softly, reading the letters. Turning back to Patrick, "Will I what–."

Patrick dropped to one knee.

Hadley inhaled and set the prongs on the counter.

"Will you, Hadley," Patrick said, opening his hand, a ring-shaped carrot slice in his palm. "Will you marry me? One last time."

Tears and laughter came at once to Hadley's face as she dipped her hand for Patrick's ring. Delicately, he slipped the halo about her finger.

Consuela had never met Hadley, so when she answered the door, the surprise was still intact. Consuela graciously stepped inside, introducing herself and commenting on the savory smell of dinner. Patrick was standing several paces away, hands on his hips, smiling at his old lab partner.

"Dios mio!" she cried, leaping backwards into Alika.

Over dinner they gave her an abridged version of the story, both Patrick's and Hadley's. Consuela was a gasper, and she accented each chapter of the tale with an abrupt draw of breath. She had to stifle tears at the parts involving Meredith. "And she still doesn't know?" she sobbed from behind a tissue.

The reason for indulging Consuela was to create another witness. In the event that their escape failed or something should happen to Alika, Patrick and Hadley wanted to have an additional guardian of truth. Consuela was handed a packet that contained papers and documents. Inside was proof of their story, Patrick and Alika's investigative work from the past year. The Simons had decided to flee, they didn't know enough about their opponent to make a stand. Both men had searched tirelessly for a link between who stood to benefit most from Patrick's disappearance. Tracing the billions and millions was proving impossible and the beneficiaries of the REI-Seven Energy deal increased daily. Even if Alika and Patrick pooled their Green Equator millions and went to court, the damage already done to Patrick would still likely trump. Their greatest hope in staying would be to send a curious mind searching in the right direction; and that was no guarantee. They would have to be patient and wait.

"I pray we haven't seen the last of you," Consuela said to Patrick with big teary eyes. She looked at Hadley and thought of Meredith. "But if I were you, I'd go too."

Patrick smiled and handed Consuela another folder. This one was thinner. They had finished dinner and were sitting in the living room.

"What's this?" she asked, opening to the first page and reading.

"It's what you've been looking for."

"You sly..." she tailed off, skimming the notes that Patrick had written for her. The contents showed the steps of Patrick's discoveries in Colombia—enough hints to un-stump the Seven Energy scientists. "Was it really just the anode-cathode pair?"

"Plain and simple."

"Damn," she said.

"What?"

"I never would have got that."

Patrick and Hadley then described their exit strategy. The move would be made Saturday night, in two days' time. The complex was most busy then, people coming and going, and it would be simpler to slip away. Patrick and Hadley would drive to Alika's apartment, enter through the backdoor, and reunite with their daughter. It was anticipated that the girl might require some time to digest the truth; the shock would be significant. Once together, they would return to Hadley's car and leave.

There would be cameras, but by the time Alika called the police in the morning, the rental car would be long abandoned. The guards at the gate rarely checked people leaving the facility, especially familiar cars like Hadley's. A few hours outside The Eco, they would board a boat in St. Augustine. It was a special charter arranged by Mars to Cuba. As the police responded to the Missing Persons report for Meredith, the family would already be airborne from Havana to Bermuda. In Bermuda, they would board a private flight to Europe; where exactly, Consuela didn't want to hear. "I believe this is where I say: I already know too much."

After hugs and kisses, Consuela left. It had grown late and Hadley's shift began in thirty minutes. She shooed Patrick and Alika out the door, catching Patrick for a kiss at the threshold. The approach tipped his hat back.

"Same time tomorrow?" she asked waggishly, retreating into the apartment.

Patrick nodded as Alika raised an approving eyebrow and turned away.

The two friends walked to the Acura, the evening humidity resting on their shoulders. Patrick's car was parked a few minutes outside the complex. Before they started the drive, Patrick rehearsed his re-proposal to Hadley.

Alika shook his head and laughed. "You proposed with a vegetable?!"

He laughed so hard that tears came. "That's brilliant."

"Thanks," said Patrick.

"You know," Alika picked up, putting the car in gear. "I've been thinking about going back to Washington. Maybe dicing a carrot of my own."

"Yeah?"

They looked at each other, aware of the miles between normality and now.

"You two will be great," Patrick promised. "Dolores is lovely."

Alika bobbed his head, breaking back into a grin. "A carrot!" He checked his mirrors and they wheeled around towards the exit.

"I thought Consuela took it well," Patrick said as they maneuvered a speed bump.

"Yeah," Alika agreed. "Thought we might lose her at the beginning there, but she held on. That was a good idea having her over."

"She is one smart cookie."

"One seductive cookie is what she is."

"Consuela?"

"Come on man."

"What?"

"Now don't tell me that you never…" Alika's voice trailed off into a frown.

"Never what?" Patrick asked.

Alika didn't respond. He was applying the brakes.

"Alika, what's the—?"

Then Patrick saw. Every muscle in his body instantly tightened. They were looking at Kyle. He was standing fifty yards ahead outside Maxwell's restaurant, bent down and talking into a man's ear. The man was sitting at a table with several other people. Suddenly, the man stood. It was Ward. He looked alarmed. Another man stood, Decklin Cross.

Without a word, Patrick popped the door handle and sprinted from the car.

Alika cursed and reversed into a parking spot, then accelerated back in the direction of his apartment, the passenger door still ajar. Ward and Decklin had not seen Alika or Patrick, but their clear connection with Kyle gave every reason to react. Alika watched in his rearview mirror as Ward and Decklin left the table and pulled phones from their pockets. Alika did the same and called Hadley. No answer.

A hundred yards away, Patrick burst through a row of hedges and ran across the parking lot in front of Building 5. Several people arriving home watched with interest as Patrick's hat blew from his head. A car began to pull out, stopping in a screech as Patrick leapt across the hood and slid to his feet on the other side. The driver honked and drove off.

Patrick reached Hadley's front door and tried the handle. It was locked. Furiously, he banged on the door. A few seconds later, Hadley opened in surprise.

"Quick!" Patrick said frantically, closing and bolting the door. "Grab what you can! We have to go!"

"What do you mean? What happ—"

"Kyle—Ward—we saw—They know we're here!"

Hadley went wide-eyed and ran to her room. There was a bag she kept packed at all times beneath the bed. She grabbed it. Patrick looked through her closet and drawers, taking only the pirate picture of Alika and Meredith. Bustling through the living room where they had just re-lived the horrors of the past nine months, Hadley and Patrick slipped out the sliding glass door and vaulted the low enclosure wall to the back porch. The moment they were over, a knock came at the door. They froze, looked around, and then hastily began to trot along the back of the building. The knocking came again, harder this time. To their right lay a field and small playground. It was dark, but outlines remained visible for the stars. From the far corner of the building, Hadley and Patrick heard a sharp crack. The door had been kicked in.

Hadley's car was parked a few spaces down from the front of the building. The parking lot was relatively still, only a woman at the far end carrying groceries from the back of her truck. They hustled towards Hadley's Ford Fusion and quickly got in. Hadley drove as Patrick spied for followers and called Alika.

"Hey!" Alika answered, whispering. "Meredith's asleep. Where are you?"

"I've got Hadley. We're pulling out back now."

"I'll gather some of her things. Come straight in."

Hadley brought the car around to Alika's back porch. His place was much larger, with formal entries on both sides.

"I'll wait here," Hadley said. "Go get our daughter."

Patrick was out and running before the car had stopped. Leaping up the steps, he came to the backdoor and cast it open, disappearing inside.

Hadley killed the lights and realigned the car. She checked her mirrors, scanning from side to side, watching for movement. She thought about Kyle; no ordinary tutor, but a spy placed next to Alika. Almost since the fire, Kyle had been present. Although there was no limit as to what he could know, the identity of his employers was at least clearer.

Alika's apartment was one floor and spacious. The kitchen was bordered by a dining room that emptied into an open living area with couches and a large flatscreen television. Beyond that was a small foyer that led to the front door. A hallway split from the location of the dining room table down towards two bedrooms and a study.

Alika was at the hallway closet when Patrick burst through the backdoor and thumped across the kitchen tile. Holding a bag of

Meredith's things, Alika stood up as Patrick came into view at the table. They made eye contact and the tension in Patrick seemed to ease. Before either one could say a word, the front door blew open with a bang.

Alika left the bag and hurried forward, coming to stand by Patrick, whose face was now flushed with disbelief. Three men were entering the foyer through the splintered frame, leaving the door ajar. The first was a large pale-skinned man that neither Alika nor Patrick immediately recognized. Kyle followed, suddenly confident and broad-shouldered. Both had handguns leveled at Patrick. Ward appeared last, looking a mix of angry and ill in slacks and a jacket. They marched through the living room, advancing with quick strides until they reached the dining room table. Ward came ahead to stand between the other two men. His hands hung defensively at his sides.

"Ward," Patrick greeted, as if testing the name. He and Alika had stayed stone-still for the few seconds it took the intruders to meet them.

Kyle had switched his aim to Alika, while the pale man, whom Alika now knew from the security entrance gate, kept his barrel trained on Patrick. Ward stepped forward slightly.

"Patrick," Ward said with strange disappointment. "What are you doing here?"

Patrick absorbed the question like a punch, cocking his head. The reality of the confrontation was shocking. There was so much he wanted to say, to ask. He looked at his old friend in confusion. All along, Patrick had held out hope that Ward was not involved. He looked at the gun and pursed his lips. "What am I doing here?" he repeated, as if the query was legitimate. "What am I doing here? To be honest, I don't know, Ward, I really have no DAMN clue what ANY of us are doing here," his voice rising. The verbal release felt redemptive after all his stacked minutes of seclusion. The guns didn't scare him anymore; he had changed since the first affront. "Maybe the real question is—how the HELL did it come to this? I trusted you!"

"Easy buddy," said the pale man in a low voice, trying to focus Patrick on his firearm. Alika took a step forward, and Kyle followed suit.

"Kyle, Lewis," said Ward urgently, putting his hands out to calm the situation. He looked back at Patrick, "Let's just relax. We can talk about this—"

"You were at Hadley's, weren't you?" said Patrick, looking dead at the pale man. "Lewis." He remembered Hadley's description of her assailants. "You tried to kill my daughter. To burn her alive."

A cruel smile spread across the man's face. Again, Ward held out his hand.

Patrick wanted to leap the table. Instead he turned back to Ward. "I don't know where to begin, Ward...what the hell happened? The fire, Colombia, Korey, the murder plot—what was it all for?"

"Patrick, it's not—"

"My family, my work, my life...Meredith," Patrick continued. "I'm an enemy of my own nation—and for what?" Months of repressed frustration were finally escaping. Alika put a hand on Patrick's shoulder as he barreled on. "I know it's about Hydrogen. Money and power. But why involve my family?" he asked. "What threat did we pose?"

"You think—?" Ward looked like he might turn away, but suddenly tensed. "This isn't what I wanted either. It wasn't supposed to come to this. I promise, it wasn't."

Patrick let out a mirthless laugh. "Then how was it supposed to be?" he retorted. "Were they supposed to kill me? Was that the mistake? Were Hadley and Meredith supposed to die too?"

"Something like that," Kyle cut in. "I was there."

"How DARE YOU!" said Alika in rage. Kyle faltered slightly, causing Lewis to momentarily turn his gun on the Samoan. "To think I trusted you with Meredith. To think you stayed in our home." Alika shook his head, threatening a charge. "I should run you through a wall."

"I'm right here," said Kyle, gripping the gun tighter, gaining courage.

"Tell these goons to get out of here," said Alika menacingly to Ward. "If we're going to talk, we don't need murderers for mediators."

Ward looked uneasily at him from across the table.

Neither Kyle nor Lewis budged.

Patrick held his arm out to Alika, and the attention shifted back to him. "Please, Ward." His voice sounded calm and uniquely composed for the situation. "You've taken enough. I don't care what happened. I don't care about the Hydrogen or any new energy company. I just want my daughter."

"I'm afraid it's not his choice," said Lewis from behind his weapon. "And like he said, it never was." The words fell like blocks of ice from his ghastly face. Alika and Patrick looked in appeal to Ward, but he avoided their gaze. "You'll need to come with us."

"To hell he will!" said Alika. "Patrick, leave."

Kyle raised his aim to Alika's head.

"Alika, Patrick, please!" cried Ward, looking defeated and small between the two brutes. "If I could, I'd let…everything…but it's beyond my control now. I did what I could."

"What do you mean?" asked Patrick. "Who *is* in control?"

Ward shook his head. "It's grown too big. You'll have to turn yourself in." His voice was unsteady. "To the police, that is. Kyle and Lewis…they're private security"

Lewis looked sideways at Ward and cleared his throat in disapproval.

"The police," Ward continued shakily. "It's the best chance you have."

"But you set him up!" growled Alika. "He hasn't done anything wrong."

"No, he hasn't," admitted Ward. "He did the right thing for the wrong people."

"Kyle, pinch," ordered Lewis, beginning to come around the table towards Patrick. Kyle began advancing from the other side. "Mr. Tucker," said Lewis to Alika. "Back away. You can stay with the girl."

Kyle kept his barrel on Alika while his spare hand went to his back pocket for a plastic zip-tie. "I will be happy to use force," taunted Kyle.

Ward looked on with discomfort.

Patrick began to back up into the kitchen. To this point, no one had mentioned that Hadley was alive. If she stayed hidden, perhaps she could still escape with Meredith. How to deflect her presence remained a problem. Kyle and Lewis were closing in. Ward appeared lame to help. Alika fidgeted at Patrick's side.

"It's okay," said Patrick, continuing to back away. He wondered if his unusual composure might compute to a last rush of peace before an ultimate end; that he was being prepared somehow for his final moments. "It's okay."

"Stay where you are!" yelled Lewis, but Patrick continued his retreat. "Stop moving!" Kyle came forward quicker, training his gun off Alika to Patrick.

As soon as he was close enough, Alika pounced.

Outside and waiting, Hadley had seen and heard nothing for almost ten minutes. She tried in vain to reserve her panic, constantly checking every mirror.

"Come on, come on!" she said in angst.

Another minute went by. And then another. She checked her phone and saw the missed call from Alika. In a quarter of an hour, their six months of preparation, planning, and secrecy had dissolved fast. Hadley considered calling inside; surely it would do no harm.

"Where are you?" she urged again, looking back up at the porch. As she hit re-dial on her phone, the first gunshots thudded from within the apartment.

When Alika's fist crashed down on Kyle's head, Lewis fired the first shot. It missed Alika's neck by mere millimeters and exploded into the drywall. Dazed by the attack, Kyle tried to swing his gun around, but Alika grabbed him from beneath the arms and pulled him backward up against his own chest. Kyle's gun flew free from his hand and into the hallway entrance. Patrick and Ward both screamed as Lewis sent a volley of shots roaring across the table. Alika ducked his head as the rounds tore into Kyle's chest.

Still yelling, Patrick charged Lewis and dove for his shooting hand. The pair crashed to the ground as Patrick struggled to dislodge the gun from Lewis's hand, railing at his arm and head. Ward remained at the center of the table, unsure what to do.

Stronger than Patrick, Lewis managed to swing his arm free, crashing his elbow sideways into Patrick's forehead. Patrick relented momentarily, but it was sufficient for Lewis to gain his balance and follow with another strike to Patrick's abdomen, causing him to double inwards.

Ward had started forward, but stopped as Lewis gathered himself onto his feet, gun in hand. He looked across the table for Alika and Kyle, both had fallen.

"Lewis!" Ward pleaded. "Please."

Lewis ignored him, staring down with hatred at Patrick.

Patrick looked up in pain at the barrel of Lewis's gun. His head spun from the blow and yet he felt no fear. All he wanted was to get Meredith to Hadley. Patrick searched for Ward and mercy, but received only another kick to the stomach from Lewis. Patrick sputtered on the floor, worried solely for his family.

"You were right, it was me," said Lewis, wiping at a cut on his forehead. "I burned the house, I killed the editor. But it wasn't supposed to be that way." His voice was cool and malevolent. "It was just you they needed gone." He zeroed the gun on Patrick's head, sneering. "My apologies for the delay."

Ward remained frozen, an observer only. Patrick held his breath.

"No," said Alika deeply, rising from across the room. He held Kyle's gun.

Lewis turned, instinctively swinging his weapon toward the voice as Alika released a single shot.

Patrick watched from the ground as the bullet split Lewis's temples and exited out the back of his head. The pale man then slumped backwards against the blood splattered wall, dead.

Alika came forward quickly, walking past Ward like he wasn't there. "Get up, Patrick," he said, extending an arm. "Get up."

Patrick dizzily staggered to his feet, holding Alika's arms.

Alika breathed abnormally, and Patrick looked down at a dark stain on his friends' shirt. The ominous blot was growing below the right side of the rib cage.

"It's fine," Alika reassured. "Go get Meredith."

"But—"

"Go," Alika repeated firmly.

A voice from near the door made all three men swivel. It was accented and came from out of sight.

"Alright in there, Ward?"

Patrick and Alika looked warily at Ward, who suddenly seemed to wake. "All fine in here, Decklin," said Ward.

"Doesn't sound like it," replied Decklin Cross, entering through the front door. He raised his eyebrows at the scene. "Doesn't look like it either." Cross took another few steps into the living room. He wore a dark gray sports jacket over black slacks and shiny shoes. "Patrick, Alika, an unexpected surprise."

The casual arrival of their old REI contact, the Australian gentleman who had not aged a day since their first meeting in San Francisco, left Patrick and Alika speechless. Having felt so close to escape, Patrick sensed an obstacle in Cross that would not be easily moved. He observed Alika's grip tighten around the gun still in his hand.

Ward took a step towards Cross. "They're leaving, Patrick and Meredith."

Cross considered Ward as a young boy, smiling at his naïvety. He then looked at Patrick. "It was never meant to come to this. I assure you."

"So I've heard," Patrick replied, still gathering his breath. "Was it you?"

The smile on Cross' face remained. "Not quite." He dropped his gaze to Alika's weapon. "No need for firepower now, I'm no threat."

"I'm okay," Alika assured, holding onto the gun.

Cross shrugged and turned his attention back to Patrick. "No, this wasn't my plan, nor was it Ward's." He buried his hands in his pockets. "We may have helped execute a few details, but the outline was already made."

"I don't understand," said Patrick.

"You wanted to start an energy company that didn't make money," Cross said, almost in accusation. "And not just any energy company, but one with a monopoly on the most promising discovery since nuclear fission." Cross grinned. "You can't do that."

"But that was just an idea," Patrick firmly replied. "A thought."

"You may say it was simply an idea, and one you may not have acted upon, but ideas can be dangerous and fickle, especially in the hands of someone like you. There is a way that things are done, an order—and costless energy does not have a place at the table."

"Be straight with us," said Alika, his breathing labored by his wound. Patrick put a hand out to support him. "Just tell us who and why."

Cross stopped to calculate the request. "I know you can see it," he said. "You must have with all the time that's passed." He paused for a response from Alika and Patrick. "The flow of money through the trade of energy cannot be stoppered. It is an immovable feast. Ask any politician, any expert, any businessman, even the man on the street—and they'll tell you that if profit was removed from the sphere of energy production and consumption, then governments, cities, and entire nations would promptly spiral into disaster. Oil, coal, natural gas, nuclear, renewables...Hydrogen, these are commodities that have no place being given away. They form an artery of the global economy. They cannot be shut down; else the whole body should wither." Cross paused again. "So it was the world's decision to afflict you Patrick, not mine, not REI's, not Seven's—we were merely doing its bidding. You were a necessary sacrifice." He glanced at Ward. "As to your family, that was Ward's initiative."

Patrick and Alika recoiled slightly.

Ward breathed in deeply. "It was to protect you, Patrick."

"Protect me?" Patrick replied.

"Didn't pan out like he thought," Cross added.

"When I found out—" Ward began, avoiding Cross' eyes. "When I admitted what your plans were for this new energy company, I didn't realize what would happen. Word got out to the Board at REI, then our investors, then their contacts, soon everyone seemed to know...and the magnitude of your intentions grew with every whisper. Not everyone came to the same conclusion, but the pressure mounted quickly—suddenly you were a threat that needed to be erased."

"So you brought my daughter into it?"

"It's not like that," Ward said with frustration. "These...," he indicated the corpses of Lewis and Kyle. "They were supposed to kidnap Meredith and then hold her until you abandoned your non-profit designs, just to give you a good scare. It was only meant to be a scare." Ward twisted his hands together. "A fright to get you to finish the Hydrogen work, take your money, and come home....that's all."

"However," Cross picked up, pointing at Alika, "Lewis and company got spooked when you turned up at the front door. They knew the original plan of eliminating Patrick and made a snap judgment on how to proceed. Thereafter...a degree of improvisation was required."

"So it was all a cover-up of Ward's Good Samaritan plan gone wrong," Alika concluded.

"A major headache for us all," Cross stated candidly.

For a few moments, no one responded; Cross' capricious summary weighing down their tongues. Cross and Ward stood about three paces from Patrick and Alika at the dining room table. "Well," Cross finally said. "On that note, I think the police will be here…"

As Cross bent to check his watch, Alika took one step and then a lunge. Before the Australian could react to the rush of movement, Alika's left fist impacted on the side of his face and Cross fell backwards in a heap, unconscious before he hit the ground. Alika stumbled and felt at his stomach, spitting a wad of blood onto the carpet. Patrick moved forward to steady him. "I'd heard enough," Alika said roughly.

Ward looked back at the fallen form of his colleague, shaken. "You have to run," he said turning to Patrick. "Anywhere. The police are on their way and Decklin was right—the power behind this is too great."

Silence passed over the three old friends. They considered the scene; Cross crumpled on the carpet, Kyle and Lewis bleeding out at either end of the table, bullet holes and blood across the walls. The last time they had been together was the autumn wedding in Vermont.

"I'm so sorry," said Ward to them both.

Patrick nodded and bowed his head. Then, with a flash, he lurched up and socked Ward in the face. Like a stone, Ward collapsed to the floor in the same fashion as Cross. Breathing hard, Patrick and Alika stood over him as a trickle of blood emerged from his nose.

"Nice work," said Alika wryly. He made way for Patrick. "Now, get out of here. I imagine the police *are* actually on their way."

"But your—"

"I'll be fine," Alika said, forcing a smile. "Just a flesh wound."

Patrick hesitated and then embraced his friend. Alika winced, but returned the hug with a gentle pat. His words grew more and more painful. "Go on. She's waiting."

There were lightning bugs that night.

Meredith lay in bed, supposedly asleep, when the first one puttered up near the glass. The field behind Alika's came alive on such evenings, winking like a metropolis seen from the sky. She stood on tiptoes to peep at these fireflies from her window. Kyle had slipped out again, which he did from time to time—amongst other curious things—but as usual, he would return before Alika. Until then, the girl would spy for the little men who played Jupiter.

When the front door burst open, Meredith knew it must be Kyle. She crept back beneath the covers, closing her eyes. Except the footsteps—they were too heavy. They bounded directly to her room, slowing before the door. Meredith felt light as the hinges engaged. Cracking her eyes, she saw Alika stick half his body through the frame. A cellphone rang and he ducked back into the hallway. The door closed gently behind him. Meredith strained her ears for clues.

Then Alika was back, rummaging through drawers and sweeping about the closet. With great speed, he wrapped clothes into his arms, bundling them up against his chest. The fashion was so curious he might have been a robber. Meredith remained in bed, too timid to interject.

A substantial fraction of the girl's wardrobe in his grasp, Alika shuffled back into the hall. Curiosity seized Meredith and she threw aside her covers. The bedroom door had shut and she gently padded towards it. The buzz of zippers, opening and closing, was the only perceptible sound. As she gripped the door handle, the house erupted with noise.

The back door flung open, and someone came loudly through the kitchen. Then the front door opened, and feet rocked the living room. Meredith heard Alika advance as well. The tides met at the entrance to the hallway, over the dining room table. Alone in her pajamas, she retreated to the bed.

Voices shot out from beyond the walls, elevating louder and louder. Yells and shouts emanated with bellicose ferocity. The girl was shaking now and wanted it to stop. One man's voice roared above the rest. Everything went quiet.

Meredith knelt and listened. There was a muffle of speech, then another cry, and then silence. She wanted to hear Alika, but the voices were building again, leaping and falling in bursts. They were too mixed to distinguish. She flattened herself to slip under the bed.

The blast from the first gun made her scream. Terrified, she curled into a ball beside the bed as the next shots erupted. Her heart beat like a mallet against her chest. After more voices, there was one final gunshot. She was too afraid to cry, too terrified to open her eyes. Part of her wanted to hide, while another felt obligated to peer down the hallway. Voices still emanated from the dining room. Alika had been out there, but fear kept Meredith still, hands held fast over her face. After some time, the door opened, and the feeling of light rushed over her once more. Quivering, she refused to look.

When hands gathered her up, the girl stirred in fright, staring up into a face. The fireflies, Alika in the closet, the voices, the guns, her father—she thought it must be a dream, her father was dead. But it was him, bearded and glowing down in paternal love.

With Meredith clutching tight, they walked from the room. Cupped in her father's arms, she could smell the burnt metal. It corroded the air. To their right was the living room, to their left was the kitchen, and directly ahead sat Alika at the dining room table. His face was placid. He breathed like he had just been running. For him, Meredith focused on nothing else. Alika nodded at Patrick as the pair approached, a gun resting on the chair beside him.

The last time Alika looked Meredith in the eyes, it was as if they had never met, but he had heard about her all his life. And with that one gaze, the girl was the morning come, the promise kept, the answer to any question he might ever ask. She was the reason for his sacrifice.

The father and daughter left him and hustled out through the kitchen. Patrick clipped down the steps, jogging now towards a car. A woman with black hair stood at the driver's side, looking on anxiously. She got in as Patrick opened the backdoor and placed Meredith inside on the seat. Once he was settled beside her, the car began to move. The girl had not said a word.

Meredith looked from her father to the woman in the driver's seat, who turned around, tears running like snowmelt down the familiar trails of her face.

Meredith was home.

Chapter 36

March 16th, 2028
Safehouse Five, New York City, New York
2:15 a.m.

I stand alone in the interview room, hands on my hips. Meredith has been escorted out to the restroom. Her drawing of The Eco lies slightly folded at the center of the desk.

The police report written by the officers who arrived first at Alika's apartment in Florida noted the presence of four individuals—Alika Tucker, Kyle Murdoch, Lewis Penrith, and Decklin Cross. The emergency call had been made by Cross and he was the only one conscious when the police entered the room. Trembling near the front door, he gave the initial account as to what had occurred. Kyle and Lewis were declared dead and Alika was rushed to the hospital. He would survive. Ward's presence was never mentioned.

Based primarily on Cross' testimony, the police concluded that Patrick had broken into the apartment and promptly shot both Kyle and Alika. Alika said he remembered very little of the encounter, only that Patrick had entered the apartment and gunshots soon followed. It was assumed that as the first security guard to respond to the report of gunfire, Lewis Penrith had attempted to peacefully contain Patrick and been slain in the process. Cross' car was parked nearby and he explained that he'd made the 911 call upon hearing the final shots, entering the apartment as Patrick escaped with Meredith out the backdoor. Detectives and police scoured the country for weeks, then months. The search was fruitless and many supposed that Patrick had crossed over the border into Mexico. The media feasted on the spread served by *The Return of Hydrogen Frankenstein*, while the rest of the nation held prayer vigils, arranged flowers, and lit candles for Meredith's safe return.

Killian's voice comes through the loudspeaker in the interview room instead of my earpiece. "Hanna, need you in here." Stepping forward, I shuffle Meredith's map in with the rest of my papers and walk back to the monitoring center. Once inside, I shut the door behind me and accept a bottle of water from another agent. Killian is in the center of the room, looking grimly my way. Something has happened. He beckons me closer.

The room remains abnormally busy for that hour. Computer screens hum and glow throughout the studio setting. In one corner, Agent Hanks is on a video call with colleagues in Boston discussing methods to exhume Hadley's grave. In front of the viewing window, which looks out at the empty table of the interview room, two operators are going back over Meredith's recordings. In an instant they can cross-check anything Meredith has said with previous testimony or test it against the FBI's colossal data bank. Along the back wall, two assistants monitor the surveillance cameras and take messages from other offices. In the center of the room, behind Killian, another agent is at an electronic table scanning copies of Patrick Simon's alleged notes for Consuela Garcia.

I ask what the problem is, troubled by his expression. He takes a step towards me. "I've tried to keep a lid on this," he says, softly and resigned. "But it's escaped. The Director... believes Meredith should be transferred." He rubs the back of his neck. "To DHS."

I firmly object. There's no need for Homeland Security to speak to Meredith. There's no threat of terrorism here.

"Unfortunately," Killian responds, "From what they've heard, they think there is. And the Director agrees."

Abandoning inhibition, I tell him that the Director and DHS can go to hell. The room goes quiet and everyone, including the agents in Boston, fixates on me. I'm angry, not just for the poaching of a witness, but for the danger this poses to Meredith. Over the years, DHS has earned the privilege of less and less oversight. In many ways this is beneficial, as they disrupt and foil thousands of terrorist plots each year, most of which the public never hears about.

Yet the DHS is also somewhat of a black hole, and not everyone operating within this darkness is wholesome.

A buzzer sounds to indicate that a car has just pulled into the rear portico. I look at Killian in frustration, then down at the camera that shows the carport. A black Lincoln SUV, opens its doors for four men in suits. They're here already. I get a chill from recognizing one of the faces. It's worse than I thought.

I step close to Killian and whisper viciously into his ear. If everything Meredith has said up until now has been true, if she hasn't made one digression from testimony or unexplained contradiction to record, and we've been at this for twelve hours…then how can we exercise the slightest amount of apathy! The average Joe on the street couldn't tell us about his day at work without tripping up a few times. Meredith has recounted close to a century of history, including the details of an intricate cover-up worth trillions of dollars. Either we've been fed an incredibly elaborate lie that Meredith has honed for sixteen years, forging hundreds of documents, and convincing her subconscious that she's telling the truth, or—

An agent at the surveillance station turns to Killian. "Coming up, Sir, four men unarmed." All eyes turn to focus on the security monitor as the new arrivals approach the room. They're being escorted by Agent Graham and two of the three agents assigned to guard the lower floor. I duck my head and swear.

Killian tightens. "She'll be fine," he says firmly, failing to convince anyone. "We'll be sure of it."

The lock to the door unhinges and seven more bodies cross the threshold. I feel myself pushed to the side as three broad men stride inside and stare unreservedly about the room. I've not had much experience with DHS, but these guys fit the bill for typical Government muscle. A single figure trails behind them, a stately individual that Meredith has only just mentioned. I've seen Decklin Cross on the news from time to time, usually in connection with the Hydrogen Consortium, a new cartel pegged to overtake OPEC before mid-century. He is in his late 70's now, grandfatherly and taller in person, and his frosted hair sits like a crown atop his head. I feel unnerved by the comfort of his manner.

A brief silence follows as the escorting agents enter and shut the door. One of the DHS agents steps forward and extends his hand to Killian. He has a bullish face and dark brown eyes.

"Director Killian, I'm Agent Bonnington, Homeland Security."

"Agent Bonnington," replies Killian, shaking the man's hand. "Please excuse our disorder. It's been a long day and your arrival is, well, less than expected."

"A long and exciting day, I'm sure," says Bonnington, looking around the center. His gaze settles on a computer screen that shows an archived security shot of a bearded Patrick Simon at the border in Mexicali.

"Agent Bonnington," says Killian, with a harder tone. "I was advised of your visit, but I'm not entirely sure my team is comfortable with releasing Ms. Simon. Our investigation is not yet complete."

From behind the three DHS agents, Cross clears his throat to interrupt. "There is nothing comfortable about this entire situation." His accent sounds more British than Australian. "And I'm sure we're all quite tired at this hour."

Killian ignores the statement and addresses Bonnington again. "Where will you take her?"

"We're not at liberty to say," Bonnington replies. "The girl still has family in Boston, so I presume she'll end up there." I have a dark feeling this means the graveyard where Hadley was supposedly buried.

"I mean no disrespect," Killian says. "But we have invested a significant amount of time in this case, and though I honor my chain of command and the purpose of DHS, there is little excuse for an individual like Mr. Cross to be present in this setting, especially—"

"Mr. Cross is not the issue," Bonnington interjects, taking a step forward. "And regarding Ms. Simon, this is not open to discussion. So I suggest you stand down."

Killian cocks his head. "Are you threatening me?"

"Of course he isn't," says Cross coolly. "He's just simplifying the equation." Cross casts a look through the window at the empty interview room. Meredith has yet to return. "Now, where is Meredith? It's been ages."

As I step forward to intervene, the room plunges into darkness. Seconds later, the emergency lights switch on and illuminate a dozen confused faces. Every computer screen has rebooted and a flashing red light indicates a malfunction in the main security system. Agents scramble as Killian yells for them to find out what is happening. The three DHS agents come forward to stand around Cross.

I move to reach Killian, but stop short, remembering Meredith's map and the curious way she tapped it so only I could see; *And it will be your move.* I go to my folder on the desk and begin searching for the paper. An agent slips past me and opens the door with an emergency key. As my hand clinches on the sheet, I look towards the agent and the outer hallway. At first, I mistake the rolling object as a pool ball, bouncing and turning across the floor. Only when it comes to rest against the wall do I recognize the concussion grenade.

I yell for cover and dive to the ground, matting my ears as the grenade launches a wave of sound and light through the open doorway. Bodies hit the floor, papers fly into the air, and chairs overturn. A few cries rise up and the emergency lights flicker.

Head spinning, I lift my eyes to see Killian returning to his feet, along with Cross and the DHS agents. The room sounds like it has filled with jelly. Grabbing the edge of a desk, I gather myself up and grab a sidearm from the rack near the door.

"Hanna!" yells Killian. "You okay?"

I reply that I'm going out, already turning towards the two nearest agents—my agents—Hanks and Graham. They stagger forward to follow me into the hall.

I check the agent who was closest to the blast. He's unconscious and bleeding from the head after falling backwards against the edge of the door. Calling back for another agent to attend, I round the corner, gun drawn. I can see the fallen form of another body at the top of the stairs. Waving Hanks and Graham forward, we move cautiously down the hall. It's the female agent assigned to Meredith. I feel at her neck. She's alive after a solid blow to the head. Graham reports that the bathroom is empty.

Pressing on, I hammer down the steps. We sweep onto the ground floor, our weapons scanning for movement. Around the corner from the stairwell, we find the last agent, unconscious and lying flat. Fragments of another concussion grenade are apparent. I step over the body with less regard, pushing open the back door to enter the cover of the garage portico. Hanks and Graham follow as we move past the Lincoln and into the alley. I order Hanks to cross over onto the front of the street and for Graham to press towards Eastern Parkway.

As we disperse, I head up the alley alone, peering frantically through the semi-darkness. There are no street lamps along the alley, but several porch lights offer visibility. Reaching the end of the lane, I turn right and begin to loop back around to where I sent Hanks. Some traffic buzzes on the more traveled avenues and up the block on Eastern Parkway, but all is relatively still as I pass through the heart of the neighborhood. My heart thunders at the thought of losing Meredith. Theories stream through my mind—were the DHS agents a distraction? Nabbing a witness from Safehouse Five was meant to be impossible.

I hustle on, checking every parked car and alcove. Coming to another alley, I freeze as Graham comes into view ahead. He's running, now sprinting up the alley, gun drawn. Past him, I have a final glimpse of a young woman being thrown into the back of a van, her hooded assailant leaping in after her. I know the face and clothing even from this distance. They've got her.

Still running, Graham fires a single shot, blasting off the driver-side mirror as the van accelerates up the alley. I begin to run, but stop almost immediately in devastation. Graham is still giving chase as the van reaches the adjoining street and fishtails out of sight. I watch as he reaches for his radio and slows to a walk while calling in the van's description. The chase is not over, but our chances will slim.

Turning around, I feel for my phone, gun limp at my side. I don't know what to say to Killian. What is there to say? Pulling the phone from my back pocket, something else falls to the ground. Bending down, I see that it's Meredith's map of The Eco. Unfolding the paper, I feel a chirp in my chest. I read the scrawled single line several times and then dial Killian. He has already heard the description of the getaway van and tells me to come back to the Safehouse. I say I might try for some witnesses. Agent Bonnington is raising his voice in the background and Killian asks me to be quick. "I can't handle these clowns much longer," he mutters, hanging up.

I look down at the address written on the note and punch it into my phone. It's an intersection along Lincoln Terrace Park, about five minutes away on foot. Up the alley, Graham has gone and I set a brisk pace due east from the Safehouse. Along the way, I tuck the gun into my waistband. A few passing taxis slow when they spot me, but carry on again when I fail to hail them. I recall from my youth that this neighborhood was never ideal for early morning strolls. Mere minutes from watching Meredith being abducted, I arrive at the appointed corner. The note held just an address, no hint of what or who I might find.

Several minutes pass. The ever-burning torches and sounds of the city create a repeating baseline in the surrounding sky. Several windows in nearby apartments pulse faintly with television light. Watching my breath billow in the streetlight, I feel the cold for the first time. The park is misty and quiet. Despite the intensity of the day, my mind buzzes with questions. Was Meredith's capture actually an escape?

After ten more minutes, when my body begins to shiver, I hear footsteps on the grass behind me. I turn around to see two men wearing overcoats and gloves. They have stopped at the perimeter of the lamplight. I slowly step from the sidewalk and pad across the grass towards them. My pulse gallops when I recognize their faces.

ucker has aged well in the past fifteen years. Tree- support a hefty frame, raised shoulders, and a full curls are clipped short and graying on the sides. He kept a low-profile after Meredith's disappearance, quitting Seven Energy to take work as a lecturer at UC Berkeley. He married Dolores and they have two children.

Ward Prince appears exhausted and shrunken in comparison to his standard campaign persona. The part in his hair is less defined and his cheeks are ruddy. Though he has developed a striking and steadfast image as a politician, I see him now for the young and unsure man of the past, the aspiring titan that Meredith described. As to his presence here, I'm stunned.

"Agent Corsica," Alika says, his voice richer than I'd imagined. "Glad you found us."

I dip my head, feeling an extraordinary respect for Alika that leaves me slow to react.

adlH

"How long can you be?" asks Ward, checking his watch. He seems less composed than Alika. "It's 2:45 a.m."

After a moment of hesitation, I finally find my words.

As long as you need.

Ward nods and looks to Alika.

"I know there are many questions that you would like to ask us," Alika begins, "And these will be answered in time. But first we need to ask you something. We need to know where you stand."

...As in?

"Do you believe Meredith?" Alika asks bluntly. "Do you believe that what she told you is true?

I do.

"And the documents she brought with her, do you believe these are valid as well?"

I've only seen several sheets, but Director Killian believes them to be authentic and I trust his judgment.

Ward continues. "And given the implications of Meredith's account, are you prepared and willing to see this case through to the end?"

I am.

"Do you believe that Director Killian is as well?" asks Ward.

Yes.

Ward takes a deep breath and focuses me in his gaze. "I can understand if you find me to be an evil man," he says, as Alika stands silent and strong beside him. "And if I'm not now, then I certainly was. I was blinded by ambition and the delights of success. I became a pawn in an ancient game of power—the world against itself." Ward pauses briefly. "There were cover-ups, there were murders, there were bribes, all manner of poor conduct and criminality was committed. Not by me, no, but I knew—I understood the rules. Throughout my career I have tried to make up, to atone for these sins and errors, beginning when I saw Patrick again in Florida—I didn't know he was alive, Hadley either." Ward takes another long breath and studies my face. It is singular to hear his signature pace and rhetoric, the same from the debates, except now in confession instead of confidence. "I'm tired, Agent Corsica, tired of seeing Meredith in my children, Hadley in my wife. It rubs my conscience raw. So often I imagine that it is my daughters cowering within that burning house, my daughters losing their mother, my daughters being told their father has done horrible things." He pauses again, bringing his hands together in front of him. "It's time for honesty, for justice, and given my current...public position, the hour is no accident."

What do you plan to do?

"Shuffle the board," Ward says, the words picking at his throat. He must know this decision will set in motion the end of his political career, if not more. "Make way for something new."

The air hums around us. I begin to grasp the depth of the coup that is about to take place. This is bigger than just one man, Patrick. This is about the oligarchy of energy that he unknowingly offended.

"We've sent portions of the documents that you have analyzed to several newspapers," Ward explains, checking his watch again. "It should help the investigation keep traction."

Ward goes quiet and Alika's baritone returns. "As I'm sure you've already determined, Meredith's sudden departure was planned. She is safe now, but given the spirited arrival of certain individuals at the Safehouse, it's clear that she will be safest in hiding until the story breaks." Alika pauses and smiles. "So until then…I trust the two of us will suffice."

Ward steels himself to the ground, nodding once in agreement.

Very well. Would you like to meet Director Killian now?

"That would be fine," says Alika. "Is Decklin still there?"

As far as I know.

Alika and Ward exchange a look, one of thrill and trepidation.

"I'm sure he will be 'absolutely chuffed' to see us," Ward says with a subtle accent.

When I call and tell Killian that I have two witnesses to bring in, he flippantly agrees to send an agent to collect us, asking if we can pick up coffee on the way back. I agree to bring back something better than caffeine. He is still dealing with the DHS agents and hangs up abruptly.

In the cool morning air, the three of us wait beneath an icy heaven. Several people walk past on the opposite sidewalk, some coming home, some just leaving for work; no one takes much notice of our unique trio. After a moment of collective thought, I turn to them with the first of many questions.

Patrick and Hadley: where have they been?

Alika and Ward share another glance.

"You should see for yourself."

Chapter 37

July 15, 2028
Fort William, Scotland
9:00 p.m.

It's been a long trip since London. The hour has grown late and the sun refuses to sleep. It hangs above the nearby loch, spread out in defiance against a cluster of mountains. I don't know where they're taking me, only who I'm being taken to meet.

I landed this morning at Heathrow airport, walking out of the arrivals hall to a waiting car. The driver never said a word, just stored my luggage and drove north for an hour to a small city named Stevenage. After escorting me into a modest train station, the man handed me a ticket for an approaching train, bowed slightly, and then turned to leave. Although I understood the secrecy of my journey, I still would have liked to hear him speak—if only for the accent.

The train took me further north to Peterborough, where a woman in a rain jacket was waiting outside a coffee shop. In similar fashion, I was passed another ticket and informed that my train would arrive on the opposite platform in three minutes. True to her word and the station master's whistle, the train departed exactly on time. When I pulled away, the woman was gone, leaving me to ride alone with my thoughts until Edinburgh, the capital of Scotland.

It has been four months since I first met Meredith at JFK airport in New York. In the intervening time, a political storm of historic proportions has pelted the US from coast to coast. Ward Prince has provided testimony and evidence to the involvement of several individuals, including himself, in the murder of Korey Devoir and the attempted murder of Patrick Simon. As the Election front-runner and an influential member of America's energy framework, Ward's revelations released a destroying angel within America's known and unknown echelons of wealth and power. Along with an exoneration of Patrick, Ward went further to expose a range of energy affronts—billion-dollar tax fraud, denied technology-transfer to foreign nations, kickback reward systems, and illegal price setting. *The Green Scare, HydrogenGate, Prince: Green Reaper*; ran the headlines.

Although the public was disappointed in their Presidential candidate, there was a degree of admiration for what he was doing and many rallied for Ward to remain in the race. There had been no pressure for him to come clean; this was no preemptive confession, it was restitution. Over half of the members on the former REI Board were detained, including Decklin Cross and James Le. Several members of Seven Energy were also indicted, as were a handful of Government authorities and police officials. Simultaneous to these arrests and summons, resignations began flowing in from all manner of private and public companies, some relating to the Prince scandal, and others on issues that may never have been uncovered; skeletons were opening closet doors from the inside.

Despite the apparent purge of corrupted circles, it seemed as though such political change was not the final ambition of this ambush. Ward alluded to further designs in a statement given last week from the steps of the Capitol building.

> *Amends, apologies, even arrests—as we reveal the extent of crimes committed by certain individuals of trust, none of these developments should be discounted. Though we exist in the age of information, an era that has seen our nation grow and integrate with the world in magnificent leaps, portions of the most vital knowledge have nonetheless been kept from you, the people…*
>
> *…I do not stand here today as a martyr, I stand here as a man who was given a voice. It was you that gave me this voice, my place at the podium, and it was you that called on me to improve your lives, and although I endeavored to be true, I believe what I have said and shown in the past few months will yet yield the greatest return on your faith…*

...The problem we face in Energy, and have faced, is not a host of evil men. On the contrary, it is honest men that constitute the majority of this working body, for there is no curse on Energy, only the stubborn persistence of a long-entrenched Elite. It is the malignant pride of a few that erodes the worthy convictions of many. I stand here today as a former member of that Elite...

...There will be many wise men and women who will yet say that our current method of energy production, consumption, and profit is adequate – it's enough. And though I would encourage you to listen to their learning, for they are not to be ignored, if others should come to tell you of another way, a different way, then do not turn your back. I offer this as an invitation, because although present practices have proven themselves in days past, an incumbent is not always worthy of the future. Such is progress, an uphill track. Yet I would submit to you that the pain of this price is promptly forgotten, swallowed up in the sweetness of the purchase.

The tracks north from Peterborough pass mainly through countryside, diverting off occasionally at cities like York, Durham, and Newcastle. England is beautiful, as are its trains. I'm impressed by their cleanliness and punctuality, as well as the selection of unusual treats on the food trolley. I bought a few things for their novelty, and admittedly for the strange pleasure of hearing more English—*Any teas or coffees?*

I emerged from the ticket gates at Edinburgh to meet another man. He was dressed much like my first driver, a suit jacket over an open gray shirt, and he insisted that I visit the station bathroom before we continued. Although not in need, I relented and left him with my luggage. I took my time passing through the restroom turnstiles, assuming that a search of my belongings was desired. Within the white-tiled room, the faint smells of cleaning products, perfumes, and biology lingering in the air, I received a surprise upon encountering a woman standing by the sinks. Her skin was lighter than mine, but we were dressed exactly alike; down to the color of our shoes.

After a dry comment about looking gorgeous, she explained that there were two identical cars waiting for us in the station and that I should go directly to the front one. I was beginning to understand why the Brits have always been the greatest spies.

Following directions, I entered the designated car, a black Volvo, and sped away from the station, skirting Edinburgh Castle and its rocky outcroppings, passing the city's parks and sandstone buildings, traveling west until Glasgow where we banked north on the A82, The West Highland Highway. That road brought us here to Fort William, wooing every mile of the way with provoking hills, Martian valleys, quenching lochs, and enigmatic grasslands. I was wrong about England, it was pretty—Scotland is beautiful.

The driver returns to our car with a *Haddock Supper* for each of us. Sitting in the Volvo, we enjoy the fried fish and chips while he talks about the history of the Highlands and inaccuracies in the movie *Braveheart*. His accent is Scottish, thicker, and patched with various intonations that escape me.

We are on our way again shortly and continuing north, then bearing west. I was hoping that Meredith would make this trip with me, but her face has returned too prominently to the news. I've met with her several times since our marathon at the Safehouse. She's with her grandparents now in Boston, trying to relax under a 24-hour bombardment of interview requests and fan mail. Like Alika and her parents, she has become a hero. Across the world, people are eager for each emerging detail of the Simon saga. Even with an inside track to the story, I too find myself wondering at its twists. In Meredith's escape at the Safehouse, it was Agent Graham—my own agent—that assisted with knocking out the security system and providing the concussion grenades—the riskiest element of the whole plan. Everything else was definitively calculated; my unit's involvement, the required time for Meredith to deliver her account, the quantity of evidence, and most key, Ward's political prominence.

The driver turns back to let me know that I will be changing cars again shortly, a promise fulfilled at a highway-side parking lot amid tumbling hills of rock and sand. My belongings are transferred to the new car and we continue. It is past sunset, yet the sky remains a cerulean twilight, adding to the mystery of this fabled setting.

Being away was never easy, Meredith told me, and there was always a buried sense of tension. After dramatically fleeing The Eco, Mars had managed to arrange another charter for the Simons at St. Augustine, as well as new flights from Cuba and the Bahamas. Arriving in Zurich, they traveled by train into the countryside, waiting for several months until the drama that accompanied Meredith's disappearance subsided. Alika had already transferred Meredith's $100 million from the Green Equator deal to a Swiss bank account in the name of Patrick's new alias. With these funds, the Simons built a new life, a secret existence known to less than a dozen people.

Meredith said life in hiding became more bearable as time passed, especially with the arrival of a sister and two younger brothers. They all went to the local school, Meredith with her new haircut and name, and in their obscure rural community, they were soon living a fairly normal life. Anthony and Rose Hannigan visited occasionally, taking more than a few European vacations, and Hadley returned to her novels, writing several under the alias *Jane Lemon*—which amazes me as I often see her books in airports. Patrick continued his work with Hydrogen for some years until branching off into another focus—what exactly, I'm not sure, Meredith told me to wait and see.

I've been dozing somewhat over the last stretch, the length of the journey pressing down on my eyelids. I wake at times, listening to the driver's brogue voice point out the silhouette of the *most romantic* castle in Scotland, the bridge at Kyle of Lochalsh, the sleeping village of Portree, and the stoic Old Man of Storr. The roads are quick and winding, one-lane in many places, and we cruise past coastlines and dark bays. We're on the Isle of Skye, he tells me, just a few minutes to go.

I rub my eyes, preparing myself. After a discussion of how they would like to proceed, I will escort Patrick and Hadley back to the United States. There is a private jet waiting in London to collect us from whichever airport we choose. The car leaves the paved road and turns down a narrower dirt track. Outside my window I see a notice indicating that we have entered a conservation area. We descend into a valley and soon enter forest, dark and dense, blocking out the unusual radiance of the night sky. The dirt track splits and we branch off to the left, following a sign that says *Caretaker*. It's midnight, and for the first time in years my phone has no signal.

Through the darkness of the wood, a well-sized cabin appears in a clearing ahead. The driver flashes the headlights twice as he pulls up and stops near the front of the house. I notice a swing set on the lawn and a large barn a little further away in the clearing. The soft glow of lamplight emanates from a front room. Nervous excitement grips me as I open my door and stand from the car.

The driver pulls my single bag out of the trunk, wishes me a pleasant stay, then promptly returns to his wheel and drives back up the road. I wait in the mild summer air, observing the home before me. A child's tricycle lies overturned near a flower bed and a roughly built birdfeeder stands vacant nearby. Sounds of nocturnal life surround me, akin to the natural whispers I heard from my tent when I was young. The front door opens and they step out together onto the driveway.

Hadley's hair is longer now, Patrick's thinner. Her face is more elegant in person, and his boyish charm has refined with maturity. Dressed in jeans and long-sleeved shirts, they look like parents. I feel a tug of emotion as they come and stand before me. There is a wind blowing above, I can hear it in the trees, but the forest and the valley shadow us from its pull.

With the same determined eyes he gave to his daughter, Patrick reverently looks over my face. The summer sky rises above us, illuminated by the wake of the sun.

"Hello Hanna."

Acknowledgements

Attempting a novel requires the writer to take a journey, one hard to explain with words. I have deeply enjoyed the wandering pace of this path and have sincere gratitude for those who have walked with me for various stretches.

To my eternal friend, Sarah, thank you for your patient support and inspiration. I look forward to all that we will build together.

For my mother and father, thank you for always believing in me and showing me great love. Your imaginations have been the seeds for mine.

Finally, special thanks to those who edited and corrected the many drafts that this story went through, as well as gave sage guidance; especially Clem, Mike, Kristin, Apolline, Roxanne, and Hunter.

Printed in Great Britain
by Amazon.co.uk, Ltd.,
Marston Gate.